CRIME SCENE
COVER-UP

JULIE MILLER

For Lissanne Jones, a fellow author, reader and friend. She sent me the generous gift of a tea sampler from Australia. I had so much fun trying the different selection of teas that I'd never seen before, much less tasted. I appreciate your kindness. Thank you!

Chapter One

Mark Taylor loved the scents of fish, grill smoke and the outdoors that clung to his clothes and filled up the cab of his truck. He and the silver-haired man sitting in the passenger seat across from him were chasing the sunset along Highway 7, speeding home to Kansas City after their annual camping-and-fishing weekend at Truman Lake.

The scenery on either side of the twisting highway was especially picturesque in the summer. The rolling hills were carpeted with endless green trees giving way to tiny towns, the steel-gray water of wind-whipped lakes and the grittier browns of creeks and rivers filled with the rain that had flooded parts of the state earlier that year. Although some of the highway had been straightened and expanded into dual lanes, Mark preferred the narrower cuts of the two-lane sections because it still felt like he was out in the country. As much as he loved Kansas City, where he'd grown up and now worked as a firefighter/EMT, there was something inherently relaxing about the slower pace of the countryside.

And something good for his soul in sharing another memorable one-on-one weekend with his grandfather, Sid Taylor.

The two men had been doing this for twenty-three

years, since Mark's fifth birthday. Grandpa Sid had done more than teach him how to pitch a tent or fish. As the youngest of four adopted brothers, with five uncles, an aunt and their families, it had been easy to get lost in the boisterous shuffle of holiday gatherings and Sunday dinners when the entire Taylor clan got together. But Sid had singled him out as his baby boy—his little buddy who shared his love of the outdoors. If Sid hadn't closed his butcher shop a few years back, Mark might have considered learning the trade so that he could take over his grandfather's business. Instead, he'd followed in his adoptive parents' and birth brother Matt's footsteps, and joined the KCFD.

As a little boy, Sid had made Mark feel like his favorite kid on the whole planet. Mark now knew that Sid had singled out each of his grandchildren to develop a special bond with, but he wouldn't trade these twenty-three years with his grandfather for another Chiefs Super Bowl victory. Their conversations over the years had been about nothing and everything. Sid had been there through the insecurities of getting to know his new family and measuring up to his overachieving brothers' standards; his concerns for his extremely withdrawn brother, Matt; some messy teenage angst; and the ignominy and heartache of his girlfriend saying no to his proposal and moving away to pursue a dream he wasn't invited to be a part of.

This afternoon's conversation was no different as they segued from the Royals trading away good players and relying too much on their farm system, to probing questions about whether Mark had started seeing anyone again, and on to a friendly debate about the success of their time at the lake.

"That bass was over twenty inches," Mark insisted,

adjusting his wraparound sunglasses on the bridge of his nose. "Maybe even two feet."

"The one that broke your fishing line or the one in your imagination?"

Mark grinned, refusing to take that gibe without giving back one of his own. "My largemouth was twice as big as that shrimp of a striper you caught."

"Why don't you just make him a mile long now, so he doesn't have to keep getting bigger every time you tell that story," Sid teased, pulling his ball cap lower on his forehead to shield his eyes from the bright June sun.

When Mark had been a boy, his grandfather had planned the weekend to his lake of choice, packed the food and driven him—filling the time with jokes and deeper conversations about life, answering questions and challenging him to make good, thoughtful decisions about any problems he might have confided in the older man.

Now that Sid had survived two heart events, the knuckles of his workingman's hands had knotted with arthritis and his broad shoulders had stooped with age, their roles had reversed. Mark planned, packed, drove. Although he still let Sid, a retired butcher and former marine, clean the fish and grill them because there were some talents the old man had that he'd never be able to surpass. He could only emulate. Like his adoptive father had before him, like his uncles and brothers had. Every man in the Taylor family had learned about hard work, honor and integrity from this guy who was still teasing Mark about his lousy lack of fish this weekend.

"I'm just sayin' my cooler has six crappie and that eighteen-inch bass on ice to show your grandma." Sid pointed his thumb to the camper on the back of Mark's truck. "Yours is, what? Holding dirty laundry?"

"Fine. I surrender. You get the Taylor Prize for Best Fisherman this year." Mark rested his elbow on the door beside him as they crested a hill and drove down into the valley where the next creek flowed. "It's a good thing I love you, old man. I wouldn't put up with this kind of trash talk from anyone else."

"Right back at ya, son." With a drawn-out sigh, Sid sank back against his seat, looking out the side window at the pin oaks and pines, and occasional glimpses of a colorful redbud or white dogwood peeking out from the dense woods as they sped past. He shifted again, as if he couldn't quite get comfortable in his seat.

"You okay?" Mark asked, feeling a twinge of concern. "Did we overdo it?" The long pause only worried him more. "Grandpa?"

"This has always been a pretty drive. No matter what time of year it is."

"Yes, sir." But Mark had a feeling his grandfather wasn't thinking about the scenery.

"I'm a lucky old dog. I've spent a lot of years with the woman I love, and I'm so proud of all my children and grandchildren. And the great-grands." Without taking his gaze from the scenery, he nodded. "Damn lucky."

Mark reached across the console to squeeze Sid's shoulder. "Are you feeling all right?"

"Too maudlin for you?" He patted Mark's hand, his familiar smile returning. "Don't worry about me. I just get tired sooner than I used to. My eighties haven't been too kind to me."

"You know I love our time together, but if these trips are getting to be too much for you, we could stay closer to home. Or do something else." Mark returned his hand to the wheel. "It's the time we spend together that matters. Not the activity. I'd be just as happy to come over and watch a game with you."

"I know." Another worrisome pause. "I just wanted to see all this one more time." Mark was about to press him on what had brought on this sudden melancholy mood when Sid sat up straight and pointed through the windshield at the wisp of a gray-and-black cloud just above the horizon. "Is that smoke?"

They crested the hill and Mark spotted a scene that no firefighter wanted to see. Two mangled cars, compressed together, lying at an angle down in the steep slope of the ditch. "There's been an accident."

"Looks like it's a head-on collision. Mark?"

Mark had already punched in 9-1-1 on his phone on the dashboard as he slowed his truck and pulled onto the shoulder of the highway above the wreck. He set his blinkers on and identified himself to the local dispatcher. "This is Mark Taylor. I'm a Kansas City firefighter. I'm on Highway 7 heading northwest out of Truman Lake." He reported the last mile marker he'd seen to give a better location. "I've got a two-vehicle accident. They've rolled into the ditch. I need fire and a bus to roll ASAP. I'm off duty and don't have all my gear with me, but I'll do what I can to help."

With the promise to notify the local sheriff's office and volunteer firefighters, the dispatcher ended the call. Mark slipped on his black KCFD ball cap, grabbed his phone off its mount and slid out of the truck. "Stay put." But Sid was already climbing out of the other side. "Grandpa."

His grandfather waved him closer. "Hand me your phone. I'll stay out of your way, but the least I can do is watch for traffic and call Dispatch while you work with the victims down there."

Yeah. Even at eighty-seven, this man was a Taylor, born and raised to serve and protect.

Mark winked and handed over the phone. "You know how the fancy new tech works, Grandpa?"

"Get out of here."

Matching the old man's grin, Mark turned down the steep slope, half sliding on the wet grass and half sinking into the water-soaked ditch as he followed the swath of muddy tire tracks down to the two cars.

A quick assessment showed him three potential victims—the teenage boy driving the rusting farm pickup truck, the woman slumped over the steering wheel and deflated airbag of her SUV, and the crying infant strapped into the back seat. With no skid marks on the road above them, he'd wager that one of the drivers had fallen asleep and drifted over the center line. Or one or both drivers had been distracted with a text or phone call. It wasn't his business to determine the cause of the accident or who was responsible—Mark's job was to get everybody out of the wreck alive, treat any injuries and get them safely onto an ambulance or to a hospital for any further care they might need.

Ignoring the mud and water at the bottom of the ditch that oozed up over his hiking boots and soaked into his jeans, Mark reached the SUV first. It was tipped partially onto its side, and he had to climb up onto the running board to see inside. The woman was out cold. Judging by the lump on her forehead and blood dripping from the wound, she'd hit her head on the side window when the vehicles had rolled. With the doors locked, he couldn't check her pulse, but her chest rose and fell, indicating she was still breathing. The car seat in the back was strapped in correctly, and the baby was wailing up a storm, prob-

CRIME SCENE COVER-UP

JULIE MILLER

COLTON 911: ULTIMATE SHOWDOWN

ADDISON FOX

MILLS & BOON

First Published in Great Britain 2020
by Mills & Boon, an imprint of HarperCollins*Publishers*
1 London Bridge Street, London, SE1 9GF

Crime Scene Cover-Up © 2020 Julie Miller
Colton 911: Ultimate Showdown © 2020 Harlequin Books S.A.

Special thanks and acknowledgement are given to Addison Fox for her contribution to the *Colton 911: Grand Rapids* series.

ISBN: 978-0-263-28059-3

1220

MIX
Paper from
responsible sources
FSC
www.fsc.org
FSC® C007454

This book is produced from independently certified FSC™ paper to ensure responsible forest management.

For more information visit: www.harpercollins.co.uk/green

Printed and bound in Spain
by CPI, Barcelona

ably good indications that the infant might be scared but hadn't been harmed in the accident.

Mark jumped down and circled around to the driver's side of the pickup. It was partially wedged beneath the SUV and sunk into the mud, and this time he had to squat down to get a look at the driver. The truck was old enough that, without air-conditioning, the kid had been driving with his windows down. Thank God the driver was wearing his seat belt. But he was bleeding from a head wound, too, and holding his chest as he squirmed in his seat, shouting for his phone.

"Where's my phone? I can't find my phone."

"Hey." The startled teen spun toward Mark, wincing with pain. "My name's Mark. I'm here to help you. What's your name?"

"Wyatt," he answered in a breathy gasp. "I can't find my phone. I think it flew out of the truck. I just got it with my last paycheck."

"Okay, Wyatt." Mark kept his tone calm and friendly as he reached inside and turned off the ignition. "I'll look for your phone in a minute. Are you hurt? Do you feel pain anywhere?"

The young man clutched at his chest. "I'm having a hard time catching my breath." That could mean a dozen things, from having the wind knocked out of him to internal injuries. The kid's unfocused gaze might mean a head injury, or he could be going into shock. Mark placed his fingers at the side of his neck. His pulse was fast, but even. That was a good sign, at least. "I'm not sure what happened. Can I get out now? I want to look for my phone. My mom's gonna kill me if I lose another one."

When he opened his dented door, Mark pushed back. Typically, he didn't want the patient moving until he'd done a thorough assessment and had a backboard to put him on. But Mark's eyes and sinuses stung with a whole new set of priorities, as smoke filtered from under the dashboard and through the vents. The same smoke Sid had pointed out earlier. Engine fire.

Mark pulled the door open himself and stood, keeping his voice calm, despite conveying a deep sense of urgency. "Yeah, Wyatt. That sounds like a good idea." The young man unfastened his seat belt and swung his legs out the side of the truck. Mark hooked his arm beneath the young man's shoulders. "Can you stand okay?"

The young man swayed for a moment before smiling from ear to ear. "There it is!"

He reached down and pulled his cell phone from beneath the driver's seat. Mark shook his head and pulled the kid into step beside him, leading him back up the side of the ditch to the shoulder of the road. Another car with an older couple had stopped on the far side of the road. While the woman talked on her phone, hopefully to emergency services, the man had been chatting with Sid. "My wife is talking to the highway patrol. I have a blanket in my car," he offered.

"Get it," Mark ordered. "Grandpa, we need the sleeping bags out of the camper." While the two older men left to fetch those items, Mark did a preliminary exam of Wyatt's head wound. Wyatt's relief might just be fueling him with adrenaline for the moment. He wasn't going to take a chance with the kid going into shock. He sat the young man down and told him to call his parents while the other man wrapped the blanket around his shoulders.

His grandfather dropped the sleeping bags beside Mark. Mark stood, turning over Wyatt's care to the other couple. Sid rubbed his shoulder, as if the joint was stiff from the exertion, and nodded toward the wreckage. "The fire's spreading."

Flames were visible now, shooting through the gaps in the warped hood of the truck and traveling up to the SUV's engine.

"Can you make it down the hill?" Mark asked, jogging to the back of his truck and climbing into the camper. On the fire engine, he'd have a Slim Jim to slide into the SUV's door panel to unlock it. He jumped back down to the pavement. Today, the crowbar from his toolbox would have to do.

"Of course I can. What do you need?" Shaking off Mark's guiding hand, Sid followed him down the slope to the upended SUV.

Mark climbed onto the running board again to peer inside. The woman was conscious now—disoriented, but aware that she and her child were in danger. "Courtney?" She flopped her right arm over the back of the seat. "Are you okay, sweetie? Mommy's here."

Mark knocked on the window, capturing her attention. "Ma'am? I need you to turn off your engine." With a nod of understanding, she turned the key, killing any sparks in the motor that could set off an explosion and turn the small fire into a deadly inferno. Mark held up the crowbar, indicating his intention. "I need you to look the other way."

She turned, raising her hand as if it might shield her baby in the back seat. Mark found the precise spot on the window, shielded his own eyes and shattered the glass with a single blow. In a matter of seconds, he swept the glass shards from the ledge of the door and reached inside to unlock all of them.

"Hang tight, ma'am. I'll be right back."

"Save my little girl," the woman pleaded, understanding Mark's intention as he opened the back door and reached inside. "Is she hurt? It all happened so fast."

"You okay, little one?" A quick check indicated that the car seat had done its job protecting its occupant. Possibly a few bruises, and the child was good and scared, but she quieted and reached for Mark as he inched inside to release the carrier from the car seat. "I think she's okay." He climbed out and handed the baby in her carrier to Sid. "Can you get her up the hill?"

Sid nodded and climbed slowly up the hill. "You come with me, sweetie. I know all about little girls. I have one named Jess. She's a big girl now. But she'll always be my…"

The familiar voice faded as Mark turned his attention to the injured mother. With the seat belt jammed, he pulled out his pocketknife and cut through the straps, catching her before she could slide to the other side of the car. Pulling her arm around his shoulders, he carefully lifted her as he stepped to the ground. Her soft grunt of pain and lack of complaining told him she was probably the more seriously injured of the two drivers. And even though moving her risked aggravating any spinal injury, the spreading flames weren't giving him any choice.

He slid once in the grass, before finding traction and completing the climb. Sid had spread one of the sleeping bags out on the ground where Mark laid the woman. He asked the other woman to hold her hand and talk to her while Sid covered her with the other sleeping bag and set the baby carrier beside her. "There you go, sweetie. There's Mama."

The sounds of distant sirens echoed through the hills as Mark ran to the back of his camper again, pulling out the small fire extinguisher he carried, and dropped back down into the ditch. The pickup's hood was too hot to touch, but it had twisted enough that he could spray the fire-suppressant foam through the gaps and douse the fire. He wouldn't have enough foam to put out two engine fires, but if he could stop the flames from spreading to oil lines and fuel tanks—

"Hey! Mister!" Mark squinted against the stinging chemical fumes of the smoke and ignored the voices calling out.

"Mister Mark! Hey, Firefighter Guy!" That was Wyatt. He turned toward the teen's panicked tone. "He doesn't look too good."

Mark followed his gaze past the two women and baby to where the other man was helping Sid move from his knees, where he'd apparently collapsed, to a sitting position. "Grandpa!"

Sid Taylor was lying flat on his back on the shoulder of the road by the time Mark reached him. Ah, hell. He was pale. His skin was clammy. The subtle signs had been there, but Mark hadn't been paying close enough attention. The pulse at his neck was thready at best.

His grandfather was having a heart attack.

"I'm feeling a little light-headed." Sid's dark eyes drifted shut. "That climb…too much…"

"I shouldn't have asked you to do it. Damn it, I shouldn't have asked." Mark dug through the front pockets of his grandfather's jeans, pulling out the small bottle of baby aspirin. His fingers shook as he twisted it open. This shouldn't be happening. They were supposed to be having fun this weekend. He and Grandpa Sid always had fun.

"Nonsense… Happy to…" For one frightening moment, his voice drifted off.

"Grandpa!" Mark bent his ear to his grandfather's nose and mouth. Was he still breathing? He flattened his palm over Sid's chest, searching for a heartbeat. Where the hell was his med kit when he needed it? Back at the station, on the truck, where it was supposed to be. He and Sid were on vacation. This wasn't supposed to happen. "Grandpa, you hang in there."

After three compressions, Sid's eyes slowly opened. But they were hazy, unable to focus.

"There you are." Mark popped the pill onto Sid's tongue, lifting him slightly and running his hand along his throat to help him swallow. "You scared me, old man. Here. Take this."

Then he laid him flat on the pavement again and resumed compressions.

Someone covered Sid with a blanket. Someone was talking on the phone to 9-1-1. Someone else was crying.

"Did we save the day?" He'd never heard that voice sound so weak.

"Yeah. We sure did, Grandpa." Mark swiped angrily at the tears that clouded his vision. "As soon as the ambulance gets here, they'll all be okay. So will you."

With a flop, Sid covered Mark's hands with one of his, brushing his fingers against Mark's wrist. His touch was cold, jerky. "My good boy. Good…man…"

Sid Taylor's eyes focused for a split second. And then they closed.

"No!" Mark continued the compressions against the old man's brave heart. "Grandpa!"

Chapter Two

Two months later

"What is wrong with you?"

Mark shied away from his brother Alex's flick on the ear, dragged himself from the gloom and guilt of his thoughts, and frowned at his oldest brother's reprimand. "What's wrong with *you*?"

Not the whippiest comeback, but it was the best he could do under the circumstances. Parked on the street in front of the empty butcher shop their grandfather had run for almost fifty years, Mark set the box he'd carried down from his grandmother's apartment above the shop on the tailgate of his truck.

Before he could push it into the bed of the truck, Alex picked up the box and carried it to the pickup parked in front of Mark's, where his brothers Matt and Pike were tying down a dining room table and matching chairs. "That's the third full box of Grandma's things you've tried to load in the back of your truck. Her things go into Matt's truck to haul out to the new house. Grandpa's things go into your truck so we can put them into storage."

Alex might be the shortest of the four Taylor brothers—all adopted into the Taylor clan when they were kids—but there was no doubting his position as the oldest. And possibly the toughest, given his early years as a gang member on the streets of Kansas City. Finding a family like the Taylors, who'd embraced each of them despite their rotten childhoods and the emotional needs they came with, had been a real blessing. They all loved their parents, Gideon and Meghan, as well as their extended family. Brought together first in a foster home and then by adoption, they loved each other, too—and would fight to the death any outsider who threatened their family. But they were still brothers—and picking on the youngest had evolved into an art form over the years.

Probably why Mark had learned at a young age never to back down from standing up for himself and expressing his own opinion. He pulled a black bandanna from the back pocket of his jeans and wiped away the perspiration trickling down his neck before tying it around his forehead to keep the sweat there from running into his eyes. The early summer morning had turned into a long, hot afternoon as it was all hands on deck to help their widowed grandmother move into a ranch-style home with no stairs.

Mark rested his hip against the tailgate. "It doesn't bother you that we're putting Grandpa Sid into storage?"

"It does," Alex agreed, his dark brown eyes a mix of sympathy and reprimand. He stepped aside while brawny Matt pulled a cooler from the back of his truck and opened it to share some iced-down bottles of water. "But we're here to help Grandma today. Moving her to a new place where she doesn't have to climb twenty steps just to get to the front door. Downsizing. Clearing out the apartment so that we can fix it up and she can sell it along with the butcher shop." He tossed Mark a bottle of water and opened one of his own. "She's the one who got left behind, little bro. She needs us to suck up whatever hurt we're feeling and help her get through this." As a SWAT cop, Alex was used to giving orders and expecting them to be obeyed. But he understood that he couldn't just order Mark to stop feeling the grief that distracted him today. "Pike, you're the logical one. Explain this to our baby brother."

The tallest of them, and the only one with blond hair, Edison "Pike" Taylor levered himself off the back of Matt's truck and grabbed one of the water bottles for himself. His KCPD K-9 partner, Hans, was upstairs with his wife and two young children supervising the packing and distracting Martha Taylor from the sadness of the day. "Don't put me in the middle of this. We all miss Grandpa. I've got a little girl who's never going to know how much her great-grandpa would have spoiled her." He rested an elbow on Alex's shoulder, a long-ingrained habit that reminded their oldest brother that he wasn't the boss here, and that, despite his best intentions, he didn't have all the answers. "Mark was there when we lost him. Maybe that makes it harder for him to compartmentalize and move past it."

Maybe it did.

Mark had saved every life that day except for the one who really counted.

His KCFD counselor kept reminding him to focus on the positive when he got stuck in his head like this. *"Try telling that to the parents of that teenage boy—to the husband and father of that mother and baby."*

"Try telling that to my grandmother. Or parents. Or brothers." Try explaining how he'd let Sid Taylor, the patriarch of this large, wonderful family who'd rescued him, die on the side of the road in the middle of nowhere.

"Hey." The truck shifted as Matt sat on the tailgate beside him. "Get out of your head. This is not your fault."

"Yeah? Just like the death of our birth parents wasn't *your* fault." The shock that flared in Matt's brown eyes was hidden away as quickly as it had appeared. Mark shook his head in apology, hating the way the words had come out of his mouth. He knew the pain his older brother carried. "Hey, man—I'm sorry. That was a low blow. You were a little kid—not even in school yet. No one blames you. Hell, you saved my life that night. It's just…" Mark shrugged. "I know you've struggled with that. When you figure out how to let that one go, you let me in on the secret, okay?"

Matt's gaze narrowed with a considering look. Then he threw an arm around Mark's shoulders and hauled him in for a tight, quick hug. Then he was pushing Mark away and rising to his feet. Ever a man of few words, Matt finished off his water, crumpled the bottle in his fist and went back to his truck. The four brothers packed the remaining boxes into their respective vehicles and headed up the inside stairs to their grandmother's apartment for the next load.

After another hour of packing, they sat down on folding chairs and the floor to share one last Sunday dinner at their grandparents' home. Mark had never left this place hungry, and today was no different. He wolfed down two helpings of potato salad and deli sandwiches, along with samples from the last batch of chocolate chip cookies Grandma Martha would ever bake in this home, where she'd lived with Grandpa Sid for almost fifty years. Somewhere along the way, Mark's mood lightened as his dad and grandmother shared family stories. Hans accepted the offering of a roast beef sandwich from Pike's son to several "Oops" and "Oh, no"s and quick corrections for both dog and boy. And Alex and his wife, Audrey, announced they were taking a class to get certified to adopt a child, which generated a round of hugs and congratulations. Mark wrestled his dad for the last cookie before discovering smarty-pants Pike had already eaten it. Then there was a round of cheers and applause when Grandma Martha pulled a plastic container filled with more cookies from a secret stash in one of the boxes.

Mark was finally laughing when his phone vibrated in the pocket of his jeans. The noise in the big apartment quieted as other phones buzzed or rang with incoming calls and texts. His mother, Meghan, a station captain; his father, an arson investigator and deputy fire chief; as well as his brother Matt—all firefighters—got the same page on their phones.

"Looks like Station 13 needs backup," Mark reported. "They're calling in all off-duty personnel who weren't on the last shift."

"Must be something big," Alex observed.

"I got the same message from my firehouse." Their mother swung her long blond braid behind her back, shifting into command mode as she shared the gist of the message while Mark read the all-call on his phone. Meghan Taylor might be diminutive in size compared to her husband and the four sons they'd adopted, but as the ranking KCFD officer, Mark and Matt automatically deferred to her. "Looks like volunteer firefighters in Platte County have lost control of a wildfire up north. The winds have shifted and pushed it into our jurisdiction. They thought they had it contained to the brushland and trees, but it's threatening a new housing development and farm homes close to the airport."

Their father, Gideon, was already putting his phone to

his ear and striding out of the room. "I'll put in a call to the city—see if we can get some water trucks up there."

Meghan crossed the room to her white-haired mother-in-law. "Martha, I don't want to leave you here. I know this is a tough day for you."

"I'll be just fine, Meg." Martha Taylor might have lost some height and gained some arthritis over the past few years, but nothing could diminish her innate strength or the bright warmth in her blue eyes. She cupped Meghan's cheek and smiled. "I was married to a marine. And we raised enough cops and firefighters to know that when duty calls, you answer. Don't you worry about me."

Alex slipped his arm around their grandmother's thinning frame. "Audrey and I will stay with her, Mom."

Pike draped an arm around Martha from the opposite side. "Hope and me and the kids, too. Grandma won't be alone."

Martha reached up and squeezed both Alex's and Pike's hands where they rested on her shoulders, and Mark suspected she was finding the comfort she needed to ease today's abrupt departure as she leaned first into one grandson and then the other. "I never have been. Go. It's because of this family that I have always felt safe."

Meghan nodded and the two women exchanged a hug and a kiss on the cheek. "Love you."

"Love you, too, dear."

Then Meghan turned to Mark and Matt. "Boys?"

Mark imagined they could be sixty, seventy, eighty years old, and their mother would always summon them with *Boys*. Mark didn't mind. He knew he was a lucky son of a gun to be included in this family. Alex, Pike, Matt and he were the boys that, because of a tragic event early in Meghan's life, she'd never been able to have. To his way of thinking, it made the bond between them that much more special because she and Gideon had chosen the four of them to be their boys.

Their father strode back into the room. "The tankers are on their way." He grasped their mother's hand. "Shall we?" He nodded to Mark and Matt. "Why don't you boys drive separately? It sounds like we might need to spread out our resources."

"Yes, sir." Matt swallowed Martha up in a hug against his broad chest and dropped a kiss on the crown of her hair. "Love you, Grandma."

"Love you, too, Matthew. Be safe."

Her blue eyes locked on to Mark's across the room. Were they sad? Troubled? Or was that the reflection of his own thoughts he saw there? "I love you, too, Mark."

He was the one who'd made this day necessary. How could she say she loved him when he'd taken the love of her life from her?

But her outstretched arms demanded he obey Alex's directive and *suck it up* to do whatever was necessary to ease their grandmother's pain. After the unfamiliar hesitation, he crossed the room and leaned down to wrap her up in a gentle hug. Her slight frame was surprisingly strong as she held on a little longer than he'd planned. "You keep your head in the game and be safe," she whispered against his ear. "I'll be all right."

He didn't deserve her kindness or forgiveness or whatever this was. Still, he tightened his arms as much as he dared because, with everything else she had to deal with right now, he didn't want to add to her burden. "You'd better be," he whispered back before pulling away. "I love you, Grandma."

Then he was jogging down the stairs, following Matt and his parents to their respective vehicles, answering the call for off-duty personnel to provide backup for the exhausted firefighters in North Kansas City.

It was time to go to work.

Time to make sure nobody else died on his watch.

Chapter Three

"Mr. O'Brien, if you could just sign—"

"Do you see how close that fire came to my model home?" Dale O'Brien ignored his assistant, who tried to push a pen and notebook with a page of typed checks toward the contractor, who was building new homes in the area at the edge of the wildfire they'd finally put out. With a heavy sigh that bespoke too little appreciation on too long a day, she hugged the notebook back to her chest and followed her boss as he approached Mark's mom, the local scene commander. Mark watched from his perch on top of the Firehouse 13 truck as the contractor pointed a stubby finger at Meghan Taylor. "I have two buyers who are ready to move into their houses, and eight more lots sold. I have a substantial investment here." O'Brien, the owner of the Copper Lake subdivision near the KCI Airport, had a right to be concerned about the safety of his construction employees and damage to the property he owned.

But a faint accusation laced the tone of the man with a gut pushing over the top of his belt buckle. O'Brien insisted on pointing out the negative instead of focusing on how Mark, Matt and the rest of the KCFD off-duty volunteers who'd answered the call for backup had cleared a trench through the neighboring farmland and watered down a protective perimeter around the new subdivision so that not one of O'Brien's fancy Copper Lake homes and construction sites had sustained any damage from the approaching grass fire.

While Matt was driving the bulldozer they'd used back onto its trailer, Mark and the other firefighters rolled up hoses and stowed their gear in the engine behind his mom. The firefighters were hot, sweaty and grimy, while O'Brien looked like he'd just stepped out of his air-conditioned trailer. He pointed to the charred shell of a tiny house on the far side of the lake that gave the subdivision its name. "This is the third fire we've had out here in less than two months. That's bad for my business. I know it's putting a burden on taxpayers and the KCFD to deal with them. But I don't know what we would have done without your help, Chief Taylor. Clearly, the local yokels can't handle it. Something needs to be done to stop them."

Meghan Taylor pulled off her white helmet and brushed aside the sooty blond curls that stuck to her freckled cheek. "It's Captain, not Chief, Mr. O'Brien. The county volunteers have been working their butts off to keep these brush fires in check. This one was in danger of jumping the interstate and causing a whole slew of new problems like impaired visibility and traffic accidents. Not to mention encroaching on airport land." Just as he had been for as long as he could remember, Mark was amazed at how tough his mother was. He'd learned long ago not to be fooled by her youthful beauty and soft tone. If Dale O'Brien didn't stop telling her how to do her job, he would soon learn that her gentle demeanor hid a backbone of steel. "You should be thanking them, not insulting them."

"Well, I didn't mean anything by it, of course." He pulled off his hard hat and scratched at his receding hairline before he came up with a new angle that sounded more concerned citizen than whiny businessman. "I was just thinking of the welfare of my men—and your people, too. I know you put lives before property, and that's as it should be. But I don't want Copper Lake to be a frequent call for you."

Mark thought the guy seemed too friendly, too eager to show that this neighborhood was his moneymaker and that he was the big cheese around here. And if he kept pointing that arrogant finger at Mark's mother, Mark was going to break it.

"Mr. O'Brien, please," his young brunette assistant pleaded. "I need to get back to the city and run some errands before my date tonight." She nodded over her shoulder to the pair of men waiting at a beat-up blue sedan near O'Brien's office trailer. While one man lounged on the hood of the car, watching the firefighters work, the other paced beside the car, more focused on the conversation between O'Brien and Mark's mother. "You promised Brad and Richie a paycheck today."

"Can't you see I'm busy, Lissette?" the portly man snapped.

This time, Lissette's sigh held a hint of impatience as she shoved the checks into his chest. "If you want me to work a miracle and make the books balance this month, then you need to pay them. Everyone else gets direct deposit, but you insisted that those two get paid out of petty cash. I won't be responsible for any shortfalls this month. You have to sign."

"Fine." He grabbed the pen, glared at the two men who were now watching intently for his response, then scribbled a line across the bottom of each check. He shoved the notebook back to the young woman and dismissed her. "Tell them they don't need to report for work again until I call them. That'll be all."

"Yes, sir."

Mark watched her hurry over to the two lookie-loos and hand them their checks. The two men made an effort to chat her up after thanking her for getting them paid, but she waved aside their thanks and hurried into the office trailer to deposit the notebook and retrieve her purse before quickly driving away.

The rest of O'Brien's men—the ones not getting paid out of petty cash—had packed up their work trucks. Maybe those two had been waiting around for the chance to get a few more hours in on their paychecks once KCFD cleared the scene. But with black smoke still coiling across the horizon, gusting winds threatening to reignite fires, and some of the access roads into the farm country and public woodlands blocked by firefighting equipment and crew vehicles, he didn't anticipate anyone getting back to work before the next morning.

Once the hose was secured, Mark slid down the ladder at the back of the Lucky 13 truck and grabbed his turnout coat and helmet. Instead of heading to his truck, he lingered to hear a little more of the conversation the contractor insisted on having with the captain.

"I warned my crew about smoking in the dry grass," O'Brien announced. "And to police the sparks from their power tools. They're supposed to work over a paved area or the dirt. But I can't keep my eye on them 24/7. Nothing out here a good rainstorm wouldn't cure. An end to this drought would make life a lot easier for all of us."

Meghan Taylor shook her head. "These fires didn't start where your men are working. The fires are coming from the other direction, across the lake where that farmland is. The wind is what moved the fire toward your property."

Mark scanned the far side of the lake as O'Brien pointed across the water to the hilly landscape. "A lot of that is my land, too. Or will be. The landowner, Mrs. Hall, is selling it off in chunks as we build the new homes out here. She's a widow now and getting on in years, can't keep up with it all. I expect when she's ready to move into the city and sell off the rest of it—I mean, it's not like she's farming it herself—I'll own the property around the entire lake. We're building quite a nice bedroom community out here. Quality homes with an easy commute into downtown."

Mark knew that his mom wasn't interested in O'Brien's sales pitch. She pointed to the empty lots beyond the newly built model home and the two houses that were already under construction on either side of the street. "You've got all the proper permits here? There's only one hydrant on the north side of the lake."

"The city hasn't repaved the street and updated the water main there yet. Those houses are on well water." Had O'Brien dodged the question about permits? Or was he still intent on impressing Mark's mom with his grandiose plans? "Once I tear them down and build new homes, the view to the north will improve one hundred percent."

Mark eyed the dilapidated string of houses on the far side of the lake. Besides the burned one, another had a listing boat dock, making those homes look like the poor neighbors of O'Brien's fancy new lakeside community. Only one of the tiny houses had a decent roof. The farmhouse at the top of the rise beyond them looked in better shape. But that might be deceptive since the front of the house was camouflaged by scaffolding. It was painted an antique white about halfway down the shingled siding of the two-story colonial, while the bottom half just looked antique, as in peeling, warped and faded. But the roof was new, a shiny warm corrugated copper that gleamed with the orange-red glow of the late summer sun. And the whole thing sat in a patch of green grass, an indicator that the homeowner cared more about the property than O'Brien claimed. Not only was the old woman fixing up the house, but she had watered the yard more frequently than any of the newly sodded properties O'Brien had built.

"I just want to know that my men are safe out here," O'Brien added. "And that they can get back to work sooner rather than later. Idle time is wasted money."

About the time Mark decided to interrupt the conversation to tell O'Brien to clear out with the last of his men, and give his mom an excuse for ending the stocky man's gripe-and-brag session, the door to the farmhouse flew open and a woman ran out.

Even if he hadn't heard the slap of the door slamming shut behind her, he couldn't have missed the flag of a copper-red ponytail flying out behind her as she ran to an old blue-and-white pickup parked in the gravel driveway. Although he couldn't make out the details of her face, the stretch of long legs between khaki shorts and hiking boots pounding down the steps and front walk screamed that something was wrong. The hackles on the back of Mark's neck went up another notch as she executed a quick three-point turn and gunned the engine, racing down the driveway toward the weathered asphalt that separated the farmhouse from the run-down lakeside buildings.

"What the hell?"

Mark was already skirting around his mom and Mr. O'Brien when the woman made a sharp left turn onto another gravel road, churning up a cloud of dust in her wake as she crested the hill and headed down the other side. Speeding her way north. Away from the subdivision. Away from the lake and the farmhouse.

Driving *toward* the brush fire.

His mom flanked him for a moment, both watching as the woman headed straight toward the danger they'd worked so hard to avert. Meghan Taylor turned her head to the radio clipped to her turnout coat and asked for a sit-rep, a situation report. "Were all civilians evacuated from the area north of the lake?" She turned back to Dale O'Brien. "Do you know who that young woman is?"

He chuckled. "Crazy Amy. She lives there with her grandma."

"Do you have a last name for her? Contact information?"

Mr. O'Brien shrugged. "In my trailer. I've got the home number for her grandmother's house in my phone."

"I need that." She tilted her brown eyes to Mark. "We have to stop her. I'll work on calling her and get over to the house to make sure the grandmother isn't still inside. You—"

"I'm on it, Captain." Mark ran to his truck and tossed his helmet and turnout coat inside before climbing in.

But a large hand clamped around the edge of the door, preventing him from closing it. Big brother Matt had a habit of showing up without announcing himself. "Where do you think you're going?"

Mark started the engine. "After that woman. She's driving straight into wildfire territory instead of away from it like anyone with a lick of sense would." When Matt's suspicious glare didn't so much as blink, Mark grumbled a curse under his breath, knowing what his brother must be thinking after their conversation earlier that day. "I don't have a death wish. But I think maybe she does."

"You don't have to save everybody."

This wasn't about Grandpa Sid and the guilt he felt. "I'm doing my job, Matt."

Matt arched a questioning eyebrow, but this wasn't the time to psychoanalyze him. It was time to act. "Make sure that's all it is." He closed the door, but he didn't release it. "Want me to go with you?"

Mark looked beyond him to see O'Brien futzing with his phone, while their mother waited for the promised phone number. "No. Stay with Mom. I can't tell if that O'Brien guy is up to something, or if he's worried about his investments burning down out here. He sure as hell has no clue how to talk to a lady. I know she can handle herself, but—"

"She's our mom. I'm on it." Matt shoved his hand through the open window to trade a fist bump with Mark. "Eyes open, bro. Keep us apprised of your twenty."

Mark tapped his fist against Matt's, understanding the friendly warning to stay aware of any shift in the winds kindling a new fire or catching behind him and cutting him off from his escape. "Will do."

Mark shifted into Drive and took off, reassured to see Matt joining their mother and Mr. O'Brien in his rear-view mirror. By the time he'd left the new pavement and circled around the lake, he'd lost sight of the red-haired woman. But there weren't that many places she could go out here, were there?

He turned off the asphalt, pressing a little harder than he probably should on the gravel surface. After fishtailing around the turn, he crested the road she had taken, and discovered the remains of what had once been a working farm. He passed an old horse paddock with charred broken railings and a stable whose roof had partially collapsed in on its brick walls. The blackened studs and surviving beams at one end indicated the fire in the paddock had climbed the exterior walls and taken down the roof. Idly, he wondered if the fires had caused the property on this side of the lake to look run-down and abandoned—or if abandoning the farming and caring for the structures had led to the fires.

But it wasn't all run-down. Beyond the stable was an equipment shed that was built in a similar design. The barn wood had a fresh coat of white paint on it, a new corrugated metal roof that matched the house, and a padlocked door. Clearly, that building was still in use, but the padlock on the outside told him the mysterious redhead hadn't gone in there.

Mark looked ahead to the rolling hills that had gone wild with brittle brown prairie grass and scrub pines that dotted the sea of brown with tufts of green. A row of charred fence posts swept over the hills like a gothic version of holiday garland. Nothing he could see was tall enough to give shelter or hide the redhead's truck. He looked to his left to see the undulating line of black crossing the nearest hilltop, indicating the line the fire had reached before the winds had moved the flames in another direction. He spotted the flames climbing the next hill, and the team of volunteer firefighters spaced along the front line to keep it from advancing. While the trench his own team had dug, and the lake itself, would protect the subdivision for now, that farmhouse and the buildings on the north side of the lake were still vulnerable. Anything between the lake and the natural firebreak of paved and gravel roads to the north and west was still vulnerable to the mercurial path of the fire.

And that woman with the striking copper hair had driven right into the heart of it.

A wary alertness pricked the nape of Mark's neck as he discovered a crossroads at the base of the next hill. He didn't have eyes on her yet, but Mark didn't hesitate to turn left. The dry earth formed a plume of dust behind her truck that was as easy to spot as the woman's red ponytail.

"Finally." He spotted the dust cloud settling around the blue-and-white pickup near a burned-out bridge over a narrow creek. The woman had stopped at the roadblock warning drivers to steer clear of the wildfire area. Mark skidded to a stop behind her battered truck. But as their cumulative dust cloud drifted past him, he saw that she was out of the truck, climbing over the barricade. When her hiking boots hit the charred grass on the opposite side, she took off running again.

Even though his truck could handle a little off-roading, with no clear line of sight to determine the current location of the fire, Mark couldn't risk driving after her. In seconds, he was out of his truck, swearing at her persistence and chasing after her. "Hey! Lady, stop!"

If anything, those long legs of hers picked up speed as she climbed up the opposite side of the embankment. Mark swore. Either she was deaf, purposely ignoring him or actually *was* crazy, like O'Brien had said.

Although he'd stripped down to his T-shirt and suspenders in deference to the heat, Mark still wore his bunker pants and boots. Their heavy, protective weight was necessary for fighting fires, but not the best gear for a cross-country race. But Crazy Amy's reckless charge left him little choice but to go after her. Lengthening his own strides, he climbed the bank of the creek and closed the gap between them.

"Ma'am?" he shouted. He was close enough to hear her labored breathing now. She'd been running hard. Or maybe the stranger chasing her down had panicked her. "I'm KCFD. I don't mean to frighten you, but you're entering dangerous territory. I need you to stop and come with me."

"I can't." She stumbled over the slick mix of dirt and ash, swore at her clumsiness and relentlessly pushed herself back to her feet.

But her tumble slowed her enough for Mark to reach her. He caught hold of her arm beneath the rolled-up sleeve of her blouse, abruptly stopping her ascent and pulling her around to face him. "I believe I'm the authority here."

She shoved long coppery bangs off her face, leaving a streak of soot on her freckled cheek. "I believe this is my land. Well, my gran's." She made a fussy noise and twisted her elbow from his grip before lunging up the hill again. "I'm sorry. I can't talk to you right now."

"Can't…?" In two long strides he was in front of her, holding out his hands, hoping to calm down this flight response and reason with her. "My name is Mark Taylor." He pulled aside one strap of his suspenders and pointed to the logo on his T-shirt. "I'm with the Kansas City Fire Department."

"Good for you." She darted around him.

"Hey!" This time he grabbed her with both hands, keeping a firm grip on each upper arm. A unique pendant, which looked like a knotted rope of silver, rose and fell with every breath against the freckles dotting her ample chest above the tank top she wore beneath her blouse. But the shiny metal wasn't nearly as bright as the gold flecks sparking against the green irises of her eyes. He glanced over his shoulder, thinking maybe that was the encroaching fire he saw flickering there. But no, she was just pissed that he'd outmuscled her for her own good. Easing his grip on her, and taking a deep breath to calm his demeanor, Mark explained the danger so she would understand his concern. "KCFD and the Platte County Volunteer Fire Department has the fire contained for now. But it covers acres, miles, maybe. And it's still burning. Plus, the way this wind is blowing, we don't know if it will stay contained or head back this way."

Mark was six-two, and even though he stood slightly uphill of her, the woman barely tilted her chin to maintain eye contact with him. That height explained the mile-long legs. "Thank you for that PSA, Mark Taylor, but I'm willing to risk it." She waved her hand as though she was shooing him away, flashing a variety of chunky rings on her thumb and fingers. "I absolve you of responsibility. Be gone with you."

She scooted around him again.

"Be gone with…?" Had he slipped into some universe populated by flakes and stubborn women who wouldn't listen? He grabbed her one more time, pulling her closer to his body so she couldn't twist away. That didn't stop her from pushing at his chest and trying. "You're nuts, lady. I'm trying to rescue you here."

"I don't need you to rescue me!" All at once the air rushed from her lungs and her expression changed. On first glance, he might have thought her unadorned face was rather unremarkable. But those green-gold eyes offered a fascinating glimpse of her emotions. They were darker now, as green as the charred landscape around them should have been. She wasn't crazy. Something was wrong. Seriously wrong. Something clutched inside him as she patted the KCFD logo over his heart. "I need you to help me."

"Help you do what? Get yourself killed?" Her hands settled against his shoulders and he felt her arms stiffen. She was getting ready to bolt again. He calmed his tone, hoping to reason with her. "You're running toward the flames, not to safety."

"Isn't that what you do? Run toward danger?"

"One of us is trained and the other isn't."

She pushed and tried to twist free. The soft, frightened moment had passed. Her eyes were sparking again. "Then be a hero and help me find my friend. She's somewhere out here in the middle of all this."

"I'm no hero." Her description grated against Mark's guilt, but he shoved his feelings aside and worked harder to assess the situation before she escaped again. "I'm just doing my job. Now tell me about your friend, and do not run from me again."

Her arms relaxed their stiff posture and he released her. "Jocelyn Brunt. College roommate. Best friend. She's the yin to my yang. Introvert-extrovert. Scientist-artist— you get the idea. Jocelyn's a researcher, working on her PhD in environmental science. She was working up near the apple trees that run along the eastern property line. She's been living with my gran and me the past couple of semesters."

He noted the direction of her pointing thumb. "The old farmhouse by Copper Lake? Weren't you ordered to evacuate?"

"Of course we were. I drove Gran into the city to stay with one of her friends."

"But Jocelyn didn't go with you?"

"Would I be here if she had?" She gestured to the top of the hill behind him, frustrated with his lack of clairvoyant understanding of her concern. "There are still several old buildings on the property. Jocelyn uses one of the old feed sheds to store her equipment when she's out in the field checking the soil and plant growth, so she doesn't have to haul it back and forth every day. I called her as soon as we were notified the fire had changed course. One of the things she studies is how fire affects different kinds of soil with different kinds of crops or grazing land like this, so I thought maybe she was taking a little extra time to pick up her data. It's my fault I didn't check in with her right away. She said she was on her way to the shed to lock up her stuff, and then she'd join us." The breeze whipped her long bangs across her face again, and Mark squeezed his fingers into a fist, surprised by the instinctive urge to brush the russet waves aside and tuck them behind her ear. "That was six hours ago."

"Did you try calling her again?"

"Of course I did. I'm not an idiot. Her phone goes straight to voice mail." She tilted her nose into the air as the wind shifted. Mark could smell it, too. Smoke. All the more reason to solve this woman's problem and get her out of the fire zone. "She could be trapped out here somewhere. I hoped that she had gone back to the house because you guys stopped the fire, but her Jeep wasn't there. What if she holed up in the shed, thinking that was safe? Or she tried to hike back to the house but got cut off by the fire? You saw that roadblock and the scorch marks on the ground—all the way down to the creek. I'm afraid something has happened to her."

Now he understood. There was another life to save. "Where is this shed?"

"I'll take you."

"No, that's not what I…" But she was already jogging ahead. Mark turned his face to the smoky sky and swore before hurrying after her. He caught her arm and stopped her again. "Fine. I'll give you fifteen minutes. You lead the way. But if I see anything I don't like, if I think you're in immediate danger, I will order you to stop, and we will leave."

"Fine." She was running again.

Mark clamped his hand over her arm once more and turned her to face him. Her eyes were deep green with emotion now—she was probably pissed at him for being so bossy. But he meant business. He took the time to radio in a sit-rep and give his team an approximate location and their destination before he spoke to the woman again. "What's your name, Red? That O'Brien guy called you Crazy Amy. I don't intend to do that."

"Dale O'Brien is a bully and a prig." She muttered a choice expletive that made Mark wonder what the pudgy contractor had done to her. But that conversation was for another time. And a different man. This was a rescue op, not a get-acquainted date. "I'm Amy Hall."

"All right, Amy Hall. I will help you find your friend. But you do what I tell you, when I tell you, or I will throw you over my shoulder and carry you away from that fire myself. That's the only way we're moving forward."

She seemed to consider just how serious he was about the over-the-shoulder threat—or maybe she was just desperate to end this conversation and get to her friend.

But then she nodded. "I can live with that." She shifted her grip to lace her fingers together with his and pulled him into a jog behind her. "Let's go, Fire Man."

It was a steeper jog down this hill, and Mark was glad he had a hold of Amy when her feet slipped from underneath her. She didn't complain about the soot mark on the rump of her khaki shorts, but simply thanked him and fell into step beside him again as they climbed to the top of the next hill.

They both halted when they reached the devastation waiting for them there.

"Oh, my God." Amy's hand tightened convulsively around Mark's. Then she released him and ran toward the burned-out shell of a Jeep. "Jocelyn!"

"Hold on."

"Jocelyn!" After a quick circle around the Jeep to inspect its empty interior, Amy dashed over to the carbonized wood planks and metal debris that had once been the feed shed.

Mark spared an extra minute to make sure the fuel lines were secure and there was no gasoline or oil pooling beneath the vehicle that could start another fire.

"Amy!" The wildfire had blazed a trail across the top of the hill, turning everything in its path to ash before moving on. If her friend had taken refuge here, or the flames had moved too quickly for her to escape, she hadn't survived.

There was only one woman he could help now.

Amy lifted a board with her bare hands, and it disintegrated. She lifted the one beneath it and tossed it aside. That board hit the ground and kicked up a cloud of black that could be charcoal dust or smoke. He climbed through the wreckage of the old shed after her. "Amy, stop! There could still be hot spots underneath the debris."

"Jocelyn? Please tell me you were smart enough to get out of…" She spotted something at the bottom of the pile and climbed over some charred chunks of metal he assumed had been Jocelyn's equipment. "Oh, no. Please no."

He saw it, too. The charred remains of a body.

"Amy, stop." Mark pushed Amy behind him and took over clearing the debris around the ghastly skeleton. "We don't know who it is. Someone else could have taken shelter. I need you to stand aside..."

But Amy was kneeling in the area he'd cleared. Her cheeks were pale at first, then flushed with emotion as a tear rolled down her cheek. Mark knelt beside her, intent on pulling her away from the remains.

But once again, Amy Hall refused to do what made sense. She reached down to tug at the blackened chain that had fallen inside the victim's rib cage. Mark draped an arm around her shoulders as she rubbed the soot off the chain's pendant to reveal a glimpse of knotted silver.

"That's just like yours," he whispered.

Amy dropped the necklace and wrapped her fist around the pendant at her own neck. "I made it for her. Jocelyn..." A sob broke free and Amy turned her face into Mark's chest. He wrapped her up in his arms and pulled her to her feet, tucking her face against the juncture of his neck and shoulder and holding her as Amy wept for her friend. "It's her. I'm too late. It's her."

As Mark held on tight, shielding Amy from the gruesome sight, he recognized something, too—scorch marks across and around the body. While his heart grieved for Amy Hall's loss, another, darker emotion welled up inside him.

Anger.

The scorch marks were the pour pattern of an accelerant crisscrossing the corpse, indicating the woman had been doused in some sort of chemical and set on fire—postmortem, he hoped. Burning alive was a hell of a way to die. And if he wasn't mistaken, the dent in Jocelyn Brunt's skull suggested something even more sinister.

Amy's fists gradually eased their death grip at the back of his shirt, but he held on as he walked her away from the dead body. Keeping Amy's face averted from the gruesome scene, Mark reached for his radio and called it in.

This fire was no accident. He needed to inform the scene commanders that at least part of today's wildfire was the result of arson—a fire deliberately set to cover up the scene of a murder.

Chapter Four

"When was the last time you saw Ms. Brunt?" The female detective with the long brown ponytail and seriously unfriendly frown tapped her phone with her metal stylus. "I mean alive, of course."

While KCFD investigators pored over the burned-out wreckage of Jocelyn's Jeep and the old shed on the north edge of the property, and a medical examiner took her friend's body to the crime lab, KCPD detectives had brought Amy back to the house to take her statement and go through Jocelyn's things.

Amy flicked her gaze over to Detective Cathy Beck's cold green eyes, but quickly dismissed the shorter woman's mood as they stood together inside the doorway to Jocelyn's bedroom. "Early this morning. Breakfast." Nervously fingering the silver knot that hung from the chain around her neck, Amy watched Detective Beck's partner, Dean Carson, toss the bedding. Less than a week ago, she and Jocelyn had sat up all night on that bed, pigging out on coffee ice cream and discussing the mess of their respective love lives and work woes. When the compactly built blond detective left the quilt and pillows in a pile and bent down to study something on the exposed sheet more closely, Amy asked, "What is he doing? He's making a mess of her things. Jocelyn didn't entertain guests here."

Detective Beck tapped something into her phone. "Did she entertain them somewhere else?"

Amy shook her head, closing her fist around her necklace. Jocelyn had kept her room organized and uncluttered. The speed with which the burly detective was destroying all that twisted a knot in her stomach. "She was focused on finishing her PhD," Amy answered. "She was excited about the fires adding a new dimension to her dissertation. All she had left was this semester and orals in the spring."

"So, Ms. Brunt was completely focused on her work." Detective Beck jotted a note on her phone. "Was there a boyfriend—or girlfriend—who felt neglected?"

"She had a boyfriend on and off." A lot of that last late-night ice cream bash had centered around Jocelyn's ex, Derek Roland. Amy shrugged. "But they were *off.* They were doing similar research, and she thought there might be a conflict of interest when it came time to present their findings to the dissertation board."

"Conflict of interest?"

Man, she really did not want to talk about the prejudices and bias that an assistant dean and group of professors could exert over a doctoral student, especially a female one. But she wanted to identify whoever had killed Jocelyn more. Her own experience was water under the bridge now. If answering questions that dredged up those uncomfortable memories was what it took, then she would do it. "Jocelyn was worried the professors might think she'd copied Derek's research. More likely, Derek would have copied hers. She was brilliant and determined, and he was…lazy. Always looking for shortcuts."

"Did Ms. Brunt ask for the time off from their relationship, or did he?"

"Jocelyn suggested they take a break." Amy shivered

uncomfortably. These questions felt like she was ratting out someone else she had considered a friend, too. But Derek's charm had worn thin when his demands on Jocelyn's time had made Jocelyn question whether he was interested in her or her research. Amy almost laughed when she considered Derek's aversion to spending endless hours out in the field. Would he literally dirty his hands in the soot and blood of the crime scene? Much less hurt the woman he professed to love? "Until after her orals. He agreed."

Detective Beck's grunt of agreement made Amy wonder if the woman with the badge doubted the mutual decision of Jocelyn's breakup. "Does Derek have a last name?"

Amy spelled out Derek Roland's last name. "He's a doctoral student at Williams University, too."

Detective Carson was pulling open drawers on Jocelyn's dresser now, touching all of her friend's things with his gloved hands. "I've got a box of condoms in here," he announced to his partner before stuffing T-shirts and jewelry back inside. "But I'm not finding any obvious signs of a struggle. No love letters or threatening notes. The only pictures are in that album beside the bed. A lot with the boyfriend." He thumbed over his shoulder as he moved on to the next drawer. "And Ms. Hall there."

"This feels like we're violating her privacy," Amy protested when Detective Carson grabbed a fistful of underwear to look underneath it. "Jocelyn was supersmart, but shy. I'm the one who got into trouble, not her. She was all about studying and work."

Detective Beck touched Amy's shoulder to keep her from crossing the room to halt her partner's search. "Trust me. Getting to know your friend—any secrets, any conflicts, any habits—is the first step in figuring out who wanted to harm her. Especially with as little forensic evidence as we'll get from that crime scene. We'll be as respectful as we can be with her things, but we need to do this."

Amy swallowed her outrage, hugged her arms around her waist and drifted back into the doorway. "I don't know anyone who would want to hurt Jocelyn. None of this makes sense."

"Our job is to help it make sense." Detective Beck's frown faded beneath the hint of a compassionate smile. "Would Ms. Brunt's things be anywhere else in the house?"

"Clothes in the laundry room. Some of her food is in the kitchen. She was a vegetarian. Gran didn't even want to touch her tofu." Amy rubbed her fingers along the rolled-up sleeves of her soiled blouse. Even though she'd washed her hands and splashed cool water on her face to ease the feverish aftermath of her tears, she realized she still wore the grubby, soot-stained clothes she'd had on that afternoon. By the time she'd gotten back to the house, the police had asked to see Jocelyn's room, and she'd had no time to herself from that moment on. "Jocelyn kept the rest of her work stuff in the shed that burned. Or in her car. She carried her life in her backpack, and she always had that with her."

"Where is her backpack now?"

"No sign of it here," Detective Carson confirmed.

Detective Beck tapped herself a note before looking up at Amy. She could only answer the truth. "I don't know."

Had she seen the backpack at the crime scene? She didn't remember seeing straps around the corpse's shoulders, but maybe even that tough nylon material could have burned to the point of disintegration. She'd like to ask Fire Man Mark if that was a possibility. She wanted to ask him if he thought Jocelyn had suffered before she died, too. She wanted to know if he'd consider wrapping those buff arms of his around her again to make the vision of the devastating scene she'd witnessed recede a little bit again.

Amy was taller than many of the men she knew. She was taller than Detective Carson over there. Her grandfather had always called her a *healthy girl*. And though she was reasonably fit from the training classes she'd taken after her last relationship had ended so badly, no one would ever call her skinny. Still, Mark Taylor had made her feel delicate, feminine, safe. It was probably the whole firefighter/rescuer vibe he gave off. But Amy was used to rescuing herself. Life had trained her to be self-sufficient, not to rely on someone else's love and support to sustain her when the going got tough. She'd forgotten how vulnerable a punch of grief could make her feel. Or how good it felt to not have to be the strong one for a change.

And that whole throw-her-over-his-shoulder caveman threat had been surprisingly…intriguing. Fire Man Mark hadn't meant anything sexual by it, of course. But some errant hormone deep inside had lit up with interest as if it had been. His words and steely-eyed glare had felt like some kind of dare—and for a split second during her search for Jocelyn, she'd foolishly wanted to call him on it.

Okay, sexy, strong and attractive in a ruggedly masculine way was all well and good for her hormones. But depend on him? That was dangerous thinking.

Accidental death, malicious intent and now murder had ripped away every support system Amy had ever counted on. With the exception of her grandmother, whose age was beginning to shift the balance in that relationship, even, Amy knew better than to put her trust in anyone but herself.

"Did Ms. Brunt keep an office at the university?"

Detective Beck's question pulled Amy from the fruitless turn of her thoughts. Amy nodded. "But Jocelyn never used it. Not when she was out in the field like she was this semester. Everything she needed was in that shed or on her laptop in her backpack."

The dark-haired detective nodded. "All right. We'll make finding that backpack priority one."

Amy's phone rang in the back pocket of her shorts. Automatically, she pulled it out, despite Detective Beck's apparent impatience at having the interview interrupted. But when Amy saw the name on the screen, her breath tightened in her chest. She knew any other questions would have to wait. "I need to take this call. Is that all right?"

The detective took a break from putting notes into her phone. "Make it quick." Then she nodded past Amy to the uniformed officer waiting in the hallway. "When you're done, would you show the laundry and food items to Officer Marquette?"

"Joss's laptop won't be there."

"I'd like someone to have a look anyway," the detective explained. "We'll check her office at the university, and with the ex-boyfriend, too." Amy's phone burned in her hand. "*Not* finding that laptop, or locating it in an unexpected place, could be as important as finding it."

"I understand. Excuse me." Amy stepped into the hallway and swiped the answer button. With half the upstairs landing draped in paint tarps and the stairwell itself lined with ladders and scaffolding from her remodeling efforts, it was almost impossible to find a private corner to have this conversation. So, she drifted to the railing overlooking the downstairs entryway and dropped her voice to a whisper. "Derek?" How, exactly, was she supposed to start this conversation? It wasn't going to be by announcing that KCPD wanted to talk to him. "Are you sitting down?"

He laughed. "Of course I'm sitting down. I'm driving my car." She could hear another voice in the background, and supposed he had the news on his radio or was listening to a podcast. The background voice suddenly went silent. He must have turned off whatever was playing. "Why are you whispering? I can barely hear you."

"Where are you? I need you to pull off onto a side street or parking lot."

"Are you kidding? I'm halfway to your place on I-29." She heard the change in his tone as he realized she wouldn't have made her request if something wasn't seriously wrong. "What's happened? I called you because I've been trying to get a hold of Joss all afternoon, and she's not picking up. I'm not even getting her voice mail. Is she okay?"

Amy could barely squeeze the word past the tightness in her chest and throat. "No. She's not. There's been... an accident."

Several seconds passed before Derek spoke again. "How badly is she hurt? Are you at the hospital? She didn't get trapped by the fires, did she?"

"Not exactly—"

"She was supposed to evacuate with you. Why didn't you make sure she got back to civilization—"

"Derek." She interrupted him as accusation filled his voice. "Someone killed her."

"What?"

"I discovered the body. The fire was a forensic countermeasure to hide whatever happened to her."

She imagined he drove another mile in silence, or maybe he'd finally pulled off onto the shoulder of the road, before he answered. "She was murdered? Why?"

"That's the question of the day, it seems." Amy wound her fingers around the polished oak railing that framed the landing, needing its solid form to lean on for a moment until she could compose her thoughts. "The police want to talk to you since you and Joss were so close. And because you know about her research, what she might have had on her laptop. Any chance you know where that is?"

"Her laptop? Why would I know that?"

She glanced over her shoulder when she realized both Officer Marquette and Detective Beck had tuned in to her conversation. She turned her back to them, trying to reclaim a little privacy. "Look, I need to wrap this up."

Suddenly, his voice dropped to a whisper to match hers. "Are the cops there right now?"

"Yes."

"Why?"

Why would the police investigate a murder? "They're asking questions. Looking for leads." She exhaled a breath she didn't realize she'd been holding when Detective Carson called Detective Beck back into the room to look at something. "You can come on out to the house if you want to hang out and commiserate. Or if you want to be with me when I call Jocelyn's parents."

"I can't deal with that right now. I can't deal with any of that."

She moved her hand from the railing to the steel pipe of construction scaffolding that rose above it from the foyer below. The metal felt shockingly cold in her grasp. It had picked up the chill of the air-conditioning, no doubt. Or maybe she was the one who was losing any remnant of warmth.

"I'm turning this car around," Derek announced. "I'll talk to you later, Amy. I need some time alone to process this first."

Man, did she understand that impulse. "Derek, Jocelyn really did care about you."

"Yeah. She cared so much that she didn't want to be with me." Amy didn't know what to say to that. If KCPD saw him as a jilted lover or jealous grad student, would they consider him a suspect? "Don't tell the police I said that. Okay?"

"Okay. But you should tell them."

She heard the extra voice in the background of the call again. He'd turned on whatever he'd been listening to and was tuning her out. "Thanks for giving me the heads-up. Call me if you find out anything else."

"I will. Derek, are you okay to be driving? Will you call me when you get home, so I know you're safe?"

"Sure. Whatever."

"I'm so sorry to be the one to tell you. I know you must hurt as much as I—"

The call abruptly disconnected. And Amy doubted it had anything to do with a dropped call. Hadn't anger been one of her initial reactions to losing Jocelyn? Why should the man who'd loved her be any different? If Derek didn't contact her later, Amy would call him to make sure he was all right. For now, she'd give him his space to get past the shock and start to grieve. Pulling her hand from the unbending steel that suddenly reminded her of prison bars rising up in front of her, she slowly slipped the phone back into her pocket, inhaled a couple of deep breaths and then gestured to the uniformed officer to follow her down the wide oak stairs.

"The laundry room is this way."

Detective Beck stuck her head out the bedroom door with one last directive for the uniformed officer. "Check any pockets. Signs of trace. You know the drill."

"Yes, ma'am."

"Careful. The stain on that railing might still be tacky." Urging the black woman in the KCPD uniform to stick to the wall on the right side of the stairs, away from the construction scaffolding, Amy led her down to the foyer. The main part of the house, inside and out, felt like a barricaded fortress, with honeycombs of metal framework circling the interior of the two-story entryway and the front of the house so that she and the two workmen she'd hired could repair and refinish the century-old interior oak paneling, as well as repaint the exterior of the old farmhouse. "Watch your head."

Amy ducked beneath the wood planks that formed a squared-off archway between the foyer and the rooms in the back that had already been modernized and repainted after a year and a half of hard work and restoration. While she enjoyed working with her hands and bringing out the beauty of the old home, it had proved to be too big a project to complete on her own. She had her own contracted art pieces to finish, including her metal sculpting and jewelry work. And with Dale O'Brien breathing down her grandmother's neck with monetary offers and subtle threats to drive them off the land he wanted to build on, the need for speed had grown even greater. She planned to turn the house into a historic masterpiece of turn-of-the-century architecture and petition the state and national register of historic places to give her gran's house protected status, preserving the only home her grandmother had ever known and protecting the natural beauty of the land where her great-grandparents had once grown apple trees and raised cattle.

Provided these wildfires—whether accidental or deliberate—didn't burn them out first.

As she straightened on the other side of the arch, she collided with a string bean of a man in faded blue jeans and work boots. Handyman #1, Brad Frick. Brad put his hand out to grab her shoulder to keep them from bumping into each other. "Careful there, Miss Amy. Look out."

"Brad. You startled me." Flattening her palm over the drumming of her heart, Amy offered the construction worker a friendly smile. Brad compensated for the receding points of his hairline by growing a long ponytail that nearly reached his waist in the back. Along with his beakish nose, he'd always reminded her of a long-legged bird—one who'd be easy to sculpt into a humorous garden decoration with the scrap metal and welding equipment she stored in her art studio.

"Hey, Miss Amy." His partner, Richie Sterling, who was changing out the paper on a hand sander on the sawhorses behind him, was too nondescript to spark any obvious artistic inspiration. Richie was average height, average weight and hid his average blond-brown hair beneath a paint-stained ball cap. About the only thing unique about him was the streaks of sunburn that seemed to perpetually stain his cheeks.

She widened her smile to include Richie in her greeting. "Hey, Richie. What are you two doing here?"

"We're w-w-working," he answered, cutting the excess sandpaper off with the blade of a box cutter. His gaze skipped from her to the female officer beside her before dropping to the gun strapped at Officer Marquette's waist. "Is that real?"

Officer Marquette nodded, resting her hand on the butt of the weapon. "Yes, sir. Very much so."

"Do you know how to use it?" Richie asked.

The woman's impassive professional face softened with a smile. "I'd better know how if I'm going to be carrying it."

"Cool." Richie lifted his gaze, although it danced over the other woman's face without making direct eye contact. "Did you ever shoot anyone with—"

"Richie!" Brad chastised his friend. "Back to work."

Nodding at the command, Richie lowered his head to attach a battery pack to the cordless sander.

"Sorry about that, ma'am." Brad turned his attention back to the nail hole he was filling with Spackle. "Sometimes, his curiosity gets the better of him. He's harmless."

Officer Marquette exchanged a quizzical look with Amy at the odd addendum before sharing her smile with Brad, as well. "That's all right, sir. Sometimes, folks are curious about a woman in uniform." The smile was gone when she looked back at Amy. "Ma'am? If you could show me the items you mentioned?"

"Sure."

But the alleged brainy half of Frick and Frack here moved a sawhorse table out of his way so he could move closer to the paneling, effectively blocking Amy and the female officer's path. "The Copper Lake construction site is closed down for the rest of the day because of the fires. I'd hate to lose whatever daylight we have left when we could still put in a couple of hours and make a few bucks." He smoothed the Spackle with his putty knife, focusing on his handiwork while he kept talking. "Don't worry. We're staying out of everybody's way. We even answered a few of the arson investigator's questions. We were hanging out on the other side of the lake when all the fire trucks showed up. Looks like that fire came pretty close to your house."

"A couple of hills away." Technically, he was in *her* way. Amy swallowed the temper flaring inside her. Wigging out right now would only draw KCPD's attention, and she was doing her very best to remain the cooperative witness and not become a person of interest. She gently nudged the sawhorse table back toward the wall, taking care not to spill the Spackle bucket or cans of stain on it. "The house would have been in trouble if the fire had jumped the creek bed."

"No water in the creek," Richie added before turning on the sander and drowning out any further conversation with the machine's high-pitched drone.

The deafening whine severed the last thread of Amy's polite patience. There were already too many people in the house, invading her space, wrecking any opportunity to mourn and plan the next tasks on her things-to-do-for-Jocelyn list. The police had already contacted Jocelyn's parents in Nebraska, but Amy wanted to call them personally to share her condolences. And someone needed to notify the university and insurance adjusters to take care of the research equipment and personal belongings that had been destroyed in the fire. The house was already filled with criminologists and detectives, an arson investigator, and uniformed officers, all poking through Jocelyn's things and asking questions. She didn't need Brad and Richie here, too, acting as though it was a regular ol' workday and she hadn't lost her best friend, and that the property she was trying to protect for her grandmother hadn't almost been destroyed.

Squashing the urge to call them Frick and Frack out loud, Amy dredged up one more smile for her part-time employees. "Hey, guys. I appreciate your work ethic—"

she thumbed over her shoulder to the front door "—but I need you to call it a night. We've had a rough day here. Hopefully, everyone will clear out soon, and Gran and I can have a quiet evening."

"Is Mrs. Hall here yet?" Brad asked, scanning the foyer from the front door to the rooms off the back hallway—as if her grandmother's presence could persuade him in a way Amy's request could not. He attacked the next hole with the Spackle, refusing to take the hint.

"No. But she called, and she's on her way." Not that it was any of Brad's business, but she added, "Friends are driving her home. I really need you both gone before she gets here."

"S-s-sorry about Miss Jocelyn." Richie stuttered an apology. "She was a nice lady."

"That she was," Amy agreed, raising her voice to be heard over the sander.

"She baked me cupcakes," Richie continued. "They weren't v-very good."

Despite Richie's effort to be sympathetic, Brad huffed a curse under his breath at being dismissed. His dark eyes narrowed when they came back to her. "I said it was no trouble to be here. We were just getting started. The clock's tickin' on your deadline. How the hell do you expect us to get all this woodwork and the exterior siding stained and painted by the end of the month?"

Amy bristled at the accusation in his tone. "Go ahead and log the time you were here this evening. But I need you to leave."

A thump from the ceiling above them made Amy wonder if the detectives and CSIs had flipped the mattress off Jocelyn's bed or were moving furniture now. With the whine of the sander, the drone of voices on every floor of the house and the footsteps of all these strangers, Amy wanted to run from the chaos and lose herself in the vast solitude of the scorched wilderness or hide away in the privacy of her art studio.

But she needed to stay. For her gran. For Jocelyn. For the truth.

The sander whined like an assault against her ear-drums. "Richie!"

He instantly turned the sander off, his smile sheepish as he faced her. "Yes, Miss Amy?"

Hugging her arms around her waist, she wondered at the sudden chill she felt. She hated not being in control of her environment, not having all the answers she needed. She hated that she had secrets that any one of these people might uncover if she couldn't get a grip on her panicked thoughts and emotions. "Just go," she pleaded. These two men worked for her. They weren't authorities she needed to obey, and she refused to be bullied by any man.

"We'll be back tomorrow." At last, she'd gotten through to Brad, even if he didn't seem particularly happy about being sent home. "Bright and early if O'Brien doesn't have any work for us."

"We'll be back tomorrow," Richie echoed. With a nod from Brad to put away the tools they'd gotten out, Amy wondered, not for the first time, if Richie had a dimin-ished IQ, or if he was just a really, really shy guy with a stutter who got even more tongue-tied around women.

She couldn't fault him on his flawless work, though. The parts of the interior and exterior that had been touched were transforming the house into a beautiful, classic showplace. But despite Dale O'Brien's determina-tion to tear it and all the outbuildings down, she needed time to recover from today's tragedy.

"Call first. You have my number, right?"

"I do," Brad conceded. "If that's what you want."

"It is. Thanks for understanding."

"Yes, ma'am. Whatever you say," Brad answered, putting on his own paint-stained ball cap and cursing under his breath. "Pack it up, Richie. We ain't wanted here, either."

"It'll only be a couple of days," Amy insisted.

"A couple of days without work means there's a bill I won't be able to pay," Brad groused. "But you do what you need to do."

Thanks for your compassion, Mr. Frick.

Amy's frayed patience took a turn into *Get the hell out of my house* territory. She bit down on the inside of her lip to keep the angry words roiling inside her from spilling out. She knew the two men weren't licensed like most of Dale O'Brien's other workers, and often took odd jobs to make ends meet. When they'd come to the house and offered their services three months ago, she'd been happy to hire them. No way was she finishing everything that needed to be done on the house by herself. Their work was solid, and their rate affordable. But right now she just needed some peace and quiet so she could try to figure out who hurt Jocelyn, and then have a good cry or cussing session to vent her grief.

But she refused to freak out or bawl in front of any of these people. Revealing her true emotions to the wrong person had made her far too vulnerable in the past. And she was done being vulnerable to anyone again.

As Brad picked up a mallet to hammer the lid back onto the can of stain they had opened, Richie stood up from the tarp he'd been folding. His cheeks glowed red in the waning daylight streaming through the windows on either side of the front door. And even though his gaze didn't linger on hers, he touched the brim of his cap and murmured, "S-sorry for your loss, Miss Amy."

Amy rewarded the compassion his partner had lacked with a smile. "Thank you, Richie."

Officer Marquette touched Amy's elbow. "Laundry room? Unless you want me to escort these two gentlemen out?"

"They'll be fine." She reached out to squeeze Richie's arm, both an apology and a thank-you, as she scooted between the two men. "This way."

After leaving Officer Marquette in the laundry room to sort through a basket of Jocelyn's dirty clothes, Amy headed into the kitchen for a bottle of cool water. But while the cops had staked out the upstairs, members of the KCFD and Platte County Volunteer Fire Department had gathered in the kitchen to discuss their preliminary findings and pore over a map on the kitchen table.

Her gaze zeroed in on the stormy color of Mark Taylor's gray-blue eyes. Although they widened for a moment in recognition, then crinkled with a smile when he spotted her in the kitchen doorway, Fire Man Taylor looked away almost as quickly as she did. While he focused in on the conversation among the other men and woman in the room, Amy went to the refrigerator to retrieve the bottle of water she craved.

Although they now all wore black uniforms or T-shirts and utility pants instead of their firefighting gear like before, she recognized Mark, the slender blonde woman and the tank-sized man standing behind her as the firefighters who'd been on the scene to protect Dale O'Brien's subdivision when she'd driven in earlier. Mark pointed to something on a map spread across the kitchen table, and a flurry of questions and comments ensued. All of them seemed to be answering to a tall man with dark, nearly black hair with distinguished gray sideburns. Although she was curious to hear the details of the fire, possibly specifics about the one that had torched Joc-elyn's car and storage shed, hearing several disturbing phrases like *no accident* and *incendiary liquids on the premises* and *where the body was found* made Amy opt for a quick escape, instead.

"Red, wait," Mark called out.

"Is that her?" another man asked.

"Amy." A strong, gentle hand wrapped around her elbow, stopping her in the door frame. She shivered at the unexpected touch of Mark Taylor's hand on her arm, feeling as though she'd spilled the cold water down the front of her. "Easy, Red. You okay?"

Red, huh? So they were doing nicknames now. She supposed that one fit. Amy wasn't sure if she'd jumped because she hadn't realized Mark had been address-ing her, or if she'd suddenly realized that the attention of every firefighter in the room had shifted to her. She glanced up at the concern lining his eyes, forcing a smile. "I'm holding my own, Fire Man."

Was it a trick of her imagination, or was the only warm spot on her body her left elbow, where Mark still held her?

"Mark?" The deep voice of the man who seemed to be in charge prompted Mark to pull her around to face the other men and woman in the kitchen.

"This is Amy Hall. She was with me when we found the body."

"And you're certain that was the ignition point of the fire?" the commander, or whatever his rank might be, asked.

"That was my observation. Although, we might need a chemical analysis to prove it. It could simply be a hot spot that was created in an effort to..." Mark released his loose grip on her arm and slipped his hand to the small of her back, where he rubbed a slow, easy circle. Nope. Not her imagination. Now her arm was as chilled as the rest of her. The elusive heat had followed the contact with Mark's hand. Amy couldn't help but tilt her chin to the firefighter at her side as his voice trailed away. She found his gaze locked on to hers, the grim set of his expression apologetic. "In an effort to hide the body." His big shoulders lifted with a shrug. "Sorry, Red."

Amy stepped away to concentrate on opening her water as her mind filled with the image of a charred skeleton and the soot-stained steel necklace she'd held in her hand. But her hands were shaking too badly to twist the lid off. When Mark plucked the bottle from her grasp and opened it for her, all she could do was nod her thanks.

"Miss Hall?" The man whom the others had been deferring to spoke directly to her, asking for her attention. "I'm sorry about your friend. My name is Gideon Taylor." Another Taylor? Wow. Small world. "When the police are finished with you, I'd like to ask you a few questions, as well. If you're up to it," he added kindly. Although, she got the distinct impression he expected her to say yes.

They didn't think she or her grandmother had anything to do with Jocelyn's death, did they? But she wanted answers as much as anyone else in this house did. Maybe more. She drank a swallow of the cold water before answering. "Of course." She glanced over at Mark, who still seemed to be apologizing for something she hadn't quite grasped yet. "I'll be outside when you're finished here. I could use some fresh air."

"I'll find you," Mark answered. His tone seemed to promise something more than simply fetching her for the next interrogation when the arson investigator was ready.

With a nod, Amy headed out to the front porch, holding the door for Brad and Richie as they carried their toolboxes down the front steps to Brad's beat-up car. Brad grumbled an order to *kick it into gear* and the other shot her a curious look. Amy followed them to the edge of the porch as the grumbling grew into a full-fledged argument about *stupid luck* and *no respect* and women not knowing their own mind. With that last insulting comment, Richie shushed Brad. "Miss Lissette helped us out today. Don't forget that."

"Yeah, but you've got to push them to do what they're supposed to," Brad groused.

"I think she's nice," Richie argued, defending whoever Lissette might be. "So's Miss Amy. You're bein' mean. And she can hear you."

Both men looked back at her from the open trunk of the car, and Amy held their gaze.

"Yeah, I heard you," she whispered under her breath.

Although she doubted her voice had carried as far as theirs, her attitude was crystal clear. Brad waved Richie into the car and slammed the trunk shut. Then he climbed behind the wheel and drove away in a plume of dust, turning onto the crumbling asphalt road at the bottom of the hill.

When the dust cleared, Amy discovered that she still wasn't alone. Beyond the burned-out shell and dilapidated remains of the old lake rental properties her grandfather had once managed, beyond the lake itself, she spotted another vehicle—a dust-coated white pickup with the O'Brien Construction logo painted on the side—parked near the office trailer at the edge of the Copper Lake subdivision.

Although the distance was too great to read any expression, she recognized the boxy form of Dale O'Brien lounging against the bed of the truck. He was talking on his cell phone, but she knew he was watching her because he touched his fingers to the brim of his white construction helmet and saluted her. Still on his phone after that little greeting, he straightened and circled around to climb in behind the steering wheel. Why was he still here? Was there any significance to him waiting to make contact with her before clearing out? Who exactly was he talking to, and did it have anything to do with her or Jocelyn or the fire?

She'd like to think he was chatting with an insurance adjuster, but she knew damn well the man had spies. Maybe he was doing his own dirty work, tracking every movement to and from the house, ready to report the slightest legal infraction, the slightest encroachment across a property line that might put him one step closer to purchasing the land all the way around the lake. He started the engine, but remained in the truck, finally focusing on his call and not on her.

Inhaling her first deep breath in hours, Amy turned her face to the fading warmth of the sun, watching the glowing ball shimmer and change colors as it sank below the horizon. Usually the pinks and oranges and hints of deep turquoise as the sky darkened inspired her with images of the art she loved to create. But tonight, the sunset simply marked the end of a very long, very traumatic day.

She heard the crunch of footsteps on the front sidewalk. "Now what have you done?"

Amy groaned at the gravelly voice accosting her from the bottom of the porch steps. So much for solitude. "Mr. Sanders. Is there something I could help you with?"

The lanky, slightly stooped older black man who rented one of their remaining bungalows down by the lake glared at her from beneath two white eyebrows that reminded her of fuzzy albino caterpillars. "I just got back to my house. There's no water pressure there."

Seriously? He wanted her to play landlord and come fix something right now? "Mr. Sanders, KCFD and the Platte County volunteers have been fighting wildfires all day. I'm guessing it will take time for the pressure in the pipes to build up again. I'll look at it in the morning if you're still having issues. You can come into the house and use one of the bathrooms here if you need to."

He grunted a noise that sounded like she'd given him the unsatisfactory answer he'd expected. A widower who'd worked half his life in a manufacturing plant in the city, he'd answered her ad for an affordable rental back when her strategy had been to fill the empty homes on the north side of the lake to dissuade Dale O'Brien from expanding his subdivision. When Mr. Sanders signed the leasing agreement, Amy thought she'd met a new friend who appreciated the quiet and emptiness of the countryside beyond the suburbs and downtown KC area. But Gerald Sanders took his loner status to the extreme, making her wonder what had happened in his life to make him such a cranky recluse. If it wasn't for complaints like this, she never saw her closest neighbor at all. He even stuck his rent check in the mailbox when she wasn't at home.

When he buried his hands in the deep pockets of his overalls, making no effort to leave, Amy studied him a little more closely. "Was there something else?"

He worked those bushy brows in and out of a frown before he asked, "Is your grandmother all right?" Was he worried about her? When had he become friends with her gran? Had the two seventy-somethings ever exchanged more than a few words?

Still, his concern was the most humane thing she'd heard him say. "Yes. She's been at a friend's all day."

"Good. When I saw all these official vehicles, I worried something might have happened to Comfort."

"I'll let her know you asked about her. She'll appreciate that."

"Like it isn't bad enough I have construction noise and your hammering coming into my house all day long. Now I've got the police and Kansas City firefighters knocking on my door, asking if I've seen anything suspicious." And poof! Just like that, the human connection she'd felt for a few moments vanished. "I rented that house out here to be alone, to get away from interruptions like that." He leaned in slightly, somehow giving the impression he was looking down his nose at her, even though she stood on the steps above him. "You want me to tell them just who I've seen wandering around the premises at night?"

Amy's hand fisted around her water bottle, crumpling the plastic in her fist. "I live here. If I want to go for a walk at midnight or work late in my studio, that's my right. And it's *my* business. I don't need you spying on me."

"Don't you go gettin' growly with me, girl. You know I'm the only tenant who's stuck by your gran after the stables and the old foreman's house burned down. You need my income. That means you need to show me a little respect. That means you keep the cops away from me. Unless Comfort needs something, I want you and all these people to leave me alone."

"You're not the only one who's being asked a lot of questions, Mr. Sanders. Why don't you go home and lock your door and be your old grouchy self without bothering me."

"Young lady—"

"I'm sorry. I'm grieving for a friend and ticked off that anyone would want to hurt her. I can't handle your accusations right now." Amy stormed down the steps and hurried past him, needing to get away from all the chaos before her head exploded.

I'll find you.

Mark Taylor's words echoed in her head as she ran. She didn't care that he'd have to chase her down again, that she wouldn't be where she'd promised to wait.

If she felt eyes on her, she convinced herself it was Gerald Sanders, or Dale O'Brien, watching her as he chatted in his truck. Or maybe Brad and Richie had circled back to plead for a paying job. Maybe Derek hadn't returned to the city after all. Maybe he was parked on some dusty side road or behind a hill, wanting to be close to the woman he'd loved and the mystery of her death. Or maybe it was the cops upstairs, or the firefighters downstairs, or…

"Damn it." Amy jogged around to the buildings behind the house, fighting the instinct that said something sinister, something much more malevolent than a bossy firefighter with an interesting face and a hot body, was keeping her in his sights.

Chapter Five

Amy stood at the vise on the workbench in her converted art studio, losing herself in the tangy scent of burning metal and the hiss and pop of gas from her oxyacetylene torch as she heated a sheet of copper to create a muted rainbow of red, pink and turquoise on the body of her latest sculpture.

She'd opened the window above her workbench to let the fumes dissipate into the still night air outside. Even though the sun had sunk below the horizon, she hadn't turned on anything more than the work light that hung from a nearby shelf, relying on the bright beam of light from her welding torch to illuminate her work. Night and shadows had settled around her like a cloak, and she relished the isolating feeling.

It wasn't comfort she needed so much as time to think. She needed time without strangers taking over her grandmother's house or familiar faces like Brad Frick and Mr. Sanders choosing this night to push her for things that were scarcely a priority for her right now.

Right now, she needed to remember. As she virtually painted the strokes of color by heating different parts of the metal to varying temperatures, she recalled her time here this morning, sketching out the whimsical piece, selecting the copper and anchoring it into place. But before she had been able to turn on her equipment and begin the actual piece, the call to evacuate the premises had come. That was when she'd made her first call to Jocelyn, warning her to get out of the wildfire's path. That was the last time she'd spoken to her friend.

That last chat with Jocelyn felt like a lifetime ago. What a hell of a long day.

Tears pooled in the bottom of the safety goggles she wore beneath her welding helmet. They tickled her cheeks as she thought of all the conversations they'd shared that had been about nothing. Now, knowing she'd never see another text about some gross bug Jocelyn had stumbled upon in the old apple orchard, or never hear another excited voice mail about a botanical or geologic theorem she'd proved that Amy didn't understand, Amy wished she'd paid closer attention—that she'd understood the importance of every message.

She shoved her gloved fingers up beneath the face shield of her helmet to swipe at the tears blurring her vision. Damn it. Hadn't she already cried enough today? Crying was more sensitive Jocelyn's thing—not wild-child Amy. They'd always been opposites. The science geek and the eccentric artist. A quiet brunette and a mouthy redhead. She and Jocelyn couldn't have been more different. And yet they couldn't have been any closer. Who would ever want to hurt her friend? Jocelyn had never been in trouble with the cops. She'd never had a run-in with her professors or been in a relationship that had gone sideways. She'd never had an unkind word for anybody.

Amy was the one who spoke her mind and fought for lost causes and made enemies.

But Jocelyn was the one who'd had her head bashed in and had been set on fire.

It simply wasn't fair. Amy pulled the torch away from the metal when she let the hissing line of flame overheat one spot to a deep blood red. She cursed behind her mask. "Nothing symbolic about that, huh? Did you see something you shouldn't have, Joss? Was there some secret you never told me? Is there a monster out there who set his sights on you? Did you know? Were you surprised? Did you suffer?"

More tears, full of anger rather than grief, steamed up her goggles.

Amy drew the flame across the copper again, determined to find solace in her work if she couldn't find answers. She had almost blinked her vision clear when the door behind her swung open and the overhead light came on. "Damn it, Mr. Sanders! Have you ever heard of knocking?" She spun around, her temper flaring. "I said I'd get to it in the morn—"

Not a bushy-eyebrowed geezer who'd gotten on her last nerve.

Her visitor was a tall, broad-shouldered firefighter with short, spiky dark hair that needed to see a comb. Or her fingers.

Amy blinked and immediately twisted the valve to shut off the gas flow to her torch and kill the flame. She eyed the bulky gloves that protected her hands and effectively kept her from touching anything. Yet she could feel the tingling in her fingertips, as though she had brushed them through the wiry disarray on top of Mark Taylor's head. Where had that impulse come from? Why was she having any impulses at all concerning the Captain Good Guy Bossy Buttinsky filling the doorway?

"Hey, Red. I thought you'd disappeared on me."

"Fire Man," she acknowledged, pushing up the face mask and removing her helmet. She set it on the workbench before removing her goggles and hanging them on the pegboard above the bench.

"Fire Woman. Didn't know you were a welder. I followed the smell of the gas and flames, and I wanted to make sure you were okay."

She stowed the torch on its metal hook and turned back to her workbench to unwind the vise and pick up the sheet of copper. She carried it over to the concrete blocks near the old garage door to cool. "Didn't know you were keeping tabs on me. I'll be sure to file a travel report the next time I go into my own backyard."

The door closed behind him. "I did knock. You probably couldn't hear me over the equipment. I take it this Mr. Sanders is a troublemaker? Need me to go beat him up for you?"

She wondered how Mark Taylor could make his deep, steady voice sound so comforting, even with the teasing and probing questions.

Amy shook her head, fighting the urge to smile. "It would hardly be a fair fight. He's closer to eighty than he is seventy. And you're what…? Thirty?"

"Twenty-eight," he answered. "I bet I could still take him."

A small laugh bubbled up, catching on the grief and anger constricting her throat and coming out in an embarrassing hiccup. "I bet you could." She pulled off the insulated gloves she wore and tossed them onto the workbench before pushing a stray tendril of her own hair off her face. "I'd say come in, but since you're already here, I'll just offer you a seat." She pointed to the stool at her drafting table and the denim couch decorated with colorful pillows along the wall opposite the workbench. "Your choices are limited, but comfortable."

He studied her face, no doubt taking in her red-rimmed

eyes and the tear tracks crystallizing on her cheeks. "Old Man Sanders made you cry?"

Amy quickly ducked her face away from his curious gaze and busied herself unzipping the faded and stained blue coveralls her grandfather had once worn. She stripped down to the shorts and tank top she wore underneath before putting away her torch, mask and gloves, ensuring the gas canister was shut down correctly and her gear was neatly stowed. "Gerald Sanders is our tenant. He lives in the white house down by the lake. He chose tonight to complain about the plumbing. I couldn't deal with him right now, so I came here to work."

"Someone actually lives in one of those places?"

She splashed some cool water from the slop sink on her face before realizing she hadn't set a clean towel out. Instead of digging through the refinished dresser that sat in the corner, she grabbed the blouse she'd worn earlier to dab her skin dry. "We used to have three more tenants until the foreman's house burned down. A single man who worked on a neighboring farm and two other guys who work on a highway construction crew. We're cheaper than a hotel for a long-term stay." She pulled the damp blouse on over her tank top and turned to face him. "They're nicer on the inside than they are the outside. And being so close to the lake has always been a draw."

"It is a pretty lake. The fishing any good there?"

"It's mostly crappie. Better for fun than eating. Grandpa tried to get catfish going in the lake, but no one's caught one that I know of. Of course, with the water levels down, nobody's fished there at all this summer."

He moved to her workbench, inspecting her tools and the cubbies and crates where she stored a variety of scrap metals and found objects. "Do you fish?"

"I used to when Grandpa was alive. I loved going out

on the water with him." She tied the tails of the blouse around her waist and picked up the bottle of water she'd taken from the kitchen to down the last of it. She hadn't known how ugly the world could be when Grandpa Leland was still alive. Now he was gone, and her life had changed drastically from the dreamy-eyed tomboy's he'd raised. "Those were simpler times. Are you a fisherman?"

She looked up in time to see a shadow pass across his face. Before she could act on the curious compassion that squeezed her raw heart, Mark straightened to his full height and reached into his back pocket.

"Sorry if I hit a nerve. Mark—?"

"Here." He pushed a black bandanna into her hand. He pointed to his own cheek, indicating the droplets of water or tears that glistened on her face. "My grandmother said I should always carry a handkerchief in case somebody needed to wipe their eyes or blow their nose or, you know, apply a tourniquet. Frankly, I use a tissue for all that. Not the tourniquet, of course. Never holds." Amy almost smiled at the silly remark, even though she understood the diversion for what it was—an attempt to deflect her concern. "I'm glad I have one with me today."

"You're trying to rescue me again." She dabbed the soft cotton against her feverish eyes and nose, relishing its soothing comfort. "I swear I haven't cried this much since Grandpa died. I'm used to being stronger than this. But thanks."

"What made the foreman's house burn? Faulty wiring? Someone falling asleep with a cigarette?"

The flare of sympathy she'd felt died with the reminder that opening her heart to someone only set her up to be hurt or taken advantage of again. Why would he ask that? Was he really here to check on her welfare? Or was this part of the KCFD investigation?

Did he really want to mention the word *arson*? The source of that fire had been confirmed, though who had set the blaze was yet to be determined.

Amy tilted her face to study him. Same KCFD T-shirt. Same broad shoulders. Same short crop of spiky brown hair. This time she noticed the interesting bump on the bridge of his nose that indicated a fight or accident in years past. And the stubble of a five o'clock beard shadowed his jaw, making the crooked grin that softened his firm mouth stand out against his taut skin. Damn her traitorous hormones for being attracted to Mark Taylor. If this man was using subterfuge to get some answers, he was awfully good at hiding it. And what secret had he shuttered away when they'd been talking about something as inane as fishing? "What are you really doing here, Fire Man? Is this part of my interview? If so, I don't know anything about the fire at the old foreman's house. Only that the two highway workers renting the place were gone that weekend, so no one was hurt."

"I'm just checking on you, if that's okay," he answered, instead of pushing for details she couldn't give and suspicions she wouldn't share. "I grew up in a family of cops and firefighters. I know days like this can be pretty intense." He looked around, taking in the rest of her supplies. He studied the works in progress, the hodgepodge of furniture, and the chains and pulley system suspended from the ceiling left over from when this workshop had been Grandpa Leland's. "What is this place? A machine shop? One of those she-sheds?"

"It used to be the garage where my grandfather worked on his tractor and other small equipment. Now it's my art studio. It has good light when I open the windows and garage entrance, doors I can lock." Which, apparently, she should have done if she'd really wanted to be alone.

"That explains the new roof and why this place has been better taken care of than the other outbuildings."

Steeling herself against the probing questions he sneaked into their casual conversation, Amy downed a sip of water and sat on one end of the couch. "Why is KCFD still here? The wildfire is out, isn't it?"

He folded his long, sturdy body down on the cushion beside her. "This isn't about wildfires and drought conditions anymore."

No. It was about murder and arson. "Tell me about it. The cops are asking lots of questions, going through everything in Jocelyn's room. I don't know what they think they'll find. She kept scientific journals, not a diary."

"Did she have a boyfriend? Maybe they're looking for a connection there?"

"So, this *is* an interview."

"I'm just making conversation."

"Does that all-American good-guy charm work for you with other women? Get them to drop their guard so they'll answer all your questions?"

He gave her an exaggerated wink. "You think I'm charming?"

It was such a nerdy maneuver that Amy laughed before she could stop herself. He surprised her by touching the tip of his finger to the point of her chin and mirroring her smile. "That's better."

For several endless moments, Amy stared into gray-blue eyes and wondered at the sudden infusion of heat that seemed to be drawn through her blood to the simple press of a gentle, calloused finger against her skin. But then she blinked, and her thoughts suddenly filled with images of the last man she'd foolishly found so captivating.

Amy pushed to her feet, carried her empty water bottle over to the bin beside the trash and crushed it in her hands before tossing it inside. Mark Taylor and Preston Worth weren't anything alike. Not in age. Not in looks. Certainly not in personality.

Preston's prematurely gray hair and striking features matched his vast knowledge of art and his travels around the world. He was sophisticated and charismatic. He'd taken Amy under his wing, encouraging both her talent and her eagerness to learn. He'd flattered her pale skin and Rubenesque figure, demanding she sit for him while he painted her. She'd felt beautiful in the studio and in the bedroom under his tutelage. She'd blossomed in his bright, colorful world.

And then one day she woke up.

Amy flashed back to her last scary encounter with the professor she'd fallen in love with. She'd never expected Preston to get violent when she broke off the affair after discovering she wasn't the only muse he'd taken to bed. She might still be in grad school, working on her PhD, if Professor Worth hadn't threatened to fail her on her art thesis and studio show. Hell, she might still be painting on a canvas instead of on her grandmother's house. Fortunately, she'd found a new medium she loved with her welded sculptures and jewelry making. There was strength in fire and metal, a strength she'd needed to get through the hell of taking down a powerful man and seeing her lifelong dreams go up in flames.

Because Preston Worth had taken far more from her than her doctorate and her watercolors. He'd taken her hopeful innocence about the world. He'd stolen her ability to trust and her willingness to give her heart to another man. She'd burned the remnants of that life down to the ground, but she couldn't purge the feelings of self-doubt and mistrust that lingered in the aftermath.

She'd reported the assault and subsequent threats meant to keep her quiet about it. She'd gotten him fired from Williams University, in fact. Amy had even gone through the preliminary stages of his criminal trial. But then Grandpa had passed, and Gran needed her, and... Preston Worth scared her in a way that most men did not. Although the charges against him had been negotiated down to lesser charges—a year in prison and probation— and he'd gone through a mandated anger management class, with Preston's temper, she could see him committing a crime of passion like she'd seen today. But Jocelyn didn't have anyone like that in her life. At least no one Amy was aware of...unless Derek Roland's personality had changed 180 degrees.

"Amy?" She startled at the brush of Mark's fingers on her shoulders. He held his hands up in apology when she spun around. "Sorry. Where'd you go?"

She wasn't about to share her trip down nightmare lane with a man she'd only known for a day, a man who was weaving a spell of attraction and security around her she couldn't afford to get too comfortable with. "I was thinking about who'd want to hurt Jocelyn and was coming up with zilch."

It wasn't too far from the truth. Mark Taylor didn't need to know that few people would have been surprised if she'd turned up as the victim today.

His gray-blue eyes narrowed as if he knew she wasn't telling the complete truth. "Are you sure you're all right? Your skin's a little pale. No aftereffects from today? I've got paramedic training. I can get my kit."

"No. I don't need first aid." Amy waved her hands, urging him out of her personal space and dismissing his concern. She folded the black bandanna into a neat square, then unfolded it again and tied it around her wrist when he refused her offer to return it. "Why are you here, Fire Man? Babysitting me? Making sure I don't run off before the chief interviews me?" If he was staying put, then she would move away. She made a show of fluffing the decorative pillows on the sofa. "Are you an arson investigator, too?"

He shook his head. "I was the first firefighter on the scene at the shed. They needed my report. I told them what we moved to get to the body, and so on. Besides, I rode up here with my brother and he's still inside, keeping an eye on Mom."

"Your mom and dad and brother are firefighters, too?"

"Yeah." He crossed to inspect the valves on the oxyacetylene and Argon-CO_2 canisters she used for different welding jobs. She knew she'd stored all her equipment according to regulation, but still, it made her feel a little less like she was under official scrutiny when he nodded and moved on to study her sketches on the drafting table. "My dad's the chief arson investigator. You spoke to him in the kitchen."

Amy hugged a turquoise batik pillow to her chest. "That sexy guy with the silver sideburns is your dad?"

"Um, I don't really think of him in those terms. But man of few words? Large and in charge?" She nodded at the apt description. "Yep. Gideon Taylor is my dad."

"You don't look like him." Except for the sexy part. She should be more worried about how her brain kept focusing on liking this guy instead of maintaining her defenses. Sure, Mark Taylor gave her interesting ideas for a piece she wanted to sculpt. His face reflected the cool tones of the overhead light and created mysterious shadows in the hollows beneath his cheekbones and jaw. Maybe she'd take up painting again, to see if she could capture the beautiful stormy-sky color of his eyes. Suddenly aware of just how thoroughly she was studying him, she set the pillow down. "And the blonde who was bossing all the firefighters around earlier is your mom?"

"I look even less like her." He reappeared beside her, holding a pencil sketch from her drafting table. "This is like the pendant you wear around your neck. Your friend had one, too. You made them?"

Amy nodded, her fingers automatically going to the matching knot of steel resting against her cleavage. "I work mostly in metals now. Everything from big sculptures to intricate jewelry."

"You know the crime lab will still have to do an autopsy on the remains. Identifying her by the necklace alone won't hold up in court. But it does give the ME a lead on whose dental records to pull."

She felt light-headed at the thought of the medical examiner doing further damage to the body she'd found. "I suspected as much. But it's her. I know it is."

"Your drawings are good," Mark pointed out after several moments of silence, no doubt wanting to divert her thoughts from the images an autopsy conjured. "So, art is what you do for a living?"

"I make decent money at it. Not enough to pay for all the home repairs I've taken on. But I could live on it if I had to." She didn't want to talk about herself anymore. She didn't want to talk about his father's investigation, either. She carried the drawing back to the table. "Who's the guy who looked like he had to duck and turn sideways to get through the door?"

"My brother Matt." He saw her frowning at the idea of him and Matt coming from the petite blonde. "We're adopted. Matt and I are blood brothers, too. Our parents died in a fire when we were little. I barely remember them. Alex and Pike are part of the Taylor tribe, too.

They're cops with KCPD. All four of us were adopted from the same foster home where Mom grew up."

Adopted? Foster care? Amy slowly revised her all-American-hero impression of Mark Taylor. Not only was his face incredibly interesting, but there seemed to be some interesting dimensions to his history and personality, as well. A fascinating subject with complex layers beneath his good-guy facade—and those impressive arms and shoulders? She wondered if he was hairy-chested, waxed clean or something in between. Any way she imagined it, he really would make an attractive model to pose for her art.

"Would you like to take a shower?" Mark asked.

Amy gasped at the unexpected question. She smoothed her hair behind her ears and shook her tangled ponytail loose behind her back, wondering if she'd heard him correctly. She'd just been thinking about how physical he was and how she'd like to strip him down to sketch and sculpt him.

But then she felt the sticky grit of soot and dusty earth clinging to her hair and realized she was a mess. "Why?" She tugged the collar of her soiled blouse up to her nose. "Do I smell?"

He laughed. "Only like anybody else who's been dealing with a fire. Seriously, you're lucky you're not downwind of me." He held his hands up in mock surrender, taking any sting from his words. "Back in the kitchen, I could tell you needed a few minutes away from all the drama. Just now you said you needed some time alone. I can clear the house if you want me to."

She arched a doubting eyebrow. "You're not the man in charge."

"No, but I'm in pretty good with the guy who is. I'd ask everyone to give you some space and stand watch outside your bathroom door. Promise I wouldn't peek." His rugged cheeks softened with the barest hint of pink. A man who blushed? Could Captain Good Guy here speak any more clearly to her artistic impulses?

"You are determined to save me, aren't you?"

"My mom does that. Bubble baths are her thing. Growing up, none of us even dared knock on the door when she was in her sanctuary. And believe me, as much as she loves us, she needed a break from the four of us boys and Dad every now and then."

Amy's meager defenses against this man were crumbling. "You're giving away state secrets, Fire Man. I know all about your family now."

He perched on the edge of the sofa, inviting her to sit beside him again. "Then tell me something about you besides working with power tools and making art. I'm the baby. Of my generation, at any rate." Oh, there was nothing babyish about him. "You got any siblings to pick on you?"

Why was this man so easy to talk to? If the police or arson investigator wanted answers from her, they'd be smart to send in Mark. Even though every survival instinct inside her warned her not to give in to his goofy charm and apparent kindness, she shook her head. "Only child. My parents died when I was little, too. A car accident. Gran and Grandpa raised me. Grandpa passed away two years ago."

That shadow of pain shuddered across his face again before his crooked mouth widened with a grin that couldn't quite erase the pain she'd glimpsed. "Family is everything, isn't it? Me? I've got uncles and aunts and siblings coming out my ears. But I wouldn't trade the madness of a Sunday family dinner or Labor Day reunion for the world." He shrugged. "Of course, I'm not sure exactly how that's going to play out now that my grandma is moving to a new home. It won't be the same."

"It's the people, not the place or the activity, that matter." A lesson her grandparents had taught her as a child.

"Yep. Still, when one of those people is missing…"

Amy nodded. "Jocelyn was the closest thing to a sister I'll ever have. Now Gran's all I have left."

"You live here with your grandmother?"

"I moved back when I left grad school at Williams University, after my grandfather passed. Mutual benefits. This way, I don't worry about her being out here by herself."

"And she had the perfect location for your art studio."

"Exactly." Amy fiddled with her pendant again, wishing she could rebuild her own heart the way she'd crafted the coiled tendrils around the abstract chunk of steel. "We're all each other has."

"I lost my grandfather a couple of months ago." The way he worked the tight line of his jaw made her think he was still in the throes of grief. "He was one of the greatest men I ever knew."

She reached over to squeeze his thigh. Exhaustion must be making her a fool to care about his pain. Or maybe it was simple empathy because of the loss she'd suffered today. "I'm sorry."

He placed his hand over hers. It was a workingman's hand, yet it was as finely shaped as the rest of his body. "Thanks."

When he flipped his palm to link their fingers together, she didn't pull away. Despite the instincts that screamed at her to guard her emotions, getting close to Mark Taylor felt so natural, so right. She felt his sadness as clearly as her own. "Are you okay?"

"Hey, I'm here to cheer you up," he teased.

Amy didn't laugh. "I told you I don't need to be rescued."

"Give me a break. It's what I do." He tightened his grip around hers briefly before pulling away and checking his watch. "I hate to do this to you, but, if you're ready, I do need you to go talk to Dad."

She stood when he did. "Might as well get it over with. I don't know what I can tell him that I didn't already tell the police."

"Just be honest. And if you don't have an answer, it's okay to say that, too." Mark helped her close the windows. After locking up her studio, they crossed down to the long gravel driveway and headed back to the house.

"I'm glad you were there when I found Jocelyn," she admitted as he fell into step beside her. "But, for the record, I would have gotten past the shock. I would have called the police and made my way back here without your help."

He grinned at her over the jut of his shoulder. "Message received. You're a tough chick and I'm a Neanderthal."

"Don't put words in my mouth. It's not an insult. I just meant that I can do the rescuing and cheering up, too."

"It's okay to let someone help you when you need it, Amy. Family has taught me that."

Then why hadn't his family helped him with the grief or guilt or whatever emotion had shadowed his face earlier?

Amy grasped his hand and stopped, silently asking him to face her. When he did, she gave in to the urge that had taunted her all evening and reached up to smooth the messy spikes of hair that stood up above his forehead. She hadn't expected a simple neatening up could feel so intimate. She hadn't expected him to reach out and capture a loose lock of her hair between his fingers and inspect its color and texture before tucking it behind her ear, either.

He was taking care of her. Rescuing her. Seducing her without even trying.

"Look, Fire Man—Mark…" She grabbed his errant hand and squeezed it between both of hers, stilling his caress, whether it had been intended or accidental. She tilted her chin the short distance necessary to meet his curious gaze. "I need you to stop being such a good guy. Nothing's going to happen between us. Nothing should. You don't want to get involved with me. I can be a lot of trouble."

"Who told you that?"

"Seriously. I don't think I'm your type, and…"

"And what?" He switched grips so that he was holding her fingers in his. This would be so much easier if she could boss him around. He was patient, yes, had a cheesy sense of humor, but he clearly wasn't a pushover. And that was part of the problem. "Are you thinking you like me, too?"

"Too?" Her eyes widened at the implication. He was feeling this foolish connection just like she was. "This has been an extremely unusual day. We were thrown together by awful circumstances. You made me laugh, you annoyed the hell out of me, you comforted me—and I'm grateful. If I leaned on you a little bit, or there's some heat-of-the-moment, opposites-attracting kind of thing going on, I blame it on the day." She wished the breeze hadn't kicked up just then, blowing the dust that billowed up from an approaching car in the driveway over them, and kicking up those coffee-colored spikes of hair her fingers itched to smooth into place again. She pulled away, wisely breaking all contact with him. "I'm not looking for a relationship. I've taken advantage of your kindness more than once today. I don't want you to think I'm leading you on."

"Fair enough," he agreed. He nodded toward her art studio. "But I wasn't the only one doling out comfort back there. Don't I get a say in this heat-of-the-moment, opposites-attracting thing, too?"

Amy was saved from coming up with another reasonable argument that would shut down this budding attraction by the sound of her grandmother's voice. "Amy?"

At the honk of a car horn, Amy turned and waved a thanks to the friends who had dropped Comfort Hall off and were now driving away. Leaving Mark behind, she hurried to meet the slender, slightly stooped woman with the circular lime green eyeglasses, a mannish snow-white haircut and cropped linen pants that gave her grandmother a distinctly boho vibe.

"Gran." Amy wound her arms around Comfort's slender shoulders and felt those familiar loving arms wrap around her in a tight hug. "I'm so glad you're here."

"Oh, baby, I'm so sorry. What a horrible accident." She pulled back far enough to study Amy's face and inspect the evidence of tears there. "Jocelyn was such a fine young woman."

She pulled her in for another hug, and Amy held on when she felt the shudder of grief tremble through her grandmother's body. They kissed each other's cheek before Amy pulled away to deliver the grim news. "It wasn't an accident, Gran. The police are in the preliminary stages of their investigation, but someone attacked Joss. The fire was an attempt to cover up the crime scene. I think her killer thought the police would blame it on the other fires we've been battling."

"Murder?" Comfort pressed a hand over her heart. "That poor girl. Who would want to hurt Jocelyn?" Dropping her voice to a whisper, Comfort peeked over the top of her glasses. "An arson fire? They don't suspect—"

"That's why I wanted to warn you about all the people in the house tonight." Amy cut her off before her grandmother could finish that sentence. She tilted her head toward the man waiting patiently behind her. "They're trying to figure it all out."

"I see." Comfort's hazel eyes darted past Amy to assess Mark's casual uniform before hugging her one more time. Gran understood better than anyone how much trouble Amy could be in if certain elements of her past came to light, whether she was innocent or not. "How are you holding up, dear?"

"I'm okay." She looked back to invite Mark to join them. "I made a new friend today. He tried to rescue me earlier."

The older woman snickered, not bothering to hide her amusement. "How did that go?"

"He's been…patient…with me." She gestured to make the introductions. "Gran—Comfort Hall—this is Mark Taylor. He's a KCFD firefighter."

Gran smiled broadly when Mark took her hand. "I can see that. Nice uniform."

"Mrs. Hall."

"Aren't you a tall, hunky drink of water." Her smile didn't dim as she drew back. "I'm available, you know." Oh, my gosh, was that a nudge on Amy's elbow? "So is my granddaughter."

"Gran!"

Mark grinned. "I believe you're flirtin' with me, ma'am."

"Is it working, handsome?"

His cheekbones warmed with a sweetly vulnerable blush.

Amy rushed to his defense, hoping to tone down the obvious matchmaking. "He's not handsome, Gran."

When Comfort arched a fine, snowy white brow above her glasses, Amy realized that her words might not have come out the way she'd intended. Not wanting to offend Mark or endure a lecture on politeness from her grandmother, Amy hastened to explain. "His face is interesting." Ever the artist, Amy touched Mark's face to point out exactly what made his looks so compelling. "Strong angles and shading. The intriguing bump on his nose. Those gray-blue eyes. The design of his face is better than handsome." When she felt the stubble of his beard tickling her fingertips, and saw those gorgeous eyes boring into hers, Amy quickly pulled away. Now they were both blushing. She squared her back against the firefighter who was doing crazy things to her vows to swear off men and wrapped an arm around her grandmother's shoulders. "We'd better get you inside. The police and arson investigator might want to ask you some questions about Jocelyn."

"Did you make coffee for them?" Comfort asked.

"No. I was trying to stay out of the way." When Comfort stopped at the bottom of the porch steps, Amy confessed the truth. "All right. I was hiding out for a few minutes, trying to get my act together. I'm guessing someone sent Mark out to fetch me."

"I came of my own volition," Mark volunteered, unable to avoid eavesdropping. "I swear."

Comfort lowered her voice to a whisper. "He seems like a nice man."

"Doesn't matter," Amy whispered right back.

A little bit of heartbreak creased her face before Comfort squeezed Amy's hand. On a mission now, she turned and climbed the porch steps. "I'd better get a pot started for our guests. You get cleaned up and come help me."

"What is it with everyone wanting me naked in a shower?"

Her grandmother turned at the front door. "Who wants to get you naked?"

"Gran!" Amy heard the words and turned to Mark to apologize. "I mean, offering me a private bath…" Nope. That wasn't any better. "I will stop talking now."

Mark nudged a pebble with his foot, the blush on his cheeks as evident as the fire heating her own. But her grandmother was grinning from ear to ear as Amy glared daggers at her. "I don't know what you two have been talking about, but it sounds mighty intriguing. It was nice to meet you, Mark."

"Ma'am."

Comfort winked behind her glasses. "Invite your friend to stay if he wants."

When the front door closed behind her grandmother, Amy quickly apologized to Mark. "That was awkward."

Being the unfailingly good guy that he was, Mark grinned and put her at ease. "Don't worry. I know a thing or two about grandmothers. Relentless matchmakers. Always worried you're going to wind up alone."

"Or unfed." She shrugged. "And unwashed, apparently."

His easy, deep-pitched laughter made her smile. Amy extended her hand. Nothing could ever come of this chemistry they seemed to share, but she had enjoyed *most* of her time with Mark Taylor. "Thank you, Fire Man."

"I was just doing—"

"Don't say you were just doing your job. I was losing it earlier, when I couldn't find Jocelyn. I *did* lose it when we did." The polite thing to do would be to release his hand. And yet she didn't. Instead she turned it over and traced the shape of his knuckles with her fingertips.

"I'm sorry I didn't listen to you then. But I couldn't think straight. I was frantic with the need to—"

"Find your friend." His grip tightened around hers a moment before he proved the stronger of them and pulled away to prop his hands at his waist. "I'll give you a pass on that one today, too. Your reputation as a stubbornly independent woman is still intact."

"Thanks." Amy tugged on the bandanna knotted at her wrist. "And thanks for not letting me be alone with my thoughts for too long tonight."

"Why does Dale O'Brien call you Crazy Amy?"

"Because he's a jerk?" The abrupt change in topic when she kept trying to say goodbye reminded her that he could be part of his father's investigation. But O'Brien was a sore spot for her. "Because I don't bow down at his feet like he's the power broker he thinks he is? I work odd hours in my studio when I get an inspiration, so he thinks I'm spying on him and sabotaging his construction sites if I'm up in the middle of the night? He doesn't understand the words *no sale*? Take your pick. And yes, I might have given him a little aesthetic advice on the design of his blocky, modern houses so that they fit in better with the lake and wilderness surrounding us. His designs are like sticking a concrete cinder block in the middle of a Monet painting. I don't think he appreciated my input. I can be obstinate sometimes."

"Really? You? Speaking your mind?" Mark teased.

"You don't know me, Fire Man," she teased right back.

"I know you don't take orders very well."

"No. But I can be reasoned with." She frowned, remembering that he hadn't been reasonable at all when he'd first chased her down during her search for Jocelyn. "Would you really have thrown me over your shoulder and carried me away from the fire?"

"Yes."

"I'm a big girl," she argued.

"I'm a big boy," he responded without batting an eye. "Picking you up would not be a problem for me." His strong arms swelled in size as he crossed them over his chest, more than proving his point.

Something deep inside Amy's womb fluttered at the blatant show of masculinity. *Not. Your. Type.* Why couldn't she keep a coherent thought around this man? Or just walk away from him? "I don't know whether that's freakin' hot or if I should be offended by your Neanderthal tactics."

"Did it get you to listen to me in a potentially dangerous situation?"

"It got my attention. But I think hearing me out, and the promise to give me fifteen minutes of your time, is what ensured my cooperation."

"So, I'm a Neanderthal and you're crazy. Makes me think we should go out sometime. People would talk."

"Probably not in the way you think." Captain Good Guy and the eccentric bad girl? People would definitely talk…about her ruining his life or corrupting his heroic ways. Amy smiled. "Good night, Mark Taylor. I'm glad I met you."

He caught her hand when she reached the top step. "I was serious about the date thing. When you're ready. After you've had the time you need to grieve."

Bless his think-the-best-of-everyone heart. That was why he thought she was refusing him? She should have set him straight immediately, but he was giving her time and space. And he wasn't professing insta-love or asking her for anything but an evening of her time. Plus, she really did like the guy…even when he was telling her what to do. Or asking questions. And his face wasn't the only interesting thing about him. She wanted to know more about the dark secrets hidden beneath his friendly exterior. She understood a lot about the differences between what she felt and what she showed the world, too. And how exactly was a woman supposed to resist those smoky blue puppy-dog eyes looking up at her?

"Give me your phone." After he pulled it from the clip on his belt, she typed in her number and the nickname *Red*. "Call or text me sometime."

"I will." When she handed him her cell, he typed in his number and the words *Fire Man*. "So you know it's me." He tucked his phone back onto his belt. "You take care of yourself. No more running *toward* the fire, okay? That's my job."

When Amy stepped onto the porch, the front door opened. The man she now knew to be Mark's father, Gideon Taylor, stepped out, blocking her path. Detectives Beck and Carson flanked him on either side. This couldn't be good. Amy bristled, straightening to every inch of height she possessed and raising her invisible defenses.

Then Dale O'Brien slipped out the door behind them, his self-satisfied smile curling around the matchstick he chewed between his teeth. Amy glanced behind her, too late spotting the white O'Brien Construction pickup parked in the shadows beyond the lights of the house, behind all the official vehicles lining her driveway. How had she missed seeing him here? Because she'd been too distracted by grief and Captain Good Guy to realize she needed to be protecting herself.

This *so* couldn't be good.

"Miss Hall?" The gravitas in Gideon Taylor's voice demanded her attention. She faced him again, feeling outnumbered, outsmarted and under attack as the three people with badges and that crud O'Brien all studied her.

"What is it, Dad?"

Amy jumped at the weight of Mark Taylor's hand settling at the small of her back. While she appreciated his support, she doubted it would last.

"Son." Gideon acknowledged Mark before returning his gaze to her. "Miss Hall, I'm the chief arson investigator for the KCFD. Our records indicate that we've been out here before investigating suspicious events on your property."

Her gaze immediately shot to the *helpful citizen* who had no doubt reported her. Dale O'Brien would do anything to get her and her gran booted off this property— even take advantage of her vulnerability on the day her best friend had been murdered.

Unless he'd had something to do with that murder? Was the man so desperate to build his Copper Lake empire that he'd kill an innocent woman to set her up like this?

"What did you do, O'Brien?" she accused, letting the anger coursing through her chase away the chill she'd felt a moment ago. She shimmied away from Mark's touch and lifted her gaze back to Deputy Chief Taylor. "It's not what you think, sir."

"Seems pretty straightforward to me." He pointed to the burned-out house down by the lake. That meant O'Brien had told him about the firepit and stables behind the house, too. "You were accused of setting fires."

Chapter Six

Mark stretched out on his bunk at the station house, but it was too early to try to sleep. He'd done his duty by the beef stew and home-baked bread his Station 13 captain, Kyle Redding, had prepared for dinner. But he'd barely tasted it, despite the warm, homey smells that had filled the station house while they'd been washing down the rig, checking hoses and stowing gear. He'd joined his brother Matt for a workout in the house's weight room but had excused himself from an invitation to join some of the men and women he served with for a couple of hands of toothpick poker. Now the sun was setting, the city was quiet, and he had no other reason to put off reading the text he'd received from Amy Hall.

He pulled up the message.

Another rejection.

His breath seeped out on a sigh of disappointment. But he wasn't surprised. He wondered how long he should chase this chemistry he'd felt with the leggy redhead. He wondered how long the image of her crying in her studio behind her welder's mask, hiding away where the chaos couldn't reach her so she could grieve alone, would stay with him.

His instinct had been to take her in his arms, just like he had up on the hill with the burned-out shed where she'd discovered her friend's body. She'd fit against him like two pieces of a puzzle locking together. The woman had curves in all the right places. Yet he could tell she was fit, based on the endurance she'd shown running those Missouri hills. She had hair like wildfire and freckled alabaster skin. She was immensely talented, worked like a badass with power tools and fire, and had a beautiful mouth that could irritate, commiserate and make him laugh. And damn, he wanted to kiss that mouth.

He'd never met anyone like her. He'd never felt this instant, intense draw to another woman before. He wasn't a player, but he had enough experience to know that the attraction was mutual.

But Amy Hall had keeping him at arm's length down to an art form. He didn't need to be a rocket scientist to understand that she was used to handling whatever she needed to on her own.

So, he'd respected her need for space a whole twenty-four hours before calling to leave a voice mail. He'd wanted to make sure she and her grandmother were all right, remind her that his dad was a thorough, but fair, investigator who knew the difference between arson convictions and alleged suspicions that hadn't been proved. And he'd wanted to apologize for Dale O'Brien being such a dickwad to raise those suspicions about her in the first place.

Yes, there'd been two fires on her property before the wildfire that day. One, she confessed to starting when she'd been burning something in the horse paddock and the fire had gotten out of hand. He'd checked the records himself. Amy had been the one to call 9-1-1 that day to contain the accidental fire.

The one at the old foreman's house was still under investigation. And though Dale O'Brien had hinted that she was responsible for setting that one, too, there was no hard evidence to indicate she'd had anything to do with it. Her denial and his loathing for O'Brien had been good enough for Mark to believe her.

But the woman was still hiding something. Something that made him all the more eager to get to know her better, that made him ache to hold her and listen or do whatever was necessary to bring a smile back to that beautiful mouth and chase the wary distrust from her eyes.

So, for two weeks, he'd kept the conversations between them light and safe and fun, getting to know the little things about her before he pushed for the something more he thought could be really, really good between them.

After that first terse *We're good. Thanks!* reply, he'd waited another twenty-four hours to ask what she charged for one of her pendants or sculptures. How long it took her to create her art. Where did she get her ideas? What was her favorite food? Did she listen to country, rock or classical music? In turn, she'd gotten him to reveal he was a Chiefs football fan. That yes, he'd been to the Nelson-Atkins Museum and Art Gallery—with a school group—and the suits of medieval armor were his favorite display. And that he preferred his grandmother's fried catfish over sushi any day.

Mark had given it a full week before asking her out.

It felt like flirting, reading all the clever ways Amy could say no to his invitations to coffee or lunch or browsing one of the big chain outdoorsman stores in the city before having dinner at the attached Islamorada restaurant. This evening's answer was no different.

In some parts of the world, they call this harassment, Fire Man. ;)

Mark texted right back. In other parts of the world, they say that persistence wins the race.

Amy's reply was accompanied by an eye-rolling emoji. And what race would that be?

The one where you finally say you'll give in to our heat-of-the-moment, opposites-attracting thing and go out with me.

You're never going to let me forget those words, are you, she answered. I can't see you tonight. I've got a university thing with Jocelyn's parents. Sort of a wake for coworkers, profs and students who couldn't get to Nebraska for the funeral. They're making a donation to Williams U in Joss's name. Strictly froufrou event. Speeches, canapés and cocktails. I've been forced to put on a dress and heels.

He closed his eyes, having no problem imagining how killer her legs would look in a getup like that, before typing a response. Need an escort? he offered. I look good in a tux.

Mark smiled at her reply. I bet you do. But there's nary a fried catfish on any of these buffet tables, so I don't know what you'd eat. She'd been paying attention to the little details of their conversations as much as he had. Besides, aren't you at work?

He answered the truth. Yes. But I'd skip out to be your arm candy.

Two minutes passed before she sent a reply. You're trying to rescue me again. You'd let Kansas City burn just so I don't have to go to this shindig alone?

Alone. There it was again. The thing about Amy Hall that kept nagging at him. She didn't seem to mind chatting, as long as he kept his distance. Based on her responses to his texts, he didn't believe it was him she had an aversion to. Just the idea of dating or relationships, in general. Why on earth was she so determined to be alone?

What had happened in her life to make her think that facing adversity by herself—with just her grandmother for backup—was her safest bet? Was it Mark's relationship to the man who was investigating the arson fires on her property that made her so cautious of doing more than play text tag with him? Was there something going on in her life that was forcing her to be distrustful of a man's interest in her? An image of the portly contractor with the misogynistic attitude toward his mother and Amy came to mind. He really didn't like that guy.

Probably shouldn't. But let's make plans for tomorrow after my shift, ok? I promise, jeans will be the dress code.

She asked, What did you have in mind?

Mark swung his legs over the edge of the bunk and sat up straight in anticipation. It was the closest response to even a *maybe* he'd gotten since they'd started these daily text chats. He had to give the right answer.

How about you and me talking face-to-face? Let's go for a walk. I'll bring the water bottles and you bring the sunscreen.

Her reply wasn't what he'd expected. Could we go back out to the shed where we found Jocelyn? Detective Beck said they took down the crime scene tape earlier today. No sign of Joss's laptop or even her backpack anywhere.

Mark frowned. Doesn't that place have bad memories for you?

I need answers, Mark. Not Fire Man. Not a joke. I'll go out there on my own if I have to. But I'd rather you came with me. You can tell me what you know about the fire. Help me sort through the debris. Maybe your dad and the police missed something.

Tension knotted at the back of Mark's neck. Her friend had met a killer at that shed, or somewhere close by. She'd been alone, too. No one was in custody for the crimes. Beyond Dale O'Brien, he wasn't even sure who the suspects were that KCPD had been investigating. Besides the awful memories of Jocelyn Brunt's murder, who knew what or who Amy would be facing out there in the remote hills behind her house. No culprit would appreciate a shapely redhead pawing through his business, trying to uncover his identity.

Do NOT go out there by yourself. We don't know who's setting those fires or who killed your friend. He waited a whole minute with no response. Red? No reply. Be safe. I will go with you. I'll call as soon as I get off tomorrow. Wait for me. Tell me you won't investigate any of this on your own. Amy?

Five minutes without any answer and he dialed her number. But when it went straight to voice mail, he got up and paced the length of the bunk room. Either she'd turned her phone off because of the reception, she was ignoring him or he was an absolute fool for worrying about her like this. He stopped at the second-floor window overlooking the landscaping and street in front of the station house. The streetlamps were coming on, telling him the hour was getting late. Still, there were steady lines of traffic moving in both directions, thanks to their location just off the interstate near several restaurants, hotels and suburban neighborhoods.

There were so many people in Kansas City. Probably

a lot of people at that hoity-toity university event. Lots of people outside this window. Why wouldn't Amy let him in? Let him be her friend. Let him be something more? He'd always had family around to help him through tough times. He'd always had his real brothers and his brothers at Firehouse 13 to back him up when he needed to take a risk.

Mark pocketed his phone before the frustration building inside him made him sling it across the bunk room. He pounded his fist against the window frame when he couldn't shut off his concern and pulled out his phone to text one last message to Amy. Just let me know you're safe. Ok? A thumbs-up will get me off your back tonight. I promise.

"What did that window ever do to you?" Mark was still waiting for an answer when his brother Matt entered the bunk room. Matt sat on his bunk, stretching his long legs out in front of him. "I'm supposed to be the quiet one. But you're making me look like a regular social butterfly tonight. Thinking about Grandpa again?"

Nope. But he should have been. Mark squeezed his eyes shut against the lousy job he was doing taking care of people lately. He scraped his palm over the top of his hair and blanked the emotion from his face before turning to face his brother. He held up his phone in explanation before stuffing it into the pocket of his BDUs. "Just waiting for somebody to call me back."

Matt picked up a car magazine and flipped through the pages, his tone deceptively indifferent. "It's *her*, then. The redhead?"

No sense denying it. What Matt Taylor lacked in verbosity, he more than made up for in observation skills. Big Brother never missed a trick.

"Her name's Amy." Mark strolled back to his bunk

to sit across from Matt. "We've been, um, getting acquainted since that day we got called in on the wildfire."

"Uh-huh."

Mark interpreted that as *I'm interested enough. Keep talking.* "Dad confirmed that there's been three suspicious fires on her property. The first one Amy admitted to—she called 9-1-1 herself. She was burning some trash in a homemade firepit that got out of hand. A couple of weeks after that, she lost a rental property, then another storage shed in the wildfire—the one where we discovered her friend's body. Dad says those last two fires were deliberately set." Matt didn't look up from his magazine, but Mark knew that didn't mean he wasn't listening. "Now she wants to go exploring and solve the crimes by herself. Two fires are a coincidence. Three fires and a murder mean somebody's really pissed off." Mark waited for some flicker of a response in his brother's brown eyes. Could he not see what the problem was? "How do I convince her she isn't safe?"

Matt lowered the magazine to his lap and met Mark's gaze. "You think someone's targeting her with those fires?"

"Dale O'Brien wants her and her grandmother off that land. If they won't sell, could be he's trying to burn them out."

Matt nodded and dropped his attention back to the article he was reading. "O'Brien was only too happy to let Dad know that she was accused of setting at least one of those fires. That guy is a real piece of work."

"He's probably the one who reported her."

Matt's grunt was as good as an agreement.

"Since she admitted to setting the bonfire in the firepit, she was the first suspect they looked at. She doesn't trust the police. Or Dad. So, she's investigating on her own."

"Sounds risky."

Mark pushed to his feet and paced toward the windows again. "Maybe it's not my place to worry, but I've never seen anyone with less backup than that woman has. I keep asking her out and she keeps putting me off. And the hell of it is, I think she likes me. Maybe she doesn't trust me enough to tell me what's really going on with her. Maybe she thinks I'm just trying to get close to her so I can report to Dad. I've been up-front with her that if I learn anything, I'd have to share it, but that's not why I want to see her."

"She's really gotten under your skin." Matt tossed the magazine aside. "Why are you trying to get close to her? You think you're going to lose somebody else on your watch?"

"It's more than that. She needs somebody, Matt." *I want her to need me.*

"You sure you're not making up a threat that isn't there, so you can get closer to her?"

Mark muttered a curse and shook his head. "I am not making this up. At least, I don't think I am. There's something dangerous surrounding Amy Hall. I think she needs help. But she's too proud, or too scared, to ask for it. So, I'm offering."

"Grandpa would tell you to trust your gut. You think she needs help? Then do something about it." Matt Taylor was a big reflection in the window as he walked up behind Mark and rested a hand on his shoulder. "But if this is just about you needing to save somebody because you feel guilty about Grandpa, let it go. The only one who blames you for Grandpa's heart attack is you."

Mark shrugged off his brother's touch. "Amy and I

have been talking or texting every day. And it's not just me being all stalkerish. She contacts me as often as I do her. We've got a connection. She's funny. And smart. She thinks *I'm* funny."

"Oh, well, now I know there's something wrong with her."

Turning, Mark smacked Matt in the arm. "Maybe you've got no interest in a relationship, but I think we could be something if she'd give us a chance."

"What makes you think I've got no interest—?"

"I'm fine with going slow, if that's what she needs. But I don't want to lose the possibility of being with her because she's too pigheaded to listen to reason."

Bracing his hands at his waist, Matt puffed up to a size that intimidated most men. But that only made Mark match his stance. He knew his brother too well to be intimidated by whatever salient point he suddenly wanted to make. "Amy's not the only woman trouble you have."

"Huh?"

"At Sunday dinner, Grandma Martha asked why you weren't there. She knew you weren't working because I was there." Matt crossed his arms over his chest and glared. "She thinks you're avoiding her."

"There were plenty of people there with her to christen the new house, right?"

"We were all there. Every uncle, every aunt, every cousin. So, it stuck out that you were missing."

"Grandpa is the one who's missing, Matt. I..." Mark turned to the window and looked down into the night. He hated that he'd caused Grandma Martha any pain. "I let the man she loves die. Why would she want me around to remind her of that?"

Matt's chest expanded as though he was about to light into Mark. But the fire alarm sounded, ending whatever butt-chewing session he'd been about to receive. Personal matters took a back seat as the call to duty rang through the building and the brothers Taylor answered.

"Let's move it, Thirteen," Captain Redding called over the intercom as Mark and Matt jogged to the stairs. "Structure fire, fully engulfed. All trucks are rolling."

"We'll finish this conversation later," Matt announced as they hurried to their gear lockers. "And put the red-head out of your mind for now, too, bro. I don't want to be saving your butt because you're thinking about a woman instead of the call."

Mark gave Matt a curt nod and picked up his gear, letting his training move him through the steps he needed to perform. He stepped into his turnout pants and boots and grabbed his coat and helmet before climbing up to his position behind the driver's seat of the first engine truck. Mark leaned forward as Matt settled behind the wheel and started the engine. "Where are we headed, Cap?"

Captain Redding settled into the seat across from Matt and punched the address into the engine's GPS system. "Copper Lake."

The adrenaline pumping through Mark's veins skidded to a halt as recognition hit, filling him with dread. "That's where Amy lives."

"Who's Amy?" the captain asked.

"A friend." A friend who didn't need more of this kind of trouble. Mark sank back into his seat before meeting his brother's stoic gaze in the rearview mirror. "You still think I'm making up a reason to rescue her?"

Chapter Seven

Amy glanced down at the last text Mark had sent her and considered sending him a thumbs-up, so that he would stop worrying. She wasn't reckless enough to search through the hills of her grandmother's farm at this time of night on her own.

But as a tipsy guest jostled her without apologizing at the reception's free bar, she couldn't exactly assure him that she felt okay. Her toes were pinched to the point of numbness in these high heels, and her patience had been pinched even further. She'd already stayed an hour longer than she'd intended. She'd traded hugs with Jocelyn's parents, shaken hands with the Dean of Arts & Science, who'd asked if she was considering reapplying for graduate school, and applauded speeches by the dean, Jocelyn's parents and the supervising professor for Jocelyn's doctoral project.

As the man who'd bumped her brushed past her again, eager to greet a friend, Amy stepped up to the bar and placed her order. "I'd like a cola. Whatever you have with caffeine. Just give me the can. I don't need a glass. And a bottle of water."

She looked over her shoulder to the blond man in the crumpled black tux and dangling bow tie who sat with his head in his hands near the exit door. Derek Roland was the only reason she was still here. When she found him out in the parking lot, trying to unlock his car with his apartment key, she'd offered to call a car for him. With vomit staining his shoes and the hem of his trousers, he clearly was in no shape to drive. But then he'd fallen onto her, trapping her against the car and swallowing her in an uncomfortable hug as he wept onto her shoulder.

Deciding Derek was too drunk and despondent to be left to his own devices for any length of time, Amy had helped him back inside with the intent of sobering him up before he went home.

Unlike her drunk, dramatic friend there, Mark Taylor probably looked freakin' hot in a tuxedo. Not that a firefighter's uniform or sweaty T-shirt had done him any injustice. Plus, he'd be more entertaining. She could certainly use a few laughs after the strain of smiling all evening, pretending she was fine being back on the campus that had once been her beloved home. She had a feeling that Mark wouldn't have gotten so stinking drunk and become a burden to her tonight, either. He was too considerate for that. He would have realized that she was grieving, too. He wouldn't have made tonight all about him.

Giving in to the temptation of connecting with Mark again, Amy pulled out her phone and reread the draft of the text she'd typed while she'd been waiting in line for caffeine.

I changed my mind. Could I see you tonight? I could use a friendly, interesting face. Are you at the station house? Tuxedo is optional. ;)

"Ma'am?" The bartender popped the tab on the cola and set it in front of her. "Your drinks?"

"Thanks." Amy sent the text before she could question the wisdom of getting closer to Mark, dropped some money into the tip jar, and wove her way through the groupings and conversations to Derek. "Feeling any better?" she asked as she sat down across from him. She set the cola in front of him and opened the water for herself. "Here. Drink as much of that as you can. I figured you could manage it better than a cup of coffee."

At least the wailing had stopped. But his eyes were red and puffy when he leaned back in his chair. He raked his fingers through his shaggy hair, surveying the dwindling crowd before settling his bleary gaze on her. "Why are you being so good to me, Amy? I don't deserve it."

Maybe not. Derek wasn't the only one grieving in this room or sharing fond memories of Jocelyn and celebrating her work and her life. But he was the only one who'd made a noisy, public display of his heartbreak, to the point that his fellow grad students and professors had turned away from the emotional drain he imposed on them.

As far as Amy was concerned, she'd stuck by him because of Jocelyn. She owed her friend that much, to take care of the man she'd left behind. Joss would have done the same. Otherwise, these killer shoes would be off, and she'd be home in bed or in her studio.

Or maybe she'd give in to the foolish urge to see Mark Taylor in person again. To feel his soothing touch. To laugh at his goofy humor. To lean on him like the pillar of strength that he was.

Right now, she had no one to lean on but herself.

"You've had too much to drink. And you're grieving. It's hard to manage one when you're dealing with the other." Amy pushed the can toward him. "Drink up. I'm calling that car for you once you sober up a little more. I don't want you barfing again in the back seat."

He chuckled and reached for the cola, downing a long drink before reaching across the table to capture her hand in his tight grip. "I've ruined the party for you. I'm sorry."

Amy couldn't help but compare his crushing grip to the gentle strength of Mark's hand. With Mark, she could have pulled away if she'd wanted. She tugged against Derek's hand. A remembered panic from Preston's attack bubbled through her blood. Maybe he was too inebriated to realize he was hurting her. "Derek, let go," she ordered. If anything, his grip on her tightened, nearly snapping her wrist. "Let. Go."

His drunken haze seemed to vanish for a split second, and his green eyes zeroed in on hers before his grip suddenly popped open and he raised his hands in mock surrender. "Sorry. Don't know my own strength, I guess. Did I hurt you?"

Amy assessed the thumbprint that would show up as a bruise on her fair skin within the hour. But out loud, she answered, "Nothing that needs a doctor. Just be more careful next time."

He nodded and took another long drink of cola. "I really have ruined your night."

"I haven't been in much of a party mood anyway, lately," she confessed. "I wanted to be here to support Joss's mom and dad. But, whenever you're feeling up to it, I am ready to head for home."

"Me, too." He downed the rest of his soda in one final chug. At least he covered his mouth when a noisy belch followed. As his foul alcohol breath carried across the table, Amy subtly rubbed the hand he'd crushed in her lap. Remembering the force of Preston Worth's attack was much harder to erase. His hand had been at her throat. His fists had been everywhere. And then there'd been that horrible fall. "You're so much stronger about all this than I am."

No. She was just a survivor. That was what she was good at.

"We all grieve differently." Amy offered the platitude before standing and circling around to link her hand in the crook of Derek's elbow and pull him to his feet. "Come on. A walk in the fresh air will do you some good, too."

"Just give me my keys and I'll go home."

"You're not driving anywhere. Now walk."

They reached the edge of the parking lot before she stopped and pulled her phone from her purse to call a car service. She spared a moment of disappointment when she saw that Mark hadn't answered her text. Was this how he felt when she got too worried about how emotionally involved she was getting and put off replying? She couldn't blame him for ignoring her and giving her a taste of her own medicine. Or was he on a call with his team? Was worrying about him battling a fire or dealing with a dangerous accident any easier than feeling guilty or hurt by the absence of any contact with him?

Wow. Where was her head these days, when her hopes and sorrows centered around whether or not Mark connected with her?

"Amy?" She quickly scrolled off her text messages when Derek bumped her arm. He was sobering up, but not as quickly as she'd like. "Wish I could get out of this damn monkey suit. Especially with the…" He stumbled against her as he looked down at his soiled shoes. "You know."

Irritation warred with pity. If she didn't believe this sad sack's love for Jocelyn was genuine, the pity might not have won. With a weary huff, Amy linked her arm through Derek's and turned him toward the agricultural sciences building. "Do you have a change of clothes at your office?"

He nodded.

"Then let's go there." Since Derek's university ID was on his key chain, she had no trouble leading him past the building's nighttime security guard and heading to his tiny office at the top of the stairs.

Once there, Derek took his bag of running gear to the bathroom down the hall and changed. Amy wished she still had an office on campus and a pair of tennis shoes or flip-flops to change into, too. But since she suspected she'd never get her swollen feet wedged inside these heels again for the drive home, she sat in the lone chair behind Derek's messy desk and waited to make sure he didn't pass out somewhere between the bathroom and loading him into the car that would take him home.

As emotionally exhausted as she was, her mind wandered. Before she fully realized what she was doing, Amy was tidying up the stack of student essay books spread across his blotter and sticking stray pens, paper clips and sticky-note pads into the desk drawer with other office supplies. She reached into her purse for a tissue to dust off the dingy keyboard and screen of his laptop, and smiled when she discovered the black cotton bandanna Mark had given her the night Jocelyn had died. Even when she couldn't reach the firefighter who had wormed his way into nearly every thought, this old-fashioned token of his Captain Good Guy persona warmed her heart and eased some of the stress of the evening.

Feeling an uncharacteristic urge of sentimentality, Amy twisted the bandanna into a long skein and tied it around her wrist. Maybe the time had come for her to admit she had feelings for Mark Taylor, that she wanted to be more than just texting buddies. That one of these days, she was going to have to sit him down and tell him all her twisted past and current hang-ups and see if he was still interested in turning their daily flirtations into something more serious.

Feeling a little lighter now that she'd admitted those feelings and was considering the risk of taking on a relationship again, starting with that date Mark kept teasing her about, Amy went back to cleaning Derek's desk. She found the tissue she'd been looking for and dusted off the screen and keyboard before closing the university-issued laptop and straightening it on the corner of the blotter.

And then she saw the second laptop hiding beneath a hodgepodge of maps and file folders. She almost called down the hall to Derek to ask what he'd done to rate two laptops, or if he'd been careless enough to lose one in this mess and had requested a replacement, when she got a better look at the second laptop.

"What is…?" She fingered the sticky bits of fuzz and glue on the laptop's outside cover where someone had peeled off a sticker. Not just any sticker, but one with the nearly imperceptible outline of two initials…a *J* and a *B. Jocelyn Brunt*.

Amy unplugged the laptop and flipped it over to find the remnants of another familiar sticker. Although the shredded bits of glue and plastic gave no indication to what had once been there, the location was exactly where Joss had put the emblem of a female superhero who'd inspired her.

Had the air-conditioning kicked on in the small office? Or was the chill racing down Amy's spine confirmation that Derek had his hands on something he shouldn't?

Amy hugged the laptop to her chest and stood as Derek leaned against the door frame. "I'm as ready as

I can be..." When he saw what was in her arms, when he saw her crossing toward him with a purpose, Derek straightened. "What are you doing?" He dropped his tuxedo jacket and slacks on the worktable beside him. "Are you going through my things?"

"This isn't *your* thing." If possible, he turned even paler and looked like he might be sick again. But Amy's sympathy had left the building. "You know damn well this is Jocelyn's. Where did you get it? How long have you had it? You do know the police are looking for it, right?"

"I know." He sagged against the door frame. "I wasn't finished with it."

He wasn't *finished*? He'd known its location for two weeks and hadn't said anything? "Damn it, Derek. The police think this could be key to finding Jocelyn's killer. And you...?" Amy muttered a curse and pushed him out of her way, heading for the stairs. "I'm turning this over to the police. And I'm telling them exactly where I found it."

"She left it in my apartment the night before she died."

Amy spun around to face him. "She left it? Jocelyn never went anywhere without this." She frowned as another thought registered. Maybe a better question was, *She stayed the night with you?*

Wait. Amy eyed her position at the top of the stairs and felt the yawning expanse down to the first floor ripple through her vision like a chimera of heat. Blinking away the dizzying sensation, she moved to the side, so she wasn't in such a vulnerable position to an impulsive shove down to the first floor as Derek shuffled toward her. Maybe the smartest question she could ask was, "Did you have anything to do with Joss's murder?"

"What?" Derek's hands shot up in surrender and he drifted back a step. "No. God, no. I loved her."

She knew better than most that love didn't necessarily mean violence couldn't also be part of a relationship. "Tell me exactly how you got this," she ordered, wondering if she was having this conversation with Jocelyn's killer. Maybe she should get her phone out and call Detective Beck. No, her key chain with the canister of pepper spray was a better option right now. Amy pulled her keys out of her purse and put her finger on the button, showing Derek that she wasn't going to be afraid of him. She wasn't going to leave without answers, either. "Tell me about the night before Jocelyn died."

Derek lowered his hands and drifted back to the door frame, as if he needed its support to stand. "Joss and I spent some time together that last week. She told me you said she should put herself first, that she should do what was right for her." His mouth tightened into a grim line as though he hadn't appreciated that advice. "Maybe she loved me more than you thought she did. She came over to talk and…things heated up."

"Are you talking breakup sex?"

"No!" For a man who was two blinks away from passing out, Derek was suddenly loud and lunging toward her. Amy aimed the pepper spray, but the walls must have whirled around his vision because he stumbled back into the doorway, clinging to the frame to keep himself upright. He might be less of a threat, but the bile toward her was still there. "I'm talking about two-people-who-are-meant-to-be-together kind of sex. I needed to know that she still loved me. I wanted her to know that once her degree was done, I would be there for her."

Yeah, yeah. True love. Emotional blackmail. Amy wasn't interested. "Tell me about the laptop."

"I woke up before her the next morning, the day she died." He shook his head and tears filled his eyes. "I just wanted some confirmation of her findings to fact-check against my own dissertation. But then she was awake… but I hadn't found the information I needed…and I didn't want her to think that was the reason I'd slept with her… so I hid it. When she didn't find it in her bag, I suggested that she left it at your place. Or in her equipment shed. Later that day—I knew she'd been evacuated because of the fire—I was driving the laptop back to your place to stick it in her room when you called me."

"You son of a bitch. You can't *use* somebody and love her at the same time."

Derek sank down against the wall until he was sitting on the floor and blubbering again. But this wasn't grief. It was guilt. Despair. "Don't you see what I've done? She must have driven out to the shed that morning looking for her laptop. I sent her to her death. She wouldn't have been there if it wasn't for me."

Could his lame story be true? Or was he trying to give himself some kind of alibi? Despite his obvious distress, Amy was done offering comfort. "You won't get any more sympathy from me tonight. You sure you didn't have an argument with her over stealing her research? Maybe you got a little rough?"

"And took her out to your place to hide the body? I'm not that gnarly old professor who beat on you!" His words struck Amy like a slap across the face. Maybe that had been his intention, his way of getting her to back off. He scraped his palm over his jaw, shaking his head. "I'm sorry, Amy. I didn't mean that. I blame the whiskey."

As he straightened his legs across the floor in front of him, apparently too weak to stand, Amy explained just how damning his words had sounded. "Derek. When you're drunk, or overly emotional, it's not a stretch to see how lashing out with words can become lashing out with a fist or whatever object is close at hand." She inhaled a steadying breath to calm her own emotions and remind herself that she was the sober one here. "I have to tell the police what you said to me. You need to call them tomorrow when you're clearheaded and tell them exactly what you told me."

"I didn't kill her."

"That's not for me to determine. But you may have been the last person to see her before her killer did. You had her laptop and everything she was working on. If you don't call KCPD tomorrow, I will send the detectives to your apartment."

"I swear, leaving my bed that morning was the last time I saw Joss before she was gone." Derek raked his fingers through his hair. Every strand fell right back into place, reminding her of the temptation of Mark Taylor's wayward hair and where she'd rather be.

Since Derek's legs were apparently jelly right now, and she was out of arm's reach, Amy felt it was safe to venture to the top of the stairs again. "I'll call a car to pick you up in twenty minutes. Meet it out front. I'll leave your keys with the security guard, so you don't try to drive yourself and do damage to anyone else."

"Damage? Amy, I didn't mean to hurt you—"

"Good night."

Amy explained the situation to the security guard at the front desk, tucked the laptop under her arm and headed outside. She'd call Detective Beck and drop it off at North Precinct headquarters in the morning, if the woman wasn't on duty tonight. She hurried across campus to the alumni center parking lot where she'd left her truck. Armed with pepper spray and a pair of heels she wasn't afraid to use as a weapon, she was hyperaware of someone watching her, following closely enough to keep her in sight without being seen. Just like the night of Jocelyn's death, when goose bumps had prickled up her spine, Amy sensed that she'd become the focus of someone's curiosity. Or obsession. Or rage.

She stopped once, turned, wondering if Derek had gotten past the security guard and was trying to see if she would call 9-1-1 and report him for being in possession of key evidence. But she saw no one suspicious, nothing unusual. There was a group of older teens, probably freshmen here for some kind of orientation or camp, moving in a loud, laughing pack from the fine arts building over to one of the fast-food places in the student union. But no Derek. No other adults on the sidewalks. No slow-moving car tracking her across campus.

Although the group of young students had come from the music wing of the fine arts building, she lifted her gaze to the windows of the art department where she'd once had a tiny office. Where she'd taken numerous classes and posed in Preston Worth's studio. Preston no longer worked at the university, but there was a light on in the window that used to be his office. A shadow moved behind the blinds and disappeared. Amy gasped for a breath. It was probably just the cleaning crew at this time of night. Some other professor worked in that office now. Preston had served his time and moved to a remote town in Montana where he taught at a community college and probably had some other impressionable young student he was preying upon. The attorney who'd handled Amy's case kept tabs on him. She would let Amy know if he was anywhere back in Kansas City. Plus, he was persona non grata at Williams University. If he stepped foot on campus, he could be arrested.

So, not Derek. Not Preston. Not anyone she could see.

Still, she had a hard time hearing anything beyond the drumbeat of her pulse pounding in her ears.

Amy swallowed her fears and turned away from the window. She was just projecting her imagination after the vile things Derek had said tonight and done to Jocelyn. "I'm fine," she whispered out loud, hurrying her pace. "Just get to the truck and you'll be fine."

Once she reached her truck without anyone showing his face or accosting her, Amy didn't waste any time climbing inside and locking the doors. She tossed the laptop and her purse on the seat beside her and started the engine, racing out of the parking lot in an effort to put Derek and her cruel imagination behind her as quickly as possible.

At the first stoplight, she exhaled a breath she'd been holding for far too long and pulled out her phone to text Mark. Was he busy at work? Had she pushed him away so many times that he didn't believe she wanted to see him?

She typed quickly before she lost her nerve and denied herself what she wanted, what she was afraid she needed. I'm sorry I gave you any reason to doubt my interest. I DO want to see you. I could use some friendly Captain Good Guy vibes right about now. Wish you'd answer. I'm stopping by tonight if that's ok.

Amy sent the message and had just typed in a search for the street address for Fire Station 13 when her phone rang. A moment's excitement, expecting to see Mark's name and hear his voice, evaporated in an instant when she saw her grandmother's name instead. What was Comfort Hall still doing up at this hour?

Amy instantly answered. "Gran? I know I'm running later than I said, but—"

"Amy. Sweetheart. You need to come home. Right now."

"What's wrong?" The light changed, and the car behind her honked. Amy steered her truck toward the high-way and home, instead of turning toward Firehouse 13. "Are you all right? Is it your blood pressure? Did you take your pills today?"

"Of course I did. I'm fine. It's not me."

Then what warranted this hushed urgency? "What's going on?"

"I've already called the authorities."

Not reassuring. She pressed harder on the accelerator. Something was seriously wrong. "Authorities? Gran?"

"You know the rental house those two road workers shared?"

"Yes?"

"It's on fire."

Chapter Eight

Fortunately, the highway patrol wasn't out in force to clock Amy flying down the interstate toward home.

Despite the urge to call her grandmother again, she resolutely kept both hands on the wheel, slowing down only when she reached the turnoff to Copper Lake. She sped past the older suburban neighborhood, gas stations and convenience stores near the highway exit, then wound through the hills and trees beyond.

"Oh, no." Once she left the lights of civilization behind her, Amy spotted the smoke, a darker shade of black roiling up above the horizon into the night sky and blotting out the familiar stars. She tried to confirm the location of the fire, logically knowing it was too far down in the next valley to be her grandmother's house. But it was still too close. And there'd been too many fires. Amy didn't breathe any deeper or ease her concern over her lone surviving family member until the hills opened onto Copper Lake itself and she saw the spotlights and swirling warning lights of several fire engines silhouetting the rental house on the north side of the lake.

She drove through the Copper Lake subdivision and was sickened to see Dale O'Brien's white truck parked in front of his office trailer. Why was he always around whenever trouble screwed with her life these days? Every light in the trailer was on, as though he was working through all the commotion without a care that his neighbors' property and lives were in danger. Several of his workers stood around their vehicles, watching the excitement and using their phones to record the devastation across the lake. With no sidewalks yet, the men were standing in the middle of the road, forcing Amy to slow her truck to a crawl to move safely past them.

"Miss Amy!" someone shouted. Amy glanced out the passenger window to see Richie Sterling's sunburned cheeks puffed up like apples as he beamed a smile and waved. "Glad to see you're okay."

"Thanks." Automatically, Amy raised her hand in a wave. Judging by their state of dress and the tool belts a few still wore, the construction workers had been here since the end of their workday. She stepped on the brake, rolled down the passenger-side window and waved Richie over. She hated to think these men were hanging around because they saw the destruction of her property and the threat to her tiny family as some kind of morbid entertainment, like drivers who stopped to study the aftermath of a car wreck. "What are you all still doing here? I didn't see any roads blocked off. Is the fire department keeping you here for a reason?"

Brad Frick appeared in the window next to his friend, sticking his beak-like nose into their conversation before Richie could answer. "It's Friday. We're all waitin' for our paycheck." He curled his work-gloved fingers over the bottom of the window, and Amy idly noticed the scrapes and bruises on Richie's hands gripping the door frame beside him. True workman's hands.

What was her fascination with men's hands lately? Brad's were hidden. Richie's damaged. Derek's hand had been crushing and Mark Taylor's strong, yes, but infinitely gentle.

Mark. Amy glanced across the lake to the firefighters battling the flames. She needed to get home. She needed to see Gran. She wanted desperately to talk to Mark.

Wait. These men were waiting for a paycheck late on a Friday night? "Don't any of you have direct deposit?"

Brad muttered something under his breath. "O'Brien says there's something wrong with the computer payroll system. He can't make it work. So, he's writin' out paper checks. Of course, Richie and me are at the bottom of his list."

Richie nodded. "Yep. No matter what job we do, we're the last to get paid."

"Shut up." Brad elbowed him out of the way. "You got any work for us, Miss Amy? We'd be happy to come out this weekend, or come in early Monday, or stay late, whatever you need."

Wanting this conversation to end and to be on her way right now more than she wanted the two men hanging out at her place with everything else that was going on, Amy halfway agreed. "Once the fire is out, there will probably be some debris that'll need to be hauled away. Of course, KCFD and the investigators will have to clear the scene. Probably not this weekend, but I'll call you as soon as I know anything."

"Appreciate it."

"Here you go, boys." Brad turned away from her truck as Dale O'Brien came out of his trailer, waving a stack of envelopes in his hand. He started calling out names and handing out the paychecks. Once the men grabbed their envelopes, they headed for their trucks and cars, thankfully turning their attention to something besides her family's misfortune across the lake. Before he was done with the checks, O'Brien handed them off to one of the men to finish distributing them and filled up Amy's window before the road ahead cleared and she could drive away. "How's your grandmother?" he asked, as if they'd shared friendly chats like this a hundred times. She couldn't help but notice the pristine manicure on the fingers he drummed against the door. "I hope this latest fire hasn't frightened her."

"Now that your men have cleared the road for me, I intend to find out. But I'm sure she's fine."

And here came the relentless sales pitch. "You know, with that old house gone, that's just one less place for me to clear when I start building over there."

"It's not your land to build on," Amy reminded him.

His belly jiggled as he chuckled. "I'd still give you a fair price, despite the loss of that house devaluing the property."

"Sounds like a great scam. Setting fires to devalue our property so you could scare us away and buy it cheap."

He straightened from the door. "Are you accusing me of something, Crazy Amy?"

Amy's knuckles were white with tension as she shifted the truck into Drive and pulled away. "Good night, Mr. O'Brien."

Amy drove on as quickly as she dared, circling around the lake, feeling soiled somehow, as she did after almost every encounter with the greedy contractor.

She skirted the spinning lights and red-and-gold engines blocking the asphalt road and cut into the ditch, driving straight across the dead grass until she reached her driveway. Once she parked and climbed out, she did an immediate assessment of her surroundings. She spotted her grandmother standing on the front porch in her robe and pajamas. Their neighbor, Gerald Sanders, stood beside her, his arm draped around her shoulders. Her grandmother clasped her hands together like a prayer and blew a kiss to Amy when she stepped out. Amy answered back by blowing a kiss before turning to the fire itself.

Although there was little breeze and the smoke seemed to billow up straight into the night, her eyes stung with the scents of sulfur and ash floating in the air. She clung to the side of her truck as a beam or wall crashed to the floor inside and she heard a noise like the snap of a dozen matchsticks before flames shot up through the roof. There was a thunderous rush of water from the main hose attached to the hydrant, and another, smaller hose, pumping water from one of the engines itself. The man in a white helmet shouted orders, just as Mark's mother had, and others responded.

Her stomach clenched when she saw the *Lucky 13* logo on the sides of every fire engine and knew Mark and the men and women he served with were here. She tried to find him on one of the hoses or stamping out burning embers with dirt and shovels between the burning structure and Gerald Sanders's home. Amy spared a quick glance of panic at Gerald's house. It appeared to be a far enough distance away to be safe unless the firefighters missed one of the embers and it floated onto his roof.

Where was Mark in all this well-orchestrated chaos? Was he safe? Was this another arson fire set by her number one suspect, Dale O'Brien, or some other lunatic with a grudge against her, putting these brave men and women in harm's way? Did that fire monger realize how much she cared about Mark?

Amy waited a few moments longer, hoping to see him and assure herself he was okay. With the dancing shadows, bright lights of the fire and engine lights on their faces or the distortion of their masks the firefighters closest to the blaze wore, it was nearly impossible for her to identify anyone.

The one exception was Mark's brother. Simply put, Matt Taylor was the biggest guy out there. He hauled an ax over his shoulder and reported something to the captain in the white helmet.

The captain shouted his response over the noise. "Tap into the hydrant across the lake if we need it. We'll pump out of the lake itself if we have to. Keep this line going until our men are out."

"Yes, sir." Matt, clearly a second-in-command, whatever that title might be, pointed to two other firefighters and relayed an order that sent them running to move one of the trucks. Then he turned to Amy, startling her. She flattened her back against the side of the truck. She thought she was staying out of the way. How had he even noticed she was here? But a few long strides brought him to her. Up close, she could see the perspiration and grime marking his face beneath his helmet. His expression was as grim as Mark's was friendly. "We've got it under control. Go up to the house."

He was imposing, yes, but he was a Taylor and Mark had joked about him, so she wasn't afraid. "Where's Mark?" she asked.

Stern stoicism aside, Matt at least had the grace to give her a straight answer. "He and Jackson are doing a room-to-room search to make sure whoever set this didn't get trapped inside."

That aching knot in her stomach intensified as she glanced beyond him to the fire. "He's inside that?"

Since he must have considered that a rhetorical question, he didn't answer. "Your house is a safe distance from the job." The job? He called this life-threatening destruction of a nearly hundred-year-old home that could potentially kill his brother a job? She supposed she had a lot to learn about firefighters. Matt pointed his gloved hand up to the porch where her grandmother and Gerald were watching. "Beyond those front steps is not. Stay with them. Keep them out of harm's way."

His deep-pitched command was not open for discussion. She wondered if he was simply giving her something to do in an attempt to alleviate the worry that must be etched all over her face, or if he thought she'd be a distraction to Mark. Whatever the reason, Amy nodded. "Thank you for talking to me. Thank you for being here."

Behind Matt, there was a loud crash as the front bay window shattered. Another firefighter cleared the glass and broken frame pieces, and Mark climbed out behind him, carrying a limp body wrapped in a shiny silver blanket in his arms. When they were several yards away from the structure, the two men laid the body on the ground. Mark tugged the mask off his face and shouted, "Medic!"

Although soot and sweat camouflaged his exact expression, there was no mistaking the direction of his gaze, seeking out Matt beside her truck, then darting briefly to her. He nodded an acknowledgment of her presence and she hugged her arms around her waist. The tension in her stomach unknotted a fraction and she knew the silliest urge to either smile or start crying.

Matt's heavy hand dropped to her shoulder, turning her toward the house. "Go."

His touch wasn't much in the way of comfort, yet she found Matt's terse order oddly reassuring. While she was relieved to see that Mark was in one piece, it was frightening to realize that someone had been caught in the fire and was seriously, if not fatally, injured. She hadn't fallen apart when she'd been the object of violence herself, and she wouldn't fall apart now when Mark, his brother and the rest of the Station 13 crew, her grandmother, and that poor victim on the blanket needed her to be strong. "Thank you."

While Matt jogged back into the fray, Mark and two paramedics unwrapped the person he'd rescued, put a breathing mask on the victim's face and began their examination. With a team of paramedics swarming around, it was impossible to identify anything more than charred clothes on the blanket. Meanwhile, Amy finally plucked those painful shoes off her feet, curled her toes into the cool grass and hurried up to the house.

Get out of here. Do something useful. Clearly, she wasn't the one who needed to be rescued tonight, nor did she want to be.

"Amy!" Comfort called to her as Amy ran up the porch steps. The two women wrapped each other up in a hug. "I'm so glad you're safe."

Amy tightened her hold as much as she dared when she felt the coolness of her grandmother's cheek pressed against hers. "I'm glad *you're* safe."

"Isn't this terrible?" Comfort finally pulled away to tighten her robe. She crossed her arms in front of her, rubbing her hands up and down her sleeves. "So many fires in such a short time. These can't all be accidents."

Amy was beginning to wonder if any of them besides the one she'd set when she'd burned up the last bits of her life with Preston Worth could be accidents. As she draped her arm around her grandmother's shoulders and let the older woman lean against her, she noticed that Gerald was wearing a pair of slippers and a pajama shirt with the jeans and sweater he must have hastily thrown on. Both of them must have been sound asleep when this tragedy started. "Thank you for being here, Gerald. I came home as soon as I heard. I appreciate you staying with Gran. I might not have worried so much if I'd known you were with her." He curled his gnarled fingers around a bar of scaffolding, moving slightly away, yet making no show of leaving. "You discovered the fire?"

"I smelled the smoke. Came up to the house to make sure Comfort was all right." He glanced down at Comfort, then quickly turned his gaze back to the fire, making Amy wonder, not for the first time, if the reclusive older gentleman had a bit of a crush on her grandmother. "Then we saw the flames and she called 9-1-1."

The three of them stood together a few minutes longer, watching KCFD battle the blaze. Thankfully, they seemed to be winning, although Amy was certain it would be a total loss by the time the fire was out. And that poor victim who'd been trapped inside.

Once the paramedics drove away in the ambulance, Comfort reached up to pat Amy's hand. "What did that firefighter say to you? Was it that nice Mark Taylor you've had your eye on?"

"Gran!" This was hardly the time for matchmaking, even if she *had* been looking for Mark among the crew from Firehouse 13. "I haven't seen Mark since the last time he was out here."

"But I know you've been texting him on the phone. He makes you laugh. That makes me like him."

"I only saw him briefly," Amy confessed. "I talked to Mark's brother Matt. He said we were safe here."

"Did he say anything about that body…?" Comfort moved her hand to her chest, mindlessly rubbing her hand over her heart. Was her heart racing? Her blood pressure spiking? "No one was living there unless we had a squatter. Who is it? How badly are they hurt?"

"They don't know any of that yet, Gran. Matt told me to make sure the three of us were safe."

"We're not hurt."

Danger aside, Amy didn't like the effect this stress was having on her grandmother's health. "Did you take all your pills today?"

"I'm sure I did. Although, I'd have to check my pillbox."

"I'll do that," Amy offered, hating that her grandmother seemed so fragile tonight. Normally, Comfort Hall was a tough old bird, but Jocelyn's murder and these arson fires seemed to be taking a toll on her. Coming just two years after her husband's death and Amy's life blowing up over her breakup with Preston, it was a lot for a woman Comfort's age—of any age—to deal with. "Why don't you go lie down? Do your breathing exercises or read a book and try to relax. I'll get your blood pressure cuff and we can check your BP, just in case."

Comfort adjusted her glasses on her nose and frowned up at Amy. "I'm worrying you, aren't I?"

"If I didn't love you so much, I wouldn't."

"You don't need this stress any more than I do. It's like Preston all over again." She found Amy's hand and squeezed it. "I want only good things for you. A good man. Happiness." She looked down at the burning house and shook her head. "Not this. I don't want this to be the legacy I leave to you."

"None of this is your fault, Gran." She tightened her hug around Comfort's shoulders. "This is your home. You were born and raised here. You raised Dad here, then me. No one has the right to force you to leave your home."

"If I find out Mr. O'Brien set any one of these fires, I'll be first in line to punch him myself." Amy thought she detected a soft chuckle from Gerald.

Amy found she could smile, too. "That's my girl. You and I are going to be okay."

Comfort reached up to cup Amy's cheek and smiled. "I am a little tired, dear. You'll tell me when the fire is out? Or if it comes toward the house?"

"Of course."

Then Comfort turned to Mr. Sanders and squeezed his arm. "Thank you for waking me, Gerald. And for staying with me. It's nice to have a man around the place again. But I'll be all right now that Amy is here."

"I wouldn't want to see you get hurt, Comfort." He covered her hand with his own before she released him and headed into the house. Once the door was closed, he nodded to Amy. "I'd better be going."

"Would you like to stay here tonight?" Amy stepped into his path at the edge of the porch, thumbing over her shoulder to the firefighters behind her. "Looks like they'll be working for a while yet."

His white brows knitted together. "It wouldn't be proper."

Matt Taylor had told Amy to take care of these two. And since he'd helped her grandmother tonight, she owed Gerald. "I'm a grown woman. And so is Gran. It's going to be noisy and smell like smoke at your place for a couple of hours yet, if not the rest of the night. Maybe just a cup of coffee? I promise I won't try to make conversation with you."

He snorted a sound that she thought might just be a laugh. His dark eyes studied her sincerity a moment before he nodded. "Well, I suppose I won't have any water pressure tonight, either." That sounded more like a joke than a complaint. Finally, he nodded again. "I'll take the coffee. Decaf, if you have it."

"It's all Gran drinks anymore." Amy opened the door and let him precede her into the foyer.

Before closing the door, she turned to give the fire

one last look, checking every firefighter until she found Mark again. No wonder he hadn't answered her texts. He was busy saving lives. He didn't have time to rescue her tonight, and she shouldn't have wanted him to. She should be stronger than that, strong enough to handle aging grandmothers and fires and Derek Roland and Dale O'Brien and whatever else the world tossed at her.

But it was hard to always be strong. It was lonely, too.

What if she was only imagining a relationship between her and Mark? They hadn't even had that date he kept pestering her about yet. Still, she felt like she knew him. And she couldn't ignore the attraction they shared.

She was setting herself up for heartache by thinking she could trust any man the way she'd mistakenly trusted Preston. But Captain Good Guy and the whole Taylor family seemed like the embodiment of trust. Mark wasn't even hers to worry about. But she did. She'd never forget seeing him burst out of those flames, knowing he'd risked his life to save a stranger.

How could she deny feeling something for Mark when her stomach was too knotted up with fear for his safety to join Gerald in the kitchen for a cup of coffee?

Chapter Nine

An hour later, Mark took the steps to Amy's front porch
two at a time. It might have been the longest hour of his
life, knowing he couldn't leave his Lucky 13 crew or the
woman he'd found in one of the back rooms of the burning house until the fire was contained and the scene was
secure. Although it had been a relief to see Amy alive and
well, he'd known a stab of jealousy at seeing Matt getting
those few minutes of conversation with her by her truck.

He was the one who cared that she was all right. *He*
was the one who'd had to remind himself more than once
that Amy was tall, leggy and built like a curvy farm girl.
So, even without being able to recognize the woman's
face, he'd known the petite thing he'd carried out the front
window behind Ray Jackson wasn't her. He should have
felt guilty at feeling even one moment of respite that the
badly burned woman the paramedics hadn't been able to
revive wasn't Amy.

A woman was dead.

Another fire had consumed Amy Hall's property.

He'd finally had a chance to read the texts she'd sent
him tonight. She'd been in trouble. Upset about something. She'd needed him.

And he hadn't been there for her. Not for any of it.

Mark draped his turnout coat over the porch railing

and set his helmet on top, scratching his fingers through his hair since heat, sweat and a whole lot of water had plastered it to his head. He knocked on the door before checking the time on his utility watch, hoping it wasn't too late to pay a quick visit. He needed Amy in his arms. He needed to see her face up close and personal to know she was all right. He needed to tell her that he was ready to take whatever this was between them to the next level.

Hell, he was already at that level. He wouldn't be worrying and jealous and anxious to touch her if he wasn't feeling *next level* for her.

He held his breath when he heard the dead bolt disengage, then emptied his lungs on a deep sigh when he saw her.

Amy had changed into jeans and an aqua blue tank top that hugged every womanly curve. He did a quick check from head to toe, finding her face had been washed clean of makeup to reveal a pale canvas dotted with freckles. That silver knot pendant rested between her lush breasts, rising and falling with every breath. And she was barefoot. Her toenails were painted a shade of turquoise darker than her shirt.

And just as he acknowledged the hammer of desire that hit him at the sight of her naked, colorful toes, she grabbed one of his suspender straps and tugged him over the threshold. The foyer was dark. The door closed, and then he stumbled back against it when she pushed at his chest, stretched up on tiptoe and sealed her mouth against his.

The tension in Mark unfurled as Amy moved her soft lips over his. Then a whole different sort of tension grabbed hold. Mark settled one hand at her waist, pulling her hips closer to his. He tunneled his fingers into the thick waves of hair at her nape, cupping the back of her neck and tilting her head back a fraction to pull her full bottom lip between both of his and demand he be an equal partner in this unexpected kiss.

Amy's hands fisted in the front of his shirt, pinching the skin and muscle underneath and sending little electric shocks of heat through his body. She leaned into him and the kiss, and Mark was aware of every soft curve pillowing against his harder frame. He felt the cold metal of her pendant caught between them. He felt the heat of her lips and tongue, testing, tasting, parting, asking and answering every eager foray, every soothing touch, every needy claim of his own mouth on hers.

It might have been seconds, it might have been forever, before he heard the soft mewling sounds in her throat. Whether they were a reluctant protest or an unsatisfied hunger, Mark felt the frustrating flexing and pushing of her hands on his chest and broke off the kiss. Their ragged breaths blended as he rested his forehead against hers. Amy's green-gold eyes opened beneath his, looking up into his gaze with a frown of confusion, a bit of surprise and a dozen questions that probably matched his own gaze.

"Hello to you, too." His voice was a husky rasp from deep in his throat. "I should warn you, my boots are pretty messy—"

Amy silenced his teasing by pressing her finger to his lips. Then she touched the same finger to her own lips in the universal sign for quiet and grasped his hand to pull him into step behind her.

She pointed to the dimly lit living room off the foyer, and he saw her neighbor, the elderly black man—Sanders something—sleeping in the living room recliner. The older man who'd upset her the last time he'd seen her must be a welcome guest now because someone had covered him in a crocheted afghan. Or maybe because of the man's age, she didn't see him as any kind of threat.

Amy pointed out the low clearance of the scaffolding that arched across the foyer, and Mark ducked and willingly followed the pull of her hand to a first-floor bedroom where she peeked in on her sleeping grandmother before closing the door and leading him down the hallway into the kitchen. He squinted against the bright lights shining down from the ceiling, inhaled the sustaining smell of freshly brewed coffee and planted his feet, stopping Amy with a tug against her hand.

When she turned to face him, Mark buried his fingers in the silky thickness of her copper-red hair one more time, angling her mouth to reclaim it with his own. He backed her against the countertop, needing the anchor to brace them both as he drove his tongue inside her mouth to taste the sweet heat of her instant response.

He'd suspected her touch would be incendiary, that his body would react like tinder to a flame. But greeting him with a kiss that hinted at desperation and relief as much as it did bottled-up desire had ignited a different kind of fire in him. Yes, he wanted her. He wanted to pull off that tank top and set her up on this counter and find out exactly where this fiery chemistry would lead them.

But more than that, he wanted to understand if she truly felt the same connections their bodies did. Kissing Amy assuaged a lot of emotions that had been roiling inside him. But it also raised questions he needed answers to. He was falling for her. Falling harder and faster than he had for any other woman. Did that kiss—did this kiss—mean the same thing to her that it did to him? Did she care? Did she want? Did she need him the way he needed her?

This time, Amy pulled away. Her uneven breathing

warmed the skin above his collar as she rested her forehead at the juncture of his neck and shoulder. She wound her arms around his waist and snuggled in, cooling passion to comfort. Mark willingly wrapped his arms around her, breathing in the herbal scent of her hair and the faintest notes of sulfur and ozone that clung to her clothes and hair, no doubt from the welding work she did in her studio. He felt a little raw himself and craved the soothing warmth and softness of her body settling against his.

"Is the fire out?" Her whisper tickled the skin at the base of his throat.

Mark had to think about that for a second. She was talking about the structure at the bottom of the hill, not the sexual chemistry still simmering inside him. Distance. He needed distance and something cold to splash onto his skin to replace the fire she generated by clinging to him if he wanted to think straight. He tilted his face to the paneled ceiling and exhaled a heated breath before pressing a kiss to her temple. "It's contained enough that I could take off for a few minutes. It won't reignite and nothing else should collapse." He shifted his hands to the more neutral position of her shoulders but couldn't help stroking the soft skin of her arms as he pulled back. Her hair hung in loose waves around her face and he brushed a long tendril behind her ear before he resolutely moved away. He folded his arms across his chest, keeping his hands firmly tucked away from the impulse to touch her. "My brother said you wanted to see me."

"I didn't tell him that. I asked about you, but…" She crossed her arms beneath her breasts, matching his deceptively impersonal stance. "Why did you kiss me just now?"

Mark arched a questioning brow. Um, hadn't she started this kissing thing? Had he misread the whole *next level* connection between them tonight? But then he saw the tightness around her slightly swollen lips and read the doubt behind her bold question. For some reason, Amy wasn't used to following her impulses. Those two weeks of texting, sharing so much, yet keeping him at a distance, told Mark a lot about her willingness to trust. But who? Men? Him? Herself? What had happened in her past to make such a wildly creative and headstrong free spirit be so guarded with her personal life?

He suspected complete honesty was the only way to earn this woman's trust. He shrugged, attempting to take the anxious concern he'd felt out of his tone. "You're too pale. I remember how scared you were when we found your friend after that last fire. I know you must have seen me carrying that body out. Figured it would trigger some bad memories. I wanted to feel your energy, know that you're okay." He raked his fingers through his hair, admitting another truth. "I was jealous of my own damn brother because he had the chance to talk to you and I couldn't."

"You were in the middle of risking your life—of saving someone else's life. It was nice of your brother to check on me."

Right. Save a life? Apparently, that was a skill he'd lost somewhere along the way. But she didn't need to know what he'd found in that house. Not yet. So, he went with a joke. "You're talking about my taciturn big brother? You sure have a funny first impression of my family. First you think my dad is sexy, and now you think Matt is nice?"

"I must have been projecting some aura that told him I was worried." She reached up to smooth his hair across his forehead. It was a tender, intimate gesture, putting her fingers into his admittedly damp and messy hair. And yeah, it took a little of the edge off his concern for her. "I was scared when I realized it was you running out of that fire."

"So, you kissed me at the front door because you were scared?"

"I kissed you because…" She pulled her hands together in front of her, as if she needed to control the urge to touch him, as well. "I needed to know that you were okay, too."

When he realized she was shaking, Mark gave up on the idea of keeping his distance and pulled her into his arms. Her hands snaked around his waist to fist in the back of his T-shirt as he palmed her head and nestled her into that sweet spot where she fit so perfectly against his neck and shoulder. "Hey. It's okay. I'm fine. Just doin' my job, Red."

"I know, Fire Man. I know you're well trained, and you have your crew there to back you up. But you shouldn't have to come here, to *my* property, to fight fires that shouldn't be happening. You and your brother and everyone else shouldn't have to risk your life because some jerk is trying to hurt *me*." He could still feel the tremors ebbing from her body, but he got the idea from her words that her fear had transformed into anger, and it was now abating as she reassured herself that he was in one piece. They stood there, holding each other for several moments before Amy rubbed her nose against the column of his throat and breathed in deeply. Her smile felt like a soft kiss against his skin. "You smell like you've been fighting a fire."

"Sorry." Right. Smoke and sweat weren't big turn-ons. Mark started to pull away, but Amy pushed her body into his and held on tighter.

"Don't apologize. I'm just glad you're here. Like you said, you were doing your job. You smell like *you*." She eased her death grip on the back of his shirt and reached up to stroke her fingers along his jaw. "Like hard work and honesty. Strength and doing the right thing."

"Uh, none of those are scents, Red."

"Maybe that's what I feel from you." She pushed away from his chest, but her fingers lingered on his face. "Like art. It's not always an exact representation, but the feeling you get from the piece. I told you that you were a work of art."

Although her purposeful exploration of his features was a surprising turn-on, there was something about her smile that seemed forced. "Is this about more than the fire? You being scared? Did something happen tonight at your fancy party?" Her fingers stilled against his cheek, telling him something had. "I just had a chance to read your last text before running up here. It's a stupid nickname, but why do you need Captain Good Guy vibes? Are you okay?"

Amy pulled away entirely. She pulled out a chair from the table and invited him to sit. "Could I get you some coffee? It's decaf. Cold water? A beer?" Nice deflection of the question, but maybe she needed a few minutes to sort her thoughts and regain control of her emotions, too.

"I'm still on duty. But I'll take the water if it's cold." While Amy opened the fridge and brought a couple of bottles of water to the table, Mark washed up at the farmhouse sink. She was already sitting in a chair around the corner of the table from his when he joined her.

Amy watched him take a couple of long, cooling drinks before she spoke. "Derek Roland, Jocelyn's boyfriend, got drunk at the reception tonight. I tried to help him out. Watched him puke. Called him a car service. Argued at his office about stealing Jocelyn's research. Accused him of hurting her." She rolled her bottle between her hands on top of the table, drawing his attention to the purple marks on her wrist and hand. "This hasn't been a great night."

When Mark saw the fresh marks of brutality on her pale skin, he caught her hand and turned it gently, inspecting the severity of the bruises. There were five of them, almost fitting the span of his own hand. "Did he do this?"

"Like I said, he was drunk." She pulled away, perhaps sensing the anger simmering in him. She crossed her legs in her chair, sitting pretzel-style and self-contained, away from his touch, and reached for the open laptop on the table she must have been perusing before he knocked on her door. "Derek had her laptop all along. The police have been looking for it. I'm supposed to turn it in to Detective Beck in the morning."

Mark rested his elbows on his knees and leaned toward her, glancing from Amy to the icons on the computer screen and back to Amy. "What am I missing here? Beck doesn't suspect you again, does she?"

Amy shook her head. She pulled her hair from behind her back and twisted it into a loose braid over her shoulder. He wondered if sitting still was ever an option for this woman. "I don't think so. But I may be the closest thing she has to a witness. I've done a cursory search through Joss's files, but they're mostly work related to her dissertation. Correspondence with her parents. A couple of applications for teaching positions at Cal Tech and Columbia University."

"She didn't want to stay in Kansas City?"

"She wants—wanted—to go where the interesting jobs are."

Mark pushed up straight again. "Did her boyfriend know she planned to leave?"

She considered that. Maybe Derek had an even stronger motive for killing Jocelyn than getting caught stealing her research. "I'll let Detective Beck know that's a possibility."

The same tension that had gripped him when he first realized Amy's bruises had been put there by a man's hand resurfaced. "Does Derek know you're reporting all this to the police?"

"I told him I was turning over the laptop."

His suspicion about the threat surrounding Amy grew even grimmer. "Did you have to wrestle it away from him?"

"No. I just took it off his desk. The argument happened afterward."

Mark wanted an explanation. There were too many crimes surrounding Amy and her fragile grandmother for him not to know the facts. She might not realize it yet, but it had become his personal mission to protect her from the things he'd seen two weeks ago and again tonight in that fire. "Give me details, Red. Why did Roland manhandle you? Why the hell are you doing KCPD's job?"

"Because I need answers. And I think I can find them faster than they can and make this all go away." Yeah, but at what cost? Putting herself in the literal line of the next fire? "Derek told me he was the last person to see Jocelyn alive. For a while there, I thought he'd done something to her. He was so distraught tonight."

"Could have been an act."

She finally opened her water and took a sip. "He confessed to stealing the laptop. But I don't think he hurt her."

Mark traced his fingers along the marks on her wrist. "He hurt *you*." It wasn't just his training that had him on his feet and opening her freezer. He found a bag of frozen peas in the door and carried them back to the table, where he placed them on her injuries to help the bruising and swelling reduce a little bit. It wasn't much, but it felt right to do something to ease her pain and give her some of the support she needed. He pulled his chair closer to face her straight on before he sat again. "Sounds like a reason for a serious argument. Could he be one of those possessive guys who thinks that if he can't have the woman he desires, then no one can?"

"Their relationship wasn't like that. At least, Joss never indicated there were any physical threats." She paused, and it took everything in him not to pull her into his arms and hold on until all this murder and arson mess had passed. "I should probably tell you…" She looked off into the shadows of the hallway beyond the kitchen. Ah, hell. Something was really wrong. It wasn't like the Amy Hall he knew to hesitate to share her thoughts.

"What?" He rested a hand on her knee, gently demanding her attention. "You can tell me anything, Red."

Her hazel eyes studied every nuance of his expression, determining the sincerity of that statement before she nodded. "I have PTSD. My argument with Derek triggered a bit of a panic attack. My first instinct after getting away was to get a hold of you."

"That's a good instinct to have."

"I don't want you to think I'm crazy or anything—"

"I'm not Dale O'Brien. You feel what you feel. You do what you need to do. That doesn't make you crazy." He squeezed her knee through her jeans. Then, with a legitimate excuse of checking her for other injuries, he tugged on her leg, and then the other, pulling her feet across his lap. He closed one hand around the arch of her foot and ran the other up to her thigh and back to her calf, gently massaging the tension he felt in her, or maybe just creating an outlet for the tension inside him. "Why do you have post-traumatic stress?"

If it had anything to do with this Derek Roland, he was going to punch the guy. But Amy sure as hell didn't need any more violence in her life. So, he forced himself to breathe deeply and kept rubbing her legs and feet as though he was soothing an injured animal.

She wiggled her toes in his grip and gave him a weary smile. "That feels fantastic. Those shoes I was wearing tonight about did me in."

"Red." He urged her to continue.

"Two years ago, my last boyfriend… It was a stupid Svengali thing that I shouldn't have fallen for now that I look back on it—"

"Amy." He needed her to focus, to spit it out before he lost the patience to handle whatever trauma she'd faced. And somehow, he knew she'd faced it on her own. That would never happen again. Not if he became part of her life the way he wanted to.

"When I discovered he was cheating, and I broke it off, he assaulted me." The massage paused for a moment. Mark thought his jaw might crack because he was clenching it so hard at the thought of anyone putting cruel hands on this woman. But the battle to maintain an impassive expression was worth it when she went on. "Beat me up pretty good. Pushed me down a flight of stairs."

Mark swore, unable to remain impassive when he imagined her lush, pale body bruised and broken. "Please tell me you reported him."

He didn't realize his hands had stopped moving until Amy pulled away, hugging her knees to her chest. "He served time. I got him fired from his position at the university art department. He tried to blackmail me into not telling the police or the dean's office by keeping me from finishing my PhD. I filed charges against him from the hospital."

"He was a professor? One of *your* professors? He already had the power of grades and success over you, and then he…?"

"Preston had an artistic temperament."

Unable to go along with her attempt to lighten the conversation, Mark muttered a very choice word about what this Preston asswipe needed to have happen to him.

The tightness left Amy's expression, her eyes widened with surprise and she smiled at his curse. "What? Captain Good Guy knows some bad words, too."

Her smile widened, and some of the tension in him faded away. She dropped her feet to the floor and rested her hands atop the fists that he'd clenched on each knee of his bunker pants. "Preston Worth is old news. You don't need to rescue me from him. He doesn't even live in Missouri anymore. He's in Montana."

"What is your hang-up with rescuing you? I'm not okay with someone hurting you."

"Derek didn't really hurt me tonight." The bruises on her hand and wrist told another story, but he held his tongue. "But his office is at the top of a flight of stairs. Fighting with him reminded me of that last night with Preston." She squeezed her eyes shut and shook her head. "And so many men have hands. I don't like most of them."

"What?"

When she opened her eyes and tapped against his fists, he relaxed his hands and she laced her fingers with his. "I like yours, though."

"You don't always make sense," he confessed. But he liked the feel of her hands tangled with his. "I'm so sorry you had to go through that. No wonder you're gun-shy about getting involved with someone again."

"I'm not afraid of you, Fire Man. I don't think you'd ever hurt me." Her gaze dropped to the clasp of their hands on his knees, and he suspected that she truly believed that. "But what would you get out of getting involved with me?"

He considered that for a moment. Sure, there was the sexual pull he felt toward Amy. And as a Taylor, he'd been raised to serve and protect others long before his firefighter training had fine-tuned that calling. He wasn't naive enough to pretend that some of this need didn't have to do with redemption. He'd failed his grandfather, and he wasn't sure he could survive failing to help anyone else he cared about. That was one reason he'd been avoiding his own grandmother. "A few minutes of peace and quiet."

For his soul. For his conscience. For his future.

Amy's eyes widened. "Talk about not making sense. Peace and quiet? With me?" Without confessing his mistakes, it was easy for her to misinterpret his answer. "I'm not an easy relationship. I have opinions." He arched an eyebrow in a universal *Duh* expression and she grinned. "I have issues. A temper. Sometimes, I freak out. And, apparently, I have an enemy." Her breath puffed out in a sigh. "Or several."

"You think I can't handle all that?"

"You shouldn't have to."

"Isn't that my decision to make?" He reached out to sift the end of her braid through his fingers. "Unless you tell me to go, I'm going to be here for you. You reached out to me for a reason. And I don't think it's because I have an interesting face and likable hands. Whatever that means."

She caught his hand and linked their fingers again. "You also give a hell of a foot massage, and you definitely know how to kiss."

He chuckled at the compliment and felt his cheeks warm. "I hadn't heard that one yet."

"You're adorable when you do that." She brushed her fingers across his heated skin. "In a manly man kind of a way. It humanizes you. Makes me think you need a little bit of protecting, too."

"And yet you still won't go out on a date with me."

She finally pulled away, tucking her legs up against her chest on the chair again, ignoring his joke. "Letting you rescue me makes me feel like a victim. And I don't want to feel that way ever again. Needing help—needing anyone—makes me feel like I'm dropping my guard or giving up. I'm strong because I've had to be. Gran needs me to be strong to take care of her, to take care of this place—to take care of myself so she doesn't worry herself into a heart event or stroke." He'd ask about Comfort Hall's health issues later, but he needed to hear the end of this story before Amy changed the subject to something less personal and painful. "Tonight, on campus, though, I couldn't seem to calm myself by doing any of the mantras or meditations my therapist taught me. I feel better, safer—centered—with you here. But I'm afraid that makes me weak."

"You don't think it takes a strong person to admit that they could use a little help? That's smarts, not weakness."

"What about you, Mark? Do you ever ask for help?" Damn it if she wasn't turning the tables on him. "Like with whatever it is that makes you so sad? I catch glimpses of it. When you're not trying to make me laugh and you're not busy being Captain Good Guy and saving the day. Does your family help you with that? Or are you trying to be all strong on your own, too?"

Mark stood, paced to the kitchen archway and over to the sink, where he finished off the last of his water and searched for the recyclable bin near the back door to drop it inside. Hell. Should he admit he felt more centered being here with her, too? More normal than he'd felt in months? He'd been so worried, but touching her, holding her, talking to her—all seemed to ease that raw, self-doubting place inside him. She'd opened up to him, let him in. He'd dated other women, one for a lot longer than he'd known Amy, and he'd never felt as close to them as he did the copper-haired tomboy sitting across the room from him tonight.

He hadn't felt like he could share the guilt he felt over Grandpa Sid's death before. But Amy was so intuitive, so caring—so strong, despite her fears to the contrary—that he was tempted to be as honest with her as she'd been with him. But he couldn't. He wouldn't dump that on her, too. Although he wasn't quite clear on the distinction between helping her and rescuing her that she took such issue with, he was damn clear on the idea that *he* wasn't the one who needed to be rescued tonight.

"Struck a nerve, huh?" He could hear her getting up behind him, closing the laptop, straightening chairs. "It's not so easy, is it? Baring your soul to someone? Trusting them with your inner truths? Admitting you can't handle everything on your own?" An edge of sarcasm entered her tone. "I still don't see what you'd get out of this relationship if you won't talk to me. Seems pretty one-sided to me."

"One problem at a time. Okay, Red?" He leaned his hips against the sink and faced her, holding on to the edge of the counter on either side of him. She stuffed the peas in the freezer door and closed it, waiting for him to continue. "I'm not ready to talk about it yet," he admitted.

"But you will talk about it with somebody?" she

pushed. "If not me, then a friend or family member? A therapist?"

Mark nodded. "I will. But tonight, we deal with the fire and figuring out who set it."

"And keeping me safe." The sarcasm left her tone and she smiled. "So you can get those few minutes of peace and quiet."

Some of the tension in him eased at her understanding. "Keeping you safe is a given." He pushed away from the counter to capture her injured hand and folded it gently into his own. "My team will be here awhile, checking for hot spots, rolling up hoses and cleaning up the debris."

"Aren't you supposed to help with that, too?"

"They can manage without me for a few minutes longer." Since she seemed to be willing to let him touch her, Mark wasn't inclined to let go. "Will you walk with me?"

They headed through the darkened house and back onto the porch. The lights from the fire trucks pointed toward the charred shell of the smoldering structure, leaving the ground between them and the house in darkness. With the omnipresent construction scaffolding casting more shadows than illumination from the porch light, the late summer night swallowed them up like a blanket.

When Mark paused at the railing to watch his crew checking for any embers that could reignite and structural issues that could collapse on the firefighters or the investigators who would be here soon, Amy leaned against his arm, resting her cheek on his shoulder.

"It's another arson fire, isn't it?" She sounded more resigned than surprised.

Mark nodded. "Looks that way. There were pour marks from an accelerant on the mattress."

"At least O'Brien can't accuse me of setting this one.

I have over a hundred witnesses who saw me on the WU campus tonight."

"He's more of a suspect than you are." He pointed to the housing development across the lake. O'Brien's trailer was still lit up, and the beat-up car of a couple of his workers was still parked beside his white truck. "He and all the men who work for him were here when we arrived. A bunch of lookie-loos. Not one of them drove over here to check on your grandmother."

"Great neighbors, huh? Thank God for Mr. Sanders. He's not the friendliest tenant, but he does seem to care about Gran. He alerted her to the fire."

"Amy…" Mark turned and sat on the railing, pulling her between his legs, to keep her close and their conversation hushed, as though his words might carry to the men across the lake. "I know you saw me carry a body out of the house—"

He thought he detected a shiver. "Can you tell me who it was? Our tenants who lived there moved out almost two months ago. Did we have a squatter? A homeless guy?"

He settled his hands at her waist, offering the support he suspected she'd need. "It was another woman. Her skull was crushed, and she was set on fire."

"Just like Jocelyn." Definitely a shiver. He slipped his fingertips beneath the hem of her tank top and felt the chill on her skin. But her hands were braced against his biceps, keeping him from drawing her closer. "Do you know who she is?"

"We got to the fire sooner this time," he explained. "The body wasn't completely incinerated, but I suspect she was dead from her injuries or smoke inhalation before we ever got to her. There was a purse with her. The plastic in her wallet hadn't melted yet, so there was a name. Autopsy will have to confirm it's her purse, but it looks like Dale O'Brien's assistant."

"Lissette Peterson?"

"You knew her?"

"Not well. We met once when I went in to argue with O'Brien. She was nice. Polite, when she probably didn't have to be."

"The woman had to be a saint to work for him."

Amy nodded, but her gaze moved beyond him to the lake. "The men who work for O'Brien were all there tonight, waiting for paychecks because he didn't know how to do the books and handle payroll. I'm sure Lissette did that for him."

"Sounds like she's been missing for some time if that wasn't taken care of." Mark released her long enough to pull out his phone. "I'll call my brother Pike at KCPD, see if she was reported missing. I'll have him check to see that your old boyfriend— What was his name?"

"Preston Worth."

"I want to make sure he's still in Montana and nowhere near you."

Amy hugged her arms around her waist and listened in while Mark made the call. Pike promised answers by morning, if not sooner. By the time he hung up, Amy was perched on the railing beside him. "I doubt if Derek ever met Lissette. You might convince me he had a motive to kill Jocelyn, but he'd have no reason to go after Lissette."

"Unless tonight was a diversion, meant to cover up his original crime and make KCPD think they have a serial killer on their hands."

"That's an unsettling thought. Poor Lissette." She shrugged. "But Derek was at the same reception I was all evening."

"Did you have eyes on him all night?"

"Well, no. I saw him before the dinner, but I didn't really talk to him until after the speeches. He was outside when I was ready to leave. I stayed longer to try to sober him up."

"How long does it take to get here from Williams U and back? Forty minutes? An hour if there's traffic?" He reached for her hand, lacing their fingers together again. "You need to share that possibility with Detective Beck, too."

"He would have had to have been acting drunk to pull that off." He saw the exact moment in her upturned expression when she realized that Roland could pull off something like that. Uncomfortable with the possibility of a friend's betrayal or his touch, Amy hopped down and started to pace. "His emotions were way over-the-top tonight. I thought it was grief."

"He could have been responsible even if he didn't leave your party." Her face was alternately dappled by bright light and shadows as she moved across the porch, making it difficult to tell if she was angry or afraid. "Fires can be set by a delayed ignition, too. You said he's a science guy, right? Anyone with basic chemistry or electrical experience could rig something like that."

She stopped in front of him with a mix of emotions crossing her face. Mostly anger, he'd say. "Are you trying to reassure me or scare me to death?"

"I'm being real with you. I don't want you to ever think that I'm not telling you the truth."

"I appreciate that." She tapped her fist against his thigh, then drummed it faster and faster until she threw her arms out in a burst of frustration. "Who is setting these fires? Is Derek covering up his crimes? Did Jocelyn and Lissette stumble across someone like O'Brien burning down buildings on our property, and this guy is silencing his witnesses?" Her temper ebbed, and the gruesomeness of what she was thinking seeped into her voice. Her fingers remained on his thigh, squeezing, kneading, clinging to him even if she didn't fully realize it. "Or are *they* the crime, and the fires are the cover-up? Is any woman in this part of the city safe? Are Gran and I safe?"

"Exactly." Mark covered her hand with his to still the pulsing movement and pulled her to him again. "I need to know why someone is trying to burn you out of house and home." He hunched his shoulders slightly, so he could look straight into those beautiful green-gold eyes. "And why I shouldn't be afraid that you're next on this guy's list."

Chapter Ten

Amy pushed her face mask up on top of her welding helmet and stood back to admire her work. Instead of celebrating that she was nearing completion on her latest metals project, she frowned. "Needs more color."

This garden alien was supposed to be a fun piece, a cartoonish figure meant to add height to her client's backyard garden. But instead of building a whimsical sculpture that reflected the young family's playful style, she'd ended up with a stark, metallic *Doctor Who* villain that looked like it had just rolled off an industrialized war machine assembly line.

She shook her head at the copper robot. "That'll scare the kids."

Heck. It scared her. Setting her helmet aside and hanging her welding torch over its hook, she glanced around her studio. For a piece this size, she needed something bigger than the broken bits of glass and rocks on her shelves. The purple crystal geode sitting on her workbench would work for the creature's nose. But she wanted a pair of colored glass bottles to add as drop earrings, or maybe she could find some old fencing to extend as antennae on top of the figure. Some colorful beer and pop bottle caps could be grouped together to make eyes and blushing cheeks.

Now that the creative juices had kicked in, Amy was thinking more positively. She pulled up the sleeve of her blue coveralls past the deep purple bruises that had worried Mark so last night and checked her watch. Sleep had been elusive after Mark and his crew from Firehouse 13 had driven away, taking all their lights and activity and reassuring company with them. After checking in on Gran and Mr. Sanders, Amy had settled in upstairs to wrestle with nightmares about crashing down stairwells and being swallowed up by flames. And then her waking mind had raced with memories and future possibilities, both good and bad, as she sorted out her unexpected feelings for Mark. Once she'd decided how easy and risky it would be to not only depend on him, but to fall in love with him, she'd gotten up early to lose herself in her art studio.

But she lacked the materials her imagination wanted her to use, and with her 9:00 a.m. appointment with Detectives Beck and Carson at Fourth Precinct headquarters, the clock was ticking. She should set the sculpture aside, put away her gear and take a quick walk to clear her head before Mark came by the house to pick her up.

Between pulling Mark into the house to kiss the stuffing out of him and sitting out on the porch and kissing him good-night, something had changed in Amy. Her resolve had shifted. She'd admitted her fears and shortcomings. She'd surrendered some of her independence and strength by needing Mark so desperately last night. She'd made herself vulnerable by sharing her past mistakes. But maybe she'd gained something, as well. She was strong enough to admit that she was out of her league with murderers and arsonists, that she stood a better chance of finding justice for Jocelyn and possibly saving other lives if she accepted Mark's help.

And, perhaps more important, she'd discovered that her heart had healed enough to let someone new into her life.

She was strong enough to risk falling in love again.

As Amy slipped off her coveralls and buttoned a cotton blouse over her tank top and jeans, she replayed how last night had ended.

"I'LL GO WITH you to see Detective Beck in the morning," Mark offered. His tone was casual, like he was making plans to meet a friend for coffee. But his calloused fingertips, tickling the skin at her waist and back beneath the hem of her top, told a different story. They clenched and released, as though reluctant to let her go. As though Mark didn't want to let her out of his sight, not even for a moment.

"That isn't necessary," she assured him. She knew the way to the precinct. She'd call a friend to come stay with Gran, or maybe see if Gerald had plans for the day. If their neighbor was good to her grandmother, then Amy could put up with his grumpy personality.

"Not negotiable, Red. Unless I'm out on a call, I'll be here to pick you up. And if I'm still out with my crew, I'll send one of my brothers. You're not doing any more of this on your own."

"Do you know how much I'm bristling at you giving me orders like that?"

His hands tightened on her hips, pulled her closer. "Do you know how much I need you to be safe? How much it kills me to know that you don't feel safe in your own home? On your own land?"

Amy reached up to stroke her fingertips across the taut angles of his cheek and jaw. She brushed her fin-

gers across his stubbled skin, once, twice, again, until she felt the tension in his expression ease.

And then he palmed the back of her head and covered her mouth with his. Her lips parted on a soft gasp of plea-sure and he thrust his tongue inside, staking a claim she willingly surrendered. Amy circled her arms around his neck and pulled her body flush against his hardness and heat. A fire ignited inside her, heavy and molten, shoot-ing sparks to the tips of her breasts where they rubbed against his chest and pooling between her thighs as she felt his response swelling against her belly.

Whistles and catcalls from the bottom of the hill, and the blast of one loud engine horn startled Amy from the madness that had consumed her.

"Mark." She flattened her hands on his broad shoul-ders and pushed some space between them. "We have an audience."

Even through the murky light seeping through the porch scaffolding, she could see the blush on his cheek-bones. Amy had no doubt her face was just as red. In-stead of moving apart, he turned his hands to squeeze her bottom and pulled her in to reclaim her lips. "They're jealous."

But despite the wanton urge to crawl right onto his lap, Amy pushed back, not wanting to give his coworkers any reason to make more noise that might wake her grand-mother or Mr. Sanders. "Won't they give you grief for this public display of affection? Especially when you're supposed to be working right now?"

"Kiss me like that again and I won't care how much they tease me."

She laughed and slipped her fingers between their mouths when he tried to kiss her again. "I'm just look-

ing out for your best interests, Fire Man. You'd better get back to work."

He pressed a ticklish kiss to her palm and eased his grip on her backside. *"I'd better."*

Amy moved away, surprised at how cool the air felt on her skin after being pressed so close to him. She handed him his coat and helmet. *"Be safe. I'll see you in the morning."*

Mark stood and set his helmet on top of his beautiful, mussed hair. *"It's a date."*

Amy followed him to the edge of the porch, hugging one of the posts as he jogged down the steps. *"Driving me to the police station is not a date."*

He faced her but continued backing his way down the hill to rejoin his crew. *"If I bring you coffee or buy you lunch, it will be."*

"Taylor!" the fire captain in the white helmet yelled. *"Get your butt down here. I need a report."*

"On my way, Cap!" he shouted over his shoulder. But he pointed to her. *"You're going to go out with me yet."*

"Taylor!"

"You'd better go."

"You're not alone, Red. Remember that." With that promise, Mark turned and jogged down the hill to speak to his captain. His brother Matt joined them. A minute later, their father, Gideon Taylor, climbed out of his KCFD SUV and strode over to the group.

No. WITH A family like that, Mark probably had no real idea of what it meant to be truly alone.

Alone was when the man you loved made no apologies for sleeping with other women, telling her she wasn't enough to make him happy.

Alone was when standing up for yourself was rewarded with a punch in the face and a shove down the stairs.

Alone was testifying against the bastard who'd beaten you and then tried to cover up his crime with blackmail that had silenced other victims.

Alone was knowing your best friend was missing and if you gave up the search, no one would find her.

Alone was protecting the woman who'd raised her from greedy contractors and dangerous fires and a sick threat that seemed to be closing in around her beloved home because there was no one else to do it.

How could she make Mark Taylor understand that she'd forgotten how to be part of a couple? How to trust implicitly that backup would be there when she needed it? How patient could he be with her while she relearned how to love? How much trouble was he willing to endure being involved with her?

How much was this going to hurt if she listened to her heart and Mark wound up getting injured because of her? How much was this going to hurt if he wised up and decided that a relationship with Crazy Amy Hall wasn't worth the risk?

Because she was tired of feeling alone. Of fighting alone.

She was ready to risk her heart on Mark Taylor. But was he ready to risk his heart on her?

With that philosophical debate weighing heavily on her heart and mind, Amy grabbed her backpack, where she carried Jocelyn's laptop, and fastened the padlock on the art studio door behind her.

Since she had time, she detoured through the surviving part of the old stables, finding a wooden tray of old skeleton keys and lock plates in the tack room that might work for her sculpture's earrings. There was no electricity in the damaged building, but with the morning sun shining through the collapsed roof and broken windows, she didn't need man-made light. Her exploration uncovered a rusted metal trowel that could be polished up and used as the creature's antenna if she could find another similar old tool somewhere on the property. Perhaps she could remove the peeling paint from the handle and repaint it a bright, vibrant color. She dusted off the items as best she could, then unzipped the front compartment on her backpack and tucked them inside. Joy bubbled up at her discovered treasures, and the idea for a humorous, more child-friendly garden alien became a finished piece in her mind.

But the image died, and the joy quickly dissipated as she turned and faced the back end of the stables. Still marked off by crisscrossing yellow tape, the charred timbers and chunks of roof piled inside and atop the old horse stalls were a stark reminder of the downward spiral her life had taken after Preston. Curious to know if she could truly put her past behind her, she walked closer, reaching over the restrictive tape to shove aside a broken door and pick up the burned frame of one of her canvases. The ruined pinewood crumbled into dust the moment she lifted it off the ground. She'd set all of her paintings she'd done under Preston's tutelage aflame that cathartic night when the first fire had gotten out of hand and she'd been forced to call 9-1-1. She'd burned the portrait Preston had painted of her. Even though the image had once made her feel beautiful, the way he'd treated her had not.

Amy shoved the old door back into the debris and brushed off her hands. Nope. Not even one flicker of regret or sorrow for the destroyed life she'd left behind. She'd proved herself stronger than her past. Tipping her chin up, she marched out of the stable, pausing at the spigot on the back of the house to wash her hands.

She was ready for her future. Ready to solve a murder. Ready to love again. She wound her fist around the knotted heart pendant hanging from her neck and smiled. She only hoped Mark Taylor was ready for her.

Amy had every intention of going back inside to wait for Mark, but when she rounded the house and saw the blackened walls and broken windows of the rental property that had burned last night, a glimmer of movement caught her eye. She paused at the railing leading up the steps and waited to see if what she'd seen had simply been a trick of the morning sunlight and her own movement.

There. Amy's grip tightened around the straps of her backpack. There was a light on inside the abandoned house. A house that had no electricity. Not since KCFD had shut off both the electrical and propane feeds last night.

Since there was no vehicle parked on the concrete pad in front of the house, Amy scanned both sides of the lake, looking for some clue as to what was going on. A looter? Curiosity-seeker? A light blazed through the windows of Gerald Sanders's living room, indicating he'd returned home and was reading his newspaper over coffee and breakfast. On the far side of the lake, she spotted Dale O'Brien's work truck in front of his office trailer. But there were no other vehicles there. No men reporting for work yet. Had O'Brien come in early? Or stayed the night? And why? Straightening up the mess of paperwork created by Lissette's absence? Or something more sinister? The man always seemed to show up when she least wanted to see him.

The light in the burned house flickered, drawing Amy's attention again. But it disappeared almost as quickly as she'd seen it. When it reappeared a few seconds later, passing by the shattered front window, curiosity and a familiar sense of anger and violation moved Amy's feet. Why the hell was the Hall farm such a target for criminals?

Someone was in that house, moving through it with a flashlight. She headed straight down the hill and crossed the asphalt. Her heart beat faster as she realized whoever was in there was looking for something. An intruder searching for treasures like she'd just found in the wreckage of the stables? An arsonist revisiting the scene of his crime, either reliving the adrenaline rush of his handiwork or retrieving something he'd inadvertently left behind?

The yellow warning tape crossing the front door and broken window hadn't stopped the trespasser from entering.

It wouldn't stop her, either. Amy pulled her cell phone from the side pocket of her backpack and pressed 9-1-1, holding her thumb above the Send key as she pushed open the front door. She couldn't go far before a collapsed wall and the skeletons of charred furniture forced her to step into what used to be the living room. "Hello?" she called out to the intruder. "You shouldn't be here. Both for legal reasons and your own safety." She heard the screech of something heavy moving across the floor from the back of the house, followed by the scuffling of footsteps. "I have the police on speed dial. I'm calling them right now if you don't leave."

"Don't do that. Please." The next thing she knew, a bright light was shining in her face, blinding her. "You shouldn't be here, Miss Amy."

She exhaled the breath she'd been holding when she recognized Richie Sterling's voice. "Richie?"

When he saw her holding her hand in front of her face, he lowered the beam of his flashlight. "Sorry about that."

"You shouldn't be here, either." She showed him that she was clearing the number off her phone and tucked her cell into the pocket of her jeans. "My family's name is on the deed to this place."

"Huh?"

"I have the right to be here. You don't." Blackened carpet, still soaked from last night's fire hoses, stretched between them. This had once been the furnished living room, and though most of the furniture here was still in one piece, it had been ruined by smoke and water. Her steps squished as she crossed the room, heading toward the back of the house, where the hottest point of the fire had peeled wallpaper, warped floorboards and linoleum, and taken down interior walls and roof braces. She stopped in front of Richie, nodding toward the kitchen and bedroom at the back of the house. "What are you looking for?"

He shrugged. "I'm not looking for anything."

"Then why are you here?" She moved around him into what used to be the kitchen. The appliances were black with soot, and the countertops had melted, but the surviving cabinets had been opened. She didn't know enough about fighting fires to tell if that had happened during the fire or after. The air here was stale with the scents of sulfur and dampness, leftovers from the blaze and its aftermath. "Are you looking for copper piping?"

"Like you use to make your funny creatures."

Amy nodded. She doubted she had a competing artist here. It wouldn't be the first time someone had broken into one of the empty buildings over the years to steal metals that could be sold on the illegal market. "I know the copper is worth some money, but you can't take anything from here, Richie. The police and fire department are conducting an investigation. You might be disturbing evidence."

She startled at the touch of Richie's hand closing around her upper arm. "You shouldn't be here, Miss Amy." He parroted his greeting from earlier. His cheeks were redder than usual as he slid his hand down to hers and tugged. "I'll walk you out."

While his tone wasn't threatening and his grip wasn't painful, Amy had suffered too many recent encounters to be comfortable with him touching her. She pulled her hand away and smiled. "That's okay, Richie. I'd better check to make sure everything's secure before I leave."

"You have to go." He reached for her again, and Amy retreated a step. He ducked his head, his gaze darting back and forth across the floor. His voice came out on a whispered croak. "It's not safe."

It certainly didn't feel safe with a warning like that. "Richie, do you know something about what happened to Ms. Peterson? Or who's setting these fires?"

"There you are." Brad Frick's surly interruption sent Richie skittering several feet away from Amy. He strode from the front door to the kitchen, not caring what mess his work boots stepped in or tracked onto the ruined linoleum. Like a parent speaking to a naughty toddler, Brad snapped his fingers and pointed at Richie. "I told you to stay out of this place." He pulled off his paint-stained ball cap and nodded to Amy. "Sorry, Miss Amy. Richie's just curious about what burned-up places look like. He likes watching fires. Thinks they're cool."

Richie's downturned face finally lifted, and he laughed. "Fires are cool. That doesn't make sense. Fires are hot."

"Get on out of there." Brad jerked his head toward the front door, ordering Richie to leave. As his lighter-haired partner shuffled past him, Brad's gaze darted toward the framed remains of the hallway and bedrooms beyond. Was he taking in the blackened scorch marks on the floor and standing timbers? Did he think watching something burn was cool, too? Had one of them set this fire? Set all the others?

Amy couldn't help but retreat another step as suspicion hammered through her pulse.

"You didn't take anything, did you, Richie?" Brad asked, his gaze coming back to Amy after he looked over his shoulder to his friend.

Richie frowned. "I didn't take anything. I didn't find it."

Find *it*? Find what? Had Richie been in here looking for something specific? Did Brad know what *it* was?

Before she could ask a question, Brad covered his receding hairline with his cap again and shooed Richie on out the door. "Come on. We'd better get over to O'Brien's and get to work." Once Richie was outside, he stopped at the door and glanced back at her. "Don't pay him no mind, Miss Amy. He's like a kid in the head. He don't mean nothing by what he says. You'd better leave, too. You wouldn't want to get in trouble with the police."

With that dubious warning, he left. A few seconds later, she heard the slam of two car doors at the back of the house and an engine turning over. With parts of the house damaged and missing, it was easy to see Brad's old blue car bouncing up onto the asphalt road and driving away.

Why had they parked behind the house in the dead grass? So they couldn't be spotted from the house? There didn't seem to be any good reason for hiding. Had Richie's slip of the tongue been something important? Had he broken in to look for something specific? Brad had known he was here. Had he sent Richie in to find something for him? Or had he been indulging his friend's dangerous fascination with fire?

There were so many things wrong with this encounter that Amy wanted answers before she went to talk to Detectives Beck and Carson. At the worst, Richie or Brad was hiding something. At the very least, they'd sneaked into a crime scene and had possibly disturbed evidence the detectives or Mark's dad would want to know about.

And since Brad's attention had been focused on the back bedrooms, and that was where Richie had come from, Amy crossed through the kitchen and walked into first one bedroom and then the next. The first had been burned from floor to ceiling, and there was a hole in the roof above her. But the second bedroom, the one where Lissette had been found, was in a whole other state of destruction.

Piles of ash littered the floor where wood furniture had stood. And the double mattress, cordoned off by more yellow tape, rested at a wonky angle beneath the missing back window. Had KCFD broken that window? Had the fire blasted it out of its frame? Or had the arsonist—and Lissette's killer—broken in that way? The wood slats beneath the mattress and box springs and plastic wheels on each leg of the bed were gone, leaving the metal frame supporting the hollowed-out mattress where Lissette must have spent her last moments.

Amy's coffee and breakfast bar curdled in her stomach. She didn't have to be an arson investigator to recognize the dark black pattern zigzagging across the mattress and pooling at the center where accelerant had been poured to hide the body. Although every surface in this room was stained by smoke and soot, more pour patterns circled the floor around the bed.

Moving closer, Amy remembered the absolute destruction of Jocelyn's remains, and her hand automatically went to the pendant on her chest, feeling the bond that had once linked them. Would she find anything similar here where Lissette had died? A piece of heirloom jewelry? The purse that Mark said had survived the conflagration? Had Lissette Peterson been burned out of existence without any symbol of a good friend or loved one to cling to?

If there was anything here for Richie or Brad or anyone else to find, she didn't see it. No matches. No melted gasoline can. No lighter like the one she used to ignite her welding torch.

Creepy though he might be, Brad was right about one thing. She didn't need to be here, either.

Amy turned to step away, to respect the dead and the crime scene, when her foot crashed through one of the charred, warped floorboards. "Ow!" She tweaked her ankle as her work boot glanced off something metallic and wedged her leg in up to her knee. "What the hell?"

A couple of tugs only scraped her skin inside her jeans. The twinge in her ankle receded as her curiosity kicked in. Giving up on keeping her clothes clean, she sat down on the floor and turned on the flashlight of her cell phone. She shrugged off her backpack and shone her light down into the gap between the floor joists. The metal wasn't part of the house's construction. It was a box—a square metal strongbox that had been hidden beneath the floor. Had that been put there by an earlier resident? Amy glanced up at the door frame. Was this what Richie had been looking for?

Would he and Brad come back for it the moment she left? Provided she could get herself out of here.

Amy pulled her phone back to call the police, but she'd be going to the police station in a little while anyway, so she could mention it then. Dale O'Brien certainly hadn't helped her reputation with the authorities any by pointing out that she, too, had set a fire. What if this box had nothing to do with Lissette's death and the fires? Maybe she'd uncovered one of the former tenants' stash of porn or pot. No, she'd make sure she had something significant here first, before she gave Detectives Beck and Carson any more reason to question her reliability as a witness or even a suspect in their investigation.

Instead of calling the police, she texted Mark.

Running a little late. I got caught at the rental house where the fire was last night. "Caught." She shook her head, grinning wryly at the literalness of her choice of words, before finishing and sending the text. My two handymen were checking the place out. I had to shoo them away.

Then she snapped a picture of the hole in the floor, the box and her boot. It didn't take her creative mind long to figure out a plan of escape. She dug the old trowel out of her backpack and wedged it between the floorboards, prying one loose on either side of her leg. They came up more easily than she'd expected because this section of flooring wasn't nailed down. Nails didn't burn. So, these boards had been loose before the fire. Before Lissette's murder. Someone had made themselves a secure hiding place for whatever treasures were inside that box.

With more wiggle room now to move, Amy reached into the hidey-hole and untied her boot. Pulling her foot out released the tension that had trapped her and allowed her to twist her boot onto its side and pull it and the strongbox up. She scooted away to a sturdier stretch of charcoal floor to examine the metal box. It, too, had been blackened by the fire, but not destroyed. Scrubbing away the soot with the butt of her palm, she uncovered the familiar O'Brien Construction logo.

"What have you done now, Dale?" she murmured. Maybe he'd paid Brad and Richie to come here to find his stash of buried treasure. She took another picture before sinking back onto her heels and pulling the box onto her lap. The simple lock was no match for the trowel blade and she quickly pried it open. "What the...?"

Inside the box was a cigarette lighter. She also found a half-empty jar of petroleum jelly that had cotton balls stuffed inside. Her grandfather had once taught her that trick on a camping trip—petroleum jelly burned, even in rainy weather, providing enough tinder with the cotton to ignite a fire for thirty seconds or so. Enough to burn until kindling could be added to build the blaze. Were they enough to set an entire building on fire? Maybe if another accelerant was added to the mix.

But even those simple tools for starting a fire weren't what made the bile rise in her throat.

There were other items inside, yellowed with smoke damage and frayed at the corners, but she had no trouble identifying a stack of photographs printed out on cheap card stock. She took one more picture before tucking her phone into her jeans and lifting the pictures from the box. "Oh, my God. Oh. Oh." She felt like she might truly be sick as she sorted through the tainted photos. If these were Dale O'Brien's, the man had some serious issues. They weren't images of architectural works the contractor had built. They weren't pictures of fun-loving get-togethers or even scenery from a family vacation.

They were pictures of women.

A lot of women. All taken from a distance. All snapped without any of the women knowing.

Pictures of Jocelyn Brunt and Lissette Peterson.

Pictures of her.

Chapter Eleven

Amy's phone vibrated in her pocket, but she couldn't look away from the haunting images to answer the text.

Her hand shook as she identified the familiar scenes of Jocelyn in her Jeep, driving through the hills on the north end of the farm. Jocelyn bent over equipment, analyzing a soil sample and entering the data onto her laptop. Lissette Peterson coming out of the construction office. Sharing a conversation with a group of workers on the Copper Lake site, smiling.

There were images of Amy, hiking alongside the fence that bordered the old orchard, gathering discarded items from the nearby highway that she could use in her sculptures. Another picture of her standing on the front porch, leaning away from the scaffolding and turning her face to the warmth of the sunset.

There were other women she didn't know. Standing on the corner of a crosswalk in the city. Walking across a parking lot at a shopping mall. There was a dark-haired woman sitting at a desk in an office somewhere, as though the picture had been covertly taken across a waiting room. None of the pictures were lewd. But they were all…invasive.

Her phone buzzed again, and she absently took it out of her pocket. Mark.

Get back to the house. On my way.

He understood the threat. All those times she'd felt as though she was being watched, she had been.

These women had been spied on. *She* had been spied on. Now at least two of those women were dead.

Were there other bodies out there? Would there be more bodies in the future?

Amy couldn't quite seem to catch a deep breath.

Would one of those bodies be hers?

"Frick! Sterling!" The sharp male voice shouting from the front of the house startled her from the terrible portents of her imagination.

She typed a quick text to Mark. Only one word. Hurry.

At the sound of approaching footsteps, Amy moved as fast as she could. She shoved her phone into her pocket. She stuffed the photos she held into her backpack, along with the trowel. She closed the lockbox and grabbed her boot and backpack. But she couldn't handle all of them at once. She couldn't handle any of them like this. Dropping her boot, she opened the main compartment of her backpack and tried to stuff the box inside, to keep searching or spying eyes from knowing she'd found it. But the box was too big, and the footsteps were too close. She unzipped the expanding feature on her pack, but with the laptop and her own things inside, there still wasn't enough room. She shoved the box into the top as best she could before slipping the straps around her arms and pushing to her feet.

"I thought I told you to meet me at…"

Amy spun around at the voice from the doorway. The box tilted in the top of her open pack and she squeezed her shoulders back, trying to keep it hidden from view. Her breath gusted through her nose as she tried to appear composed, unassuming, not worried one whit about Dale O'Brien standing there, snorting a laugh at her expense.

"Crazy Amy." He propped his hands at his bulky waist and stepped into the room, eyeing her from head to toe. "One shoe off and one shoe on. Nothing weird about that. At the scene of another fire. If the police ask, I'll have to tell them I found you here."

"I'll have to tell them you were here, too," she countered, sounding bolder than she felt. "Why are you looking for Brad and Richie? Why did you think they'd be here—on my property?"

"I saw Brad's car parked behind the place. Thought I'd come over and chase them back to work." He swiped his finger along the charred frame of the door, studied the soot that came off and then pulled out a white handkerchief to wipe off his skin. "Some of my men are less inclined to come early or stay late with this rash of fires."

"And murders."

"And murders." He walked over to the bed. Amy picked up her boot and scuttled away, keeping more than an arm's reach between them. "I hear this is where your boyfriend found Lissette. Shame to die like that. She meant somethin' to me. She was a good employee. And she was…sweet. My men all liked her."

She thought of the pictures in her bag. Someone had liked her a lot. "Lissette was friendly to me."

"She would be." O'Brien studied the burn marks around the mattress, breathing in deeply, before he pulled off his hard hat and wiped the sweat from his forehead and cheeks with the soiled handkerchief. Or was he dabbing at tears? Could he be remembering Lissette's last moments? Or was he truly grieving for a friend? "Always friendly, that girl. Always sticking up for the underdog."

Amy's phone buzzed in her pocket again, but she

didn't want to take her eyes off O'Brien as she drifted half a step toward the door. "You and Lissette were close?"

"You mean, was I boinking her?" He plopped the hard hat back on his head, his crass response erasing even that small bit of compassion she'd thought about feeling for him. "Nah. Wasn't for lack of trying. She said I was too old for her." Amy kept inching toward the door but found him circling the bed to keep the distance between them from increasing. In fact, whether it was intentional or not, he was moving her toward the back wall now, away from the exit, unless she wanted to try to muscle her way past him. Muscling hadn't worked against Preston Worth. It hadn't worked against Derek Roland. She doubted it would work against a man O'Brien's size, either. "Besides, she had a strictly hands-off policy with the men she worked with. Most of them respected that."

"Most of them? Who didn't?" Was climbing onto the mattress and diving out that window an option? It couldn't be that far to the ground outside a single-story house. As long as the mattress didn't collapse beneath her. And she could move faster than the overweight man. Amy shifted closer. "Did you respect her wishes?"

Instead of getting an answer to her probing questions, the metal box chose that moment to shift out of her bag. Her scrambling efforts to catch it before it hit the floor only rattled the contents and pushed it away from her. It tumbled to a stop at O'Brien's feet.

"What do you have here?" He picked it up before she could snatch it away from him. "This looks like one of mine." He turned it over to inspect where she'd rubbed the soot off the remnants of the O'Brien Construction Company logo. "You stealing from me?"

She should have been moving toward the window, not trying to retrieve the box. Because now she was close enough to smell O'Brien's coffee breath and stale sweat. And there was no mistaking that he meant to corner her in this room.

"You're kidding, right?" Amy sassed, as though fear wasn't pounding through her veins. If that box was his, then that fire-starting kit and those pictures must be his sick obsession, too. She stepped back toward the window.

But suddenly he was right in front of her. The backs of her knees bumped against the mattress. "I've had a couple of them go missing over the past few weeks."

"First you accuse me of arson, and now you accuse me of stealing?" Amy pulled up to her full height, even though she was shaking inside. "Are you sure you want to claim that box? I found it hidden under those floor-boards. I think Richie might have been looking for it." She pointed to the hole in the floor, hoping he'd at least turn, if not move, toward it. But the big blob didn't budge. Amy tilted her chin. "Question is, was he searching on his own accord? Or was he doing a job for you? Is that why you wanted them to meet you early this morning?"

He tucked the box under his arm. "My property, my business."

"So, you admit you know what's inside," she accused.

"You have been nothing but trouble from the first time I met you. If it was just your grandmother, this whole farm would be mine by now. I'd own every inch of Copper Lake."

"It's a good thing I'm around, then, isn't it?"

"That's a matter of opinion." He was close enough to share his unwanted body heat now. Another centimeter closer and she'd be falling onto the mattress where the dead woman had lain. "You want me to tell the police or KCFD that you were in here poking around—"

"You're trespassing, O'Brien." Mark Taylor's deep voice uttered a succinct warning from the open doorway.

O'Brien grinned at Amy's gasp of relief before turning. "Well, if it isn't the boyfriend."

Mark flashed his KCFD ID badge in his wallet and waved Amy over to stand beside him. She hurried around O'Brien as fast as her bruised ankle allowed. Mark caught her by the arm and pushed her behind him without taking his eyes off the bullying contractor. "Get out of here before I call the cops," he warned. "I have several of them on speed dial."

O'Brien chuckled. "You need to keep a shorter leash on your wild-child girlfriend, Taylor. She's messin' with things that don't belong to her." He held out the box and rattled the remaining contents. "Neither of you have any legal claim to whatever's inside this box."

Mark's hands fisted at his sides. "Your other option is for me to lay you out flat. And after the way I've seen you talk to my mother and Amy, I would love to."

O'Brien's amusement faded as he considered the validity of Mark's threat. He wisely decided that Mark could make good on besting him in a fight. He hugged the box to his chest and put one hand up, placating Mark as he sidled past them. "Hold your horses there, Taylor. I don't want any trouble. I'm going. I've retrieved what belongs to me." He looked past Mark's shoulder to Amy. "But you may want to investigate who stole it from me in the first place."

"I never took anything from you," Amy argued. She reached around Mark, but his arm straightened across her stomach, keeping her back. She latched on to the sleeve of his T-shirt, instead, pleading with him. "I found it under the floorboards. You can't let him leave with that. It's important."

"Did you take that from Amy's property?" Mark demanded.

O'Brien moved toward the door, keeping his eyes on Mark as he held up the box. "It has my name on it, doesn't it?"

"But there's evidence," she insisted. Not that it had been legally obtained, but it had to help with the investigation, didn't it?

"Evidence of what?" O'Brien taunted. His smarmy smile returned. "Nothing you can prove, darlin'."

Mark glanced over the jut of his shoulder at her, silently asking how far she wanted him to push this. At least she still had a handful of photos left in her bag. Plus, the pictures on her phone. It was more than she'd had a few minutes ago. If O'Brien wanted to claim that box and incriminate himself, she'd let KCPD deal with his explanation. Amy squeezed Mark's arm, thanking him for giving her a choice. "I just want him to leave."

"Done." With a curt nod, Mark pointed to the door. "I'll show you out."

Mark followed at a measured pace as O'Brien clutched the box and hurried his steps. Amy retrieved her boot and sat on the floor to untie it and pull it over her tender ankle. A minute or two later, she heard an engine starting and the crunch of gravel, and assumed O'Brien was driving away.

When Mark strode back into the room, he was on his phone. "Yeah, Matt. If you and any of the other guys can come out here and keep an eye on things while we're gone, I'll owe you a solid. Thanks." He disconnected the call and knelt in front of her. "My brothers and a couple of my crewmates are going to set up a round-the-clock watch on your place. We won't leave until I know some-one's here whom I trust." His hand settled on her knee as he scanned her from head to toe and back. "Should I ask why you're in the middle of a crime scene that was cor-doned off by KCPD and the fire department last night?"

Jeans and a KCFD T-shirt didn't make his broad shoul-ders and stern jaw look any less authoritative than he did in his black uniform or decked out in his full bunker gear. But those smoky blue eyes spoke of caring and concern and a compassion that soothed the edges off her fear. She could talk to those eyes. "I saw someone was in here and came to check it out. Suddenly, it was Grand Central Sta-tion. Richie Sterling, Brad Frick, Dale O'Brien. Any one of them, or all of them, could have been looking for that box. Or something else the police missed. I had to see what was going on."

"You *had* to?" He moved his hand to cup the side of her face and then captured the copper braid that fell over her shoulder. "Are you injured?"

"Turned my ankle when I fell through the floor. Noth-ing serious."

He immediately went into paramedic mode, inspect-ing her ankle before determining she was probably going to live. When she didn't protest, he tied her boot for her. "Keep this on. This is the last place you want to be run-ning around in stockinged feet."

"Mark, that's not important. Look what I found." She pulled up the pictures on her phone. "These were in that strongbox. I had already taken a few of them out. There was a homemade fire-starter kit there, too. Probably not enough to burn down a house, but enough to start some-thing small. Here." She showed him the images on her phone. "Is that significant?"

"You're right. A cotton ball soaked in petroleum jelly

wouldn't burn long enough to take down a house. But it does show that someone likes playing with fire." He considered something for a moment. "If you stuffed the lit cotton inside the gas tank of a car…"

"It would torch it, like Jocelyn's Jeep?" It had been totaled, just like the equipment shed.

Mark nodded.

"I found more." She pulled the loose photographs from her backpack, but Mark pushed them away when she tried to hand them to him.

"The fewer people who touch those, the better. Show me." Mark's expression turned grim as she thumbed through the photographs.

"I want to show these to the police, too. What do you think they mean?" Amy shook her head. "What am I saying? I know what they mean. I've felt like someone's been watching me on and off for a long time now, but I didn't know he was taking pictures."

Mark muttered a curse. "You think someone's been spying on you out here? For how long?" He reached for her hand. "Never mind." He pulled her to her feet and slipped his arm around her waist, pulling her hip against his. "Can you walk?" Amy nodded. She doubted she even needed his steadying support as she barely limped along beside him, but she wasn't about to push away his solid warmth and sheltering strength. Her ankle might be fine, but her knees were still shaking after that encounter with Dale O'Brien. "I'm going to put in a call to my uncle Josh or Cole at KCPD. My brothers Pike and Alex aren't detectives like they are. I want to find out how they think we should handle this. Are you the only one who's touched these photographs?"

They stepped out into the sunlight, and Amy breathed

in the fresh air, and the clean, freshly showered maleness that was all Mark Taylor. "Since I've been here, yes."

"Do you have any big plastic bags at your house?" She nodded. Mark opened the passenger door to his truck, spanned his hands around her waist and lifted her in.

"I guess you *can* pick me up." She was half teasing, remembering the threat he'd made the first time they'd met. But she was also thinking of the gentleness and caring behind all that strength.

He winked. "Wait until I throw you over my shoulder." But before she could respond to the flirtation or even smile at seeing the intensity of his protective mode ease a fraction, he had closed the door and jogged around the hood to climb in behind the wheel. It was a quick drive to the top of the driveway, and then Mark was at her door again, winding a supportive arm around her waist and helping her up the steps into the house. "Get me those bags," he ordered, taking her all the way into the kitchen when she told him their location. He set her backpack on the table and hovered around her while she opened the drawer and got him the requested items. "I've learned enough from my brothers and uncles about police work to know that we shouldn't be touching things they might be able to get fingerprints from. While I'm doing this, you change your clothes and get your grandmother ready. Unless you need me to help you?"

Amy shook her head. "I can manage just fine. But I don't think Gran's awake yet."

"Then get her up. We're all going into the city this morning."

"Why?"

"Why? Because I'm not leaving any woman out here alone with that piece of scum O'Brien and everything else that's going on. I've got a place she can stay for a couple of hours while you and I are talking to the detectives."

"Okay." She made it to the kitchen archway before she stopped and turned. "Mark?"

He paused in his bagging of those disturbing pictures. "What is it?"

"I had a plan to get away from O'Brien."

"I'm sure you did."

"I'm strong and I'm smart. Maybe braver than I should be. I don't need you to rescue me." He set the bag down on the table and turned to argue something about being alone and getting hurt and somebody needed the hell to keep an eye on her. But his words fell silent when she crossed the room and wound her arms around his waist. Her forehead nestled in at the crook of his neck and collarbone, and she turned her ear to the strong beat of his heart. "But I do need you to hold me."

She felt the tension in him vanish as his strong arms folded around her and pulled her close. "Anytime, Red." He nuzzled his lips against her temple. "I will hold you anytime."

They stood together like that for countless moments until the warmth of Mark's body seeped into hers, chasing away the chill that even the summer day hadn't been able to reach. "I was scared," she confessed, knowing she was in a safe place to share the truth. "Of Brad and Richie. The timing was just so weird. I hate to give the man any kind of satisfaction, but I was scared of O'Brien, too. I'm scared of whoever took those pictures. I don't know who I should be afraid of, but I am."

"I know, Red. I know. Your last text scared me, too." He rubbed warm circles against her back, then settled his hand with a possessive familiarity over the curve of her hip. "And then I walked in and saw he'd cornered you against the back wall—"

"I wasn't giving up without a fight."

"Neither was I." When he started to pull away, Amy whimpered a protest. But the sound quickly became a groan of pleasure as Mark framed her face between his hands and kissed her. Deeply. Thoroughly. And far too briefly for a woman who was learning to love and trust this man more and more with every passing moment. She clung to his wrists as he leaned his forehead against hers. "Don't worry about the box O'Brien took. We'll get this guy with or without it. I just need you to be safe. Because, as far as I'm concerned, you are the only thing that's important."

Chapter Twelve

It didn't hurt that Mark's oldest uncle, Mitch Taylor, was the chief of police.

After a phone call to his uncle Josh to ask how Amy should handle this meeting with Detectives Beck and Carson, Mark dropped Comfort Hall off at his grandmother's house. Although Amy seemed inclined to stay a little longer and chat after he'd made the introductions, he'd reminded her of the time, dropped a quick kiss onto Martha Taylor's cheek and hurried Amy back to his truck, leaving the two older women standing in the front door of Martha Taylor's new house.

Josh must have mentioned something to Mitch because a phone call straight from the chief's office had suddenly changed Cathy Beck's doubting demeanor. While her partner, Dean Carson, copied the pictures off Amy's phone and took the photographs and Jocelyn's laptop into evidence, Detective Beck started treating Amy more like a witness than a suspect, jotting down notes of Amy's account of this morning's events at the burned-out house and her run-in with Derek Roland on the Williams University campus. They agreed that the arson fires and murders were connected, although it would require more digging to determine if the murders were the reason the fires had been set, or the fires were the reason the murders had happened. Or, as Detective Beck postulated, was the killer taking advantage of some firebug's handiwork? Motive seemed to be the key to solving these crimes. Apparently, the motives for setting a fire and killing an innocent woman were quite different. If they could pinpoint why these women were being targeted, or why the fires were all on Hall property, they could narrow down their suspect list.

Mark's fingers were going numb from clutching them into fists while Amy described Roland's erratic behavior toward her, and the way she'd confronted the two handymen and Dale O'Brien this morning. Someone with a sick, selfish plan had been watching Amy, taking pictures of her, possibly setting her up to be his next victim. And he hadn't been there to protect her from any of it. It wasn't until Amy reached across from her chair to rest her hand over his fist that he realized just how tense sitting through this meeting and feeling like he'd failed her was making him.

Muscles leaped beneath his skin at her intuitive touch, calming him, centering him. When he forced his hand to relax, she laced her fingers together with his, linking them together while she answered Detective Beck's last question. Now his fingers were tingling where she touched him. Probably just the nerves waking up from the tight grip he'd held for too long, but maybe because, well, it seemed this woman's touch had awakened a lot of things inside him.

He squeezed his hand gently around hers where it rested on his thigh, and wondered how in the hell he was ever going to save her when a) she insisted she didn't want to be rescued, and b) he needed her quirky caring and trusting touch to save *him*.

"Thank you, Ms. Hall, Mr. Taylor." Detective Beck

stood up and circled around her desk to shake Amy's hand. Mark stood and shook her hand, as well. "Thanks for keeping an eye on her. Although, I wish you'd leave the detective work to Dean and me. Don't suppose I can stop you from poking around your own place, though, can I."

"Just keep me in the loop if you can," Amy said. "Jocelyn didn't have an enemy in the world. I really want whoever did that to her to pay."

"We'll do our best."

Before they headed back out to his truck, Amy went to use the restroom and Mark seized the opportunity to stop by the officers' lounge to pay a visit to his two oldest brothers. He accepted a cup of coffee and gave Pike and Alex a brief rundown of everything that had happened out at Copper Lake and Amy's home, and why they were here at precinct headquarters. Since he'd already called in favors from Matt and his Lucky 13 crew to watch the place while he was gone, he asked his KCPD brothers to help with something else.

Alex didn't typically carry a notepad on his SWAT uniform, so he scribbled himself a note on a paper napkin. "Sure. I'll make a couple of calls to verify that Preston Worth is still living in Montana."

"And hasn't shown his face in Kansas City anytime over the past few months."

"Hasn't…shown…his…face…" Alex copied the words and underlined them.

Pike doctored the bitter coffee with a shot of milk before bending his long legs and settling onto the vinyl couch. His K-9 partner, Hans, lay down at his feet. "You think this old boyfriend could be seeking retribution against Amy?"

Mark leaned against the door frame and downed half

of the nasty brew. He'd been going almost forty-eight hours on just a couple of naps since his KCFD shift had started two days ago. He was off the clock now, but he didn't intend to crash and leave Amy alone without him guarding her back just because his stomach lining was tired of downing caffeine. "He's at the bottom of my suspect list. Those pictures tell me this killer is patient, calculating. The fires had to have been planned—the targets are specific to the old Hall farm, and we'd have somebody on our radar by now if anyone unfamiliar with the place was seen there. Worth sounds like a temper tantrum waiting to happen." Mark forced himself to take another sip. "But so help me, if that man does show his face anywhere near Amy, I'll have to ask you two to look the other way."

Alex grinned. "We'll let you have a punch or two before we arrest him for violating his no-contact order."

"It was an abusive relationship?" Pike asked, possibly remembering the trauma his wife had suffered growing up.

Mark nodded. "Amy told me he put her in the hospital. Then he tried to blackmail her into not reporting him."

"And he's the one who lost his job and ended up serving time." Alex raked his fingers through his dark curly hair and huffed a noise of admiration. "That woman sounds like she's got some backbone. Think you can handle her, baby brother?"

"I can handle her just fine," Mark answered, refusing to be baited by his teasing. "She says she needs me, and I don't intend to let her down."

"Hold on a minute." Pike braced his elbows on his knees and leaned forward. "Matt said you were struggling with some kind of savior complex because of Grandpa

Sid. Taking risks you shouldn't, getting involved with a woman you barely know—"

"I *know* Amy in every way I need to." Mark straightened where he stood. He didn't have to defend his feelings for Amy, but he was doing it anyway. Because denying his feelings for her would be a lie. "I've talked more to Amy Hall in these past two weeks than I have to any other woman I dated for months. How long did you have to be with Hope…or Audrey—" he included Alex's wife in his argument, too "—before you knew you were in love with them?"

Tactical error! Mark saw the transformation from concerned argument to surprise to amusement at his expense on his brothers' faces.

"You're in love with her?" Pike asked. He and Alex exchanged a knowing look. "Uh-oh."

Mark crossed the room and tossed his empty coffee cup in the trash with more force than was necessary. "My point is, I'm not doing this for Amy because I feel guilty about Grandpa and I think I have to make amends. She needs somebody. She says she needs me. I want to be there for her."

"We're not questioning what's in your heart, baby bro." Alex moved in beside him, slapping a hand against his shoulder. "Well, not about Amy."

Why did Pike moving in on the other side of Mark make him feel like he was about to get some kind of intervention on his love life? "You didn't answer my question. Do you love her?"

Mark glanced up into blue eyes and down into brown before he answered. "How do you know?"

"You know," Alex assured him.

Pike's reply was more helpful. "Does anything scare you more than losing her?"

Mark squeezed his eyes shut and remembered the blinding anger he'd felt when he'd caught O'Brien trapping Amy in that burned-out bedroom. He remembered the utter destruction of an innocent life when they'd discovered Jocelyn Brunt's body and when he'd found Lissette Peterson dead, bound and burning in last night's fire. He remembered the angry bruises on Amy's hand and wrist and the pictures someone had taken of her, watching her, stalking her. His gut was tight with dread as he connected the dots and imagined some bastard breaking Amy's stubborn will and silencing that beautiful mouth.

Yeah. Losing Amy scared him more than anything.

"I love her."

Pike squeezed his shoulder. "She can't do any better than you, baby bro."

Alex squeezed the other shoulder. "We'll get this guy," he promised. "You're a Taylor. You'll keep her safe. We've got your back for whatever you need."

"Thanks."

And then, because they were brothers and they loved each other and they knew each other so well, Alex ended the supportive moment with a punch to Mark's shoulder. "Then, if you're not moping over this woman, and you're not feeling guilty about Grandpa Sid, why did you make Grandma cry?"

Mark groaned and shoved them both off. "This is not the time, Alex."

Pike stopped him at the door and showed him an old family picture in his wallet from when they were newly adopted kids. "See this picture? She's smiling. You made her cry, dude, by skipping her open house. You didn't even give her a reason why. Not cool."

"I've already had this conversation with Matt."

Alex nodded toward the curvy redhead coming down the hall to join them, but he had one more lick to get in before the conversation ended. "Then you know what you need to do to make it right."

Amy arched a questioning eyebrow as she walked up to the three of them. "Am I interrupting anything?"

Alex grinned. "I see what's to like, Mark. Nicely done."

"Excuse me?" Amy was an only child. She had no idea how relentless the teasing among a team of brothers could be.

Mark reached for her hand and pulled her into the break room. "Red, these are my brothers Alex and Pike."

He knew when she touched her necklace that she was a little anxious about this introduction. She was grounding herself, reminding herself she could deal with this. And she could do it with her beautiful smile. "Wow. Uncles? Brothers? Are you related to every cop in Kansas City?"

Alex, who was shorter than she was, took her other hand and winked. "Just the good-lookin' ones like me."

Pike nudged Alex aside to shake her hand, as well. "Ignore him. He's married, adopting a baby and not nearly as charming as he thinks he is. I'm Pike Taylor. Beautiful wife. Two kids. Big dog. I'm the brains of the family."

"You wish." Alex shoved him right back.

"You two work this out on your own time." Mark slid his hand behind Amy's waist, steering her toward the elevators. "We have to go."

"Nice to meet you, Amy," Pike called after them.

"Talk to Grandma, Mark." Alex was more direct as he followed them to the elevators. "I can't handle her crying over you because you skipped her party, and she thinks you're avoiding her."

Several minutes later, Mark and Amy were in his

truck, cruising onto the highway toward his grandmother's house east of downtown KC. Mark was deep
in thought, about Grandpa Sid, about his brothers' concern that he was alienating the one family member he
loved the most, about his feelings for Amy.

Probably because his brooding radiated off him and
filled up the truck cab, Amy reached over to adjust the
air-conditioning and broke the silence. "Wow. Your brothers are sure protective of your grandmother. Saving the
day seems to be a trait that runs in your family."

He grunted. She was tapping into a well of emotions
he wasn't sure he could keep a cap on anymore.

"Why didn't you go to the party?" she asked. "Did
you have to work?"

Mark's fingers tightened on the steering wheel. He
felt her eyes on his hands, knew she had some kind of
weird fascination with men's hands and wondered what
message she was getting from his white-knuckled grip.

They'd pulled off on the exit to Lee's Summit Road
before Amy spoke again. "Is this about your grandfather's death?"

"Don't you push, too." The cap had been opened, and
the emotions were steaming to the top.

"If you haven't noticed, that's kind of my nature.
You're hurting. Apparently, she's hurting, too, if your
brothers are that worried." Her gaze darted between his
eyes and his hands. "If you want to stay for a while and
talk to her, I don't mind. Gran and I can wait in the
truck."

Mark shook his head and turned south. "I want you
and Comfort to stay with Grandma. At least for a night
or two. One of my uncles or brothers can be there to keep
an eye on you. You and I should go back to your house
to pack some things for her. I'll stop by my place on the

way back and pack a bag so I can stay out at the farm. I don't think we should leave it unattended."

"One, no one is chasing me out of my own home. And two, do you feel responsible for your grandfather's death?"

"What?" The truck swerved toward the next lane as his hands jerked on the wheel. That vat of emotion was completely uncorked now. "I *am* responsible." He wasn't sure if it was his brothers' badgering or the fact that he'd already shared so much with Amy that he felt he could talk to her about anything. He pounded the steering wheel as the guilt and pain came pouring out. "You've seen a glimpse of what a big, loving, crazy family I have. I took him away from all that."

"Did you murder him?"

"What? Of course not. He had a heart attack. We were…" He shook his head. His jaw hurt because of how tightly he was clenching it. "I don't want you to see me hurt and angry like this. I don't want you to ever be afraid of me."

"Pull off into that parking lot, Mark. We need to talk." Oh, man, she was tough. On the outside. But he knew how vulnerable she could be, too. She pointed to the next turnoff. "Do it, Fire Man."

He glanced across the seat. If she had on that bossy, let's-run-into-the-fire look on her face, he would keep driving. Instead, she looked frightened, sad. She cared that he was hurting. He couldn't resist the woman who looked at him with those hazel eyes as though she believed he could make her world better.

Slowing the truck, he pulled up beside an empty ball field in Adair Park. Before he'd even turned off the engine, she was unbuckling and climbing onto her seat. She reached across the center console and placed her hands over his, gently willing him to let go—of the steering wheel and of the guilt and pain battling inside him. "For what it's worth, you are too kind, too Captain Good Guy, for me ever to be afraid of you, Fire Man. Now talk."

He pulled her hands to his lips and kissed them. She waited patiently for Mark to unfasten his seat belt and push his seat all the way back. She didn't protest when he reached across the truck to pull her onto his lap. With her long legs stretched out across the console, she wound one arm around his neck and stroked the angles of his cheek and jaw with gentle fingertips. Although the sweet weight of her hip nestled against his groin stirred other ideas, he reveled in her tender ministrations. She was warm and caring and strong and irresistible. Mark felt the hard shell that guarded his emotions crack open and crumble into dust.

Maybe she was right about the whole rescuing thing. *He* was the one who needed to be rescued. *He* was the one who needed to trust that his heart and his secrets and his future would be safe with *her*.

After several moments of simply touching her hair and putting his faith in those green-gold eyes, Mark drew his hand down the smooth skin of her neck to capture the chain she always wore between his fingers. He traced the path of the chain down to the pendant of knotted silver around a small heart and treasured the warmth it had drawn from her skin into his palm. The symbolism of trusting Amy with his own heart and all its twisty complications wasn't lost on him. She had made this beautiful thing. She had made his heart come alive again.

And she still waited for him to speak.

"Grandpa and I were…" He hated to say the touchy word around her, but she wanted the truth. "We were *rescuing* some people from a bad car accident. The strain was too much for his heart." Her sympathetic gasp couldn't stop him now. The comfort of her hand stroking his jaw couldn't stop him, either. "I saved everyone else that day. Didn't save the one man who mattered the most."

"Was he as old as Martha?"

"A couple years older. Why?"

Her fingers trailed down his neck to rest against his chest. "My grandfather was seventy-nine when he passed. His doctor said every heart has only so many beats in it. Whether you were helping those people who needed you or not, maybe his heart was done. It was his time."

He released the pendant and curled his hand around the curve of her thigh. "Great. So, you're saying he would have died in my truck driving home from the lake. *Still* my watch."

"You need to talk to your grandmother about all this, Mark. You're both grieving. Instead of fighting each other, you could be healing each other."

"It hurts."

"Hell yes, it hurts." She slipped her arms around his neck and hugged him tightly, briefly, before sitting back in his lap. Her hands framed his jaw. "I was in the middle of Preston's trial when my grandfather died. You don't think I wanted to be there for him? You don't think I felt guilty that all my trouble caused him so much stress that it probably contributed to his heart attack?"

He rubbed his hand up to her bottom and down to her knee, wanting to draw her even closer. "You didn't tell me that's how you lost him. I'm sorry."

"Look, Mark, I know I'm not the poster child for smart choices and easy answers, but I do know about surviving. I know about all the fear and guilt and grief that goes along with that." She stroked her fingers across his lips, and he felt the tugging need to kiss her all the way down to his groin. "The number one thing I've learned is to be with the people who love you the most. When Grandpa Leland died, Gran needed me. She didn't need me wallowing in self-pity. She needed someone to take care of. She needed someone to grieve with who understood just how much it hurts to lose someone you love. She needed someone to love when Grandpa Leland died. So did I. So do you." Tears glistened in her eyes, but she blinked them away before Mark's thumb could catch one. "Getting over a loss like this—it's not going to fix itself overnight. But it will get better. I promise. If you're anything like your grandfather, I know he was a good man. I can imagine the loss you feel. Let your grandmother take care of you a little bit. Let her talk and share memories. And you do the same. Don't deny her—or you—the chance to heal together."

When her fingers tried to brush his hair into order, the last of Mark's strength snapped. He crushed Amy in his arms, buried his nose in the herbal scent of her hair and finally shed the tears that had been locked up inside him.

Her arms circled around him and held him tight as she whispered soft comforts against his ear and gently rocked him. Mark shook with the depth of his grief. He released some of his guilt into the depth of her strength. And still she held on.

He loved this woman so much. He needed her. He wanted her. Whether it was yin and yang, Captain Good Guy and the bad girl, intuitive and creative and grounded in training and duty, she completed him. Amy Hall made Mark Taylor whole again. This woman who had seemed so alone knew more about being together with him than he ever knew he needed.

Somewhere along the way, the intensity of his emotions turned to passion, and the generosity of her comfort turned to a blinding need to know all of her.

Mark seized her mouth in a searing kiss that ignited a fire behind his eyes and in his heart and in that potent male part of him that wanted to link them together in the most elemental way. After a quick scan outside to assure the privacy of their surroundings, Mark tilted his seat back as far as it would go and pulled Amy on top of him.

He palmed the back of her head and squeezed her bottom, fitting her to him in all the right places. He thrust his tongue in her mouth and traded sparks of desire, claiming and taking as equal partners. His jeans grew uncomfortably tight as her thighs settled on either side of him and gripped his hips. Her breasts were beautiful, pillowy mounds that flattened against his chest, her nipples beady pearls that branded him through the clothes they still wore.

Too many clothes, too tight a space, perfect woman, consuming need. Not the way he'd imagined making love to Amy. But he had a will, and he would make a way. He cupped her hips and lifted her slightly off him, loving how she arched to keep their lips together even as he unbuttoned her blouse and filled his hand with a full perfect breast. He caught the tip between his thumb and hand and she finally tore her mouth from his and gasped a hot, breathy moan. "Not fair, Fire Man. This is supposed to be a two-way… I want to…"

When he unhooked her bra and moved her to capture the pale pink tip in his mouth, he discovered she had trouble saying any words at all. She hummed. She moaned. She made him crazy, kissing and nibbling on any part of him she could reach. Her fingers tightened against his scalp when he moved her to claim the other breast.

She knew where this was going because she uttered a

single word—"Protection?"—before tugging at the hem of his T-shirt and scorching her hands across his flank and chest.

"Are you sure?" A rational part of his brain tried to fight its way through the fire raging inside him. She unzipped him and her hand found its way inside his jeans to cup him, and Mark discovered he was the one struggling to talk. "Can't…be…too…good here."

"With you, it'll be perfect." He guided her hand to the back pocket of his jeans and she pulled out his billfold. "We'll do it pretty next time."

"Next time. I like that."

"Shut up, Fire Man." Together, they opened the condom, pushed aside jeans, shorts and panties. Mark cracked his knee on the steering column, but barely felt it. Amy's elbow hit the automatic door lock the next time he lifted her. "Soon. Now."

And then he lowered her on top of him. She was hot, wet, perfect. Her moans were music to his ears. Her greedy hands roaming all over him were incendiary. Once they were linked as closely as a man and woman could be, Mark thrust inside her. Her soft, freckled breasts bobbed in his face as they found the rhythm they needed to bring each other to a swift, fiery completion. As Mark released himself on one last, powerful thrust, he slipped his thumb between them to tease her sensitive bundle of nerves and ignite the tremors that cascaded all around him. "Yep. Great…hands…" Overcome by the strength of her release, she gasped his name and collapsed on top of him.

Mark wrapped his arms around Amy and whispered, "You're beautiful."

A few minutes later, spurred by the reality of all they needed to do and the possibility that they might be discovered, despite the empty parking lot and trees that blocked his truck and the ball field from the road, Mark sat up, spilling Amy into his lap. She scrambled over the console and Mark straightened his seat. He put the condom back into its wrapper and dropped it into the trash while she adjusted her clothes and combed her fingers through the loose hair he'd pulled from her braid.

"Well, that was cathartic," she teased, buttoning up her blouse. She'd missed a hole and was buttoning it crooked, reminding him just how sweet and sexy and desirable she was. When he pointed it out, her face turned an endearing shade of pink and she started again. "I don't think I've ever been that…spontaneous."

"You?" Not that Mark was having an easy time getting his shorts straightened inside his jeans again. "I figured you were the adventurous type."

"I've only been with one other man, and that didn't turn out the way I—"

He pressed a finger over her kiss-stung lips and tried to make that memory recede. "I'm sorry. Forget about him. I'm sorry he hurt you. But I'm glad he's gone so you can be here with me now."

"Me, too." She reached across the seat and feathered her fingers through his hair, trying to make him look presentable, too. "With Preston, the emotion wasn't there. I realize that now. It's a lot more intense when I believe the guy wants me, and just me."

"Believe it." He caught her hand and pressed a kiss to her fingers before releasing her to fasten his seat belt and start the engine. "You'd better tone down the blush on your cheeks so our grandmothers don't guess what we've been doing."

"I'll stop blushing if you will."

No doubt. Even though his emotions had been tempered and his desire temporarily quenched, he was still hot for this woman. "I am in love with you, Amy Hall."

She settled back in her seat and buckled up. "Now, *that* scares me."

"It shouldn't. You're the bravest woman I know. I would never pressure you to jump into something you're not ready for. And I would never hurt you the way your professor did."

"I know that. What scares me is that I think I'm in love with you, too."

Mark reached across the seat to take her hand, holding on tight to his future.

Now, if they could track down an arsonist turned serial killer, he and Amy might just have a chance to make that future happen.

Chapter Thirteen

After his *conversation* with Amy, it was surprisingly easy to sit down at the kitchen table with Martha Taylor and apologize for distancing himself from his grandmother. Her bony, arthritic hand, marked by age spots and years of hard work, never left his as she gently clasped his fingers across the table.

Mark was beginning to understand Amy's fascination with hands. They said so much about a person. Strength, gentleness. A link of family and trust. Shared history and new feelings. A loving touch versus a hurtful one. He had an affinity for certain hands, too. Like the freckled hand that eased his pain and stoked his desire. Like the one holding his now.

"It's my job to save people. I didn't save him."

"You didn't let your grandfather die," Martha insisted. "He didn't think that and neither do I."

Mark shook his head, wishing he could make things right. "I was running around while he was making like the Hulk, pulling equipment out of the truck and taking care of that baby. I was so busy taking care of everybody else and putting out that fire that I wasn't paying any attention to his distress. I took him for granted, Grandma."

She turned her blue eyes to the sunlight streaming through the kitchen window for a moment before she sighed and faced him again. "You mean, you took it for granted that my Sid was always going to be there for you?"

"Don't get into semantics about generations and life spans. I should have saved him. I should have been there for him when he needed me most. And I wasn't."

He could never argue that his grandmother wasn't a wise, intuitive woman. "So, you've been avoiding me because you feel guilty? I thought maybe you were afraid that I was going to leave you, too. That you were mad at us for being old and no longer the vibrant, fun-loving grands you could do no wrong with."

"Mad?" Mark was stunned that she'd even considered him feeling that way. "I love you. Come on. I'm your baby boy. You know that."

"I do." The teakettle on the stove whistled, and he waited patiently while she got up and poured the water into a teapot and carried it and a tray of cups back to the table. "Your grandfather had a serious heart event fifteen years ago. I nearly lost him then. Sid and I both knew that he was living on borrowed time—and he was determined to make the most of that precious gift of a second life. He wanted to live and love and laugh and see his grandsons grow into fine young men." Standing beside Mark, she cupped his cheek. The tears in her eyes would have gutted him until he realized she was smiling. "I am grateful beyond measure to know that he had you with him when he died. That he wasn't alone. That he left this world doing something important, saving lives. That he had the grandson he loved so well and was so proud of with him at the end. It helps me know that he died a happy man." Mark hadn't thought he had any tears left in him, but when they spilled over, his grandmother wiped them away and pressed a kiss to his cheek. "Thank you for being with him, Mark. Thank you for that precious gift."

"Ah, Grandma." Mark pushed to his feet and wrapped her up in his arms.

She hugged him back. "That's what I needed. A big bear hug from my favorite grandson."

"Favorite? You say that to all of us."

Her frail arms tightened around him for a precious moment before she relaxed against him. "I do. Take it or leave it," she teased.

"I'll take it." They laughed together. "I miss him, Grandma. I miss him so much."

"I miss him, too." After a few moments, she pulled away, brushing a few last tears from her cheeks. "But do you know how angry he'd be if he thought you were throwing your life away? Taking unnecessary risks? Refusing to live and love and laugh the way he wanted you to?" A stern matriarchal finger poked the middle of his chest. "Do you know how hurt I'll be if I lose you, too?"

She curled a finger, urging him to follow her over to the cabinets. "I don't remember my birth parents. But I do remember being lost, and a little scared of the world until Mom and Dad adopted Matt and me—Alex and Pike, too. When I found out you and Grandpa were part of the deal, I was on cloud nine. Being the youngest of four brothers, though, I got lost in the shuffle sometimes. But Grandpa—and you—always had time for me."

She opened the cabinet and set four plates in his hands. "Those are the memories you need to cherish, Mark. It's okay to be sad. But don't waste time with regrets."

"That's about what Amy said."

"Sounds like a smart girl." She handed him silverware and napkins and ushered him back to the table. Somehow, Martha Taylor was one step ahead of him. "Now, where is that young woman of yours? If she's half as fun as Comfort is, I need to get to know her."

"She's a little different, Grandma."

"Good. That means she's interesting." After the table was set, she nudged him toward the back door, where he'd left Amy and her grandmother inspecting the contents of Martha's late summer garden. "Go. Invite her in. You and the Hall women are all having lunch with me today."

"I'd like that." Mark grinned and kissed the top of her head. "I love you, Grandma."

"I love you, too. Oh, and, Mark?" She stopped him with his hand on the doorknob and touched her fingers to her white hair. "Maybe you and Amy should comb your hair after you…enjoy each other's company."

"Grandma!"

Hell. Nothing got past that woman.

She chuckled. "I think your grandfather would have liked her, too."

Mark knew he was blushing when he stepped outside.

ONCE THEY TURNED off the highway and slowed their speed to drive through the hills toward Copper Lake, Amy cracked open the window of Mark's truck and breathed in the hazy air. It smelled of dried grass, pungent earth and asphalt, but there was something about the chill of the truck's air-conditioning, or maybe it was the idea of returning home to where innocent women died and creeps spied on her that left her shivering.

"You doing okay?" Mark asked, slowing as they drove through the Copper Lake subdivision and construction zone.

Amy's gaze zeroed in on Dale O'Brien's office trailer and the familiar company truck parked out front. Brad Frick's car was there, too, making her wonder what connection the men shared—why they'd all been in that burned house this morning, why they'd been so anxious to get her out of there. Were they just three slimy, opportunistic morons? Or did they share a more sinister connection?

Brad leaned against the car, flicking away a cigarette as they drove past. Amy curled her fingers through Mark's when she felt his touch on the back of her hand. "So much has changed today."

"Some of it for the good, I hope."

She nodded and faced the much more pleasurable scenery of Mark's angular face. "Of course. I don't regret what happened between us. I'm just not sure if I'm ready for what happens next. We haven't even been on a real date yet."

He turned north to circle the lake. "What happens next is we pack a bag for Comfort. I might not be able to convince you to leave, but at least she'll be safe, spending a few nights with my grandmother. Then I'll grab my bag and bunk on your couch until this guy is caught. That date will happen. I promise."

"Is he going to go into hiding or leave town if you're here with me?"

"I'm not setting you up as bait to draw this guy out."

"I don't know if I can handle another murder," she confessed. "I'm not even sure I can handle another fire. O'Brien has to be behind it somehow."

Mark released her to turn into the gravel driveway and pulled up beside his brother Matt's truck. "The detectives are already on his case and have subpoenaed him to turn over that strongbox you found this morning."

"It's probably long gone. At the bottom of the lake or buried somewhere else."

"Then they'll arrest him for obstruction of justice."

He set the brake and shut off the engine. "Either way, he won't be getting close to you again. Not while I'm around."

Yeah, but would Mark always be around to rescue her? He had to go to work sometime. He'd have family events to attend. And was what they were feeling really love? Or *love for now* because she'd helped him past an emotional hurdle, her situation fed his Captain Good Guy genes and the chemistry between them was undeniably hot?

Amy nodded, wishing she could see things in black-and-white as clearly as Mark apparently did. She knew just how complicated relationships could get. And while she truly believed he would never physically hurt her, would Mark tire of the drama she brought to his life?

"You are not the introspective type," Mark said, waiting to open his door until she gave him an answer he liked. "So, get out of your head and start talking to me."

"I'm just tired." It wasn't a lie. She'd been through a physical and emotional wringer today. "I'm tired of having to keep fighting. I'm already tired of the fight that I know is ahead of us." She pointed to the big man getting out of his truck and circling around to greet them. "Let's see what Matt has to say."

"Amy." Mark captured her hand before she got out the door. "Like I said before, you're strong. You're my grandmother kind of strong."

She smiled. "That's a nice compliment, Fire Man."

But she wasn't sure she believed it.

Without so much as a hello, Matt Taylor stuck his fingers into the back pockets of his jeans and launched into a concise report. "Nobody's been in or out that front door since I got here. Your neighbor left after four o'clock. Only people I've seen have been the workmen across the lake. There was another car out here. Driver had long blond hair. He drove off in a rush as soon as I got out of my truck to talk to him."

"Derek Roland." Amy shoved her fingers through her hair and rubbed the tension gathering at the base of her skull. "Maybe he came to apologize."

Mark slipped his hand beneath her braid to take over the quick massage. "Or to find out what the police said about him stealing your friend's laptop."

That was a more likely scenario. And certainly, someone built like Matt Taylor with his spooky impassive glare would be more than enough of a threat to send a man like Derek scurrying back to whatever hole he'd crawled out of. "I'd better get Gran's suitcase out." She squeezed Matt's sturdy forearm as she moved past him. "Thank you for keeping an eye on things."

The glare softened with the hint of a smile. Matt tipped his head toward Mark. "You keep an eye on this one."

The change in Matt's expression felt like a hard-won seal of approval.

Amy smiled. "I will."

As Amy headed up the porch steps and unlocked the front door, she overheard Matt's words to his brother. "I hear you squared things with Grandma."

"We talked."

"Good man."

Apparently, *that* was another form of approval from Matt. And a goodbye. But Amy's attention had already shifted with concern as the two brothers shook hands and Matt climbed into his truck and drove away.

Amy was waiting inside the foyer when she heard Mark jogging up the steps behind her. Her eyes had started watering as soon as she'd stepped inside. She frowned at the haze hanging in the air. Something acrid stung her eyes and nose. "Brad and Richie must have left one of the stain cans open."

When she ducked beneath the scaffolding to check the sawhorses where they stored their tools and refinishing supplies, Mark grabbed her arm and jerked her back behind him. "That's not an open can of paint." A muscle ticked along his jaw as he tilted his nose into the air and sniffed. "Something's burning."

"What?" The tension she felt in his grip radiated through her. She looked up the stairs and around the foyer, searching for flames and smoke. "Are you sure?"

When she looked back at Mark, his eyes were focused on the landing above them. "Up there. Could be electrical. Could be some kind of delayed ignition. And we just fed it an influx of oxygen when we opened that front door. It's probably been smoldering since early this morning, before Matt got here. He never came inside, so he never noticed it." He crossed to the bottom of the stairs, pulling her with him. The haze at the top of the stairs was thicker, a swirling mist of grays that grew darker toward the ceiling. "Smoke will fill the upper levels first. It's had all day to work its way down to the first floor. What's up there?"

"Bedrooms. A guest bathroom."

"Is there an attic?"

Amy nodded. "You access it through the closet in my bedroom. On the far right."

Mark pulled her into a quick jog beside him as he ran back outside. "Come on. I've got a fire extinguisher in my truck."

He vaulted into the bed of his truck and unlocked the metal storage unit there. "Call 9-1-1. Tell them there's a second-story or attic fire. I won't know for sure until I find the source." Fire extinguisher in hand, he jumped down to the gravel and reached around her to open the driver's-side door. "Get in."

"You're not going back in there."

Just like he had this morning, he lifted her onto the seat. "Firefighter, Red. If I can put it out or contain it, I will. If not, help will already be on the way."

He pushed the door lock and closed it. Amy didn't waste any time playing the damsel in distress. The moment he turned his back, she shoved the door open again. "Shouldn't you wait for backup? Bad things happen in fires around here. At least let me come with you."

Three strides brought him back to the open truck door. "I can't be worrying about you *and* the fire. I'm not the one someone's been spying on. Stay safe. Lock yourself in." He pushed his phone into her hand. "Find my brother Matt's number and call him back here. He can be here faster than Firehouse 13." Amy nodded, already pulling out her own phone to dial 9-1-1. Before she could place either call, he reached through the open door, palmed the back of her head and pulled her to him for a quick, hard kiss. "I love you. Lock the doors. Call."

Then he was running back into the house. Amy remembered him bursting through the flames with Lissette Peterson in his arms. He'd been in full turnout gear that night. Jeans, a T-shirt and fire extinguisher were hardly enough protective equipment if he came across another woman he had to rescue.

Swallowing her fears and saying a prayer for his safety, Amy scrolled through his phone and found Matt's number. He picked up on the second ring. "Miss me, baby bro?"

"Matt? Amy Hall here. There's a fire somewhere upstairs in the house. Mark said to call you for backup. He's already inside. I don't want him in there alone."

She heard tires screeching on the pavement. Matt's reply was as reassuring as it was brief. "On my way."

Amy didn't take her eyes off the house as she dialed 9-1-1 and reported the fire to the dispatcher. The early evening sun reflected like inlaid gold off the top-floor windows as she visually imagined Mark charging up the stairs and searching through every room and the attic until he located the source of the fire he'd detected.

She'd just tilted her gaze to the open ventilation slats in the attic just below the peak of the roofline when one of those gold windows shattered and rained shards of glass down on the porch roof and ground below. "Oh, my God." The flames she'd been searching for earlier shot out through the broken window, like billowing arms reaching out for the oxygen it craved. She knew Mark was fit and fast, but he hadn't flown up the stairs and couldn't have reached her bedroom that quickly. "Mark?"

"Ma'am?"

"I see flames now," she reported to the dispatcher. "Second-story front window. Mark Taylor is inside. He's an off-duty firefighter. Send help. Send lots of help."

Someone else was in the house with the man she loved. She looked at the two phones in her hands. She couldn't call him and warn him.

She'd do it herself.

"Send the police, too!" Amy yelled before hanging up and stuffing both phones into her pockets. She dashed up the stairs and shoved open the door. A wave of smoke washed over her, filling her lungs and eyes. "Mark!" She coughed her lungs clear and ran to the bottom of the stairs. "Fire Man! He's here! He's already in the house with you!"

She heard a thud and a grunt and something metal and heavy rolling across the landing floor. "Mark?"

Fear propelled her up the first few steps, but she halted when she saw movement in the smoke above her. She squinted to bring the ghostly figures she saw moving through the smoke into focus. Two men. Was one carrying the other away from the smoke and flames? Were they fighting?

Before she fully understood what was happening, she saw Mark's inert body fold over the railing like a rag doll. "Mark!"

He hit the top level of the scaffolding with a smack and then the framework of metal tilted forward, wobbling, tipping, until the whole thing toppled over and crashed into the foyer. Amy jumped back against the wall as boards and metal poles and tools and cans hurtled down to the floor, bounced, broke apart and collapsed into a pile of burning tarps and dust and smoke.

"Mark!"

No, no, no, no, no! He couldn't be dead. Not her Fire Man. Amy raced down the stairs and climbed into the destruction, stepping where she could, flinging aside debris and crawling underneath the mangled scaffolding where she couldn't. She found Mark buried in the middle of it all. Lying so still. She bent over him to see blood oozing from a wound at the side of his head. She put her hand over his heart. It was beating, strong, fast. He'd taken a horrible blow to the head and was knocked out cold. There was a tear in his jeans where he was bleeding from a cut. But he was alive. *Please, God. Stay alive!*

"This is not how we're going to end," she vowed, rising to her feet and kicking aside the burning tarp that had landed near his feet. She could see the shiny gleam of the liquid someone had poured over it, liquid that disappeared as the flames drank up the flammable chemical. She was seriously coughing now, struggling to take in a full breath of air, but she was breathing. And as long as she was alive, she would fight. For this man, for her grandmother, for Jocelyn and the other women—she would fight. She curled her arms beneath his shoulders and pushed with her legs, pulling him away from the brightest of the flames, dragging him through the foyer toward the front door and fresh air.

All that breadth and strength she loved when he was awake and holding her now pulled against her like dead weight. She screamed with the exertion of dragging him to safety. When she butted against a cage-like wall of broken scaffolding, she set him down as gently as she could and shoved with all her might against it. Her eyes were burning and watering so badly now, she could barely see. She could barely catch her breath. She leaned over him to touch his heart and make sure he was still alive before summoning the last of her strength and rising to push the debris aside, since she couldn't pick him up and carry him over it.

She grunted as she pushed, then stumbled to the floor as the section of scaffolding suddenly rose into the air and flew into the stairs. What was happening? Had Matt arrived? Was someone here to help her?

Amy was looking at a scuffed pair of men's work boots when she pushed herself up onto her elbows. "He's hurt. We have to get him out…"

The man upstairs. Mark hadn't been alone.

She scrambled onto her bottom and scooted away, wanting to protect Mark from the man she guessed had pushed him over the railing. "Stay away from him." Her words were a feeble croak that scratched through her throat and triggered another coughing fit. "You didn't have to hurt him. Is it me you want?"

A scraped and bruised hand reached down to help her stand.

Amy followed the arm up to the man's face.

Sunburned cheeks puffed up as the man smiled down at her.

"I don't understand. Richie?" Brad Frick's friendly, simpleminded sidekick.

Not help. A killer. Jocelyn's killer.

When she didn't take his hand, he squatted in front of her. His tone was as friendly as ever. "I've got a special place all set up for us in your art studio."

"My studio? Us?" Why wasn't this making any sense? "Did you take pictures of me, Richie? Do you like taking pictures of women?"

"Yeah. Pretty women. I like them."

Amy's skin crawled. There was something wrong in this man's head, something she doubted she could reason with. "Did you take pictures of my friend Jocelyn? And Lissette over at the construction site? Did you kill them?"

"Stop talking. Walk with me." He grabbed her arm.

Amy shrugged him off and crawled to Mark's body, willing him to wake up, wanting to tell him she loved him, wondering if she had any chance of living through this night. Other than the blood on his head and leg, he looked as though he was sleeping. And she might never see his beautifully interesting face or feel his strong arms around her again.

"Miss Amy," Richie prompted. "You belong to me. I want you." He coughed behind her. Odd. Somehow, she'd expected an arsonist to be immune to smoke and fire. "The fire will hide my mistake," he said, as though burning Mark's body would be a reassurance to her. "Mr. O'Brien paid Brad and me to set fires. I liked it. Brad liked the money, but I thought it was fun. Now I use them to hide my mistakes."

Jocelyn was a mistake. Lissette was a mistake. Now Mark—and maybe she, too—would be the latest mistake covered up by Richie Sterling's fires.

"I won't leave him," she protested, hoping she could order Richie away from whatever he had planned. "You'll have to go without me."

"That's not how it works." He whined a little like a frustrated child who hadn't gotten his way. "I want you to walk with me to your studio."

Amy's pendant fell out of the neckline of her blouse and dangled in front of her as she bent over Mark. Her studio. She caught the pendant in her hand and tugged the chain from around her neck. Matt Taylor and the rest of Firehouse 13 were coming. She just had to stay alive long enough for help to arrive. Long enough for Mark to wake up and do his Captain Good Guy thing.

"Rescue me, Fire Man," she whispered against his ear before she pressed a kiss there and slipped her necklace into the pocket of his jeans.

Richie's hand clamped down around her upper arm in a bruising grip and he pulled Amy to her feet. She shoved at his chest and struggled against him. "I don't want to be another one of your mistakes. Richie, you have to let me go."

"Walk." He held up the mallet he must have struck Mark with. Blood dripped from the tip onto the antique oak floor. "Or I'll hit him again."

Chapter Fourteen

Mark was regaining consciousness as his brother Matt hauled him onto his shoulders and carried him from the burning house.

As soon as he laid him on the ground outside, Mark rolled onto his hands and knees, coughing the smoke and chemicals from his lungs and drawing in deep breaths of pure oxygen from the breathing mask, which Matt held over his nose and mouth. Ball bearings pinged back and forth inside his skull with every cough. But once his vision had cleared and the world stopped spinning, Mark staggered to his feet. "Where's Amy?" He looked toward his truck. The door was open, and the cab was empty. "Amy!"

Matt caught him by the arm and probed at the aching goose egg at his temple. "I haven't seen her. Hold still."

"I sent her out to wait in my truck. There was a guy upstairs. I don't know what he hit me with." Oh, no. Hell no. He turned back to the porch. "Amy must have ignored my warning and gone back in to help me. Amy!"

But Matt planted himself on the steps in front of him, blocking his path. "Uh-uh." He thumbed over his shoulder. "Fully engulfed. Neither of us is going back in there until the team comes with full gear."

Mark could see the flames shooting through an up-stairs window and thick black smoke puffing out the front door. He turned 360 degrees, looking for a flag of copper-red hair. But there was nothing. He had her. The bastard who'd killed those women and taken pictures of Amy had her. "Lucky 13 isn't here yet?"

"They're en route. Two minutes out, according to Redding."

"Good. She hasn't been gone that long, then. He can't have gotten far."

"Gone?" Matt's tone was calm, but urgent. "Where? Where's Amy?"

Matt patted his pockets for his phone, then swore when he remembered he'd left it with Amy. "I can't call her."

Matt pulled out his cell. "Use mine."

Then Mark felt the lump in his front pocket. What the hell? He pulled out Amy's necklace, studied it in his hand. "She never takes this off."

A memory stirred in his foggy brain. *Rescue me, Fire Man.* He'd heard the words like he remembered a dream when he was about to wake up.

"I know where she is." He stuffed the necklace into his pocket.

"All right, let's go."

"No." He put up his hand to stop his brother. There was more than one threat here, and Mark couldn't stop them both. Amy had already lost enough. "I don't want to panic him, in case he hurts her." He ran around the side of the house, glimpsing the copper roof of Amy's art studio. "You got an ax in your truck?"

Matt was back in a matter of seconds and handed it to him. "You sure you don't want me to do this? I'm ninety-nine percent sure you've got a concussion."

"No. You take care of the fire." Mark swung the ax, gripping the handle in both hands before moving up the hill. "This is personal."

AMY SAT ON the edge of the sofa, chewing at the ropes Richie had tied around her wrists. He seemed inordinately interested in standing up to the copper garden alien she'd been sculpting. He thumped his chest against the sculpture's copper chest piece and laughed when it rattled. He picked up nearly every piece of glass and trash she'd sorted into various cubbies, sliding a couple into his pockets and tossing aside others.

Her first goal was freeing herself from the ropes that were cutting into her skin. The next step would be finding a way to unlock the padlocks he'd installed inside both the front and garage doors. Of course, she'd have to get past Richie himself first. And while she believed she could outthink him, he'd already proved that she couldn't outmuscle him.

And then she wanted to get back to the house. She wanted to get Mark out of there before the flames consumed him, before he suffocated, before she lost him forever. As tears stung her eyes and panic welled inside her, Amy angrily shoved them aside.

One problem at a time.

Now Richie had discovered her welding equipment. He clicked her lighter on several times, grinning each time it sparked a tiny flame. Fortunately, he set it aside before moving on to the tanks. He turned each valve on, hissing along with the release of the gas, inhaling a sinusful from each tank. "You shouldn't leave them on like that," she warned, keeping her voice as friendly as possible. Since the windows and doors were all locked shut, she could smell the gases gathering inside the building.

"It isn't safe. It will eat up the oxygen and you could pass out. Or cause an explosion if you're not careful."

She dutifully dropped her hands to her lap when he turned to her. He still carried that mallet he'd used to hammer paint cans shut, swinging it through the air and pounding it down on different surfaces inside her studio, as though he enjoyed hearing the different sounds of smashing, bending and breaking.

"I like fire." Why wasn't that a surprise? "I don't know if I like explosions."

When he picked up a pry bar to pop off the brass tokens she'd used for eyes on her alien sculpture, Amy went back to work on the knot at her wrists.

"You found my treasures. You took them from me and gave them to Mr. O'Brien. I want some of your treasures to put in my box."

"I'll give you anything you want here, Richie. Just let me go."

He dropped his gaze to her hands in her lap, shaking his head as if he knew what she'd been doing all along. "You weren't nice to me. You gave away my treasures."

The strongbox with the incriminating evidence. She'd thought Dale O'Brien had murdered those women. He'd just been anxious to remove anything that would link him to the fires. Maybe he'd even suspected that Brad or Richie had killed Lissette, but if anyone found out he'd hired them, they might think he was the killer. "Those are your pictures? Your fire-starting kit?"

"The cotton balls are just to start the fire. But stain and turpentine burn really well once you get it lit." He sat down beside her, bumping his leg against hers. She didn't bother trying to slide away because he still held the mallet, and she'd seen the dent in Jocelyn's skull. "Mr. O'Brien paid Brad and me to burn down your stuff.

Drive down the property value, or plain ol' scare you away from wantin' to stay. He said you and Miss Comfort had something he wanted." He plucked her braid from her shoulder and ran his fingers along its length. "You have something I want, too."

Amy breathed deeply through her nose, swallowing the urge to gag or run away as Richie caressed her hair.

"So, O'Brien is responsible for those fires." She intended to get that man arrested and as far away from her and her gran as she could. If she got away from Richie. Amy pushed the doubt out of her head. *When* she got away from Richie. Except for the ropes. And the locks. And the mallet. "You killed my friend Jocelyn. And Lissette."

"They were nice to me."

"You killed them because they were nice to you?"

"Like you're nice to me. Touching me. Smiling. Talking." His hand fisted around her braid, pulling painfully on her scalp. "Only you don't mean it any more than they did." He leaned in and rubbed a wet, juvenile kiss against her neck. "You're gonna be nice to me, aren't you, Miss Amy? The way you were nice to that fireman of yours?"

Amy watched his grip loosen on the mallet as he pulled her hair to turn her mouth to his.

No. No man was going to hurt her again.

Summoning her courage, letting her anger at too many injustices fuel her strength, Amy rammed her elbow into Richie's nose. As he cried out in pain and grabbed at his face, she rose, grabbing the mallet and slinging it as hard as she could across the room.

She ran to her workbench. She knew the weapon she needed to keep Richie away from her. She knew the tool she needed to cut her way through those locks. He'd already done half the work for her by turning on her oxyacetylene tanks. As long as the air hadn't truly filled with gas, she could do this without blowing herself up.

"Miss Amy!" With blood dripping from his broken nose, Richie lunged after her. If he hadn't wasted precious seconds looking for his weapon of choice and not finding the mallet, he would have reached her. "That wasn't nice!"

She dived for the lighter. Although she was hindered by her bound hands, she'd done this so often that she created a spark on the second strike. She grabbed the nearest hose.

Richie's hands were in her hair when she lit the torch and whirled around, bringing the cutting fire down over his arm and freeing herself. The torch hummed with power as she swung it again, aiming for one of those sunburned cheeks.

He staggered back, burned and bleeding, as she dragged the tank from its shelf. It crashed to the floor, disconnecting the hose. The torch went out and she dropped it, reaching for the lighter and igniting the second torch. It was impossible to aim the torch and carry the canister to the door with her hands tied.

Hold him off with the torch? Or run to the locked door?

Richie had the mallet in his fist again when he kicked aside a stool and screamed at her. "Why won't you be nice?"

Amy dropped the torch and ran to the door. "Help me! Somebody help!"

She rattled the padlock in useless frustration, wondering why Richie hadn't tackled her to the floor and smashed her head in already. Then she turned.

And realized the error she'd made.

Richie Sterling had dropped his mallet and picked

up the burning flame of her welding torch. He ran the flame across her workbench, setting the wood on fire. Her drawings and desk went next.

"Richie, please!" She ran to the garage door and had no luck with the lock there, either.

He was going to burn this whole place down. He didn't care if he died. So long as the woman who'd been too mean to love him or make out with him or whatever misguided obsession he wanted to live out died, too.

He was at the sofa now, lighting it on fire and watching the flames.

The pry bar.

Amy blinked away the tears she had no time to shed and searched the floor to find the pry bar Richie had used and discarded. She'd slipped it behind the latch of the garage door when she heard a crash from the studio's front door.

She spun around as the wood splintered. Richie turned, too, holding the blinding torch in front of him like a flamethrower.

Something heavy smashed into the door again, breaking through. She saw the glint of a shiny ax head reflecting the flames from the fire. It disappeared and then crashed through the door again, sending it flying off its hinges.

And then Mark was there. Battered and bleeding, strong and every bit the heroic nickname she teased him with. "Amy!"

"Mark! Look out!"

Richie rushed toward him, but Mark was ready. Before the flame ever reached him, he jabbed the ax forward, hitting Richie square in the chest and knocking him back into the flames. He screamed and tried to escape, but the fire he loved was climbing the walls, surrounding him, consuming him.

Amy ran to Mark, pushing him toward the broken door. "Gas!"

He smelled it, too. He glanced down at her bound hands, and then, without so much as a grunt of effort, he swung her up into his arms and ran. The studio exploded behind them, knocking them both to the ground. His arms snapped around her to break their fall and they rolled several feet until they came to a stop with Amy lying on top of him.

Mark squeezed his eyes shut and tipped his head back into the dry grass, obviously working through some kind of pain.

"Mark?" Amy tried to frame his face between her hands, but the ropes wouldn't allow her to do more than cup his chin and run her fingers across his lips. "Mark? Are you okay? How badly are you hurt?"

His smoky blue eyes popped open and he lifted his head to kiss her. They were breathless from exertion and the kiss was short, but there was no doubting the clarity in his eyes or the laughter bubbling up from his throat. "Damn, woman. You *are* a lot of trouble."

And then they were sitting up and she was laughing, too. He untied her wrists and inspected the rope burns there. "Your pale skin shows every mark." He kissed the injuries, kissed her mouth, even as she tried to inspect the knot and dried blood at his temple.

"Do you get hurt every time you fight a fire?"

"I'm fine," he assured her. "I will be fine," he corrected. "Now that I know you're safe."

"How? How did you know where to find me?"

He dangled her pendant from his hand—his beautiful, perfect hand. "I got your message."

A trio of firefighters ran past them with a hose. When one of them stopped to ask how badly they were hurt, Mark waved them on to her studio. "Man inside. Probably didn't make it."

With a promise to check to see if Richie had survived, the man ran on. Mark reached for Amy's hand and pulled her to her feet. "Come on. We're in the way here. I want the medics to check you out."

"You, too." She'd make sure of that.

But the Lucky 13 fire engines parked in her driveway and in the yard in front of the house weren't the only flashing lights she saw. "Are those police cars at Dale O'Brien's place?"

"I bet they're taking O'Brien and Brad Frick in for questioning."

"O'Brien paid Brad and Richie to set fires on our property."

"I suspected as much."

"Richie saw the fires as an opportunity to hide his crimes when his...obsessive crushes...didn't work out." Mark pulled her to his side and got her walking toward the ambulance again, avoiding the firefighters who were fighting a losing battle to save her grandmother's historic home. "I don't think he understood how people work, how to interact in a normal, healthy way. I almost feel sorry for him."

"I don't. I almost lost you because of him."

"*I* almost lost *you*."

"Matt will make sure the paramedics clear me, or he'll drive me to the hospital himself."

"I like Matt."

"No. You like *me*."

"I do. So does my grandmother. That's a good sign, I

think." She jerked when a timber cracked and fell inside the house. "Gran's going to miss that house."

Mark kept her tucked to his side as they watched the destruction. "I think she'd rather have you than the house."

Amy turned her face to Mark's shoulder. "So, are we ever going to go out on that date?"

"I'm the one who keeps asking." He pressed a kiss to her temple, then turned her away from the sad loss of her childhood home. "I think this is more than a heat-of-the-moment, opposites-attracting kind of thing."

Amy nodded. "I guess you had to rescue me after all." She laid her hand over the strong beat of his heart. "But I need you to love me even more."

Mark pulled her into his arms. "Done."

* * * * *

COLTON 911: ULTIMATE SHOWDOWN

ADDISON FOX

For April, Carley, Christine and Roxane.
Sisters of the heart. Always.

Prologue

It's called a safe house for a reason.

Sadie Colton had told herself that endlessly and she was no closer to liking it or believing the seriousness of the words. And she was sick to death of being cooped up with nothing but her awful thoughts and even worse self-recriminations.

How could she have been so stupid?

And not just sort-of-flighty-edging-toward-stupid stupid. Oh no, she was in that special league of foolishness that bordered on too ridiculously stupid to live, nullified only by the whole safe house thing.

That meant she was stuck. Physically *and* emotionally.

She tossed a few paperbacks into a packing box. How could she not have known? Was she so desperate for a relationship that she'd ignored every single sign her fiancé was a piece of crap? Worse, that he was the head of an entire criminal empire, a loan sharking organization called Capital X.

And she'd had no idea.

Not. One. Single. Clue.

She was a freaking crime scene investigator, for

heaven's sake. That—*hello?*—meant she hunted clues for a living. Clues she uncovered and then used to solve crimes with the most minimal of information…

But if she tried to solve for "X" in Capital X, all she got was *Capitally Duped*. Worse, she was obviously clue*less* about her own life.

The same scenes that had kept her company flooded her mind once more. The time she'd spent with Tate, so convinced he was the man she'd waited her whole life for. Followed by the stunning realization the man she'd been so close to binding her life with was not only a bad guy, but had only been with her to get close to the Grand Rapids PD and her family's business.

Colton Investigations was one of the premier private investigative firms in the country and did work for both the Grand Rapids PD as well as private citizens locally and nationally. It was painful to acknowledge, but she now knew her family name and connections had been the only things Tate Greer had seen when he'd looked at her. And he'd preyed on her deep-seated desire for love and a family of her own as his way in.

Only now it had all blown sky-high. One of Tate's top goons at Capital X, Gunther Johnson, had been pulled in by the GRPD a few months ago. And now the team was after Tate. Sadie had gone from dupe to target, as kidnapping her would give Tate a huge bargaining chip against her family. Both the biological one and the metaphorical one she shared with the GRPD.

So here she was, squirreled away in some hidey-hole while others were doing the real work of catching Tate and taking down his criminal empire.

Her mind drifted to what her colleagues in CSI as

well as the broader GRPD might think of her. Men and women who worked so hard to keep the good citizens of Grand Rapids safe and who were, even now, dealing with a criminal enterprise that had roots that went deeper than anyone really knew.

What did Tripp think?

Although she'd avoided personal flights of fancy since the faint stirrings of attraction she'd tamped down on in her early days with the force, Lieutenant Tripp McKellar helped run a tight ship at the GRPD. He'd also always had the uncanny ability to make her pulse kick up a few notches when she was in his presence. Even once she'd fallen in love with Tate, she'd never been fully immune to the lieutenant's appeal. She'd never do anything, of course—Tripp fell firmly in the off-limits category and always had—but she couldn't fully ignore that little flutter she kept secret.

Now he likely thought she was a ridiculous fool, not to mention a drain on department resources. All while he'd been working overtime on the RevitaYou case. The very case that had brought Tate's shady dealings into the light.

What was supposed to be a virtual miracle worker of an antiaging supplement, turning the clock back ten years for anyone who took the product, had been exposed for its dirty underpinnings. RevitaYou not only *wasn't* a miracle, it was a dangerous one at that. Its "restorative" properties came with a nasty side effect—death due to castor oil in the product that turned into ricin. It gave RevitaYou its functional properties but had horrifying side effects. The product inventor, Landon Street, had already been caught, but the damage his product had wrought was already extensive. Add distribution via a pyramid scheme masterminded by Capital X, and Tripp was dealing with an incredibly vile business.

Her family had been helping however it could, but the shady powerbrokers behind the scenes had been running her eldest brother, Riley, ragged as he tried to manage the investigation, help their foster brother, Brody Higgins, who'd gotten mixed up in it all, *and* run Colton Investigations.

And here she was, the proverbial princess in a tower, locked away and unable to help anyone.

A princess who was about to go on the move.

Again.

Her family had decided she needed to relocate to a new safe house and, having been out of the loop for the past month, she'd agreed.

At least she got to see her twin, Vikki.

"You said you were thinking you'd re-up for another five years." Sadie looked around the room, marveling at how relieved she was to be leaving the small space.

Her twin was a JAG paralegal and had always taken her military service seriously. But Vik juggled a lot and Sadie was surprised to realize how much she hoped her sister would slow down a bit and remain closer to home.

"I know I did. I've so loved the Army job, but it's time for me to make a change. I want to focus exclusively on CI. This way I can support Riley without always feeling so torn between my active duty time or working for CI."

"I never looked at it that way," Sadie said. "You really haven't had a break in a long time, have you?"

Sadie understood that battle. Riley was regularly trying to recruit her full time to the family cause. And while there were definitely appealing aspects to working for the family business, she loved her work in CSI and wasn't ready to give it up.

"No, but I get fun in where I can," Vikki said.

Fun.

Sadie remembered fun. Once upon a time. Before she'd fallen in love with Tate Greer and had believed a bright future still awaited her.

The low growl of her stomach had her glancing in the direction of the kitchen. She didn't skip meals.

A fact she'd worried over while engaged to Tate.

She actually *liked* her curves, but Tate had a way about him that had always left her a little intimidated. Like she should count herself lucky, somehow. Not lucky like how-great-is-it-I-found-the-love-of-my-life lucky, but more of a my-luck-is-going-to-run-out-if-I-do-something-wrong lucky.

And really, she admitted to herself, that wasn't any sort of lucky at all.

A fact that only added one *more* check in the box on the list of self-recriminations over why she'd ignored the small but insistent voice in the back of her mind.

Seeking a diversion from her low thoughts, Sadie pressed Vikki about the man she'd fallen in love with. "Speaking of fun, what have you heard from Flynn since last week's takedown?"

"I won't talk about it anymore, Sadie."

Sadie felt that small flash of anger that flared whenever she had an argument with her twin, but the misery that hovered deep in Vikki's gaze had Sadie holding her tongue.

Vikki and Flynn had been through a lot. The RevitaYou case was personal to Flynn and she had to imagine the man was dealing with a lot. Especially the news that his family member was instrumental in the development of the drug. "I still think I'm right. Landon was his half brother, for heaven's sake. That's a huge family deal. I'm sure Flynn needs time to process, and to do all the Army paperwork for why he was involved in the apprehension while he was on leave. Then you'll hear from him. When he knows it's right for both of you."

Sadie didn't get the sense Vikki agreed with her but she let her twin talk it out a bit before shifting gears to more inane topics like how she was going to keep busy.

"Time to go, Sadie." Her brother Riley walked into the room, his impatient gaze scanning the luggage. "You sure have collected a lot of stuff for being locked down the past several weeks."

"We'll get it in the car ourselves, don't you worry," Vikki batted back at their brother.

Riley scanned the room. "I'd rather wait until the FBI gets here. Give it five minutes. I'm going to do a quick sweep of the house and use the restroom."

Sadie knew they needed to be careful. The threat was real, no matter how much she wanted to believe otherwise. But all this process…

Moving to a new safe house. Waiting for an FBI escort. She let out a small sigh as the sound of vehicles echoed from outside the door. It was all too much.

"That's our cue." Vikki picked up a box.

Whether it was the desire to taunt her brother or just

the mindlessly boring stretch of time yawning in front of her, Sadie picked up another box and tilted her head toward the door. "I'd love to have the truck packed before Riley's out of the bathroom."

As usual, her twin was in sync and Vikki pushed through the door, propping the screen with her foot. Sadie juggled the box, walking through the door as a low growl registered from behind Vikki's shoulder.

"Don't move or your sister's dead, Vikki."

Sadie saw it happen. She heard the words and registered the press of a gun to Vikki's temple, all while the carefully packed box dropped with a thud on the front porch of the safe house.

The same man stared pointedly at Sadie. "Either of you make a sound, you're all dead."

"Take her. Now!"

Sadie felt big hands close over her shoulders but wasn't able to do anything but stare. She was shocked stone-cold still by the voice of her ex-fiancé, echoing in the cold December air. Her feet finally moved as she registered the hard press of a gun to her back, pushing her forward.

"Hi, honey." Tate Greer grinned at her from where he stood beside a large SUV. The menace lacing that smile was only matched by the equally threatening sight of the semiautomatic held high in his right hand. "You're coming home with me."

Chapter One

Tripp McKellar rubbed a hand over his growling stomach, the only acknowledgment he gave to the long hours he'd put in these past two days.

Sadie Colton was missing.

He'd sworn to her family he'd find her, but the continuously ticking clock—one that came with no answers to her whereabouts—had him working overtime with no solution in sight.

And the increasing fear he wouldn't get to her in time.

As dark images flashed through his mind, Tripp pushed them aside, just as he had for the past few days. Just as he had pushed aside his attraction for Sadie these past several years. His full focus needed to be on finding her.

Despite the increasingly dark thoughts that clouded his mind, he remained equally hopeful Tate Greer was playing a bigger game. Why kidnap her if the man wasn't going to use it to his advantage? Sadie was only a bargaining chip if she were alive, and Tripp held on tightly to the fact that Greer knew that.

Only, Greer hadn't reached out yet, outlining his demands. Nor had he given any indication he was going to.

That left Tripp right back at square one.

Sadie was missing, in the hands of a dangerous madman, and he was no closer to finding her than he had been thirty-six hours ago when she'd been first taken.

Her sister Vikki had fired the warning shot over the bow, convinced her twin was in trouble despite the repeated checks the GPRD had made on Sadie in that safe house. Although he trusted his team, he trusted the Colton family, as well, and Vikki Colton was known for her cool head and her love of her family. Tripp and his team had moved in the very night Vikki had sounded the alarm and were too late.

Too damn late. He uttered a dark curse before he stood and marched over to his office wall and the oversize map of Grand Rapids and the surrounding county. No matter how scared he was for Sadie's safety, he had to *think*. Really think, instead of giving in to the continued self-recrimination that had kept him company for two days.

He'd been working the RevitaYou case for several months now; the various marks on that map reflections of what he'd already learned. "Think, McKellar," he muttered to himself. "What do you know?"

His gaze scanned the map once more, following a radius around the safe house. He still hadn't figured out how Greer had found it, which would be his next order of business once he got Sadie back. He'd already dealt a few months ago with a corrupt cop in his department. Joe McRath's death had sent some serious ripples through the GRPD, and they were still dealing with the emotional fallout and loss of trust.

Corrupt cops had a way of doing that.

And now he had a problem with a department safe house? How the hell were some of the worst criminals in the county getting their hands on sensitive information like that?

It was an urgent problem, but one he had to deprioritize until he found Sadie. And while he'd like to bring in help to uncover the mole, he didn't know whom he could trust to ferret out the answer.

A problem for a different day, he reminded himself as the frustration threatened to swamp him. In the meantime, he had to go on the information he had.

Several points on the map were marked with red pushpins, representative of Capital X crimes. The thugs rarely took out hits in public. Rather, they enjoyed preying on their victims then taking them to a secure location to rough them up. That was how the Coltons had gotten involved in the first place. Brody Higgins, a young man who'd been a part of their family after moving through the foster care system, had gotten in with the Capital X crowd. He hadn't known the depth of Capital X's depravity until it was too late. What started as a demand for money a mark had inevitably borrowed with no ability to pay back, slowly morphed into an exercise in torture and abject pain.

But it also meant there was very little creativity with respect to where the bodies were dropped.

Thinking about their torture methods—and the immediate danger to Sadie, who had been engaged to their boss—had his stomach curling, but Tripp pushed it back. What was on this map he could use? With that foremost in his mind, he evaluated the red pushpin locations again. Once they'd narrowed in on Capital X as a crime organization, they'd begun to understand some of their patterns. With each layer of investigation, they'd added more pushpins to their map.

There were three clusters. One near the spot where Capital X henchman Gunther Johnson had been captured. One in a run-down public park on the outskirts of the city. And one at a large lake outside of Grand Rapids.

Was it possible?

Tripp quickly calculated the distance between the safe house and the lake, and estimated there couldn't be more than about fifteen miles between them.

Had Sadie been that close all along?

With an image of the lake and surrounding area filling his mind's eye, Tripp snagged his coat off the back of his chair and slipped it on, covering the holstered weapon strapped to his back. The clutch piece at his ankle was an additional weight of security as he headed for the door.

They still had one of Capital X's henchmen in custody. It looked like it was time to have a little talk with Gunther Johnson.

SADIE STARED AT the walls of the small room she'd been in for who knew how long and counted off what she knew in her head. Tate's unexpected arrival had been the start of this ordeal. She'd been fed three meals since then, and another two today, so two full days hadn't yet passed.

Nor had she seen Tate.

A tactic or something else? Was he out making misery on others? Worse, was he plotting and planning against her family? Against the GRPD?

Thoughts of her coworkers filled her mind's eye, from the dispatch staff to the detectives' squad to her fellow crime scene investigators. She meticulously cataloged each of them in her head, saving the best for last.

Tripp McKellar.

Whether it was the despair of the past few days or an inability to hold her mind back any longer, she'd finally given her thoughts of their tall, imposing lieutenant free reign in her mind.

She cared for him and always had. Perhaps he was unattainable, but that didn't make her feelings any less real. Or her attraction to him any less powerful. How funny that with Tate's true nature revealed, it only served to highlight even further what a good man Tripp McKellar was.

No flashy persona or bad-boy good looks like Tate. Instead, there was raw honesty, framed out in a square jaw, dark blond hair and blue eyes that had seen sadness yet had never become bitter. He was full of strength without being hard-edged. There was power in that, Sadie acknowledged to herself.

Real power.

It also left her with a very real, very tangible, counterpoint to Tate Greer. The pill of his betrayal had been terribly bitter to swallow, but she'd spent a lot of time thinking about their relationship during the long, lonely days in the safe house. She'd dissected it, forcing herself to really look deeply at what choices she'd made, voluntarily.

It had also given her time to think about the things she'd overlooked.

"YOU COULDN'T HAVE KNOWN, Sadie. No one could have." Vikki's voice was gentle but the grim set of her face carried the same conviction Sadie had felt since the moment Tate's true nature had come to light.

"I'm a trained cop. I should have known," Sadie shot back.

"How? Is clairvoyance in the job description for either role?"

"No, but I do know how to consider the angles. How to evaluate data and pull clues from it, no matter how little evidence I have to go on. Yet I allowed Tate Greer into my life—" Sadie flung a hand wide "—into all our lives. And for what? Because I was so damn happy to finally have a man?"

That look of fierce protection on her twin's face shifted, remolding itself into a mask of pure and utter fury.

"Don't talk about yourself that way. I won't hear of it or tolerate it. You're a good person, Sadie. You've got the biggest heart of anyone I know. More, I know you. Know who you are and how you see the world. Do not let some jerk like Tate Greer, a man who has proved himself to prey on others, taint that. Or make you question yourself."

THE REMEMBERED CONVERSATION winked out of her mind, replaced by the breath-stealing fear she'd never see her sister again. Although their conversation at the safe house suggested Vikki and Flynn had a lot to figure out, her twin had fallen for Flynn Cruz-Street, the US MP who worked on the same Army base as Vikki did. After he was attacked on base by his captain, who had discharged his weapon, Vikki had been immersed in the case as the JAG paralegal.

All because of RevitaYou…

Sadie considered that, turning it over in her mind.

Some wonder drug. A supposed miracle pill that was killing people.

A shady operation helmed by her ex-fiancé, masterminding it all.

And all of it unraveling, right here in the hands of Colton Investigations and the Grand Rapids PD.

Sadie let out a hard sigh.

How had they missed it for so long? A question Tripp was no doubt asking himself. They didn't know each other well, but she had no doubt this case was causing him lost sleep and a level of personal heartache only someone who demanded so much from himself professionally could manage.

Even now, she could picture the hard set of his jaw as he worked through the problem. She'd talked to him a few times since the RevitaYou case had broken, her own family deeply integrated in the investigation. Her oldest brother, Riley, the head of Colton Investigations, had been working the case since former foster kid Brody Higgins had come to them for help.

The Coltons had taken the misguided eighteen-year-old in after he'd aged out of the foster system but wasn't quite ready to be on his own. Her father had believed in Brody's innocence of a deadly crime, but had been murdered before he could prove it. Even with Graham Colton's pull as the district attorney, it had been a hard fight to see Brody proven innocent. It had been a tough road, but it had made them all appreciate their father's life's work that much more.

And, whether by accident or fate, it had led to the formation of Colton Investigations.

It might now be her brother's life's work, but all of the children of Graham and Katherine Colton took part. The fight for justice, instilled in them by their father, ran deep in the blood.

So when Brody had come to Riley back in July, confessing his part in the RevitaYou scheme, their collective, underlying desire was to berate the young man they'd all come to see as a brother. But as the case wore on, and Brody had disappeared after being attacked by Capital X—*Tate's*—goons, Sadie had come to realize it was something else entirely.

RevitaYou was not only a pyramid scheme, it was killing people. Good people, like Teri Joseph, the wife of Flynn's former captain. And several other victims whose names had been linked to the drug and whose photos, even now, she was sure were pinned to Tripp's crime board at the police station.

Brody had found out about the negative aspects of RevitaYou far too late. He'd fallen for the sales pitch and the mind-bending results the drug produced in the first few weeks of use. Because of it, Brody had rushed to invest, taking funding from Capital X to support his "investment." Only there wasn't any investment to be had, only a pyramid scheme and a violent organization waiting at the other end to collect. One that used the darkest corners of the internet to do its work.

Sadie shuddered, the image of Brody being brutalized at the hands of Tate's men spearing through her.

He was still alive—it was hard to get money out of a dead mark—but Capital X sure loved making life miserable for those who couldn't pay. Since that was the essence of their business model—either pay back a loan at exorbitant rates or get your fingers broken, one by one—their operation was never at a loss for capital.

Or, apparently, marks to do their bidding.

And she'd missed it all. Missed Tate's romancing her to get close to Colton Investigations as well as the GRPD.

Missed the fact that he'd disappeared for stretches at a time that she'd chalked up to a businessman needing the space to run his business.

And she'd sure as hell missed every single sign that suggested he was a violent sociopath whose need to control everything and everyone around him went bone deep.

Now she was here, and her family knew she was missing, and Tripp was trying to solve the case, and it was all a raging mess. One with violent undertones that—as the hours passed—she convinced herself had no pathway to a good end.

"Way to be a defeatist, Colton," she muttered to herself. And just as tears threatened, she heard her father's voice in her head.

What do you know, Sadie Pie? Not what you think, but what you know...

With her father's reassuring voice still ringing in

her head, Sadie pushed down—*hard*—on the idea that she'd never see her twin sister or her family or anyone else she cared about. Instead, she forced herself to go through what she *knew.*

Because she might not be guaranteed a happy ending but she sure as hell wasn't going to willingly proceed even further into a nightmare.

That meant she had to think. She had to be smart. And she had to quit worrying about all the reasons she was in this mess and start thinking of ways to get herself out of it.

Although Tate and his henchmen had subdued her the other night at the safe house, they hadn't drugged her. That had given her a rough estimate in her mind of how long it had taken them to arrive at wherever she was now. She wasn't any more than fifteen or twenty minutes from the safe house.

With a map of the county spreading out in her mind, she worked it through, the safe house the epicenter of her mental images. Fifteen to twenty minutes one direction took her to downtown Grand Rapids, but it had been too quiet outside for her to think they were in the city. With one direction checked off, she analyzed the others. As she worked it slowly in her mind, a vague memory of the drive to summer camp shot up to surprise her.

She hadn't wanted to go that first year and the drive to Sand Springs Lake had seemed over before it had barely begun. Her mother had assured her that not only would Sadie have an amazing time at camp, but if she needed anything, her parents were only twenty minutes away.

Twenty minutes away...

Was it that easy? Was she really that close?

Willing her pounding heart to slow, she ran the map through her mind's eye once more, following the various directions to the land formations that stretched out. And came up with the same conclusion the second time around.

She remained absolutely certain she wasn't downtown. And she'd bet anything she was nowhere near the suburbs that speared off in another direction from the safe house. That only left Sand Springs Lake or more distant suburbs broken up by farmland in the final direction. A secluded lake in December made a heck of a lot of sense.

Sadie searched her memory for any conversation she and Tate might have had about the area surrounding Grand Rapids, her summer camp experiences, holiday vacation cottages, or anything else that might have been said in passing conversation. In retrospect, that should have been another clue—that she and Tate really hadn't *talked* about anything. As the urge to berate herself welled up again, the tiniest fraction of a memory hit her full-on.

"My loathing for the great outdoors started early in life. Summer camp to be exact."

Tate smiled before running the tip of his finger over her hip. "Not a nature girl?"

"So not a nature girl."

"Like I couldn't have guessed that."

Sadie heard the slight sharpness through the joke but pushed it down. Did she have to take everything so seriously? Ignoring the prick of discomfort, she laid a hand over his, lacing their fingers. "Well, you can thank Sand Springs Lake for beating any sense of natural adventure out of me. From archery to rowing, I hated it all. I can still imagine all the creepy things floating on the bottom of that lake, just waiting for me if we accidentally tipped our canoe."

"There's not much in that lake. A few secrets, maybe." He leaned in then, pressing a kiss to her neck and distracting her from the conversation.

HE'D DONE THAT a lot, she'd realized in her month-long, mental, deep-dive dissection into the sad, tragic tale of Sadie Colton's engagement to Tate Greer. If he hadn't been asking her questions, he'd been distracting her with sex. And in her naïveté she hadn't even been aware it was happening.

She'd had a lot of time to think about that, too. It was uncomfortable emotional work, but she'd made herself look at her responses to Tate—and her willingness to ignore signs—assuming it was due to her lack of prior relationships. While it had become comforting—and way too comfortable—to wallow in those memories, she had to acknowledge this one paid dividends. Not only had they discussed Sand Springs Lake and Tate had made that weird comment about secrets, he had swung back around to that discussion after sex. And he'd mentioned loving the lake and spending time there as a kid.

If he'd loved it then, it stood to reason he'd love it as an adult. And he'd equally recognize that a lake used by summer camps didn't have a lot of need for the area once the weather turned cold.

A secluded lake would be highly beneficial for his purposes. It kept him close enough to Grand Rapids to get in and out of the city for business, and it kept him secluded enough to manage his dirty deeds far away from the notice of law enforcement.

A heavy thud echoed through the walls and Sadie heard the harsh laughter of Tate's goons. She still hadn't gotten names for either of them so had dubbed them Fred and Barney for lack of anything better. The names had fit if for no other reason than one was big and brutish-looking and the other was spark-plug short, with a round barrel chest and empty eyes.

She'd filed away other details, too. They spent minimal time with her, bringing in her food and ignoring any question she asked. It was eerie how they were able to be present yet completely absent.

As if they'd been brainwashed by Tate to do nothing but carry out his orders.

For all her upset at how Tate had played her, there was a bigger part of Sadie that recognized those same lifeless eyes and automatous countenance could have been her if she'd ended up with Tate Greer. Much as it pained her to imagine it, the thought also gave her strength.

And much needed purpose.

The door swung open and Barney walked in. He barely glanced at her as he crossed the room to set a plate of food on a small table. Sadie could see the outer room beyond the door, and wasn't sure if it was an accident that Barney had left the door open or a small of-

fering from the universe, but decided worrying about
it only wasted time.

She had to move.

So with speed born of desperate purpose, she did.

TRIPP RACED TOWARD Sand Springs Lake, located on the
outskirts of Grand Rapids. It was known around the
state as a summer destination, with a variety of kids'
camps populating the perimeter as well as a canoeing
outfit that had become quite a draw in recent years. Despite a swelling population when the weather warmed,
the entire area remained fairly isolated in the winter.

As each mile ticked past, Tripp vacillated between
the satisfaction that he was right, and he'd get Sadie
back, and the horror that if he was wrong he'd only
add more time to the hours she'd been missing without discovery.

Just like Lila.

Tripp shook his head.

It was nothing like Lila.

Nothing at all like knowing someone he'd cared for
had been gunned down in cold blood by someone with
a vendetta. Not against the pregnant woman at the end
of the bullet, but against the man she'd loved, cared for,
and had chosen to spend her life with.

Tripp scrubbed a hand over his face, the two-day-old
beard scratching against the tips of his fingers.

*Focus. Don't let the memories come. Don't listen to
the lies they weave beneath the truth you know.*

Wasn't that what his therapist had told him? The
professional he'd finally given in and gone to see at the
urging of his chief, Andrew Fox. He'd given it an honest

shot, despite his skepticism, but in the end, other than a few coping mechanisms for times of extreme stress, Tripp could hardly call the sessions time well spent.

What could a therapist do, really? A criminal Tripp had put away, but whom the justice system had set free on a technicality, had gunned down his pregnant fiancée. Instead of coming after Tripp to settle the score, the bastard had found another way.

One far more meaningful and destructive.

Other than coping day to day through life, there wasn't anything else to do.

That was why he had to help Sadie. He'd made a promise to her family. Moreover, he'd made a promise to her and each and every member of the GRPD when he'd sworn he'd fight to protect them.

And if there was that small matter of how he'd always noticed her, a small shot of attraction he refused to act on simmering just beneath the surface, well, he'd accept it. Use it, really, to keep himself focused.

Because damn it, he was getting her back.

His cell rang, penetrating the urgent thoughts. He hit the Bluetooth button on his steering wheel just as he made the last turn onto the two-lane road that led to Sand Springs Lake. "McKellar."

"Where the hell are you?" Detective Emmanuel Iglesias's voice shot through the car's speaker. "Michaela just told me you put out a call for backup."

Although playing a hunch, Tripp hadn't been foolish enough to go in alone and had called Dispatch before leaving. But he had refused to wait around for anyone to join him. Every second was precious and Sadie didn't have any to waste.

"I did."

"Out to Sand Springs Lake? You think that's where Sadie is?"

Tripp had endless respect for the detective, but also knew he was on sensitive ground. With Emmanuel planning a wedding to Sadie's sister Pippa, he wanted to give them hope without overpromising.

Even if he felt this hunch clear down to his marrow.

"It's a hunch, but it's a good one. I triangulated all of Capital X's victim drops over the past five years. And there's a lot to be said for an isolated lake in winter."

"Damn it." Emmanuel swore again, harsher this time. "She's been under our damn nose for two days?"

"That's what I'm betting on." Tripp slowed and cut his lights. He'd get out and walk if he thought it would help, but the area around the lake was big enough he'd waste precious time on foot versus risking the possibility of someone seeing or hearing a random car.

"Listen. I need you to work with Michaela on the coordination with the team. She's working on it but we need more cops on the perimeter if these jerks cut and run."

"There are three entrances to the lake area."

"Then let's get going and put teams on all three."

Tripp cut the call, his sole focus on what was visible through his front window.

The hollow husk of a summer camp came up on his left. The main building came first; a long, nondescript structure silhouetted by the moon. Small cabins were also discernible in the distance beyond the main outbuilding. Although the location was private, Tripp ruled it out for now. Based on Capital X's former crimes, he figured they'd need a private place of their own to shake down their victims. Squatting in an existing structure— even in the off-season—would risk unwanted attention.

He rolled down his window as he drove on, the dirt path going a long way toward muffling his approach. Despite the temperature, he wanted a shot at hearing anything that might carry on the cold night air. The path took him on a curving route around the perimeter of the lake and he passed the turnoff for one of the entrances Emmanuel had mentioned. GRPD didn't have men in place yet, but he had confidence in Iglesias that they'd be there.

For now, all Tripp could do was focus on Sadie.

Unbidden, a memory of coming upon her one evening came to mind. He'd run down to CSI himself to check on some ballistics results he needed and she'd been dancing around the room, oblivious to anyone else. He'd been captivated, happiness seeming to flow from her as she bopped along to whatever noise filled her earbuds.

He'd backed away, wanting her to have her privacy instead of possible embarrassment at being discovered by the boss, but the memory had stuck with him.

And the feeling of standing, for the briefest moment, in all that bright, vivid sunlight.

Willing that she'd find that happiness again, Tripp pressed on, the leafless trees allowing him to navigate easily with only the moon. A blast of frigid December air blew through the window but he ignored it. Chill was a small price to pay if it got him to Sadie.

It was only as he navigated another bend in the road that he heard it.

The unmistakable sound of a gunshot ricocheting through the clear night air.

Chapter Two

Sadie screamed as she caught sight of Tate, standing over Fred's body. The grisly scene had her stomach leaping into her throat and she sent up a silent prayer of thanks for her crime scene training. It couldn't erase the fact that her ex-fiancé was standing over the body of a man he'd just killed, but it did go a long way toward helping her keep a steady head.

A fact that nearly vanished when Tate swung the gun toward her. "Going somewhere?"

"You surprised?"

She had the slightest moment of triumph as she saw genuine shock cross his face before it winked out. Just like any bit of decency or goodness he might have once possessed.

With the shock gone, it left room for that cold sneer she resented with everything she was. "When did you grow a spine?"

How had she missed this?

And in what world was there a human who thought Sadie Colton lacked a spine? Yet even as the thought flashed in her mind, she had an answer ready to rise up and meet it.

She'd done that. She'd been so enamored of finally having her "true love" that she'd sublimated everything about herself for him.

It was such a useless, circular path, yet she found she couldn't stop treading over it again and again. How had she been so incredibly blind to who this man was?

A liar. A cheat. And now confirming what she'd already suspected, a killer.

"I've had one. You've just been too busy crushing me beneath your boot that you never took the time to look."

Tate's sneer—and the slow, lascivious slide of his gaze down her body and right back up—had her skin prickling in disgust. "I looked plenty, baby. And I never heard you complaining."

"Why did you kill him?"

That sneer turned even darker, twisting the face she'd once found bad-boy handsome into something downright devilish. "He's useless. And he let himself be followed here. I just got word disp—" he broke off, saying no more. Only Sadie didn't need more.

"We're not exactly hard to find. You think you're the only person who knows about Sand Springs Lake?" Her gamble was rewarded with Tate's near growl as he stared down at Fred.

"The bastard give you that information, too?"

"I figured it out all on my own. You didn't take me that far. Where else is this secluded this time of year? And who's working inside the GRPD for you?"

For the second time in a space of minutes, Tate's gaze flashed with that mix of surprise and something just a tad bit more. She wouldn't go as far as to say respect—

he clearly wasn't capable of feeling that for anyone—but there was something there.

And Sadie took heart that maybe Tate might have the slightest indication he'd underestimated her.

Well aware she had little to lose, Sadie kept on pushing. "How do you manage to find people to work with you if you go around shooting them for telling you the truth?"

"I shot him for incompetence. The truth was just an inconvenience." That subtle sense he saw something new in her seemed to hover between them once more before he added, "And with the right tech, baby, you don't need to find squealers anymore."

Sadie eyed the gun still leveled at her chest, even as she filed away that tidbit for the GRPD. "Would you mind putting that down?"

"I very much mind."

Any shred of smug satisfaction she might have felt evaporated, faced with the very real knowledge Tate cared as little for her as he had for Fred. Up to now, she'd believed she was an asset to him, but she might have been overestimating the degree to which their former relationship might influence his decision to keep her alive.

"It dawns on me that you're uniquely positioned to help me out, despite Fred's incompetence," he said.

That gun never moved, nor did Tate's gaze.

"And how would I do that?"

"What does the GRPD know about Capital X? And—" Tate leaned in closer "—what does your brother know?"

She knew he meant Riley and his role running Colton Investigations. Riley had earned a place of respect from the GRPD, his willingness to work with them and support their efforts going a long way toward fostering a good working relationship between the two.

Because she'd let him into her life, Tate knew that, too.

And the fact that he was asking meant his "all seeing" tech wasn't quite as mighty as he'd want it to be.

An aggressive bark from another part of the house drew her attention and was enough to remove Tate's scrutiny. He swore before moving toward the other room in the direction of the dog. "I'll be right back."

Although her instinct was to stay as far away from the gun and that ominous sound as possible, after two days, Sadie still didn't have a good sense of the house. The chance to learn a bit more of the layout wasn't something she could pass up.

Besides, she'd prefer to avoid staying anywhere near Fred's body.

So she followed Tate, not caring if it pissed him off. She needed as much information as she could get and sitting around like a wilting flower was not that way.

Tate had moved into a larger combined kitchen and living area, his attention momentarily focused on the dog. The German shepherd was gorgeous but dangerous-looking. A reality that only heightened when the dog caught sight of her, his ears perking as his lips quivered with clear threat.

Sadie was so shocked to see the dog holding still at Tate's command, the words were out before she could stop them. "Since when do you have a pet?"

Tate kept the dog in place, but shifted his attention to her. "One more thing you don't know about me because you weren't meant to know. But Snake and I go back a long way."

"You named your dog Snake?"

Tate's flat expression wasn't amused. "What does the GRPD know about Capital X?"

Sadie considered how to play this. While she wasn't proud of her time with Tate, she had learned how to handle him. She could only hope that she knew enough tactics to buy herself a bit more time.

"You've been tracking them for months, securing intel off your informants. You likely know more than they do."

He hesitated for the briefest moment and Sadie sensed her compliment had hit the mark. Tate wasn't going to back off, but the subtle distraction was a help.

Every moment counted.

And she made the most of this one. Through the kitchen, visible beyond the dog, was a door. The heavy wood had a glass-paneled top half. She could see no bars or trappings through the panes to suggest it was further blocked by an outer door.

That door had to be her goal.

"I want to know what you know." Tate had dropped the gun during the interaction with the dog but he quickly lifted it again. "Now!"

"I don't know anything."

The gun never wavered as Tate moved closer. "You were never straight with me. Always hiding behind your family and their connections and the big bad badges at the GRPD."

"I wasn't the one who spent our entire relationship lying."

"Oh no?"

His audacity—the fact that he could stand there and suggest she hadn't been honest with him—was a joke. "You got with me for no other reason than to ferret out information you could use for your criminal activities. I never meant anything to you."

"Not like you ever gave me anything. You and your brothers and sisters are so tight. Colton Investigations." He nearly spat the name. "You're thick as thieves, only you're all so damn pure you'd never put a hand on a piece of anyone's gold."

"While I'd hardly apologize for that to anyone, I'm sure as hell not going to apologize to you."

Sadie had no idea where it was coming from—especially with that gun still in dangerous range—but she simply couldn't stand there and take it any longer. Maybe a month in a safe house, with nothing to do but ponder all the ways she'd lost part of herself to Tate Greer, was finally finding its due.

And maybe she might even get a few of those pieces she'd given away back.

"What the hell do you know, Sadie!" The harsh shout spilled out of Tate like a violent waterfall. The dog never moved, but she sensed the tense set of his body—ready to leap at the slightest signal—even as Tate stepped closer.

Sadie knew she should keep her gaze on the gun but she was unable to look away from the veneer of sheer hate that covered Tate's face. The dog whined beside him, a small growl that affirmed all she suspected about the animal's training. And still, that gun remained leveled at the center of her chest.

A hard slam echoed through the house along with a rush of winter air as the door in the kitchen flew open.

Despite the gun, her gaze shifted to the door and the possibility of a new threat, only to find Barney stomping into the kitchen.

"Cops found us."

Tate swung around to face his other goon as Sadie saw another man tromp into the kitchen. He was as big as Fred had been, with hulking shoulders and a lethal-looking semiautomatic hanging from one meaty hand. Although Sadie had minimal exposure to the black market weapons trade in Michigan, she'd reviewed enough crime scenes and studied enough wounds to know what that type of weapon did to the human body.

An involuntary shiver skated down her spine as she weighed what she had to do.

Tate was shouting at Barney over the announcement there were cops, and the new henchman was adding his perspective, suggesting how to handle the threat. All three men were *right there*—along with their weapons—but so was the open door.

While she knew it was a suicide mission to try to run, it was still a better option than staying put.

With one final glance at the door, Sadie focused on the dog. He'd stayed in the position Tate had put him in, his training so absolute he hadn't moved. Sadie hoped that rigid training would be enough to give her the head start she needed.

Without giving herself one more moment to think, she bolted, her unerring focus on the door and the freedom just beyond.

TRIPP HELD HIS POSITION, the small copse of trees about fifty yards from the house his hiding place. The crystalline air had aided his listening in on the argument being waged inside the house, while also giving him time to assess their firepower and position.

He knew Sadie was in there.

He might not be able to see her, but he knew she was there. He'd heard her, her sweet voice floating through that cold night air. She'd been kidnapped and locked away by a madman, but what he'd been able to make out had held steady and solid. Tripp fought that sense of helplessness—the one that kept threatening to drag him under like a massive wave at the beach, complete with deadly undertow—and kept his attention on the house. This wasn't the same as losing Lila, he reminded himself over and over.

It. Wasn't. The. Same.

Instead, he needed to find a way in. But based on the two goons he'd already seen enter, he knew he was outnumbered.

Damn it, how had they missed this? An organization like Capital X, operating right under their noses. He was well aware organized crime was a consistent bane of police squads the world over, but the fact that Capital X had managed to stay under the radar for so long was a concern.

And Sadie Colton had somehow landed right in the middle of it all.

His mobile phone buzzed at his hip and Tripp picked it up, hoping for news that backup was on the way. Iglesias hadn't disappointed.

Team in place. Lake surrounded. Waiting for your Go.

Tripp tapped a message quickly in return to update the detective on his status.

Confirmed location. Sadie inside house on southwest corner of lake. I've got eyes, 50 yards out.

He typed a few more commands, until they ultimately agreed to surround the house from all angles. In under ninety seconds, Tripp felt the sensation of movement from behind him.

"Right where you said you'd be, McKellar."

"Took you long enough," Tripp muttered as Iglesias's tall form came into view.

The detective held up his hands. "You just put together a major op in less than an hour. Not all of us are superhuman, McKellar."

Tripp took grim satisfaction in the compliment. "The only goal is to get her out."

"I know, man." Iglesias patted Tripp's back. "I know. Pippa is beside herself. And since I already promised my fiancée I'd bring her sister home, you know I've got your back."

It would be little comfort until they had Sadie back, but it was a solid reminder that the entire department was invested in getting her home safe and sound. Iglesias had an added personal connection in his engagement to Sadie's sister, but he was as committed as the rest of the GRPD.

Sadie was one of their own.

Tripp pointed to the house. "Two guys went in a few minutes ago, armed to the teeth. Semiautomatics strapped to their sides and firmly in hand. Assumption is that Sadie is in the house, along with Greer. Gunshots echoed from inside, but I've heard her fighting with Greer, which suggests he targeted a different victim."

Iglesias shook his head. "He is one nasty bastard. Pippa said she and her sisters all got a bad vibe on him from the jump, but this goes way beyond not liking your sister's boyfriend."

Tripp wasn't sure why the word *boyfriend* chafed so badly—especially since he already knew the bastard in question had been Sadie's fiancé—so he ignored it. He needed his full focus on the mission. "We all get played from time to time."

"Yeah, I suppose we do," Iglesias said.

Tripp quickly outlined his observations from the past half hour.

"How many gunshots did you hear?"

Tripp fought to keep his voice clinical, with minimal inflection despite the personal nature of the op. "Just the one, and then I heard Sadie's scream. Then I heard the fighting."

"What does he want with her?"

"What he wanted before—access."

Tripp knew it for the truth. Sadie Colton was in a prime position to help Greer. Between her CSI role in the GRPD as well as being a member of the Colton family, and therefore connected to Colton Investigations, she had a lot of information a criminal could glean.

And Tate Greer knew it, too.

"Greer saw her as the way in." Tripp continued his assessment.

"Damn it." Iglesias shook his head. "Pippa was afraid this might be the reason he got close to her so fast."

"She thought Greer was trying to infiltrate?"

"No, nothing like that. But she was concerned with how quickly Sadie had fallen for the guy. As Pippa told me, it was like one day he just sort of showed up and within a matter of weeks her sister was smitten and talking of love and marriage."

While Tripp had never personally bought into it, he knew that people did fall in love quickly. In an instant, some said. If he was honest with himself, he had felt a spark of attraction for Sadie from the very first day they'd met.

He could still see her, the eager recruit joining the GRPD, determined to make her mark. She had done well enough and he had been impressed by her hard work, her dedication, and her unwillingness to rest on the laurels of the Colton name. But in the end, she'd really found her calling with crime scene investigation. She had showed an early knack, identifying some key evidence in a case she had worked her rookie season. She'd finished out that first year, giving her all to the force, but after her full commitment, it hadn't taken her long to ask for a transfer into CSI.

And she'd thrived there.

Although he no longer saw her every day, as a lieutenant in the department, he got regular updates from her division. Sadie was well respected and that work ethic they'd all recognized from the start proved itself over and over. She had uncovered a major piece of evidence that had put a large drug ring away within a matter of months after her joining CSI. She'd followed that up with some careful tech work that had put away a child predator. And just this past spring she'd worked round-the-clock to help uncover evidence to catch a serial killer.

Sadie Colton had found her calling in CSI. Their department, and more broadly, the entire city of Grand Rapids, was better for it.

"Rest of the team is in position." Iglesias interrupted Tripp's wandering thoughts.

"Tell everyone to hold the perimeter. You and I are moving in."

Iglesias relayed the information and Tripp heard a series of affirmatives through the detective's comm device.

The low level of persistent adrenaline that had haunted Tripp's system since the discovery Sadie had been taken spiked sharply as they moved from their hiding place. With determined steps toward the house, his sole focus was on getting her out safely.

"You ready for what's on the other side of the door?" he said softly to Iglesias.

"Damn straight."

Tripp figured there weren't many more on the team who would be as committed and he was glad Iglesias had his back.

Tripp pointed to the entrance to the cabin still about twenty yards away. "They both went through that door, but the gunshot came from the back of the house. Assume we're entering the kitchen and need to push through into a living room or great room of some sort."

"Got it."

They had closed the distance, the door nearly in sight, when loud barking echoed from inside the house. It wasn't the excitement of a chase or a game of fetch, but the harsh, violent bark of a dog on the scent of its quarry.

Tripp braced for that new dimension as he anticipated a large, aggressive attacker prepared to take them down at all costs.

And that's when he saw her.

Hair that he knew was just a shade darker than strawberry blond streamed behind her as she ran hell-for-leather out the door that had held their full focus. She was headed straight for the dock at the edge of the lake. Two hulking men were just behind her, oblivious to Tripp and Emmanuel's presence, struggling to catch up. Moonlight illuminated the deadly glint of waving weapons in each of their hands.

Tripp went into motion, racing toward her pursuers as he ignored the very real threat of that barking dog or the additional risk there might be more goons exiting the house. He ignored it all; his only focus on getting her back. All with the element of surprise in his favor.

But even he couldn't hold back a shout when Sadie jumped into the ice-edged water that surrounded the end of the dock.

SHOCKING COLD PIERCED her skin with all the finesse of a thousand ice picks. She knew it would be cold. Had braced for the loss of breath as she'd plunged into the water.

But hell, damn, and all the really good curse words she and her sisters practiced behind her brothers' backs, was it cold.

The ice picks quickly gave way to sledgehammers and Sadie wondered how it was possible to even think let alone find a way to survive in this.

Only she did. She would.

Somewhere between the leap into the lake and the

impossible cold, her mind went on autopilot. She'd gotten the jump on Tate and his henchmen and taken it as a small stroke of luck that they'd been so absorbed with their infighting it gave her a head start. It wasn't much, but the few precious seconds was all she'd needed to get a move on the footrace. But it had been a split-second decision to head for the lake.

If her memory served—and the trauma of going to summer camp had haunted her far longer than she wanted to own—there was a large dock at the edge of the lake. She'd also remembered the way the water eddied around the base, creating a small pocket of air between the wooden planks and the water.

That air pocket was her goal. If she could get in there, she could continue to breathe and hide until Tate, his henchman and the dog moved on. If…

Damn, it was cold, those icy sledgehammers doing their job. She could see the wooden dock. Could feel the water lapping around her, only instead of it feeling gentle as it did in summer, it felt like thick, heavy sludge as she fought her way across the lake.

Focus, Colton.

The order snapped through her mind, her own voice threading with that of her father. And her brothers.

Focus.

Battling the cold, she pushed herself on. She had no choice.

In a battle between hypothermia or her psycho ex-fiancé, she'd take the cold all day and twice on Sunday.

Assuming, of course, her body would cooperate.

She ignored the heavy pull in her limbs and forced herself forward.

The dock is your goal. The dock is your goal. Over and over, she kept that thought in place as she pushed on. The icy water dragged at her limbs, making her lethargic, while the drag of her wet clothes added to the thick pressure against her skin.

She would make it.

She *had* to make it.

Snake's frantic barking seemed to waver, growing dimmer as her full focus remained on propelling herself forward.

Her arms were so heavy. And she was going so slow.

The water was black around her, the bright moonlight that had illuminated her run toward the lake falling behind the clouds.

Was she even going in the right direction? Confusion had her stopping for a moment, her arms thrashing as she fought to catch her breath. Why was it so hard to draw air?

For the first time since jumping on impulse, something hit her chest with a swift fist.

What if she didn't make it?

What if…

"Sadie." The deep voice drifted toward her, bouncing off the water with a weird echo. "Sadie!"

Why did it sound like Tripp?

Sadie flailed her arms once more, shocked when she felt the hard edge of a dock pylon.

Did I make it?

She willed herself to focus, her gaze sharpening as her hand fought for purchase against the base of the dock.

And that's when she heard her name again.

"Sadie!"

As she looked up, large hands came around her upper arms, dragging her from the water. "Are you okay?"

I wasn't wrong. That thought dimly registered in the back of her mind as Sadie took in the broad, reassuring form of Tripp McKellar. His chiseled features and firm jaw were the last things she saw before her body convulsed in a hard shiver.

And then she felt nothing except the strong arms that came around her and the tight press of his body against hers.

Chapter Three

She's safe.

Tripp held tight to Sadie's small, shivering form and ignored the oppressive wetness that soaked his jacket. He'd survive. And, damn it, so would she. They hadn't come this far to accept any other outcome.

But she was so cold. And the shivers racking her body were nearly convulsive, she was shaking so hard. He had to get her out of her clothes and into something warmer.

The rest of Tripp's team had moved in on the cabin and grounds, the shouts of Greer's men still littering the air. All fought loudly against the bonds GRPD officers had already put on them. The two goons Tripp had seen going in had been captured as well as two lookouts discovered on the back side of the property.

But nowhere in the melee near the cabin could he see Tate Greer.

There was no way Tripp could have come this far and missed his quarry. Yet to go after him meant he would have to leave Sadie, and that was unacceptable.

When another hard shudder had her shaking against his chest, he knew the decision was made. With determined steps toward the cabin, his only goal was to get her somewhere warm. It was only the hard clutch of her hands against his forearms that had him stopping. "No."

He glanced down, the blue tingeing that heartbreaking face more than evident in the unclouded light of the moon. "We have to get you warm, Sadie."

"I… I-I'm n-not going b-back in there." Although it was a struggle to get the words out, her desperate desire to stay out of that cabin was clear in the stiffness of her body.

"We need to get you out of those clothes."

"No c-cabin." Her grip tightened on his forearm. "Car. Y-your car is f-fine."

The battle to take her someplace warm might be his goal, but there was no way he could ignore her distress. Knowing an ambulance would be there soon weighed even more in her favor. With quick movements, he swept her up in his arms. He thought there might have been a slight protest on her lips but it died as he carried her toward his vehicle.

"Where?" she finally asked, the lone word seemingly stuck in her throat.

"We'll go to my SUV until the ambulance gets here."

"Th…thank y-you." She whispered the words before laying her head against his shoulder.

All the adrenaline that had carried him for the past two days shifted somewhere deep inside him. That insistent, driving need to save morphed into something new: the desperate, fervent desire to protect.

He knew that feeling. He'd had it once—so long ago he'd forgotten the sensation until Sadie's head had come to rest against his shoulder. The desire to keep those he cared for safe and secure.

Until he'd failed at both.

Those long hours of therapy his chief had suggested had ultimately helped Tripp find closure and acceptance in one part of the truth: he and Lila had only gotten engaged because of the baby. He'd still loved her, in his way, and he'd been wildly happy about their child. But in the long run, they'd likely not have made the most stable environment for a kid.

A truth he could accept now but couldn't go back and change no matter how often he beat himself up over it. He'd been committed to seeing things through, determined to make a life with Lila once they welcomed their baby. What he still had never fully worked through was the reality that Lila and their unborn child had died because of *his* life's work.

Yet he still chose to do it day after day.

And he'd never fully reconciled what that said about him.

The department-issued SUV he drove was just where he'd left it, and Tripp set Sadie gently on her feet as he opened the driver's-side door. He quickly turned on the engine, blasting the heat before he swung around to the rear door to retrieve his first-aid kit. He also had spare clothes in the back, but the first step was to get her out of the wet ones she wore.

"I'm going to help you with these," Tripp said, moving to her side where she leaned against the open driver's-side door, tossing the first-aid kit onto the seat behind her. He kept his tone careful—neutral, even—

but knew that to help her he had to strip her of every article of wet clothing.

Her soft grunt was all he heard in return as she fumbled with the hem of her sweater. The thick wool clung to her and flopped against her fingers where she struggled to grab hold.

Tripp took her hands in his. They were ice against his palms and he fought to keep his voice steady against the rising panic he still might have been too late, even with Dispatch's call into 911. "Let me."

With careful movements, he lifted the sweater up and over her head. Her skin had that same bluish tinge as her face, visible in the dome light, but he kept going.

Next he reached for the waistband of her jeans. The denim was thick and heavy, and he ignored the brush of soft skin beneath his fingers as he undid the button and released the zipper. He worked the material down her hips and held each calf as he removed the denim from her legs. It was only then he realized she wasn't wearing shoes, just a thin layer of socks.

Everywhere he touched, her skin was that horrible, clammy cold. He removed the socks then shifted to her underwear. His job was to help people no matter the circumstance. He could, and more importantly he *would*, do that.

But he was also acutely aware that he was going to see Sadie naked, which set off something strange deep and low in his gut. Something that reminded him when this was all over, and she was warm and well, he wanted to see her again.

Ignoring the flash of need that welled at the thought,

Tripp put his arm around her and focused instead on reassuring her. "Hang on. I have a blanket in the kit."

He reached around her to the first-aid kit he'd tossed onto the seat. The thin solar blanket in his extensive supplies was right where it should be and he ripped the packaging off to unfold the thin yet effective material. Moving to stand in front of her, he wrapped the material around her shoulders. "I'm going to remove your underwear now. Okay?"

She stared up at him, her grip tight on the edges of the blanket, and nodded. "Okay."

With deft fingers, he reached behind her and unclasped her bra, making sure to keep his gaze on hers. Once the material sprang free, he reached down and removed her water-soaked panties. Leaving all her clothes in a pile beside the SUV, he opened the back door and set her against the seat. "I'm going to go around the other side, then pull you onto my lap. We need to get you warm."

Once more, she nodded, but it concerned him she didn't even put voice to an "Okay" or a "Yes." Hurrying around to the opposite side, he slid into the rear passenger seat then reached across the space for her shoulders. The small figure huddled beneath that wash of silver material tugged at his heart, but he willed it aside.

His only goal was to keep her warm until the ambulance arrived to take over.

Tripp gently pulled her onto the backseat so that she settled on his lap. His shirt and coat were still wet from where he'd held her, but the solar blanket ensured she wasn't touched by any of it. He gently tugged her long hair out from where it lay against her neck, determined to remove any bit of wet or cold from her skin.

Just like when he'd carried her, she settled against his chest. Heat blew heavy out of the SUV's front console and he positioned her so that she was in the direct line of the vent. He then settled his chin on the top of her head and rubbed his hands over her shoulders and down her arms, willing circulation and much needed heat to return to her body.

Then it was time to wait.

And hope like hell he'd acted fast enough.

THE UNCONTROLLABLE CHATTERING that had gripped her since emerging from the lake finally subsided. She still felt bone-deep cold, but that sense of her body turning on her, taking on a mind of its own, finally faded.

With each stroke of Tripp's firm, flat palm against her body, Sadie felt a bit of herself return.

And with it, the dawning sense that she was basically naked in Tripp McKellar's lap. A fact that was mostly immaterial to her situation—he was the consummate professional—but was still one that had burrowed deep and decided to unfurl with heat.

And need.

It was amazing, really, how she could even think of that in this moment, yet if she were honest with herself, it was there.

Her attraction to Tripp had always been there. Yes, it had been muted and, basically, ignored when she'd become engaged to Tate, but it had never really died. Now that she'd distanced herself from Tate's influence, she'd had plenty of time to acknowledge that the allure of the GRPD lieutenant had never really gone away.

And what was to be done about that?

The large male body that fitted around hers was the epitome of safety and protection. Even more, there was a gentle, caring quality to his ministrations that pulled at her. Tripp McKellar was a good man. She'd always known that, but to actually be on the receiving end of that tender gentleness was impossibly wonderful.

Even as it felt impossibly right.

"I'm getting you wet." Sadie was surprised by how small and croaky her voice sounded.

Tripp shifted, his arms tightening around her. "I'm fine. Are you starting to feel warmer?"

"A little bit." Although she was still chilled to the bone, sensation was coming back into her limbs.

"The ambulance should be here soon. We'll get you fixed up and make sure that dip in the lake didn't do any damage. Iglesias is with me and by now he'll have called your family, too."

"I wasn't in there that long."

"It's December. Any amount of time is too long."

He was right, of course, but she still wouldn't have changed the decision. The chance to break away from Tate had been too good to pass up and she'd taken her shot when she'd had it. She was just thankful that Tripp and his backup had been waiting for her.

"How did you know where to find me?"

"I think a better question is why did it take me so long."

Sadie didn't miss his use of the word *me*, despite

the fact that he had an entire department working behind him.

"No, I think my question is the right one. How did you figure out it was Sand Springs Lake?"

"I triangulated all of the offenses that we could identify as Capital X over the past several years. I've done some more work and I have realized that the crimes seem to fit into three distinct clusters in the county."

"And this was the most isolated of the three?" Sadie asked.

"Exactly."

Sadie considered it, struck anew when Tripp mentioned Capital X's crime*s*—as in plural—that her ex was behind it all. Would she ever get over this feeling of how badly she'd been played?

Stupid much, Sadie?

Yes, she'd had a month to think about it, to digest it, and try to come to some bit of reason for it all. But it remained nearly impossible to hear anything over the constant pounding of self-blame she couldn't seem to shake off.

Or drown out.

Or ignore.

Her entire family had been leery of Tate from the start, her twin sister, Victoria, most of all. Vikki had been kind about it at first, pressing Sadie often to know how the relationship was coming along and if it made her happy.

Since she and her sister had *always* known what the other was feeling, the continued questioning had finally taken its toll. No matter how large a smile Vikki had pasted on or how innocent her tone, Sadie had known the truth. It had all been an act. All designed to try to figure out what Sadie had seen in Tate.

And she *was* happy. Or had been.

For a few precious months, at the start of the relationship, she'd been practically giddy. Falling in love with a man she'd never expected to meet. Tate had the sexy, bad-boy look she'd always found appealing in movies yet had never imagined for herself. And as she'd gotten to know him, she'd seen that the sexy façade was only the beginning. They'd talked of so many things and, after every conversation, she'd been certain there was so much more to him than what was visible on the surface.

And she'd equated each of those conversations to herself and the woman no one seemed to see beneath her surface.

Yes, she was good, sweet, hardworking Sadie Colton. She was the baby of the family, her birth minutes after Vikki's ensuring she was the youngest Colton. Whether it was her status as youngest or her eagerness at work or her relatively upbeat personality, everyone saw her as the sweet, cheerful, girl next door. But no one seemed to see her as a woman. One with needs and desires and ambitions of her own.

But Tate had.

Only instead of falling in love with those qualities, he'd twisted them and used them to his own ends.

"Hey there. You okay?" Tripp's voice whispered over her ear, the light tickle sensation enough to pull her from the dour direction of her thoughts.

"Yeah."

He shifted until he could tilt his head just so to look directly at her. And in his vivid blue gaze Sadie saw a flash of redemption from the ugly direction of her thoughts. It was quick and fleeting, but it was there all the same.

Maybe—*maybe?*—this man saw her as a woman, too.

The flash was gone in less than a heartbeat, but that lingering idea took root somewhere deep, helping to warm her from the inside out.

"You sure about that?"

"I am. I'm starting to warm up. The heat helps." She swallowed hard, once again aware of the fact that nothing but a thin layer of blanket separated her naked butt from his lap. And with it, the heat that had slowly worked its way back into her body crept up her neck. "Thank you for taking care of me."

The edges of those compelling eyes crinkled with his gentle smile. "All in a day's work."

In that moment, Sadie realized she could stay there forever. Right there, wrapped in his arms, warm and secure. Whatever emotional damage Tate had done, it would never be enough for her to believe that Tripp McKellar was anything but a good and decent man. There was no pretense here, no false front.

Only goodness and truth.

Sure, he had a past. She knew about the woman he'd been engaged to shortly before Sadie had started on the force. Knew the sadder end that had seen her gunned down by a criminal let out of the prison system too early.

She'd watched from a distance as Tripp had dealt with it all. The pain that came from survival and the will a person needed to move on, day by day.

But he'd done it. He'd moved on, focused on his work, the city of Grand Rapids and ensuring his team had all it needed to do the job.

It was how he'd known how to find her.

Suddenly tired, Sadie laid her head back against his shoulder and closed her eyes. She could never be with this man romantically, but she could admire who and what he was. And she could quietly, without anyone knowing, use him as her own personal lodestone, showing her the way to true north. There *were* good men in the world. Good, decent men who didn't use others or betray them.

If that was all Tripp McKellar could be to her, then she'd take it. Because it was a hell of a lot more than she'd ever had before.

Tripp held tight to Sadie and wondered over the mix of emotions he'd seen in her eyes. Despite the jump in the lake and the harrowing ordeal of the past few days, there was something so resilient about her. Something so warm and open.

Even as he clearly saw the pain she lived with.

Was it due to the stark truth that her former fiancé was a scumbag?

Tripp suspected that was part of it, yet not all. He'd watched her for a long time, quietly observing her at work or out in the field, and there was something else buried deep below that compelling green gaze. It was like a river of solitude flowing beneath the woman who always seemed to be in the thick of things. She was the first to arrange an impromptu, interdepartment pickup game of soccer in the park or an after-work round of drinks.

Yet through it all, he'd always sensed there was something she held back. Some inner longing that no one except him seemed to see.

Not like he could talk to anyone about it. Even if he wasn't so maniacal about privacy, determined to give others theirs even as he fiercely guarded his own, it wasn't exactly coffee conversation with his coworkers.

Did you notice that Sadie Colton looked sad today after the soccer game?

Did you see Sadie Colton, head bowed down over her lab desk, earlier this afternoon?

Sadie Colton's big smile never quite seems to reach her eyes, does it?

So instead he'd filed all those questions away, keeping them to himself almost like a warning. He had no right to dig into her business and even less to pry into her personal life. That meant his questions went unanswered and his observations were nothing more than a curious pastime.

Lost in thought, it was a surprise when Sadie suddenly struggled in his arms, shifting hard against his lap. He ignored the sudden jolt of discomfort as her body came into intimate contact with his and instead fought to steady her. "What's wrong?"

"Tate. He's gone."

He briefly considered downplaying it, waiting until he had a full report—and full confirmation—from his team that Greer had gotten away. But he couldn't do it. Regardless of his need to protect her, she was a cop and she deserved the truth.

"I think he is."

Sadie's focus remained on the activities taking place beyond the SUV's window. "I can see some of what's going on over there and it struck me that I can't see Snake." Tripp nearly asked who or what Snake was before she added, "The dog."

"Greer has a dog?"

"'Pet monster' is a more apt term. He's huge, ruthlessly trained and clearly lethal."

It was new information on Greer that was helpful, but it also made what Sadie had endured that much worse. He'd envisioned Greer's tactics would be harsh and unyielding once he took anyone prisoner. Adding the power of a trained animal into the mix only further supported that assessment.

"Did he turn the animal on you?" Tripp asked. He hadn't seen any evidence of abuse when he'd removed her clothes, but that didn't mean she hadn't been intimidated or taunted. A fact that had his vision hazing as the image formed in his mind's eye.

"Tate's been gone since the night they kidnapped me. I've only seen his goons at mealtime since they stuffed me in that cabin."

The anger faded slightly at the news she'd been largely ignored since her capture. "And he came back today?"

"Tonight. That was the first time I'd seen him since he arrived at the safe house. The first time I'd seen the dog, too." She shook her head, a small, rueful laugh filling the space between them. "I had no idea he even liked animals."

From her description of Snake, Tripp wasn't sure he'd

lay "animal lover" at Greer's feet, but he kept the observation to himself. They had to focus on what they knew and that empty sense of remorse in her tone wouldn't benefit from him piling on more questions she obviously didn't have answers to.

Nor would this overwhelming sense of anger he couldn't quite rein in. There would be time for it all later. Right now, he had to concentrate on getting Sadie safely to the hospital and on the road to recovery. As if to punctuate that thought, the lights of the ambulance suddenly filled the night, flashing red and blue as the vehicle pulled up into the clearing beyond the house.

In those flashing lights, Tripp knew something else with terrifying clarity.

Every minute they didn't have Tate Greer in custody was another moment Sadie was in danger. Because after tonight, there was no way Greer would be willing to let her live—and no way that Tripp would let him get to her.

Chapter Four

Sadie kept her gaze on the cabin in the distance as the medics prepared to strap her onto the gurney. She knew Gus and Gage, the two medics who treated her now, and appreciated their attention to her modesty as they covered her with more blankets before helping her onto the flat bed.

There were things to say to Tripp, starting with a thank-you for saving her life, but they'd have to wait. For now, she had to think.

Where had Tate gone?

If he'd gotten away so quickly, there had to have been another hidey-hole nearby. That meant once again they'd underestimated just how well set up he was and the depths of his network.

He obviously ran a successful business. It might be a criminal enterprise, but she'd do well to start thinking of it through a new lens: as a business enterprise.

And corporations, she knew. After watching her brother build an incredibly successful business, she had firsthand knowledge and a strong sense for how a solid enterprise ran.

Well funded. *Check.*

Well resourced, with provisions for any number of scenarios. *Check.*

Well led. *Check.*

While she hated to think of Tate as a leader in the traditional sense, she needed to view him that way. It was yet another facet of his talents and personal charisma, and it was something she was uniquely qualified to assess.

"You doing okay, Sadie?" Gus's smile was gentle as he settled her into place. He had a blood pressure cuff in hand and was already gently shifting the thick blankets to get to her arm.

"Getting there."

"You're lucky Lieutenant McKellar was there. He did everything right, getting you out of those wet clothes and into the warmth of the SUV."

"He did." It was a memory that would live with her forever, the tender way he'd cared for her, with no thought to his own comfort. One she'd take out at quiet moments and remember with fondness.

It was only as Gus went to work in tandem with Gage, checking all her vitals and directing her to follow the movements of his finger or to stick out her tongue, that Sadie forced herself back to the problem at hand.

She had no doubt Tate's henchmen would remain silent and uncooperative with the GRPD. If Tate didn't already have them quaking in fear, Fred's death would provide added incentive. The PD needed to shift gears and approach the problem from a new angle.

The bright lights of the ambulance as well as Gage and Gus's conversation faded into the background as Sadie let the idea of Tate-as-leader into the forefront of her thoughts. It was a talent she'd had since she was a small child—the ability to shut out the world as she worked through a problem—and she took full advantage of it now.

Her body still ached, a fact that was increasingly clear as her circulation and warmth returned, so she'd let her mind go somewhere else. Somewhere useful. A place she hadn't been in far too long.

With that driving sense of purpose filling her thoughts, Sadie barely felt the shift as the ambulance began to move, headed for the hospital.

TATE WATCHED THE flashing ambulance lights fade away into the darkness and considered his next move. The one that would take his meddlesome, irritating ex-fiancée down a few more pegs.

He'd initially thought to just kill her, removing her as nothing more than an irritating nuisance. Quick. Effective. Easy.

But that was too good for her now.

For all she'd just pulled and the trouble she'd caused him, she deserved a lot worse. And he was hell-bent to be the man to give it to her.

Sadie had been the perfect mark, he thought as he ordered Snake into the large kennel he kept at his personal safe house. Sweet and innocent, those big cow eyes lighting up with interest and affection and—just as he'd planned—love in short order. It was just too bad she was such a damn goody-goody, his expected access to both the GRPD databases as well as Colton Investigations severely limited by her by-the-book personality.

She kept her work files on serious lockdown—an IT

director's dream employee. She changed her password regularly and she made the damn thing impossible to figure out. No "Tate1234" for her. No way. She hadn't even used his name once in her password updates.

Nor had she given many details about her family. Oh, he'd heard the sob story about how her brother Riley, in lockstep with his siblings, had started Colton Investigations after the tragic deaths of their parents. How they'd banded together to help Brody Higgins, an innocent foster kid her late father had taken a special interest in.

It had been particularly sweet to know that same dumb kid was one of Tate's biggest dupes in the entire RevitaYou/Capital X scam. A scam that had been going smoother than silk before the Coltons had gotten involved.

Now it was all upside down. His number two, Gunther Johnson, was sitting in a jail cell, the cops had figured out how deadly RevitaYou was and Tate's cover had been blown.

He had contingency plans, of course, but there was no foolproof plan that could make up for how quickly it had all collapsed. That was why he was going to make sure Sadie went down with him. He'd given her the perfect role. Loving fiancée to one of the city's most successful businessmen. And she'd betrayed him.

It was unforgivable. And because of it, she was going to pay.

TRIPP GLANCED AROUND the waiting room at the county hospital and wondered how the Coltons had seemingly managed to multiply overnight.

The eldest, Riley Colton, had been the first to arrive with his pregnant fiancée, Charlize. He had been quickly followed by the rest of Sadie's siblings, each with their own significant others. They were all there except for Sadie's sister Kiely, who apparently couldn't get a babysitter on short notice. The entire Colton family seemed to have coupled up lately, and while Tripp wouldn't consider himself on the pulse of local gossip, it had been impossible to ignore the heavy strikes of Cupid's arrow on this one family.

Working with Emmanuel, he'd seen firsthand the man's relationship—and hard fall into love—with Pippa Colton. And Sadie's twin, JAG paralegal sergeant Vikki, had recently fallen in love with Army Sergeant Flynn Cruz-Street.

They were all there, concerned about their sister and equally concerned at the news Tate Greer had gotten away yet again.

Tripp was already expecting the quiet outreach when Riley approached him. The family had settled in, anxious for news of Sadie's condition. Coltons were scattered across the waiting room, and the moment he left to get a cup of coffee, Riley followed.

"Can I buy you a cup?" Tripp gestured toward the large machine.

"Yeah, thanks." Riley seemed to hesitate for a moment before diving in. "I know she's going to be okay. She's young, and strong, and I know that all works in her favor. But I also need to know what happened to her."

Tripp knew that need, understood it intimately, and so he would play it straight with Riley. "She's fine, physically. Greer didn't get a hand on her, and for that we can all be grateful."

"Why do I hear a 'but' in there?"

"Because the psychological is going to be a lot harder. She spent a month in the safe house, mostly alone, and even that wasn't safe enough." That same raw anger and fury-fueled frustration welled up once more. "And that's on me."

Riley took the cup Tripp handed to him, his eyes wide. "On you?"

"Damn straight. I put her there, and it's my responsibility to make sure she stays safe."

"I could say that right back at you. She's my sister. My family. It's my responsibility to make sure she stays safe, too."

"In a government safe house?" Tripp shook his head, no intention of getting into a pissing match with Riley. "Greer found her on my watch. I need to get underneath the why and the how."

"You can count on me to help, however I can. This isn't on you, man. Greer and Capital X's tentacles run far deeper than we know. And they've been burrowing in for a lot longer than any of us realized."

The comment might have been meant to make him feel better, but Tripp took minimal comfort. Nothing could change the fact that Sadie had been kidnapped from an environment he'd controlled. And he was going to make it his personal mission to find out who had facilitated that access.

After, of course, he put that bastard Tate Greer behind bars.

"I do want to talk to you about some ideas we've

been working up for RevitaYou," Riley added. "I think we may have a way to get Wes Matthews back on US soil."

Tripp's mind flashed to the crime board in his office. If Tate Greer was the man behind Capital X funding RevitaYou, banker Wes Matthews was the linchpin in the operation. He was the centerpiece of their investigation. Get him and they had a chance to get to the bottom of it all—and they'd get Tate, too. "That's gotta take some doing. Matthews doesn't have a lot of incentive to come back."

"That's where my new soon-to-be sister-in-law, Matthews's daughter Abigail, has been a tremendous help." Riley tilted his head in the direction of the waiting room. "She talked to Griffin about trying to help, and he convinced her to bring her ideas to all of us. She and her father have always been estranged and I get the feeling she'd have been just fine ignoring him for the rest of her life. She has helped us immensely."

Tripp considered what he knew of Sadie's siblings, and the news that Griffin was cooperating so closely was something of a novel development. Falling in love with Abigail and her foster daughter, Maya, had changed him. Clearly for the better. "I'm glad to hear it, man. But I guess I'm a little surprised to hear Griffin is helping out the family business."

"It's amazing, actually." Riley clearly warmed to his subject. "I feel like I have my brother back. I know it was hard for him, an adopted child in the midst of five more kids, but we love him. We've always loved him. All of us. And now it feels like we might have him back.

"I guess it's the beauty of having an amazing woman in his life."

At that comment, Tripp couldn't help but think of Sadie. *She* was an amazing woman. Hadn't tonight proved that? Not just what she'd survived, but the gumption and the attitude that had carried her through it all.

Vikki poked her head in the door, her excitement palpable. "Riley. The doctor just came out to see us. We can go back and visit with her."

Tripp gave Riley a solid pat on the shoulder. "Go. Go see your sister. We can pick this up later."

Riley didn't wait, just headed for the door. It was Vikki who hesitated, calling after her brother as he passed through the door. "You go on. I'll be right there."

She moved forward, coming right up to Tripp and laying her hands over his. "Thank you. Thank you for finding and saving Sadie."

The steady need to protest that he'd nearly been the one responsible for losing her died in his throat. Vikki was so earnest—so determined—and for the first time he let himself slightly relax that Sadie was safe. He still wasn't convinced that Tate Greer wasn't going to try again, but for the moment, she was safe.

Now, all he had to do was make sure she stayed that way.

SADIE BATTLED THE mix of exhaustion and impatience that fought for purchase in the back of her mind. She was thrilled that her family was there and took deep comfort in the presence of all of them. But she also wanted to see Tripp.

She *needed* to see him.

It was the strangest thing, but ever since the doctor had given her the news that she was going to be okay, she'd wanted to see Tripp. To tell him herself.

It was because of *him* that she was going to be okay.

If left to her own devices and Tate's demented criminal activities, she could've drowned in the lake. And deep down inside, she recognized the truth of that.

Yes, if given the chance she would run from Tate Greer all over again.

But she also couldn't deny she'd made a narrow escape, all because of Tripp's quick thinking and amazing police work that had put him at the lake in the first place.

Vikki must've sensed her exhaustion, because she finally put an end to the fun. "Okay, loved ones. I think Sadie's had enough. We can come back tomorrow morning. And since Kiely couldn't get a babysitter on short notice, Flynn and I will swing by to see her and Cooper and let her know our girl's okay."

Her siblings hugged her, each in turn, Pippa hanging on an extra few beats before she let go with a promise. "I'll bring the donuts first thing tomorrow morning."

"I'm holding you to that." Sadie smiled. "And there'd better be chocolate-frosted ones."

"Why bother buying donuts if you don't buy chocolate-frosted?" Pippa shuddered in mock horror before moving to stand with her fiancé, Emmanuel.

"Clever girl." Abigail leaned in to give her a quick hug. "And it also ensures that your brother will be here bright and early, too. Assuming Maya doesn't wake up when we get home and pay the babysitter." Sadie's future sister-in-law said it all with a smile, before jokingly giving Griffin the lightest edge of her elbow to the middle of his stomach. Griffin used the shift in position to wrap his arms tightly around her, and it made Sadie's heart happy to see them together.

To see all her siblings, together with their significant others.

"Come on, come on. The donut mandate has been laid down. Now it's time Sadie got some rest." Vikki maneuvered them all out with a drill sergeant's precision, before walking back over to stand by her bedside.

"I'm so glad you're all right." The stern voice vanished as quickly as it had come, replaced with a quaver Sadie rarely heard coming from her twin. "I've been so worried."

"Vik, I'm okay. Really, I am."

It wasn't a lie, exactly, but Sadie wasn't silly enough to think there wouldn't be repercussions. But right here, right now, gathered up in the love of her family, she simply refused to focus on any of it. "Now get out of here and go kiss that hot guy of yours."

"You're my sister! You're my priority and I'm worried about you."

Sadie waved a hand. "Well, I'm fine now. And I'm ordering you to go kiss Flynn. If I had a man like him, that's what I'd be doing."

The tease was enough to bring a smile to Vikki's face, removing that crestfallen, ashen look that had been there only moments before. While there would be plenty more to say, for now, Sadie knew that had to be enough.

She kept her smile bright until Vikki was out of sight and then let it fall. She was happy for her brothers and sisters. Deeply happy, and so pleased that they had found such wonderful men and women to share their lives with.

But it did hold up a mirror to all she didn't have.

She *hated* thinking that way. It was so against her nature to begrudge anybody anything, especially those she loved as much as Riley, Griffin, Pippa, Kiely and Vikki.

Yet, try as she might, their happiness was also a counterweight to all the pain she was dealing with over Tate. She'd believed herself happy, as well, preparing for an upcoming wedding, only to find it all had vanished. And in the worst, most embarrassing—and dangerous—way.

She felt the first tear well up as a light knock came on the door.

"Hey. You up for a little bit of company?"

Tripp McKellar stood in the doorway, tall, broad, and exactly what she needed. "Hi. Yes, that would be nice."

She quickly brushed away that last tear, refusing to let him see such an embarrassing bit of selfish emotion, before meeting his gaze across the room. "What are you still doing here?"

"I wanted to see how you were. I didn't want to interrupt when your family was here."

"So you've been waiting this whole time?" It was absurdly touching, the idea that he'd hung around, waiting to see her.

"I just needed to see you for myself."

"That's funny, because you were the person I wanted to see, too. The doctor gave me a clean bill of health. And it's all because of you."

Those compelling blue eyes shot to the floor and with it his face settled in harsh lines before he seemed to compose himself. "You saved yourself. Don't forget that, Sadie."

"As nice a thought as that might be, I think we both know it's not true. If you hadn't been there, my jump into the lake would likely have ended very differently." It was strange to say it—that knowledge that a split-second decision could have had such a horribly different outcome—but that didn't make it any less true.

"I'm just glad you're okay."

Sadie wasn't quite sure where the impulse came from, because it was probably better just to let him leave, but she waved him forward. "Why don't you stay a few minutes?"

He didn't hesitate, just nodded as he walked into the room and took the seat beside her bed.

"I'd like to ask you a question, but I need you to promise that you're going to tell me the truth."

"Of course I'll tell you the truth."

"You haven't heard my question yet," she said with a smile.

He answered that with a smile of his own, one of those rare ones that lit the depths of his eyes. "Okay. Fair. What do you want to ask me?"

"I need you to tell me everything you know about Tate Greer."

"Sadie, come on. What good is going to come from that?"

It was basically the answer she had expected, which was why she'd pressed for honesty. "The good is that I'll finally know. The good is that I'll finally understand what I got myself into." She reached over and took his hand in hers. "I need to know."

"You're still a member of the GRPD. This case isn't exactly a secret."

"Not something out of a case file, but in your own words, Tripp. Please."

Whether it was the urgency in her voice, or the personal nature of her touch, she wasn't sure. But Sadie knew the moment she got through to him. Resignation painted his face before he took a deep breath. "He's not a good guy, Sadie. But I suspect you already know that."

"Yes, I do." It was only as her eyes shot down that she realized she still had her hand over his. She pulled it back, even as she couldn't deny how nice it had been to touch him.

"From all we've been able to figure out based on the most recent evidence, Tate has been revealed to be the head of the Capital X organization. Likely its founder, too. They engage in some really nasty loan-sharking and do whatever they have to to enforce their rules."

"And murder?"

"When it serves their purposes."

Just like Fred, she thought. "I'm sure your team has already found him, but Tate shot one of his henchmen when I was there."

"I'm sorry you had to see that. We did find him, but we didn't yet know the reason why he was dead."

"Tate claimed Fred had been followed and that the cabin was being closed in on. Tate shot him for sharing the news."

The memory sent a shudder through her and those earlier tears she had managed to hold back welled up once more.

"I called him and the other guy who was looking after me Fred and Barney. He was the big one, Barney was the little one, and they seemed to be a duo, you know?" She sniffed hard, even as a few more tears dropped silently down her cheeks. "I have no particular affinity for either of them and I know they chose their paths. But the man I was going to marry, to bind my life with, shot one of them in cold blood. I don't know how to reconcile that in my mind."

All the tears she had been so determined to hold back finally fell with all the finesse of a dam overflowing in spring. It felt like she kept traveling the same ground—endlessly—yet all she could ask herself was how she could've been so stupid. How she could've missed it all.

She was so wrapped up in her emotions that it took a minute before she realized Tripp had shifted some of the wires and her IV to settle in beside her on the bed. His big arms came around her, just as they had in his SUV, and he pulled her close.

"Shh. It's okay."

"It's definitely not okay. I'm a cop. And CSI. I should've known better."

"I'll let you in on a little secret. It's something I don't tell anybody."

She twisted a bit in his arms so she could look at him, curious about what he was going to say. "What secret?"

"Much as we try to be, no one in this job is omniscient. No one's a mind reader. And no one can anticipate another human being's every move. It's just the way of things, as hard as it is to accept."

"I should have known."

He pressed a light kiss to her forehead. "Someday, I promise you, you'll understand and accept why you didn't."

It didn't make sense, and Sadie wasn't even quite sure she believed him, but sitting there in his arms she felt better. For the first time in weeks, she could see the real possibility that, someday, she might feel like herself again.

And she had Tripp McKellar to thank for it.

Chapter Five

Tripp held tight to Sadie, for the second time in less than twelve hours, and marveled at how good she felt nestled in his arms. He'd only meant to comfort and care, yet somewhere between pulling her from Sand Springs Lake and pressing a kiss to her forehead, something inside him had broken wide open.

And the balance between his rigid self-control and the interest he'd had in her for years had decidedly shifted.

Attraction or not, he was still a leader in the Grand Rapids PD and she was not. Her CSI role meant she didn't directly report to him, but he was still her superior as far as departments went.

It was time he remembered that.

He carefully disengaged himself from the wires, gently settling her back against the pillow. "I think it's probably time for you to get some rest."

Those pretty green eyes were dazed, her brow knitted in confusion, before she nodded. "I probably should."

"I want you to think about what I said. You don't need to keep beating yourself up, Sadie. You couldn't have known. Really, you couldn't."

He sensed her protest, her lips opening, before she closed them. "Thank you for saying that."

"Now, get some rest. I'll come back and visit in the morning. I've even heard a rumor there might be donuts."

The mention was enough to get a smile out of her. "Oh, there will be donuts. If I know Pippa, there will be enough to feed the entire hospital."

"Well then, I'll definitely be back for that."

"Oh!" Her sleepy eyes went wide. "I did get something else."

"Got what?"

"Tate believed Fred was followed because he heard it on GRPD dispatch. When I pressed if he had someone inside he mentioned how good his tech was." She yawned, her sweet face scrunching up at the involuntary motion. "And that's all I got."

All?

That was huge and it went a long way toward answering how Greer might know about the safe house, too. But looking down at Sadie Colton's sleepy countenance, Tripp knew now wasn't the time to get into it all.

He patted her foot underneath the blankets, the move silly and awkward after what they had just shared, and figured that was his cue to leave. He'd nearly made it to the doorway when she spoke behind him. "Thank you, Tripp. For everything."

He turned at the doorway, surprised to see how small she looked amid the sheets and the big bed and all the monitors. It was such a counterbalance to a woman who always seemed so alive. So robust. "Sleep. Feel better. I'll be back in the morning."

When her eyes drifted shut as she nodded, Tripp took it as a good sign. She needed to sleep. To heal. Even with the doctor's excellent prognosis, she had been through a traumatic ordeal. Escaping from it all into sleep would do wonders.

He walked down the hall, nodding to the cop placed at the entrance to the ward. He recognized the man, an eager second-year who continually impressed everyone with his hard work and dedication to the job.

Sadie was in good hands.

Even if the fact they'd needed to post a guard at all was a bigger problem. As she'd accurately assessed even before they'd put her into the ambulance, Tate Greer was still out there. And for as long as he was, Sadie wasn't safe.

Making his way along the corridor, Tripp glanced into the waiting room. It was now empty of Coltons, but had turned over with a few new families, all as equally anxious to see their loved ones as the Coltons had been to see Sadie.

Tripp considered them all and couldn't help but remember his own time in one of those waiting rooms. He had sat in one of those seats once. The night Lila had been brought in, he had waited, like those families were waiting, only the news at the other end had been the worst of his life.

We're sorry, Lieutenant McKellar. We did all we could...

Sustained blood loss from the severity of her gunshot wounds...

At only fifteen weeks of gestation... We were unable to save the baby...

It played through his mind on a loop, the memories shockingly easy to rise to the surface, even so many years later.

The real surprise: how hard they hit and the fact that he needed to take one of those seats now for a few minutes to gather himself. Tripp stared down at his shaking hands, unable to believe he could still be so affected by the memories. Hadn't he worked on this? Hadn't he believed himself past this?

Would the grief and the guilt ever fade?

Taking slow, deep breaths, he willed the air in and out of his lungs, calming himself the only way he knew how. As he slowly came back to himself, Tripp had to admit that this was only partially about Lila and the baby.

It was also about Sadie.

He cared for her. Had cared for her for a long time. No matter how many times he told himself he shouldn't, he *did* care for her. And tonight he had almost lost her. That shook a man down to his core.

Was it finally time to tell her how he felt?

It all felt so futile, yet at the same time his ability to deny his attraction was rapidly fading. Because even beyond basic attraction, he had deep feelings for her.

That was the most dangerous thing in the world.

Hadn't he made a vow to himself? He'd never risk someone's life again because of his job. He'd cared for Lila and it had been hard enough to lose her. But even without spending any real time together, he knew his feelings for Sadie ran far deeper than they ever had for Lila.

And he had no idea what the hell he was supposed to do about it.

Rubbing a hand over his face, feeling the scratch of a day's worth of beard, he got up and headed for the vending machines. He didn't need any more coffee, but the jolt it provided would be enough for the drive home. Besides, what would a little caffeine hurt? He didn't sleep very well anyway, so what did it matter?

He walked down the hall, following the same path he had taken with Riley Colton earlier. Step by step, he willed the old hospital memories away until they were locked in that quiet place he kept them. He dug out some coins and pressed the directions on the coffee machine, then shoved his hands in his pockets to wait.

It was only as he turned, an oh-so-brief matter of a split second of overlap, that he saw a big frame pass by the alcove for the vending machines. There were still people in the hospital, coming and going. Yet there was something in that slithering form that captured his full attention.

Coffee forgotten, Tripp moved.

And feared that Tate Greer had come back to finish the job.

Sadie shifted and tried to get comfortable, but between the wires and the lightly beeping machines and the lingering troublesome thoughts, she wasn't having a lot of luck with sleep. She knew she could ring her call bell and a nurse would give her something to sleep, but she never cared for medicine of any kind. Something about artificially induced sleep just felt wrong. Off-putting, somehow. It worked for some, but she was just afraid it was one more way to lose control over her situation.

She'd had enough of that lately, thank you very much.

And then there was Tripp.

Had she been imagining things?

It was sweet that he had stayed to check on her to see how she was. If that had been all, she would tell herself she *had* just been imagining things. But the way he'd settled next to her on the bed and held her close…

Well, it was everything.

Did she dare hope that he had feelings for her, too?

Damn it, Sadie Colton, dream much?

It was silly. *This* was silly.

And still, she couldn't help feeling…*something*.

On a heavy sigh, she readjusted and tried to get comfortable. "I will sleep," she whispered. "I *will* sleep."

She had nearly done it, too, the world going dark around her, when something she couldn't identify made her eyes pop wide open.

The lighting was set to dim, but it was still easy to make out any and all movement. And the large, hulking form that had just slipped into her room was definitely moving. A scream crept up her throat, nearly spilling out when Tate's firm, unyielding hand came over her mouth.

"Shut up or I'll kill you now."

She struggled against his hand, but the dark, dangerous look in his eyes brooked little argument.

"Now, we are going to finish what we started back at the cabin. I want to know what you know. And I want to know what the GRPD knows."

She kept her gaze on his, calculating as quickly as

she could what to do about the situation. If he'd gotten this far, it meant he'd quickly—and silently—dealt with the guard positioned outside. Tripp hadn't made a big deal about it, but Riley had, stressing there was police presence on-site to watch out for her.

So what had happened? She might have been drifting off to sleep but she'd have heard something if there had been a fight. She even knew the officer they'd put in the hallway, remembering him when he'd come in to introduce himself.

"Nod once if you understand me," Tate snarled.

She nodded, still trying to buy herself time. He'd see it if she tried to buzz the nurse, and she'd prefer to avoid dragging any innocents into this if she could.

He removed his hand but it meant little when he lifted his other hand and a gun glinted in the dim lighting. Brandishing it to make his point crystal clear, he hovered even closer, like the brute he really was. "Now tell me what the cops know."

The gun seemed to dance before her eyes, but she refused to cower in the face of this relentless evidence that he was a horrible human being. "They know the same as I do. That you're a monster."

The hard slam from the butt of the gun against her jaw was swift and immediate punishment, the contact enough to make her bones rattle and stars cloud her vision.

"Bull. I know you know more than you're telling me. Unlike all the time you spent with me when you knew nothing. You didn't even know who I was, Little Miss Crime Scene Investigator. What a top-notch worker bee you must be."

Since the words matched a bit too closely to what she'd already berated herself for—endlessly—over the past month, she forced herself to ignore them. She also ignored the pain coursing through her jaw, refusing to show him anything but disdain. "Believe me, I've caught up."

Tate leaned in even closer and Sadie scrambled frantically for something to do. While she didn't want to endanger a nurse, she needed some way to issue a panic alert. Her hand fumbled along the inside of the bed, desperately trying to find the small red button they'd told her about earlier when suddenly Tate went flying.

Shock morphed quickly into a desperate desire to help when another person bodily removed Tate from her bedside. It was Tripp. Even now, the two men lay on the floor, struggling in a death grip for the gun in Tate's hand. She scrambled for the call button by touch, hitting the small panic alert before she sat up.

With an eye to the rolling stand that held her IV fluids, she figured she could use it as a weapon if she needed to. Only Tate gave her an easier opening. As he and Tripp rolled on the floor, Tate managed to maneuver himself on top. Sadie watched in horror as he lifted his gun. She didn't think, only acted. With a hard push to the heavy wheeled tray beside her bed, she shoved it as hard as she could into Tate's back.

It was awkward and not nearly heavy enough to do damage, but the recently filled pitcher on top added some advantage. Aside from spewing water over both men, the entire pitcher also hit Tate in the back of the head as the tray fell on him.

Tripp didn't waste time, using the shift in momentum

to slam the gun from Tate's hand. The weapon clattered to the floor and both men grunted as they continued their physical battle before Tripp reached out blindly, trying to drag the fallen table to hit Tate once more.

Sadie screamed as she struggled to put her feet on the floor. She would be of minimal help in a fight, but she'd already begun looking around the room for something to strategically up the stakes in Tripp's favor. The vase of flowers her sister had set earlier looked like a good option and she walked toward the small desk that held the arrangement.

Pain swam in her head from Tate's pistol whip to the jaw, but she kept moving. Tripp needed her. So did the cop Tate had gotten past in the hall.

Shouts echoed from outside the room and she knew help was coming, but still she pushed on. With the vase in hand, she moved back to the struggling, wrestling men on the floor and waited for a clean shot to drop the vase on Tate's head. When an opportunity presented itself, she didn't wait, slamming the heavy vase into the back of Tate's skull.

It made a satisfying thud but barely slowed him down as her ex suddenly struggled off Tripp, rolled away and headed for the door. The sudden shift in direction was so abrupt, it took Tripp a minute to react. By the time he'd reached the door, he collided with two incoming nurses.

"Ms. Colton!" one exclaimed as the other nurse took firm hold of Tripp's shoulders.

"Let him go." Sadie waved at them, but the second nurse wasn't having any of it.

The throng of shouts finally died down enough

for Tripp to point toward his hip. "My badge is in my pocket. I'm a lieutenant with the GRPD." His teeth were nearly clamped shut as he continued to grind out directives. "And you're letting the perpetrator against Ms. Colton get away."

The nurse finally stood down, releasing him, but Sadie knew it was too late. With a resigned sigh, she nodded at Tripp. "Go. I'll explain what happened here."

He ran off and she turned to face the two surprised women.

"There should be an officer in the hallway. We need to get him immediate help."

For the third time in less than twenty-four hours, Tripp cursed himself for the unrelenting danger that continued to find Sadie. It had been bad enough that she'd been taken from the safe house. Worse, that she'd nearly died in the lake. But *this*? To be nearly snatched right out from under him?

There was no way he was willing to trust her safety to anyone else. Not anymore.

He'd given chase after leaving Sadie's room but Greer had a significant head start.

And Greer was crafty, he'd give him that. The bastard had felled the cop on the ward with a quick pressure syringe and basically kept on moving. Straight into Sadie's room. If Tripp hadn't stopped for that cup of coffee…

If he hadn't had that moment of quiet remorse in the waiting room…

He didn't want to think about it.

Just like that moment she'd jumped in the lake to escape, Tripp knew the vision of that hulking form hovering over Sadie, alone and vulnerable in her hospital bed, would stay with him forever.

He slammed back into Sadie's room, his badge now visible high on his jacket. Backup was on its way and he'd already spoken to security for the hospital. The nurses had taken his officer into an exam room and had assured Tripp he'd be all right after they woke him from the sedative.

Now he just needed to convince Sadie that there was no way she was staying here.

Tripp came to a halt as he crossed the threshold. She was no longer huddled on her hospital bed in her hospital gown. Instead she was sitting on the bedside chair, having changed into a fresh set of clothes. One of her sisters must have brought them to her, because they certainly weren't the wet ones he had removed from her a few hours ago.

"Going somewhere?"

"I'm not staying here." She dragged a boot onto her right foot. "I'm not sure why I've remained this long."

"You can't go home."

"Then I'll go to Vikki's. Or to one of my other siblings'. But I'm not staying here. I already had one of the nurses remove my IV."

The lights were fully on in her room and underneath the harsh fluorescence, he could see the dark bruise on her jaw. "What happened?"

"Tate decided to introduce me to the butt end of his pistol."

Once more, Tripp shook at the evidence of what

could've happened to her. Hell, based on that dark bruise, what *had* happened to her... It was too much.

"You're coming home with me."

She stopped as she slipped on the other boot and stared up at him. "What?"

"You'll stay with me. I know how to keep you safe and I have my place well outfitted."

"What is that supposed to mean?"

"I know how to take care of myself. I'm a lieutenant in a major city's police department. Believe me."

He did know how, and he had also gotten better since Lila's death. Between extra security on his home and his own rigorous self-training, he felt certain he'd do a better job caring for Sadie than one of her siblings.

"Tripp, this is crazy talk. I can't stay at your house."

"Why not?"

"Because—" She stopped before standing to her full height. "Because I'm not your responsibility. I'm a grown woman. I'm also a cop, or I *was* one, before I shifted into my field. I know how to take care of myself."

Although the past month had seemingly suggested otherwise, she did know how to take care of herself. And to her larger point, she was trained. She knew how to handle a weapon, she knew self-defense and, most of all, she wasn't required to accept his help.

But he didn't know how he could live with himself if something happened to her.

"I know all those things. And I believe them, too. The last month has been anything but normal, but your situation isn't indicative of your ability to defend yourself."

"Thank you."

"But I would feel better if you were with me."

"Why?"

"Because I don't want to see anything happen to you." *Because I care about you. Because I've always cared about you.*

He didn't say those things. He *couldn't* say those things. But somewhere way down deep inside, that was all he wanted to say to try to convince her.

"I don't want to be a burden to you." She pressed on, but he could see her conviction wavering ever so slightly.

"You're not a burden. More than that, you have more knowledge of this case than anyone else. Even if you didn't, I would help you. But, selfishly, I'm going to ask for your help. I need all I can get right now."

"You want my help?"

"Of course I do. You know Greer better than anyone. I bet if we sit and think about it, you can point to certain times when you may have picked up information. Windows, or gaps in our knowledge, you may be able to fill in. If he was in or out of town… If he told you he was traveling… Or even casual conversation that didn't mean anything at the time but might be beneficial to us if you look at it now."

And if it meant Tripp had to listen to details about the quiet, intimate evenings she'd spent with her former fiancé, then so be it. He needed the help and, more importantly, he needed her safe. If it took a few uncomfortable conversations to ensure that, he'd deal.

"I was thinking about it before." She sat on the edge

of the bed. "Maybe we've been considering him and Capital X all wrong."

Immediately intrigued, Tripp prodded her. "How do you mean?"

"Well, it's easy to think of him as just a criminal. But he's a businessman, too. Heck, that's what I thought he was up until the big reveal."

He almost laughed at her description of finding out who Tate really was, but decided it wasn't quite the right moment. So he went with honesty instead. "That's what I'm talking about. That kind of thinking. That's what I need right now."

"And I'm not going to be a burden?"

"No."

"And you're not just saying that?"

"No."

A small grin edged the corner of her lips before she winced, laying a hand on her jaw. "Ow. Don't make me smile like that."

He knew she was trying to lighten the mood, but at the sign of her pain, he made one more internal vow.

Whether he liked it or not, the RevitaYou case had become personal. And when he finally got his hands on Tate Greer, there was no way he was going to give the man any mercy.

No way in hell.

Chapter Six

Sadie yawned and ignored the shooting pain in her jaw as she tried to remember the last time she'd been this exhausted. She'd pulled some all-nighters when she was in the police academy. She'd studied overtime and in every free moment she could find when she was learning the ropes for CSI. But none of it had felt so all-consuming.

And so emotionally draining.

Neither had it come with that bone-deep chill that still lingered from her dive into the lake.

"We're almost there," Tripp said. "The turnoff for my neighborhood is in two more lights."

"Sorry. I guess I yawned out loud."

He grinned, the smile visible in the light of the streetlamps. "It was hard to miss."

She had always wondered about where he lived. Now that she had the chance to see his home, she could admit to some excitement. Tripp had always been a mystery at work. He was kind, a hard worker and a true champion for his people, but he kept himself aloof.

Separate.

It made him mysterious and, she admitted to herself, even a little bit sexier than he already was. Which was

silly, because not knowing about people didn't necessarily mean that lack of knowledge was a good thing.
Look at all she didn't know about Tate, for example.

"What's the frown for?"

"Nothing." Goodness, she needed to stop this train
of thought. Not only was it frustrating and repetitive,
but clearly those negative feelings were stamped all
over her face.

"Look, I know we don't know each other incredibly
well, but I'm a good ear. I don't really talk to others,
and I certainly don't share confidences."

He made the turn at that second light he had refer-
enced, pulling into a nice older neighborhood on the
outskirts of Grand Rapids. Sadie had been here before,
she realized. A friend of hers from high school had lived
nearby and she'd visited often when she was younger.
Although the trees were bare now, the neighborhood
boasted huge oaks and the most gorgeous fall foliage
when October came around.

It suited him well, she thought. There was something
solid and sturdy about the neighborhood. Just like Tripp.

"It's not that I don't want to tell you, or anyone, really." Sadie started in, stopping as she tried to think of
the right words. "I mean, I have my sisters, and we talk
about pretty much everything pretty much all the time."

"I'm not trying to pry into the sisterhood."

She smiled at that and his sweet attempt at lighten-
ing the mood. "I promise I won't make you pinky swear
on anything, nor will I make you do my hair. But that's
not actually what I meant."

"I can do a mean braid, if I do say so myself."

"I'll remember that."

She hesitated and wondered if she dared to say what was on her mind.

Oh, what the hell.

"It's just that I can't stop thinking about what a bad decision I made. And how horribly duped I was. It's embarrassing, you know? Like, really embarrassing. Like, I-jumped-into-a-freezing-cold-lake-to-escape-the-jerk-I-thought-I-was-going-to-marry embarrassing."

Now that she'd gotten into it, the words wouldn't stop.

"I realize I should be incredibly upset because he tried to kill me. And I am. Don't get me wrong, I *really* am. But it's like one more example of how shortsighted I was. How stupid I was. And all that keeps going through my mind, over and over, is one question."

"What's that?"

"Was I so happy to finally have a relationship and someone who wanted to marry me that I didn't pay any attention to what was actually going on?"

Tripp navigated the neighborhood streets until they reached his driveway and he hit the opener for the garage door. He pulled in, his attention on the rearview mirror until the door closed fully behind them. It was only then that he turned off the ignition and turned to face her.

"I don't know how you feel. I haven't been in that situation and I won't insult you with some dumb platitudes designed to make me feel better, not you. But I will tell you something and I hope you take it to heart."

When she'd started in on her tirade, she'd expected he'd do nothing more than politely listen to the pressure cooker he'd unknowingly unleashed.

But the serious look in his eyes, visible in the dome lighting, told another story.

"What's that?"

"You're a remarkable woman, Sadie Colton. I've thought it since the first time I saw you at the academy and I've thought it every day since. You're sharp and smart and you care about people. You believe in people. And because of it, you're one of the finest members of our department. You do right by others and you want to see justice brought for all who deserve it.

"I can't tell you how to feel, but I can tell you how others see you. And I can tell you how I see you. And it's not as some helpless damsel in distress or some silly duped woman. Tate Greer is a criminal and he behaves like a criminal. And you, unfortunately, were collateral damage. That's his fault, not yours."

He flipped off the dome light and reached for his car door handle, admonishing her before he got out. "Stay where you are. I'm going to come around and help you."

The normal urge to argue or to tell him she was fine never made it past her lips. Because she was still so shell-shocked over his speech.

He thought she was remarkable.

Her.

She was still trying to make sense of those words when he came around and opened her door.

Tripp wasn't sure what had gotten into him, but now that the rush of words was out, he wasn't sure if he should be embarrassed or pleased by Sadie's response.

Or lack thereof, if the fact that she hadn't moved from her seat was any indication.

"Once you're ready, step down carefully. If you place your foot on the running board, I'll help you from there."

Sadie did as he asked, planting her feet as she shifted herself out of the passenger side. Her movements were slow, but he was pleased to see she seemed to have full range of motion as well as some pink color back in her cheeks.

Even if that rosy glow competed with the purple bruise lining her jaw.

Ignoring the hot rush of anger, Tripp took hold of her hands and helped her step down. Just like earlier, the gesture was simple and meant to help, but Tripp couldn't help but feel there was something more to it. Something monumental.

That was a train of thought he definitely needed to pull off the tracks if she was going to be living with him for the next few days.

"There are just two steps up to the garage door. If you wait, I'll help you up them and into the house."

He went around to the back of the vehicle to pull out a few of his work items as well as the small bag her sister had brought to the hospital. But by the time he closed the rear door to his SUV, Sadie was already at the steps.

"Hey there. I told you to wait for me."

She turned to him, perched on the second stair. It basically made them eye level, but she had the slightest advantage in height. From her perspective, she looked down on him, a small smile at her lips.

"I want to do this, before I lose my nerve."

Before he could even register her words, she leaned

in and pressed her lips to his. It was a quick kiss, and rather chaste, but something inside him imploded.

Unable to stop himself, his free arm wrapped around her, holding her in place. Without questioning if he should, or even if she'd welcome the gesture, he returned his mouth to hers. She hesitated for the briefest moment and he nearly pulled back, but her arms came around his neck, her lips opening beneath his.

Desire and a delicious sort of shock rippled through him as the kiss spun out. Heat, need and the culmination of what felt like endless years of wanting combined to create something he had never felt before. A soul-deep desire that made all the principles he held on to so tightly seem almost silly.

He didn't need or want a relationship in his life… right?

Somewhere a small voice inside kept trying to remind him of that, but Tripp disregarded its steady drumbeat. And then he ignored it completely as he dropped the bags from his one hand, lifting that arm to join the other at her waist. With the additional leverage, he pulled her closer, reveling in the way she seemed to melt into his arms.

Her lips were playing over his, pulling sensation after sensation. Like that runaway train he had worried about, the emotion sparking between them was electric.

And wildly raging out of control.

It was Sadie who finally broke the kiss, her pretty green eyes hazed with passion. "I guess that means you didn't mind."

"No, I didn't."

She reached behind her for the doorknob. "I should probably go in now."

As she still fumbled for it, Tripp reached past her, his forearm brushing her waist, to turn the knob. "You should. I can help you, if you need it."

She shook her head, sudden shyness taking over her normally ebullient personality. "I'm good. A friend of mine from high school used to live in this neighborhood, and I think your house has the same layout. I can find my way."

He bent to pick up her bag, handing it over. "The bed in the spare room is all made up. And there are towels in the attached bathroom."

"Thanks."

She turned then and slipped into the house. While he hated to see her go, Tripp was strangely relieved. In the cooling aftereffects of their kiss, reality was rapidly coming back.

He'd kissed Sadie.

Well, she'd kissed him, but then he'd kissed her.

The dangerous swings of emotion he had carried for the last several days had erupted at the touch of her lips. It was a distraction he didn't need. More, with the threat to her well-being still out there, it was a distraction that could prove lethal.

Yet no matter how hard he admonished himself, he couldn't deny how good it felt to touch her. To kiss her.

He gave her one more minute and then followed her into the house, setting the alarm behind him.

As he heard the light creak of someone walking over the floors above his head, Tripp acknowledged he couldn't deny how he felt at all.

It was good to have Sadie here with him.

Even if having her here, close enough to touch, would be the hardest test of his life.

SADIE CAME AWAKE the next morning in a rush, the same way she had woken up every other day of her life. Only this day, she was different. Wildly different. Because last night she'd kissed Tripp. More, she had *initiated* the kiss with Tripp.

Although he had caught up quickly, she thought, unable to hold back a smile.

She hadn't intended for things to go quite so far and, if she hadn't been so exhausted, likely wouldn't have worked up the courage to kiss him at all. But her guard had been down and he had said those lovely things in the SUV, so she'd gone for it.

And then been beyond surprised to find such a willing partner in the kiss.

Oh, could he kiss. Whatever she'd imagined, the strong lips with their gentle-but-firm pressure and the warm, secure feel of his arms around her had been beyond anything she'd imagined. And over the past several weeks, she'd imagined plenty.

Only to find that reality had been so much better.

Sitting up, Sadie tested her body, curious how many aches she would find. She was lightly sore all over. Yet, all things considered, she felt pretty good. But oh, her face. She raised a hand to lay it against her cheek and felt the tender, warm-verging-on-hot skin beneath.

Damn it, Tate had done a number on her. She could only imagine what her face looked like and was dread-ing her first glance into the mirror. If it appeared half as bad as it felt, she was prepared to look pretty awful.

Hitting her had been a nasty move, designed to make her feel small. And it had worked. Only now, with the bright sunlight of a winter morning streaming through the windows, it made her angry. She meant what she had said to Tripp the night before. She *did* want to help him. And in light of what he had suggested, working together through a timeline of the past several months in the investigation into Capital X, she likely did have something to contribute.

Tate had thought he was so clever, concealing everything he did from her, but there had been some cracks. They had spoken of travel and he'd mentioned a lot of the places he had been to. He had almost bragged about it, really, talking about the things he had done and seen.

She could use that. If they could triangulate some of the locations, they might have a better chance of tracking where Capital X's interests might lie.

Regardless of what they turned up from her memory, she was also a pretty decent whiz with the computer. She could dig as much as the next person, and she was determined to help Tripp find what he needed. They would put Tate away. And she was first in line to be part of the team to do it.

With that resolution keeping her company, she got out of bed and crossed to the bathroom. Flipping on the light, she moved before the mirror, offering up a small prayer as she went.

"May it not be too bad," she whispered before opening her eyes. And watched them widen in her reflection as she took in the purple and blue that ran down the edge of her jaw.

Wow. She breathed out, shocked to realize that it actually looked *worse* than it felt. That was saying something.

Determined to find the silver lining—and realizing it was rooted in the fact that her jaw wasn't broken—Sadie quickly washed up and headed back into the bedroom. She put on a fresh change of clothes then headed for the kitchen. Coffee would make it better.

Then she'd hunt up a pad of paper and start writing down what she knew.

It was only as she came into the kitchen that she found Tripp at the table a few steps ahead of her. He had his laptop open and a series of photographs laid out on the kitchen table. He was also scribbling notes on a legal pad beside his computer.

"You're up early."

He glanced up from his notepad. "I could say the same about you. Have you had enough sleep?"

"I'll probably crash again later, but right now I'm good." She pointed to the coffee maker on the counter. "Can I get you a refill?"

Tripp stood at that, snagging his mug from the table. "You don't have to wait on me."

"It's coffee. I think it's okay."

He'd left a mug out for her on the counter and she filled it before turning with the pot to replenish his. It was only as she turned, morning light streaming through the window, that she caught his dark glare.

"What?"

"That bruise on your cheek." Tripp came closer, ignoring the outstretched carafe in her hands and instead setting his mug on the counter with a hard thud. He then reached for her, tilting her face so he had a better view in the light.

"How sore is it?"

"It hurts, but I'm fine."

He ran tender fingers over her jaw, from just beneath her ear all the way down to her chin. The light touch sent shivers down her spine and Sadie had the abstract thought that if given the chance she'd happily stand there with him every morning for the rest of her life.

Oblivious to her thoughts, Tripp gestured with his mouth, his movements reminiscent of the Tin Man after a dose of oil. "Can you move it back and forth?"

Sadie followed suit, nearly laughing out loud at the image.

"What's so funny?"

"I'm waiting for you to pull out your oilcan, Dorothy."

It was enough to break the moment and he dropped his hand from her jawline. "Very funny."

"I'll be fine. Nothing's broken and, while it hurts, it'll heal."

"We should get some ice on it. I should have thought to do that last night."

Last night.

When they'd kissed.

If she'd been even half thinking when she'd come into the house, she'd have thought of it herself. She'd fallen into bed, so exhausted from the day, that it had never crossed her mind.

"I'll do it in a bit. Right now I want to enjoy my coffee and see what you're working on." She turned to re-fill his mug before setting the coffeepot back on the burner. "I've been out of the loop on everything for the past month. Fill me in."

He looked about to argue before grabbing his mug and following her to the table. "What has Vikki told you?"

"We communicated by burner phone when I was in the safe house, so I know a few things. But why don't you give it to me through a cop's eyes?"

She took a seat, reaching for one of the photos he'd placed on the table. A name was pinned to the bottom: Landon Street. Sadie turned the photo over, curious to the details. "This is Flynn's brother, right?"

"Half brother. He's the man who came up with Re-vitaYou."

That meant he would soon be Vikki's half brother-in-law.

"We've got him in custody," Tripp continued, "but he's not saying much."

"He probably knows what'll happen to him if he snitches on Tate's organization."

"Possibly. He's also likely biding his time in hopes he can work a deal. He's a scientist, after all. He prob-ably doesn't see himself in the same criminal class as the group he went all-in with."

Sadie figured a deal was highly unlikely, but at this point, the entire RevitaYou case was like something out of another dimension anyway. The depths of depravity as well as the strange layered mess of it all was tough to navigate.

Sadie took a sip of her coffee, a new idea playing in

her mind. "It's weird, you know. How intertwined my family has become with this case."

"How do you mean?"

"Well, the inventor of RevitaYou is Landon Street. And his half brother is now my twin sister's fiancé."

"Funny coincidence?"

"A happy one, too. But curious, don't you think?"

"People find their way to each other in any number of ways."

Sadie knew he was right, but even so, it struck her as odd. Her five siblings had all reached the age of maturity and none of them was married. And now here they all were; after just a matter of months working the RevitaYou case, all were coupled up with people intimately involved.

"It's still a bit odd. Vikki's engaged to Flynn, whose brother invented the product. And Griffin is engaged to Abigail, whose father was the banker behind the pyramid scheme. And even Kiely found her true love, Cooper, because they were working the case together at the FBI."

"They also dealt with the kidnapping of Cooper's son because of it."

Sadie thought of sweet little Alfie and how excited she was to see her soon-to-be nephew again. "They did. Which only adds to my point. My family is so deeply layered in this case and has been from the start."

"Riley told me about your family's relationship with Brody Higgins. That personal connection is why you're all involved. And things have progressed from there."

He was right. Trying to find some weird connection

made little sense when it was clear how her siblings had met their significant others.

"Okay. So personal connections aside, things have been moving forward. And between you and the GRPD, Colton Investigations, the JAG investigation that solidified Landon Street's involvement, and the FBI, it stands to reason this would be locked up by now. Yet the sands keep shifting. Every time it feels like there's a lead that will wrap the whole thing up, a new dimension opens up."

"You're on point with that one, Colton."

"Thanks, McKellar. So what do we know and where are the gaps?"

Over the next hour, Tripp walked her through the case. Every detail he had, from what had actually happened all the way through to his personal theories. He showed her his notes and replayed a few of the interviews they'd done with both Landon Street as well as Tate's henchman, Gunther Johnson, in custody.

"Then Street and Johnson are where we need to begin today."

"We?" Tripp glanced up from where he'd scratched another note on his legal pad.

"Sure. You said you wanted my help. Gunther Johnson is our first stop."

"You're not going to talk to him."

"Sure I am." Sadie made a point to keep her voice light and breezy, even if steel had gathered in her gut.

The RevitaYou case had lingered too long. They needed answers and they were losing precious time before key criminals either cut bait and got away or more people died from the drug.

Or both.

"You know how deep Greer's tentacles go. Johnson only ratted him out to get out of Murder One charges. He's not going to give up anything else."

"Then we gently persuade him to."

"I'm not sure gentle and Gunther Johnson belong in the same sentence."

"I just want to ask him a few questions about who and what he knows. He's one of Tate's lead guys, which means he knows where the money is and where the bodies are buried."

Tripp reached for his mug, setting it back down when he realized it was empty. "Which amounts to further ratting out Greer. Sadie, this isn't going to work."

Sadie stood to get the pot of coffee, returning to the table to refill both their mugs. "Sure it will. I have an ace up my sleeve. Tate didn't tell me anything, but Johnson doesn't know that."

"You're going to play him."

Even with the pain in her jaw, she couldn't hold back the big, broad smile. For the first time in months, she began to feel like herself. "Like a well-tuned fiddle."

Chapter Seven

Tripp unlocked the door to his office and wondered, not for the first time since waking up, when he'd lost his mind. Was it when Sadie had kissed him? Or before? Maybe when she'd huddled in his arms in the SUV after jumping in the lake? Or maybe it was those quiet moments in her hospital bed.

Or hell, maybe it had been that very first day he'd seen her, rookie-crisp in her uniform.

Whether or not he could pinpoint the moment, it really didn't seem to matter. The woman was in his blood and she made a damn fine argument to boot. And he was about to expose her to a one-on-one interview with Johnson. So far, the man had been a rock. Unchanging and absolutely unwilling to talk on almost anything related to Capital X.

Sadie followed in behind him and took a seat in one of the chairs opposite his desk. "Run through it with me again, will you?"

Tripp closed his door then turned to her. "Shoot."

"Gunther thinks he's being loyal by not spilling on Tate's activities. And he's been here for—what?—about two months."

"About two and a half."

"So he's out of the loop."

"He is. Although…" Tripp stilled, a new thought taking root. "What if he's the one who got Tate access to the safe house?"

"You think he influenced somebody here?"

"Possibly. I've been racking my brain but I never once considered that Gunther could have been his way in."

"It's an interesting angle. Who here has access to him?"

Tripp mentally ran through the roster. Although he knew most members of the department, he didn't know everyone. And it was impossible to know everyone's personal situations, which were usually the key. He had long believed in the fundamental decency of his fellow cops. But if someone fell on bad times, it was not difficult to be taken advantage of by a persuasive criminal with nothing to lose.

"I need to look into it. Check anyone who has been with him."

"I can help you with that later. If you get the files, I'm happy to cross-reference them with the team."

"You don't have to do that."

"Sure I do. Gotta earn my keep. And we'll add in the tech angle Tate let slip to me, too. See if we can figure out what or maybe who he's hacked." She winked at him, the move positively cheeky. It was refreshing to see, especially after her confession in the SUV last night. Tate's betrayal had done a number on her and while Tripp didn't fully understand what she was going through, he was human. He could imagine how something like that would put a boulder through her self-confidence.

That made it all the nicer to see Sadie safe and excited about the case.

And while he might not fully understand, he meant what he'd said. He was impressed with her every day and knew how talented she was, as a cop and as a lead investigator for CSI. She had skills and smarts, and the GRPD was lucky to have her.

He wasn't crazy about putting her in front of Johnson, but maybe it was what she needed. An emotional shot in the arm to begin to heal some of the damage Greer had caused.

"You ready to do this?" Tripp asked.

"Let's do it."

"All right, then. Like we agreed, I want as few people as possible to see you."

She nodded. "I know. Head down all the way to the interrogation room."

"And you wait in the viewing room until you get my signal."

"That's the plan."

"Okay, Ms. Colton," Tripp said as he stood from his desk. "Get ready to lead the witness."

Tripp waited until Sadie was settled into the viewing room before he opened the door to Interrogation Room One. Johnson was already in the room, having been brought up by one of Tripp's detectives.

"Mr. Johnson, Chief Fox told me you're waiving the right to counsel."

"Sure. Whatever."

Gunther sprawled in his chair with that special sort of disdain only a young man could truly manage. Tripp had read Johnson's file so many times, he had it memorized, but he'd still refreshed himself while briefing Sadie.

Johnson was only twenty-two and, by all accounts, had been working for Greer at least four years. He'd worked his way up to being one of Greer's deputies in that relatively short period of time. The only reason he'd even given Greer up was that he was facing a murder rap.

Tripp would do his job—he always did—but it killed him to see young men like this, their lives wasted before they'd even begun.

Sad situation or not, the kid was scary. His hulking frame had to be at least six-three and, for as big as he was now, he'd likely still fill further over the next year or two. He was bald, with ice-blue eyes that seemed almost devoid of life.

Resigned to the fact that this one was likely beyond saving, Tripp got to work. "Your rights were read to you, but I will ask you again, do you understand them?"

"Yes."

"Do you continue to waive those rights?"

"Yes."

"All right. Let's begin. You've already shared with me and my team that you work for Tate Greer. That correct?"

"Sure is."

The minimalist answers were what Tripp had expected, so he pressed on. "In the course of doing your work for Mr. Greer, when did you learn about the product RevitaYou?"

"I didn't learn about it."

"You don't know anything about it?" Tripp prompted.

"No."

"Have you heard of it?"

"No."

Tripp recognized the blocking and the bravado for what it was, so he kept on. "Surely you had to know something. You're one of Tate's lead guys. If his pyramid scheme did well, didn't you stand to get a cut of it?"

For the first time, he saw the ire rise in Gunther's cold eyes. "I keep my head down and I do my job."

"Killing people?"

Gunther finally looked up, that ice flashing hot before the kid banked it. "Making sure Mr. Greer's business interests are seen to."

It was a new angle, but Tripp had to give the kid credit. He was hardly incriminating himself by making that claim. Taking the "I'm just a lowly employee, I keep my head down and do my job" angle was surprisingly smart.

Had he thought of it on his own? Or had he been coached?

"I think we've established that Mr. Greer's business interests aren't aboveboard."

"Guy runs a business, man. You got a problem with that?"

"Last time I checked," Tripp said, "most businesses don't require murder in order to be successful."

Gunther crossed his arms but didn't respond.

"You've been in here awhile, Gunther."

"Yep. Getting moldy."

"While that businessman you're so loyal to has been out running free and clear."

Once more, Tripp saw that little shot of heat frisson through Gunther's gaze. He didn't say anything, but Tripp took satisfaction he'd hit his mark with the image that Tate was still out while Gunther sat around. It was all the prep Tripp needed and he gestured at the two-way glass for Sadie.

Gunther's attention shifted toward the door as it opened. Tripp didn't miss the shot of appreciation that filled the young man's gaze when Sadie walked in.

"I've asked my colleague to join us, Mr. Johnson. May I introduce you to Sadie Colton."

Gunther lifted his hands as high as he could, the cuffs that encased his wrists limiting his movement as the chain slid through an anchor attached to the table. "Hey."

"It's nice to meet you, Mr. Johnson," Sadie said. She didn't say anything else, just settled herself beside Tripp at the table. As she did, she angled her head so that her bruised jaw was visible to Gunther.

It didn't take any time at all for the kid to comment. "Quite a bruise you got."

"Hurts like hell, too." Sadie added a fierce grin to punctuate the point.

"You run into a wall?"

"No. I took the butt end of your boss's gun."

Although Tripp hadn't pegged the kid for much compassion, he didn't miss the way those broad shoulders stiffened at Sadie's news.

"Do you know who I am, Mr. Johnson?"

"I just met you."

"And I, you. But that wasn't my question."

Just like with the comment on her face, she let her question hang there, more than willing to wait him out.

"Sure, I know who you are. You're the boss's fiancée."

"*Ex*-fiancée."

Once again, Gunther didn't respond and it gave Sadie the opening she was clearly waiting for.

"You know, it's funny how it all worked out. You ratted him out and then I was forced to realize what a nasty-ass criminal he really is. You know—" she leaned forward conspiratorially, getting into it "—my family tried to warn me about him, but I didn't listen."

"I don't rat people out."

"Right. You just happened to tell the Grand Rapids PD that Tate Greer is the head of Capital X."

The kid struggled to sit straight, that lazy slouch gone. "I didn't tell anybody anything they didn't already know."

"I'm not quite sure Tate would see it that way. In fact, based on my conversation with him just yesterday…you know—" she tapped her jaw "—the one where he gave me this? He's still pretty steamed about it all."

She kept up that low, steady conspiratorial tone. "Between you and me, I think he's starting to panic."

"Dude doesn't know how to panic."

"Oh, sweetheart, everybody knows how to panic."

Just as she had played the conversation from the start, Sadie let those words hang there. And like a fish swimming past a baited hook, Gunther took it. "You think you can touch him?"

"I think we already have. I think that's why he's panicked."

Tripp watched as Sadie spun her argument, her demeanor sweet as cotton candy yet layered with threads of steel.

"That's why he hit me. He knows the cops know something. And between you and me, he's right."

Although the rest of him might remain frustratingly stoic, Gunther's eyes said all they needed to know. "Cops don't know nothing."

"Sure." Sadie nodded. "You keep thinking that."

"If they do know something, why isn't Greer rotting away in here, too?"

"You've worked for Tate long enough to know that. He always has a hidey-hole or two set up. He'd never expected we'd find that one at Sand Springs Lake. I'm sure he thinks you gave him up on that, too."

The explosion came exactly on cue. Gunther slammed a hand down on top of the table. "I didn't do that!"

"You sure? It would be easy enough for Tate to think that."

"I didn't do it."

"He's a man of action, isn't he? Shoot first, ask questions later. That's what he did to one of his goons. The big guy was shot dead on the floor."

"Tommy's dead?" Like a balloon popping, the air flew out of Gunther's bravado. "Big guy? Dark hair? Always wears a suit."

"That's the one."

"He was identified as Thomas Brackett." Tripp took the opportunity to layer on the details of Tommy's death. The description drew Johnson's attention from Sadie and gave her time to catch her breath. All while she waited like a patient tiger, ready to strike.

Sadie shrugged, the move deliberately casual. "He never gave me his name, so in my mind I named him Fred and the short guy who works with him I named Barney."

"Little guy's name is Rick." Gunther's words were flat. "They were a team. Worked for Greer for a long time, too."

"And clearly that loyalty was rewarded." Sadie's voice was low and quiet, and there was something beneath her words that had Tripp turning to look at her.

It was in that moment that he saw the truth. She had put on the casual charm and ready bravado for the meeting, but she wasn't unaffected.

Not his Sadie.

"What do you want from me? I don't know anything."

"Sure you do. But I respect the fact that a man needs time to think about things. Why don't you do that?"

With that, Sadie rose and walked out of the room.

It was inspired and Tripp had to give her a lot of credit. He had seen many an interrogator press too hard or go too long. Sadie had done neither. Instead, she was leaving Gunther with plenty to contemplate.

Tripp raised his hands. "I'm done, too."

When Gunther didn't respond, Tripp stood and walked to the door. He opened it and gestured one of the cops waiting outside into the room. With a last look at Gunther, he said, "You can take him back to his cell. We're done in here."

SADIE FLIPPED THROUGH Gunther Johnson's file once more as she waited for Tripp in his office. Although she had read it already, after meeting the man face-to-face, she was hunting for any new perspective she could find.

How could someone's life be so ruined, so young?

It was a question that had haunted her since walking out of that interview room. One she hadn't been able to shake since.

Though she still considered herself young, not even yet thirty, she felt light-years away from Johnson. She had a job helping others. She had a family she cared about. And while things had certainly gone beyond sideways with Tate, her gaze had been firmly on her future.

Yet young men like Gunther traded their futures for violence and some sort of temporary accolade from an employer who couldn't care less about them. Worse, one who found him disposable. It was a strange sort of belonging, doing business in an organization like Capital X. It didn't make sense. And on a bigger level, she knew it would never make sense to her.

With that sobering thought, her mind drifted to Brody. For far too long, she'd only seen him not as a foster brother, but as the young man her father had been helping before her parents had been senselessly murdered. Although the cases weren't related, she'd conflated them in her mind in a sort of resentful stew that had taken her several years to get past.

A fact that shamed her now.

Especially because all her siblings had pretty much taken to Brody. He hadn't been ready for the pressures of real life, nor had he had any resources. Save one.

Her father, Graham Colton.

In his role as district attorney, her father had taken an interest in Brody's case, determined to prove his innocence in a murder trial. It was a crime her father had been convinced Brody hadn't committed. His tenacious work ethic had ultimately proved the young man innocent.

It was Graham's belief in Brody—and her siblings' desperate need to find some meaning after their parents' deaths—that they'd taken Brody in as their own.

And ensured that he would have a better shot at a future than being left to his own devices.

It had mostly worked. Brody had built himself a future, ultimately going to college and law school and working hard to make something of himself. He was only a year younger than she and Vikki, but he'd always seemed younger, somehow. And when she wasn't being stubborn, frustrated and—she'd own it—acting like the baby of the family, she knew he deserved better.

Something she'd come to understand since the RevitaYou case had been cracked wide open. Brody wanted more out of his life, but it was his investment in RevitaYou that had knocked him down.

Terribly.

And every step he'd worked for and pushed for over the past decade had seemingly vanished overnight.

She knew her feelings about Brody weren't simple— especially the quiet one that liked to sneak in and claim he'd taken precious hours of her parents' time in the months leading up to losing them—but she knew she needed to think differently.

Vikki's voice echoed in her head—just like it did every time Sadie mentally went down her Brody rabbit hole. *You can't live his life for him, Sadie. And you need to cut him a break every now and again.*

Although she had spent a lot of time working toward Vikki's approach to Brody, she couldn't deny he still had a future. And a rather bright one, in fact, once they got past this RevitaYou mess.

Something Gunther Johnson would never have.

Tripp closed his office door behind him, their continued secrecy at Sadie's presence in the office still in full effect. "Why the sad face?"

"Just a lot to think about."

"Gunther Johnson?"

"Yes, mostly."

"Mostly?"

"I was thinking about Brody, too."

Tripp's gaze narrowed. "Brody Higgins?"

"That's the one." She waved a hand. "It's complicated emotions."

"I know I said it before, but I'm a good listener."

He was, but in this case she wasn't quite ready to share. She wasn't proud of how she felt about Brody and wasn't quite sure how to put voice to those frustrations without her own biases coming out.

"Maybe some other time. What I was really thinking about was Gunther Johnson. And the fact that he's basically traded every bit of his future."

Tripp took the chair next to her, one of the two seats opposite his desk. "I was thinking along the same lines as we talked to him. He's set his future on a boss and an organization that see him as disposable."

"But he doesn't see it," Sadie said.

"No, I don't think he does."

"It puts one more check mark in the Tate-is-a-world-class-jerk column."

Tripp cocked his head, and she saw the thoughts playing through his mind. Curious, she pressed on. "You don't think so?"

"Oh, I won't argue the world-class jerk point. In fact, I've used a few more choice descriptions. But I'm not sure I would let Gunther off so easily, either."

"He's a kid."

"He *was* a kid when he started at Capital X. Now he's a young man. Let's not lose sight of the choices he has made and continues to make."

"You mean like not helping us?"

"That, yes. He's been in here for two and a half months and, other than seeing a shot at reducing a Murder One charge, he hasn't done a whole lot to help himself."

While she didn't want to give her bleeding heart too much credit, she couldn't ignore Tripp's counter-argument. And it would be highly perilous to give too much sympathy to a dangerous criminal like Johnson. "Something to think about."

"Yeah, it is. One of the unexpected bonuses that come with this job."

She heard his light chuckle, one without any trace of humor, before she continued. "Does it ever get to be too much?"

"Some days."

"What do you do about it? On those days when it gets to be too much."

It was something, Sadie realized, she really wanted to know. How did Tripp manage the pressures of his job? Both the dangers he put himself in, and the human depravity he saw on a regular basis.

"Believe it or not, a burger usually helps."

Whatever she was expecting him to say, that wasn't it. "Thinking of your stomach?"

"Always." He leaned back and patted his delectably flat abs. "But, seriously, a beer on the back porch as I get the grill going? It usually helps."

They hadn't talked about their kiss the night before. In fact, they had both sort of silently agreed to ignore it. But in that quiet moment of camaraderie and solidarity, Sadie couldn't resist a bit more human touch.

Extending a hand between their chairs, she turned it palm up. "Want to go home and make a burger?"

He hesitated, and she thought he might be looking for a way to avoid making contact. Until his large hand came out, taking hers firmly in his own. "I think that's an outstanding idea. Let's go."

GUNTHER JOHNSON STARED up at the ceiling of his jail cell and considered the conversation with Sadie Colton. He figured Tate was pissed about the whole Capital X thing, and the exposure Gunther had unleashed, but he'd done right by the boss, hadn't he?

He was the one who'd got Greer the address to the safe house. And he was also the one who'd kept his ears wide-open since he'd been inside this hellhole.

But killing Tommy?

It sent a shudder through him. And, damn it, it made a man think, too. Tommy had been a big man in the organization. Tate had always joked with him, making it seem like Tommy was indispensable.

Then he'd killed the guy?

Gunther'd had the briefest suspicion that Sadie had been lying about that, but her description of Tommy was spot-on. And there was no way she had made up that bruise on her jaw. While he didn't have sympathy for the cops, he'd never taken Greer for one to go around hitting women, either.

And *damn*, the boss had played her. Gunther had watched it all from afar and knew way more than he had let on to the cops. Tate had worked her and worked her, making her feel so special, telling her how important she was. And all the while he'd kept poking around in her files, trying to get more details on the GRPD and on her family.

Yeah, Gunther knew who the Coltons were. Everybody in this part of Michigan knew who the Coltons were. And that was what Tate had wanted when he'd gone after their precious baby girl. Information from the easiest in he could find.

Gunther had quietly listened when Tate would laugh about her, mentioning an upcoming "date" or weekend trip she was all excited about. Greer had laughed and laughed, like she was the dumbest mark he'd ever seen.

Only she hadn't seemed dumb today. In fact, if he had to guess, she was smart as hell and was now nursing a serious vendetta against Greer.

It made her dangerous. And, he wasn't ashamed to admit to himself, sort of hot. Those sexy green eyes had sized him up and he'd liked it. But he wasn't dumb enough to let his dick do the thinking. Sadie Colton was in that interview room today for a reason and he had to figure it out.

Before he ended up as dead as Tommy.

Chapter Eight

Tripp took a long drag on his beer as he checked the temperature of the grill. He could already feel some of that relaxation and sense of calm returning, just like he'd told Sadie.

Even if the woman was driving him a little out of his mind.

He glanced down at his hand where it rested on the edge of a chair that went with his backyard dining set, and could feel the way her smaller one had fit so neatly in his earlier. He'd nearly held back when she'd stretched out her hand, but after the day they'd had and the underlying sadness of their conversation about wasted futures, he hadn't been able to resist.

A situation he continued to find himself in, more and more.

Determined not to dwell on the things he couldn't have, Tripp considered the conversation with Johnson. Sadie had been impressive, her interview skills incredibly advanced. Whether it was her role as the youngest of six that had made her a good negotiator, he wasn't sure, but she'd hit all the right notes.

She had also left him something to think about when it came to whom Johnson had had ready access to.

Tripp had pulled the log files for the past month before they'd left his office and included anyone who had been on duty at the prison or had checked in for any reason. He wanted to settle into them after dinner.

Sadie came through the back door and out onto the porch. Even though it was December, he had set up heaters at both ends and it made for a cozy space outdoors.

"You've got quite a setup out here." She looked around. "Those space heaters are incredible. I never would've expected you could sit out here, no matter how many heat sources you put up."

"It's a bit of an oasis. Add that I like to grill and needed to find some way to do it year-round."

She slid a plate of uncooked burger patties beside the grill. "Nicely done. And proof that one should never underestimate a man's ingenuity when it comes to his ability to cook meat outside."

"You've made a study of it?"

"My brothers love it. Griffin, especially." Sadie smiled at that, and he saw the clear and genuine affection on her face. "Though I suspect he's grilling less now that he's got Abigail and baby Maya in his life. I've really missed seeing that little one for the past month. She's got to be changing every day. And I missed her first birthday."

Tripp saw the brief bit of sadness and tried to cheer her up. "You've got two things in your favor on that count. First, she likely didn't realize it was her birthday. And second, a well-placed gift from a doting aunt is always a happy occasion."

"You're right." Sadie picked up the beer he'd left for her on the table and took a sip. "You're also surprisingly optimistic. I'm not sure I would've thought that about you."

"You think I'm a downer?"

"No." She seemed to consider her words. "But you are serious. And I think I'd likely misjudged that seriousness for negativity."

"I have my days."

"We all have our days. But here you are in the midst of a highly stressful case and yet you've still found numerous opportunities to make me feel better." She lifted her beer to his in a toast. "Thank you for that."

He clinked his bottle to hers. "You have to admit, you kinda make it easy. You are the sunshine of the Colton family."

She set her beer down, a look of horror on her face. "Oh no, that's what you really think of me?"

"What's wrong with that?"

"Sunshine? The next thing you'll tell me is that I'm cute like a baby kitten and should be patted on the head for my efforts."

"That's not what I meant. Although, what's wrong with being cute?"

"At the risk of borrowing too heavily from Susan Sarandon's rant in *Bull Durham*, let me tell you, a woman would far prefer to be called sexy than cute."

"Can't you be both?"

"In my experience, people tend to prefer to put you in one category and leave you there."

He suddenly realized they weren't talking about cute *or* sexy, but something that ran far deeper. Something that felt a lot like the lifelong expectations others carried for you.

"It's hard to be the youngest?"

"Probably no harder than being the oldest or the middle or anywhere in between. But when it's your life, it does have its challenges."

"Your family cares about you."

"Yes, they do." She smiled, with a benevolent sort of acceptance. "And I love them back. But it doesn't change the fact that we drive each other nuts on a regular basis."

"It's nice to have that."

"You don't?"

He didn't, and while it wasn't something he thought about often, faced with someone who had five siblings, it was interesting to compare. "No. I was a late-in-life baby and it was just me."

"I would imagine that has its challenges, too. We may have our fair share of sibling spats, but they're there for me. And I can't imagine life without them."

"Like you said, we know what we've lived. I don't think about it all that often. Mostly, in conversations like this one, when it's hard to really picture myself in your situation."

She studied him, keenly interested in what he was saying. Although he got that sort of ready acceptance at work, it was rare to have a personal conversation with someone so present, so thoroughly in the moment.

"What situation is that?" she asked.

"The assumption that because they dote on you, they don't see you as a fully capable person."

He wasn't sure where he was going with this, nor was

he sure why he felt it was his business to butt in. But that hadn't seemed to stop him with any conversation they'd had so far. In fact, an odd intimacy had sprung up between them, where he didn't really feel the need to hold back the things he was thinking.

"It's not an assumption, to be honest. It also comes from their actions and the things they say."

"What do they say?"

"About what? My job? My personal life? Where I'm going to live? Who I'm going to live with? What my future looks like?" She stopped, a broad smile suffusing her face. "Gee, that's sort of whiny, isn't it?"

"I wouldn't use that term."

"Then your mother clearly raised you right. But even if I quit my bitching, I can't say I'm entirely in the wrong about them. My brother Riley had a really difficult time when I went out for the force. And Kiely and Pippa, as the older set of twins, love playing mother hen to Vikki and me."

"You don't do the same for them?"

Her eyes went wide at the suggestion. "Of course not. Like they would take that from me."

"Then you didn't see what I saw. Last night at the hospital, for instance. I was waiting out in the hallway and I could hear the way you maneuvered the end of the conversation. You were quick to shoo everybody on after they'd hovered too close. They listened to you."

She reached for her beer, her gaze fully focused on him. "There you go again, making me feel good. And seen."

"Because you are."

"So you say. But I think it's something else. *You* see

a lot, Tripp McKellar. It's interesting and affirming, and a little unnerving."

There was that idea again, about being seen. He'd gotten the sense the night before that he'd touched her with his words in the SUV. Statements that he took as simple fact, about her competence and her capabilities. Yet she clearly saw it as so much more.

"That's probably because I'm prying again."

"No, I wouldn't put it that way. You see things, because you're an observer. Things that sometimes the person in the middle can't see very accurately or without being clouded by their own judgment."

"Only-child observer syndrome?"

"Maybe." She tilted her head, considering. "Maybe it's something more."

"Too many years on the force, being suspicious of anyone and everyone?"

"That one probably has a bit of merit. But it makes you a good detective."

He saw the split second of hesitation, curious as to what she held back. Every moment they had spent together over the past twenty-four hours had suggested Sadie hesitated over very little. Yet even with his curiosity, he couldn't quite reconcile that with the serious way she looked at him.

Ducking away from her close observation, he tilted his head toward the edge of the patio. "I should probably get the burgers on."

He moved to the grill but stopped when her hand reached out and settled on his forearm. "I do think it's something else, Tripp."

Without his even asking, she continued. "I think

you're a good man. An all-the-way-down-deep good man. And I'm afraid there aren't nearly as many of you as I had believed there would be when I grew up."

"I don't know. I think your brothers are pretty good guys. I also know a few of the guys your sisters are marrying and they seem like fine men, too."

"I agree. I think there's good in all of them. But right now, I'm talking about you. And what I see."

Captivated, Tripp couldn't resist asking, "And what do you think you see?"

"I don't think. I know." Her hand fell away, but that serious gaze never left his. "You're the man who does right by others, no matter the cost to himself. It's heroic. And absolutely unusual."

Her words struck a chord and, while a very big part of him was grateful for the way she saw him, an even bigger part refused to believe her. It was sweet that Sadie saw him that way, but he knew the truth. If he truly was a hero, Lila would still be alive. His child would be alive and in kindergarten by now. And he wouldn't carry around this endless emptiness in his heart.

But he didn't say those things.

Even if, in that same place in his heart, Tripp knew he was right.

SADIE SENSED THAT she'd overstepped but had no idea why. She'd meant what she'd said and had been as complimentary of Tripp as he'd been of her the night before.

Yet somehow she felt the genuine praise had fallen flat.

It was tempting to think the intimacy they had developed over the past twenty-four hours was a mirage. It was something she might've let herself believe, even a few days ago in the safe house while berating herself over her failed relationship with Tate.

But Sadie refused to go there, allowing that self-defeating behavior to define her reaction.

She hadn't imagined the quiet moments that had passed between them, which meant Tripp's denial was steeped in something else. But what?

She knew he had something tragic in his past. Although she hadn't been on the force when it happened, personal details always had a way of coming out. Was he still mourning and grieving the loss of his fiancée? Because if that were the case, then she *had* overstepped.

And the intimacy she had pressed for had been ill placed.

She would do well to remember it and focus instead on the reason she was staying with Tripp. It was a protective measure, nothing more. Tate Greer was still out there and she still had a target on her chest.

With the excuse that she needed to go back in to set the table for dinner, Sadie headed inside. She puttered around in the kitchen, pouring them both drinks and hunting up some fixings for salad. By the time he came in ten minutes later with the cooked burgers, she had a big bowl on the counter and plates set out for them.

She kept her smile bright and her tone equally light and airy. "Those smell delicious."

"Making burgers is one of my few skills. I feel pretty confident in telling you that they will be."

"With a sales pitch like that, how can I resist?"

They settled in at the table and Sadie sank into small

talk. It was a skill she had honed over the years with her family and she was pretty good at it, if she said so herself.

Although they had begun to find their way as adults, especially over the past year or so, there had been plenty of tension between the six Colton siblings after their parents died. Adopted as a child, Griffin had always battled feelings of being separate from the rest of them. And she and her sisters, while there was deep love between them, had the typical ups and downs that a group of four women could have for one another. From drama to secrets and back to drama again, often in the course of one conversation.

And then there was Riley.

The oldest, the head of Colton Investigations, and by default, their resident leader. There were times they loved him for it and there were times they resented him for it. Often, Sadie thought ruefully, at the same time.

But through it all, they'd each figured out a way to deal with one another. And for Sadie, that had meant lighthearted conversation and a way to navigate through all the emotional land mines that lay beneath the surface of their family unit.

With that skill firmly in hand, she put it to good use over dinner.

For his part, Tripp seemed to take the conversation in stride. He laughed when she talked about various members of the CSI team. Who was overly serious and who was working on the side to become a stand-up comic. Even one who came in each Monday with a dating story that could make a person's hair stand on end.

Tripp listened to it all, laughing and offering his own

version of events when they shifted gears to discuss other colleagues. But nowhere during dinner did they get back to that easy intimacy and layered conversation they'd shared before.

It was like a switch had flipped off, Sadie thought as she rinsed dishes before putting them into the dishwasher. And she had no idea how to get the old Tripp back.

"You don't have to do that."

"It's fine. I'm one of six kids, Tripp. Every one of us rotated through cleanup duty."

"Back to sibling politics again?"

She didn't miss the curiosity in his question. "It's been drilled into me since birth. I guess I never really realized, though, how much I depend on them. Or mention them, for that matter."

"It's nice."

Tripp's phone went off, putting a pause to their conversation, and Sadie finished loading the last few dishes as he answered the call.

"Riley. How are you?"

"Speak of the devil," Sadie muttered. What was her brother doing calling Tripp? The two men knew each other and worked well with one another when it was required, but, best she knew, Riley didn't make it a habit to call GRPD members after hours.

Was he checking up on her?

Although she didn't need anyone's permission to stay at Tripp's, she had given Pippa an early morning heads-up. Not only was she her calmest sister, but since Pippa was also on the hook for the morning donuts, Sadie had wanted to save her the trouble. Pippa had promised to spread the word about where Sadie was staying, especially since Sadie was still without a cell phone.

"Your brother's coming over, along with Ashanti Silver," Tripp said as he put his phone away.

"CI's tech expert?"

"Yep. They've got an idea for how to draw out Wes Matthews once and for all."

Although Sadie knew the players broadly in the RevitaYou mix, a month out of the loop had been a bit too long to go without new information. "I know Wes is the man behind the pyramid scheme. His daughter, Abigail, was embarrassed but honest about that from the get-go as she got to know Griffin. What's their idea?"

"It was suspected for a while that he was still in Michigan, but the FBI has officially debunked that. Latest intel suggests he's hiding out in the Bahamas."

Realistically, Sadie knew the man needed capture. But as she thought about Abigail and Griffin creating their new life with baby Maya, there was a part of her that wanted to spare them the upheaval. All while keeping Abigail's father at a distance.

"I hate what this must be doing to Abigail."

"Your brother has an idea and if it works, she will be able to put it behind her soon enough."

But would she?

It was a nice dream, to think that you found closure. And focusing on Maya's future would undoubtedly help Abigail in the healing. But looking to the future or not, the reality of her father's crimes would have their day. They'd have to.

Wasn't that the root of what she was experiencing

over Tate? Realistically, Sadie knew she was better off without him. *Far* better off.

But the embarrassment of being so wrong, coupled with the betrayal of genuine feelings, wasn't something that was so easily healed.

In the end, Sadie admitted to herself, it just hurt. More than she could ever have imagined.

TRIPP SETTLED RILEY and Ashanti in his living room before returning to the kitchen to get drinks for everyone. Riley had already hugged Sadie and affirmed for himself that she was okay, insisting she sit with them and recount the events at the hospital.

The drinks had given Tripp a polite excuse to escape. And also think about Sadie.

Something had shifted during dinner, before taking a decided left turn over the dishes. He'd thought they were getting along, but something had clearly spooked her. Although he knew the events of the past day, as well as the entire month before, were likely catching up to her, it seemed like something else was bothering her.

So much more.

And he felt wholly responsible for whatever "that" was.

Tripp brought the requested drinks into the living room, passing them out when Riley spoke up.

"I realize my sister is probably downplaying what happened last night. Which is why I want you to know that this comes from me and all the rest of my siblings," Riley said. "Thank you for being prepared and for making sure that she's okay."

"I'm fine, Riley." Sadie laid a hand on his arm, in that way of hers that was so warm and natural. "Truly, I am."

"Because of Tripp."

Sadie looked about to argue before her jaw snapped closed. In fact, if he wasn't mistaken, it looked like she might be biting down on her back teeth. Although he hadn't ignored what she'd said earlier—*We may have our fair share of sibling spats, but they're there for me. And I can't imagine life without them*—watching the byplay between brother and sister gave Tripp a new appreciation for what she must deal with as the youngest in the family.

Anxious to change the subject and take the spotlight off her, Tripp shifted gears. "What is this idea you have to pull Wes Matthews out of hiding?"

"He fancies himself as something of a playboy," Ashanti started in, clearly as happy as Tripp to divert attention off the family politics. "We've been working with Cooper and the FBI, and we're going to use that weakness to catch him."

Sadie looked to Riley for confirmation. "We're talking about Abigail's father?"

"Yep." Riley nodded. "He's quite the ladies' man. Kiely learned that firsthand when one of his discarded women, Meghan Otis, kidnapped Alfie out of some weird need for revenge."

"Which only reinforces my point," Sadie said. "Is he really going to be dumb enough to risk extradition?"

"No extradition needed," Ashanti said. "I put a few feelers out and he's nibbled on every one of them. If he's so dumb to go diving into a honeypot while in the midst of fleeing, he deserves what he gets."

It was hard to argue with Ashanti's logic. And while a big part of him was determined they play every bit of this by the book, Tripp couldn't deny the fact that it made a lot of sense for Colton Investigations to handle this part of the work. As a private enterprise, CI could function in a way that neither the Grand Rapids PD nor the FBI could.

A little coloring outside the lines, as it were.

He was still glad to know the FBI was involved. Cooper Winston was one of the best agents the Bureau had. The man was solid, aboveboard and, as of recent events, also engaged to Sadie's sister, Kiely.

Even with his reassurance that Cooper was on the case, Tripp was concerned that the team followed all proper protocols. Especially if they didn't want Matthews getting off on a legal technicality later.

"You're not doing anything illegal to capture him, are you?"

Ashanti warmed to her subject. "I've done nothing to coerce return contact."

"What have you done?"

"I started with the suggestion I had a rather sizable fortune from my older late husband that I was looking to invest."

"And he bought it?"

Ashanti smiled as she took a sip of her soda, her warm brown eyes taking on a decidedly fierce quality. "At the risk of undervaluing my mad skills, he didn't just buy it, he swallowed the whole damn hook."

"Unbelievable," Tripp muttered. They'd spent the past three months trying to think of any number of ways to lure the bastard out and maybe they never really needed such schemes at all.

"Or highly believable," Sadie argued. "Looks like no matter how smart Wes Matthews thinks he is, he's still dumb enough to fall for the oldest trick in the book."

Ashanti tilted her soda toward Sadie's, clinking glasses. "Score another one for an old classic. Because once again, the honeypot does its job."

Chapter Nine

Sadie sat beside her brother and willed her teeth to unclench. To her credit, she'd tried doing that all evening, but Riley was making it difficult. Since he was also oblivious to how much he was annoying her, she was seriously considering adding bodily harm to her to-do list.

That only made her feel guilty when Riley pulled her in close for a hug after Tripp and Ashanti left the room to go into the kitchen.

"Are you sure you're okay?"

"Riley, I'm fine." His hold remained as tight as a python's but, strangely, she didn't care. "I'd tell you if I wasn't."

He let go at that, pulling back to stare down at her. "Now you're just lying to me."

"No, I'm not."

"Sure you are. But since it's a family trait to keep one another in the dark about anything bad, I'll try to forgive you."

Sadie thought about that, especially in light of her earlier conversation on the back porch with Tripp. "Do you think we do that?"

"Of course."

"*Lie* is a rather harsh word choice."

Riley patted her knee. "I'll do you one better, then. How about 'gloss over the details'?"

Now that one she'd buy.

"It's the Colton love language. Make sure no one else knows just how bad the situation is."

Sadie laid her head on his shoulder and let out a small sigh. "How is Brody holding up in all this?"

"On the rare occasions we hear from him, not very well."

She lifted her head at that news. "What do you mean *when* we hear from him?"

Riley got that look on his face—the one that said he was about to gloss over details—and she put her foot down before he could go there. "Riley, come on. I know I've been out of the loop for the past month, but you have to tell me."

He let out a sigh, but based on his head nod and the serious look on his face, Sadie knew she was about to get the truth. "I think he's scared and I think his situation is pretty bad. We know he's hiding out."

"From?"

"Greer. And Wes Matthews. He put money into that pyramid scheme and because it's a big fat lie, he hasn't made a profit. Now they want their money back and made that abundantly clear with their usual starting point of broken fingers."

Once again, Tate's real job reared up and slapped her in the face. Capital X didn't take kindly to investors who couldn't pay them back. They were willing to make large loans, but they wanted payback in full, in a timely manner, and with serious interest.

In spite of her earlier, confused thoughts about Brody, she couldn't understand his reasons for staying away. "He came to us for help when this all blew up. Why won't he stay with one of us? We can help him and keep him safe."

"When any one of us has been able to talk to Brody, that's what we've tried to tell him. Vikki has got a couple of texts and Pippa got a phone call. But that's about it."

"I don't understand this." Sadie thought about the young man who'd been a presence in their life for nearly a decade. Despite her uncharitable moments, she loved him. They all did. Didn't Brody know how much they cared for him? And that they were his family? "Why won't he let us help him?"

"My money is on embarrassment, which, before you tell me I'm wrong, you know is true."

"I don't know any such thing." Sadie pushed back, surprised that was how Riley saw the situation. "Why should he be embarrassed?"

Riley stared at her dead-on but his voice was gentle when he spoke. "Why have you been embarrassed? About Greer?"

She sat back on the couch, that family urge to brush it off welling up sure and strong. "I'm not."

"Sadie—"

"Come on, Riley, it's not the same."

"How is it different? Greer is an ass and he took advantage of you. Why should you feel any embarrassment about that? At all?"

"You don't understand."

"I understand plenty. What I don't understand is why you seem to think you're responsible."

She didn't want to have this conversation. She certainly didn't want to have it *here*, with Tripp a room away. And she really *really* didn't want to have it with her brother. But Riley wasn't backing down and it seemed like Ashanti had Tripp occupied in the kitchen.

"Because it *is* embarrassing."

"The man is a criminal."

"And I almost married him!" Sadie caught herself and lowered her voice. "Do you have any idea how awful it is to think about that? To think that I had almost run off with him to Vegas and bound my life to a criminal. A man who murders people, Riley."

She felt the tears working their way up and did her best to swallow them back. "Where would I be right now if Vikki hadn't caught wind of it all?"

Riley pushed back, unwilling to back down. The paternal role was one he took often as the eldest sibling, but there was something different this time. He seemed *more* insistent. And even more determined than usual to make her see reason. "She did catch wind of it. And Kiely got Johnson to spill the details on Greer's involvement with Capital X. Disaster averted."

"Hardly. I still lost over a month of my life, stuck in a safe house because of him. And believe me, I had plenty of time to think about my poor judgment."

"He played everyone, Sadie. Why is that on you?"

"Because 'everyone'—" she made air quotes around the word "—wasn't desperate enough to rise to his bait. And *everyone* wasn't so freakishly eager to be married that they missed every sign that he's a horrible person."

"None of us knew the real Tate Greer."

"Yeah, but none of you liked him, either. Only, I refused to see it or even acknowledge it. That's all on me. Every time one of you tried to tell me that there was something off about him, I ignored it. And instead, I kept pushing forward, thinking how lucky I was and how in love I was. That I finally blossomed from that nerdy little kid who shoved her nose in books and had long stringy hair and now here I was, finally getting my man. My hot man who loved me. How wrong I was."

Tripp and Ashanti chose that moment to return to the living room. If either of them noticed the heated conversation, they were polite enough to ignore it. Sadie was grateful for that, but she couldn't deny her sense of social equilibrium had been badly blown off course.

Falling back on a polite excuse—she refused to use the word *lie*—Sadie stood, effectively ending the conversation with her brother. "I'm sorry to do this, but I think I'm going to wrap up for the night. I'm still a little tired."

"We should probably get going," Riley said, standing, as well. "But before I leave, let me give you your new cell phone."

Sadie made all the polite niceties, oohing and aahing over the phone her brother had procured for her, but all she really wanted was the quiet of her own room. She nearly had it, too.

She made it through an extra-long hug at the door with her brother, along with his promise to bring Charlize over to visit later in the week, and then he and his tech expert were off.

That left her and Tripp awkwardly standing together

in the foyer as if they'd just waved off their guests, which they *had* just done. Only, there was no "they," nor were the two of them a couple, jointly entertaining visitors.

Seeking to break the awkward silence, Sadie returned to their earlier conversation. "What do you think about the plan to draw Matthews out?"

"I was skeptical when Riley first said CI was working on something, but it sounds like they're on to a plan that has a shot at working."

"There aren't many who are as good as Ashanti."

"The same can be said for your brother. He runs a good shop."

"That's high praise, coming from a cop."

"I mean it."

Sadie backed up a few steps, fumbling for something to say. "Riley said we're supposed to get snow tonight."

"News is calling for about six inches overnight."

Since she was dangerously close to fumbling her way through a conversation about the weather, Sadie opted to cut bait. "Okay...well then, I'm going to go up."

"Sure. Let me know if you need anything."

She nodded before heading up the stairs.

It didn't take a genius to know that she needed something. But she'd be damned if she was going to ask for it.

TATE STOOD OUT past the edge of Tripp McKellar's property and watched the headlights as the car pulled out of the driveway then vanished down the street.

Interesting.

What was Riley Colton doing visiting the good lieutenant?

Since running from the hospital the night before,

Tate had spent his time trying to figure out where they'd moved Sadie. He knew hospital security would be looking for him if he showed his face there, but that hadn't stopped him from calling the main switchboard to talk to her, playing like he was a concerned friend.

The volunteer who'd answered the phone had seemed confused when he'd continued to insist that Sadie was a patient there. He'd used that confusion to his advantage. The woman finally gave in after he'd pressed and prevaricated, becoming more and more frantic when Sadie couldn't be found. The ploy had worked and the woman had finally told him that Sadie had been checked out.

That information had affirmed his belief that the GRPD was once again looking out for her.

He hadn't bothered going back to the safe house. Between the destruction he and his men had wrought as well as the fact the site had been compromised, there was no way they would take her back there. So he'd spent the rest of the day casing out Coltons, which hadn't produced Sadie, either.

It was only when he'd replayed the battle with McKellar over again in his mind, and all that had gone wrong in the hospital room, that it struck him.

The cop was watching out for Sadie.

Police officers might not normally list their personal information in the local telephone directory, but he had ways to find the information he needed. And getting an address hadn't been that hard.

Imagine his surprise at seeing his sweet little ex giving big, wide-eyed glances to the cop as they merrily cooked up dinner on the back porch.

Tate had no lingering feelings for her, but he sure

as hell couldn't believe the little bitch had moved on so quickly. She'd barely known how to act on a date when he'd first started hitting on her. She'd been so nervous and awkward. She'd learned—quickly, too—but it wasn't like she was the soul of experience.

And here she was already with someone else?

Tate shook his head at the irony, laughing to himself before he muttered, "Once you get a taste for it, sweetheart, you just can't help yourself."

He'd done that.

Given her the taste for a real life and a real relationship, while giving her a taste for sex, too.

Sadie was cute enough—she'd even tried to be sexy and playful once she was comfortable with him—but in the end, none of it had been about her anyway. She'd been a sweet diversion while he'd gleaned the information he'd needed, and now he was done with her.

The practical part of him knew he'd be better off just taking her out. He knew her whereabouts and he really needed to just take his shot.

But something held him back.

His goals hadn't changed. He still wanted her to pay for the sheer trouble she'd caused him. But watching her tonight, out on the back patio with McKellar, he realized he wanted something else, too.

There was still something wholesome and honest about Sadie Colton and he had the strongest need to crush it. To obliterate it so that she didn't just die, but that she ended so badly no one would ever be able to talk of anything else.

She could have avoided it. If she'd only played along and done his bidding, she wouldn't be in this situation. But in the end, she'd been weak, listening to that damn meddlesome family of hers. And there was no way he'd let that insolence and disobedience pass without punishment.

Sadie had to pay.

And after she did, the rest of the Coltons would, too.

Every one of them would know, every single day for the rest of their lives, that their precious sister died because of them. It was the only way he'd walk away from Capital X a winner. And Tate Greer always won.

Always.

Tripp stared at his laptop, but the names blurred together on the screen.

He hated this. Hated thinking there was something going on with someone in his department. But there was no way around it. Someone had given Tate Greer the information to the safe house and Tripp was determined to find out who had put Sadie—hell, all of them—at risk.

"Are you still working on that?" Sadie padded into the kitchen, thick, fluffy socks on her feet. Her hair was pulled up on top of her head in a messy bun and Tripp admitted to himself that she had never looked more beautiful.

"What are you doing up? I thought you were going to sleep."

"I tried."

Tripp understood the ways a person's body could betray them under stress. "It's a difficult time. Even when you're exhausted, sleep doesn't always come easily."

"I suppose." A small smile drifted across her face. "Even setting up my new phone didn't tire me out enough."

"Technology. The great distractor."

She shrugged. "Not this time. Anyway, I'm just going to get some water. Do you want anything?"

"I'm good."

Tripp tried to focus on his screen, but his gaze kept drifting to where she puttered around the kitchen. An oversize GRPD sweatshirt covered her to mid-thigh and underneath it she wore yoga pants. She looked like the girl next door.

Although he never considered himself someone with a type—and his limited dating life since Lila's death had been more about quietly seeking a mutually willing partner for an evening of comfort and sexual release—he had to admit the look worked for him.

That meant he needed to focus on his computer and off Sadie. He didn't need to be attracted to her. He needed to protect her.

Even if he was still curious about what she and Riley had talked about earlier, it hadn't escaped his notice that the conversation had been intense. Sadie had looked on the verge of tears. That, based on the stress she had experienced over the past month, and particularly the last few days, wasn't necessarily a surprise.

But still he wondered.

Sadie came over to the table and took a seat. "Are you finding anything?"

"No, which isn't necessarily a bad thing."

"It would be a really tough blow to think that someone in the department had given up the safe house address."

"Especially coming on the heels of Joe McRath."

Tripp knew he couldn't take McRath's betrayal solely

on himself. He had a captain and an entire team of people to work with. But it was difficult to know that a man he had respected had been dirty.

"After it happened, Pippa said Emmanuel was struggling with it, too."

"It's hard enough knowing a cop you worked with and trusted wasn't who you thought he was. But the stakes are life and death in our business. McRath traded on the wrong side of that."

That same anger that had accompanied him for the past few months—ever since Emmanuel and Pippa had brought the situation with McRath to light—flared high and bright. It was like a hot coal he'd held on to for endless weeks now. He'd gotten used to the steady pain, but every once in a while something forced him to really think about it again.

To acknowledge the reality of what they'd dealt with as a department.

"You doing okay with it?" Sadie asked.

"I have to be."

"That wasn't my question."

"No, I'm not fine with it. Not at all. I hate looking at my fellow officers with questions. I hate thinking that one of them could have fallen on hard times and is even now making a bad decision. Just like Joe McRath."

"Don't forget good, old-fashioned greed. Sometimes a person doesn't need hard times as an incentive."

Based on when Sadie started as a rookie, Tripp had always pegged her about five or six years younger than his own thirty-three. But in her comment, he heard all the pain and suffering that had narrowed that gap far faster than the standard passage of years ever could.

"You're right." On a hard sigh, Tripp pointed to his computer. "This little exercise doesn't help. I need to trust the people I work with, and combing through names, considering each of them, doesn't instill one iota of belief or conviction."

"I'm sorry."

"You don't have to be sorry. And you know as well as I do that the world isn't black and white."

"No," she sighed. "It isn't."

Maybe it was because the world wasn't black and white. Or maybe it was just because he wanted to know…

"It looked like you and your brother were having a pretty serious conversation earlier."

It was curious that she didn't immediately stiffen or turn defensive. Though Tripp did hate that his question seemed to make her sad.

"It was pretty serious. I know he's worried about me, and I appreciate that. I worry about him, too. I worry for all my siblings. We look out for each other, because we're family. But none of us can walk the other's path. We can't take away the realities and the pain of living."

"I'm sure Riley understands that."

Sadie snorted. "Understanding and practice are two different things."

Tripp knew it wasn't his business. At all. Yet still, he nudged. "Is that all?"

Sadie stared down at her glass of water before that pretty green gaze settled squarely on him. "For someone who doesn't answer a lot of questions, you sure do ask quite a few of them."

"I can stop."

"I'm not asking you to stop. But I want to make sure you're ready and able to accept the answers."

He sensed he was standing on the edge of a very shallow ledge. But that didn't stop him from pushing for an answer.

"Try me."

SADIE KNEW THIS was her shot. On some level, she'd been waiting for it since her first day as a rookie at the GRPD. Even then, she'd been captivated and awed, and yes, attracted, to the impressive leader that was Tripp McKellar. As the years had passed, after she'd transferred out of the squad room and into CSI, she'd watched him.

And always, she'd harbored that little flame of attraction.

She'd believed herself unable to act on it. The nerdy kid image of herself that she'd carried into adulthood often did a number on her self-confidence. Add that they were both in their place of work *and* Tripp appeared to keep his personal life deeply private, and she'd never felt she even had a shot at a relationship with him.

So she'd kept her feelings to herself.

She'd waited, year after year, until Tate Greer had found her, alone and vulnerable and the perfect foil for his dirty deeds.

Tracing a finger along the rim of her glass, Sadie shared some of what was racing around in her mind. "The past month has given me a lot of time to think. To dig deep into who I am, what I want out of life, and how I see myself."

"You were dealt a tough blow with Greer's deception. I see what we're dealing with as a department, and it's not nearly as personal as what happened with your relationship."

"Maybe not," Sadie said, considering. "But just like you said, it's discouraging to think of our fellow officers as potentially not being who we think they are. It makes us question ourselves." She briefly hesitated, but knew it was up to her to finish. "Imagine how much deeper that goes when the subject is personal."

Sadie wasn't sure why she had started down this path, yet somehow, she knew it was the right one. Whatever these feelings were that she had for Tripp, she also trusted him. Saw him as a friend. More, saw him as a confidant.

"It's the things in our personal lives that have the power to cut us down at the knees. And when you have spent much of your life feeling awkward and unlovable, I can tell you, it cuts you off at the waist."

Whatever Sadie expected, Tripp's immediate protest wasn't it. "Unlovable? Sadie, that's not true. Not even close."

"It's completely true. I did have those feelings and I had them for a long time. I felt that way about myself and Tate was able to use that."

"But you're a beautiful, confident woman," he argued. "I don't see how this connects."

He had no idea how much those words meant, but Sadie refused to be diverted from her point. "While that's nice to hear, it doesn't change the way we see ourselves inside. I was the proverbial nerdy kid, with my nose always buried in a book. I wasn't athletic and, outside my family, I didn't have a lot of friends. You carry that with you, Tripp. It doesn't go away just because you pass a certain age."

"But you just said it, you were a kid. You're not one anymore. I've watched you since you were a rookie. You're one of the hardest working people I know. You're competent—*highly* competent—in your job. And you go after what you want. I'm not dismissing how you feel, but I'm also telling you what I see now. Here. Today."

Although her family, particularly her sisters, had tried to tell her the same, the words did have more impact coming from Tripp. But should they?

Yes, it was wonderful to have affirmation from a man. Particularly one she was attracted to. But hadn't that been what had happened with Tate? He had showed her a bit of positive reinforcement and she had mistaken it for love.

Tripp *was* different. She held on to that, even as she searched for the real lesson beneath all the heartache.

Because whatever emotional lessons she was supposed to take out of this experience, she knew for a fact that one of them was *not* comparing Tripp McKellar to Tate Greer.

Still, the thought had taken hold. It was wonderful to be told that she was competent. Confident. And beautiful. Especially by a man that she cared about. But *she* had to believe those words. She had to find those feelings within and believe them for herself. Not because they were said to her by someone else.

But because *she* really, truly believed them.

Chapter Ten

Tripp was still thinking about Sadie's late-night confession the next morning as he put coffee on. She'd headed back up to bed shortly after their discussion, leaving him to his endlessly roiling thoughts once she was gone.

While that's nice to hear, it doesn't change the way we see ourselves inside... You carry that with you... It doesn't go away just because you pass a certain age.

He was well acquainted with emotional baggage. Admittedly, he'd never imaged Sadie Colton as having any. That was monumentally unfair, but true all the same.

Yet wasn't he the same? He still carried myriad feelings about Lila and their baby. But even before that, he'd had conflicted mindsets on his family and his upbringing. He'd been loved—he never questioned that—but they'd lived a quiet life. His parents had only been able to have him. Many families thrived with only one child, but he'd always felt his mother harbored a low-burning resentment she hadn't been able to have more kids. By the time he was old enough to understand it or to even ask her about it, she was gone.

That brought him back to Sadie. She was one of the brightest lights he knew. And he'd always thought that about her, regardless of his secret feelings for her. She seemed like someone who tackled life head-on and kept a cheery disposition all the while.

But now, in the cold light of their conversation, he was forced to wonder if he'd not only done her a disservice, but had also failed to see her as a whole, fully feeling person.

He knew the story of the Colton family. Her parents, Graham and Katherine, were killed in a story that had grabbed headlines for months. Her father's role as Michigan DA had ensured the story remained top of mind for everyone in Grand Rapids, from the point it happened all the way through to the trial that had put the murderer away for life.

The pain of losing a loved one was hard enough. He knew that and lived it every day. And he also knew that those feelings only grew more intense when the loss came from such senseless violence.

He still struggled with the reality of moving on. And yet he hadn't given Sadie the same consideration.

The woman who'd dominated his thoughts suddenly filled his kitchen and he watched, curious, as she padded into the room. She was freshly showered, her strawberry-blond hair in loose, damp waves around her head. She walked to the counter where the coffee was finishing the last few moments of its brew. She blew out a breath when it was evident she had to wait, before turning in a huff. "Do you sleep?"

"Of course I do."

"Because I've seen no evidence of it yet."

He wasn't sure what had brought on the rush of

frustration but opted for humor to deal with it. "You're cheery in the morning."

"I'm horribly grumpy in the morning."

"You weren't yesterday."

"I was happy to be alive. Today I'm just irritated."

The coffee maker made its final gurgle, indicating it had finished, and Sadie turned back to the counter, reaching for the pot like a lifeline. To her credit, basic manners had her taking two mugs out of the cabinet and pouring him one, but he was still thinking over what she'd said.

I was happy to be alive.

In the midst of his musings, he'd set that one aside. And it was jarring to have it shot back at him, and so matter-of-factly.

"Doesn't that bother you?"

"Hmm?" She was busy doctoring her coffee, pouring in copious amounts of cream.

Suddenly frustrated, Tripp walked over and snatched his mug off the counter. She wasn't wrong, but the fact that she could say it so casually over a cup of coffee was a surprise.

"That yesterday you were just happy to have your life."

"What?" Genuine confusion marred a few subtle lines into her forehead, while a small furrow dug in between her eyebrows. Her reaction also seemed to magnify the purple and blue bruise that ran down the length of her jaw, a dark, lingering souvenir from her hospital stay. "What are you talking about?"

"You, Sadie!" The words were out like a shot, coffee sloshing over the rim of his mug as he slammed it on the counter. "You. And the fact that you almost died this week and you're casually assessing it like writing out a grocery list."

The coffee that spilled over was still piping hot and he moved to the sink to run cold water over his hand. The heat covering his knuckles had nothing on the rising ire that filled him.

"I'm not casually assessing anything."

"Could have fooled me." Tripp grabbed a kitchen towel to dry his hands before tossing it back on the counter.

"What's that supposed to mean?"

He whirled on her, well aware it wasn't the right moment for this conversation. But he was frustrated, and all of it had bubbled over, needing a place to land. "It means what it means."

"That I'm not taking this seriously? That I don't value my own life? That I'm not aware of what's going on around me like the clueless woman I've been for the past six months?"

Her voice rose with each question and Tripp had the first flicker of recognition that he might have an equal partner in the battle clearly brewing between them.

He knew he needed to stop. Knew it, down to his bones. Yet no matter how that thought beat in his mind, thrumming in time to his racing pulse, he couldn't pull back.

"We're back to that again? That you're some poor, clueless woman because your boyfriend was an ass?"

Shock waves rippled through the room, radiating out from where he stood. Only, this pulsating disturbance had a directed target, and he saw Sadie nearly stumble in place before something hard and stubborn seemed to lodge in her spine. She set her coffee cup down, oh so carefully, on the counter, before standing to her full height.

"I knew you were cold, Tripp. But I didn't know you were an ass." She turned to leave, the easy camaraderie they'd had for the past thirty-six hours vanishing with her, when Tripp moved.

Just like the words he hadn't been smart enough—or hell, capable enough—to hold back, he wasn't able to stop himself. His hand snaked out, grabbing her elbow to keep her from leaving the kitchen. His touch was light, meant to stop her versus hold her in place, but battle lit her green gaze as she turned to face him.

"Leave me alone, Tripp."

He let go immediately, even as those hard breaths continued to build in his chest.

He needed to back off.

He needed to take control of himself and the situation.

He needed...her.

The already heated air between them shifted instantaneously, the hum of battle transmuting into something so full of need his own knees nearly buckled.

And then they moved. Both of them in unison. United in the same goal.

Tripp wasn't sure if he pulled Sadie into his arms or she moved into them, but as his mouth came down on hers, he knew it didn't matter.

They were both exactly where they belonged.

SADIE FOUGHT TO catch her breath, but the press of Tripp's shockingly impressive chest against hers, as his mouth kept up that delicious pressure, made steady breathing an impossibility.

And she didn't care.

All she wanted was *him*. And this sense of belonging that went beyond her deepest fears, straight toward something she hadn't felt in a long time.

Hope.

Somehow, some way, in the midst of some of the worst days of her life, Tripp had found a way to restore the one thing she'd never realized she'd been living without.

Only she knew it now.

And she was desperate to keep the feeling going.

Although she wasn't a short woman, his tall, muscular frame seemed to dwarf her where he wrapped her in his arms as he pressed her against the counter. Her hands had gone to his waist and it was with excitement she realized that their close proximity meant she could explore that impressive physique to her heart's content.

Never one to waste an opportunity, she did just that, her hands drifting over the thick sinews of his back before tracing the hard lines of his shoulders as his mouth continued to ply hers with long, sumptuous kisses that pulled at something deep inside her.

Something real and raw, and completely amazing.

Sadie opened herself up to him and, as she fervently drank him in, recognized something else.

She *needed* him.

It was a rogue thought that was just heady enough to pull her from the moment.

Tripp sensed the shift and lifted his head. "Sadie?"

"I—" The urge to sigh was strong but she held it back. "How did that happen?"

And how do we make it happen again? Not because we're fighting but because it's as natural to us as breathing.

"I'm not sure," he finally said, his gaze still stark and hungry with unmet need.

"But you were so angry."

"I wasn't—" He stopped himself before he nodded. "I was angry. But you just seemed so laid-back about everything. The current situation. And then you went right back to that place where somehow it's your fault."

Sadie stepped out of his arms and away from the counter, increasingly aware that thinking was difficult in such close proximity.

"Nothing about my life or how I feel is laid-back. Of all people, I thought you understood that. Clearly, I was wrong."

"Sadie. Don't walk away. You asked me why I was angry."

"And now I know."

His bright blue eyes clouded over, that crystalline gaze going cold. "You can be mad if you want, but I'm not wrong."

"You enjoy sitting on that high horse?"

The anger that had tinged his words before was nowhere in evidence. Instead she felt the chill slash through her with each syllable. "I'm not sitting anywhere. I'm staring at a woman who is bright and wonderful and who needs to quit feeling sorry for herself and start realizing that she's in danger."

"Your compassion absolutely spills over."

"You don't need compassion. You've got five brothers and sisters as well as a host of soon-to-be in-laws to give you that. It's my job to give you the truth. To keep you safe."

"Keep telling yourself that, Tripp. Say it as often as you like. In the end, you'll realize that they're just words. Safety. Security. Sanctuary. It's all an illusion anyway."

Before he could reply, she shot out of the kitchen and up to the spare bedroom. It was time she got to work on not needing him so much.

"He's so hot." Vikki's voice rang with authority and, since she'd said the same thing at least four other times in the past half hour, Sadie was getting close to kicking her twin. Lightly, of course, and only hard enough to push her off the double bed she sat at the end of.

"You're not listening, Vik." Kiely interrupted from her perch on the rolling desk chair in the corner of Tripp's spare bedroom. "Because attractive or not, Lieutenant Hottie can't be bothered to listen to Sadie."

Vikki waved a hand, seemingly unconcerned. "He jumped straight to doing, and that goes a long way in my book."

"There is something to be said for doing." Pippa's smile was dreamy, hearts and unicorns practically circling the air above her head where she sat on the floor. "All the doing."

"Fat lot of help you three are." Sadie added a satisfying harrumph before slamming back onto the pillows she'd propped against the headboard.

"We might be more helpful if you came up with

some argument other than 'Tripp McKellar is an ass,' baby sister."

"I'm the same age as you, Vikki," Sadie shot back. It was an argument as old as they were, but it never stopped Vikki from using it in times of discussion. Or family disagreements. Or, well, ever.

"She's a stickler for those extra minutes," Kiely said before adding, "A fun fact you can use when you turn forty."

"In twelve years. I'll be sure to wait with bated breath." *If I make it that long.*

Sadie fought off the terrible image that came to mind at the dismal thought. She was here now. She was with her family now. And Tripp—despite his ham-fisted way of dealing with whatever this thing was between them— was determined to see her stay that way.

Now.

If only her loved ones could see how crazy he made her…

"Much as I'm enjoying how readily we all feel we can and should—" Kiely eyed Vikki "—deliver love advice, we're here to game-plan."

Leave it to Kiely to get down to the heart of the matter, Sadie thought. Her sister had earned her stripes as a freelance private investigator, working with Colton Investigations, the FBI and any other qualified organization that could afford her. She had her finger on the pulse of just about everything and she had a way of subtly pulling everyone in line.

"Riley filled you in on how we're going to try to take down Matthews." Kiely directed the statement at Sadie, even as all her sisters nodded in unison.

"He was here last night with Ashanti."

"It's a good plan. But one that is going to take some really tight planning and flawless execution," Pippa added, her dreamy-eyed stare vanishing as that of a hard-nosed attorney took over.

Although Sadie had been somewhat skeptical of the idea last night, she was even more so in the cold light of a new day. "Do you all think it will work? Is Wes Matthews, mastermind behind RevitaYou, so dumb to fall for a honeypot?"

"Yes," all three of her sisters said in unison.

The unanimous agreement was swift, followed by all three of them talking at once.

"He's a total pig," Pippa said.

"Abigail's trying to hold up under all this, but even she agrees her father can't stay away from a beautiful woman," Kiely added. "That horrible Meghan Otis just one terrible example in apparently a long line of them."

"He's a man," Vikki scoffed in the loudest voice, as if her answer said everything, even as the gaze that landed on Kiely was clearly sympathetic. They'd all come to love Alfie in the short time Cooper Winston and his small son had been in their sister's life, and everyone knew how dangerous Meghan Otis had really been.

It was that last remark that Sadie keyed in on. "We know I'm no expert on men, so maybe you're right."

Sadie saw the judgment flash across Vikki's face before her sister firmly tamped it down. The urge to press her was strong, but Kiely had already launched in. "Cooper's on the FBI task force focused on bringing Matthews in. They missed him twice in the Bahamas, but they've got tabs on him. The outreaches Ashanti has made so far have worked. We've got him nibbling on a baited hook. And if Matthews behaves as he has in the past, it'll work again."

"What are the next steps?" Pippa asked.

"Ashanti's begun to make subtle outreaches on how to meet in person. She's added a few…ahem—" Kiely's normally indefatigable demeanor flagged a bit. "A few choice stock photos to sweeten the deal."

Although she'd had limited sexual experiences before Tate, Sadie was well aware men were visual creatures. Obviously the added incentive of suggestive photographs was needed to get Matthews to give up his hiding spot.

And still, it seemed like they were missing something.

"You still don't look convinced, Sadie," Pippa noted.

"It's not that I'm not convinced. Matthews is a pig and, if his own daughter believes this is his weak spot, it's well worth pressing the advantage. But it feels like we're missing something."

Alert, Kiely leaned forward from where she sat on the desk chair. "Go on."

"So, Brody got pulled into this relatively early on. The pyramid scheme had been active long enough that some people had a successful outcome, which was a plant to entice more investors. But it was also in place long enough to start tanking results for the next round of investors."

"Which was Brody," Pippa added.

"Exactly. And he got the loan from my scummy ex-fiancé to finance his way in."

"But we know all this, Sadie. That's why Brody came

for help in the first place." Vikki blew out a hard breath. "Even if he refuses to take it now."

Brody's disappearance had been a sore point for Vikki from the start. Sadie knew that, but she'd already warmed to her point, her CSI training to look beneath every surface kicking in. "And we've got Landon Street, who made the product effective but highly deadly."

Her sisters nodded in unison, still seeming to follow where she was going.

"So in the planning of all this, who's supposed to get out of here with the big score? Matthews works up the pyramid scheme but Tate is the funding and the muscle? Yet now Matthews is gone? And despite Tate's sick focus on me, he has to be thinking about pulling up stakes. There's no way he can stay here any longer."

"That's true," Pippa agreed. "I hadn't thought about it like that, but you've got something here. It's like Wes is off scot-free and Tate's stuck holding the bag."

"And we also already know the product has its limits." Sadie continued with her argument. "Even if they get a few million so far off of investors, it's all Tate's loan money to begin with. Where's the real cash coming from?"

"Not everyone needs funding from Capital X," Kiely said. "Some of it came from people with genuine money to burn."

"That's it!" Sadie sat forward, the next layer of the scam they were about to create coming to life in her mind. "That's how we get them both."

"Both?" Kiely pressed her.

"Wes and Tate. Keep going with the honeypot because it's obviously a powerful lure. But we need to turn the two of them against each other, too. There's only so much money at play because a lot of it was Tate's to begin with. He's going to want even more than his criminal interest rates to get out of this deal with a profit. Especially since it's blown his entire operation to hell and back."

"You don't think either of them has an exit strategy?" Vikki asked.

Sadie considered the question, even as she used what she already knew about Tate to form her opinion.

"I think each of them thinks he's smarter than the other. So they might have an exit strategy, but it's predicated on each thinking he has all the money in play. And that's where we come in."

Pippa stood to pace. "This is good, Sadie. Really good. If we can get them to turn on one another, we can tug all the loose threads. How it started in the first place. How they're finding their so-called investors. And where they've been hiding the funds they already have in hand."

"We can even get Brody's money back." Sadie sat back hard against the pillows, an image of Brody's dejected face in the front of her thoughts. Although she'd been hard on him at first, assuming he was too focused on money instead of making strong choices, she'd come out the other side of that line of thinking. Brody had unfortunately been duped, on a project he'd believed couldn't fail. As someone who'd been duped herself, through a "grand romance" with Tate Greer, she was hardly one to judge.

And maybe that was the bigger lesson anyway. Maybe it wasn't about judgment but about helping someone out of a tough spot. One they hadn't asked to be in, nor actively sought out, but one they'd ended up in despite their best efforts.

Kiely's phone dinged and she frowned, staring down at it. "I need to go pick up Alfie from day care. He's got a fever."

She was out of the chair immediately, her sole focus on leaving. Sadie rose and walked to her sister, quietly excited to see Kiely's concern and obvious love for her soon-to-be stepson. And, if recent discussions were any indication, *actual* son once she and Cooper were married and she could adopt Alfie as her own.

Wrapping her in a soft hug, Sadie pressed a kiss to Kiely's cheek. "Text me and let me know how he's doing."

"I will." Kiely hugged back—hard—before stepping away. "I'm sorry to rush out."

"Go." Sadie smiled. "Now."

In a matter of minutes, Kiely was gone and Pippa was up and readying to leave, too. "I'd rather stay and talk, but I've got a judge I still need to see to get a case on the docket before the holidays."

Sadie hugged Pippa before her sister could talk herself out of leaving. "You get out of here, too."

With no one left but her twin, Sadie turned to Vikki. "You're holding out on me."

"When have I ever done that?"

"A lot the past six months. Before that…" Sadie made a scrunched-up face before lightly scratching her temple in a mock gesture of thinking really hard. "Never."

"I'm not holding out on you."

"You are and I'd like to know why."

Vikki patted the bed, a clear invitation for Sadie to sit. "I'm worried about you."

"Now? But I'm safe."

"At this moment, yeah, sure. For good?" Vikki took her hand once Sadie sat. "I'm not so sure."

"Vik—"

Vikki squeezed her hand, the motion enough to stop Sadie from saying more. "Hear me out."

"Okay."

"I love you and I know you've been through a lot. Way more than anyone should ever have to go through."

"I hear a *but* in there."

"I told you to hear me out."

Sadie blew out a harried breath but shut up. Vikki had her "older sister" voice on and she knew she needed to listen.

"I did hold out on you. I did it a lot while you were dating Tate. I never liked him and it's not because I didn't want you to be happy."

"So why are you telling me now?"

"Because I couldn't say all I wanted to. I know I told you to be careful and I was hesitant about the engagement, but it was more than that. I never liked him. But—" Vikki broke off, her voice choked with tears. "I never thought he'd be such a monster. Or that he'd try to hurt you like this. If I'd had any clue, I'd have said something. Hell, I'd have run him out of town on a rail myself."

"None of us knew."

"Yeah, but my twin sense never stopped tingling around him. And I held back on you. I'm sorry."

Vikki pulled her into a tight hug and Sadie held on

just as strong. She'd held back her own tears up to that point but let them fall as the heavy emotion of the moment finally caught up to her.

"I'm sorry, Vik. So sorry I was so blinded by him."

Vikki squeezed her once more before pulling back. "You really need to stop apologizing for him. For your feelings. For all of it."

"But—"

"Nope." Vikki shook her head and wiped away tears. When she finally spoke, her voice rang strong and true. "I'm not holding back now, either. Not now, not anymore, and *not* about this."

"Not about what?"

"You didn't do this, Sadie. You didn't bring it on yourself and it didn't happen because you didn't have a lot of dating experience."

"But I—"

Vikki shut her down, barreling through the conversation like a GRPD cop hot on a chase. "Experience has nothing to do with a manipulative bastard like Tate Greer. He saw a way into our lives and he took it. I hate to break it to you, but it could have just as easily happened to Pippa or Kiely or me. You were the one he somehow flagged as his mark."

"I don't think the three of you would be so stupid to fall for him."

"Then you sorely overestimate a woman's power to overlook an attractive man who shows her attention."

"What's that supposed to mean? If he was ugly, I'd have ignored him?"

"No, no. What I meant was that I remember those first few weeks the two of you were dating. You talked about your conversations and the way he made you laugh. How kind he was and how much thought he put into each date. I was jealous."

"Of me?"

Although Sadie had built some level of confidence, she'd always seen Vikki as the glamourous one of the two of them. She had the blond hair and more slender figure, taking after their mother, while Sadie had thicker curves and the less flashy strawberry version of blond.

And until this moment, she'd never had reason to think any other way.

"Yes, of you. So were Pippa and Kiely."

"What? No way."

"Yes. We all did."

"So when did you stop feeling that way?"

"When I saw how he spoke to you. It was like after he'd done the work to get you to fall for him, he'd stopped trying. And the real him began to peek out from the edges."

"I know."

And she did know. Hadn't that been the most puzzling part of the relationship? Those early, halcyon days had been so much fun. Tate had been sweet and attentive, kind and considerate. But the veneer had eventually begun to crack. She'd told herself it was because they'd moved into a new phase of their relationship. One where things weren't quite so new and where they'd begun to settle into life without the bright, shiny haze of new love.

But it had bothered her all the same.

Only she'd ignored it. She'd convinced herself that

it was inexperience. That she had no reason to be discontent. Or to complain.

Or to feel she deserved something more.

"Which is why I like Tripp so much," Vikki said.

The change in topic was swift and, if Sadie knew her twin, deliberate. "This has nothing to do with Tripp."

"It does if you let Tate Greer stand in the way of something amazing with Lieutenant Hottie."

"Stop calling him that."

Vikki reached out and brushed Sadie's hair over her ear. "Okay then. I'll call him something else."

"What's that?"

"A shot at happy-ever-after."

Chapter Eleven

Sadie thought about Vikki's words long after her sister had left. Long after the afternoon light had faded into a dark winter night. And long after the scent of dinner had drifted up the stairs.

Tripp had left her alone and, somewhere deep down, Sadie knew she needed to be a decent houseguest and go talk to him. Yet still, she'd stayed put in her room.

Part of her felt slightly childish, but a bigger part of her needed the time alone. The discussion with her sisters had been good for her. The time together and the comfort that always came from being with them had given her a chance to see things in a new light.

But with that light, she'd been forced to examine some of the things she would've preferred to keep buried. For the past month, every thought of Tate had been equated with personal inexperience. How odd then, to have Vikki suggest something else. A new view Sadie hadn't considered before.

Up until now, she'd taken the situation fully on herself. And while she suspected she would never be entirely free of the sentiment—and the embarrassment seemingly intertwined within—her sisters had also helped her look at what had happened with fresh eyes.

Tate had done her wrong. And rather than allow that battering litany to run in her head that she'd somehow allowed it, or somehow asked for it, Vikki and Pippa and Kiely had helped her to see things differently.

The knock on her door pulled her from her thoughts. "Come in."

Tripp poked his head into the room and as she caught sight of his face—that firm jaw and serious blue gaze—Sadie was surprised to realize she had missed seeing him. Oh sure, they'd talked about him all day, but it wasn't the same as seeing him again.

That took her right back to the morning and how it had felt to be wrapped in his arms.

To have that firm chest pressed against hers.

To have those lips caress her own.

"I just wanted to check on you. I made some dinner."

"Thank you. I'm sorry I didn't come down, but I—"

"It's okay. I'm glad your sisters were here. That the four of you had a chance to spend some time together."

"Me, too. Their visit gave me a chance to, um, process a few things."

"That's good." His brow furrowed. "Right?"

"Yes, very good. It also gave me time to work my way up to that apology I owe you."

Tripp opened the door more fully, leaning a shoulder against the door frame. "I think I'm the one that probably owes you an apology."

"Nope. I think this one's all on me. And I need to say a few things."

He considered her for a moment but said nothing.

Just as she had earlier, Sadie felt so completely *seen* by him. The way his gaze drifted over her. The way his attention was fully on her. It was heady. And it was real, somehow. But it also reinforced all the reasons why she really did owe him an apology.

"I didn't want to listen to what you were saying earlier. But you were right."

"About what?"

"About Tate. About what happened with him, *because* of him."

"No, Sadie, I overstepped."

"For the record, I don't think you did. But I am curious why you tried to convince me otherwise."

He never moved off the door frame, but the casual nature of his pose belied the fierce light that leaped into his eyes. "Because I think you're pretty great. I always have. And it galls me to see how somebody who isn't worth your time could make you feel so badly."

"Thank you for that."

"You're welcome."

Tripp looked about to say something but held back. Instead of speaking, the two of them continued to stare at each other, the pulsing need that had arced between them in the kitchen this morning filling the air once again.

A part of her wondered if she should turn away, yet another part of her—a much bigger, deeper part—knew she couldn't.

This was Tripp. A man she had feelings for. And, if their kiss in the kitchen was any indication, feelings that weren't entirely unreciprocated.

But what to do about it?

With all the other stresses in her life, it would be so easy to simply reach out for it. To take the physical comfort she knew she would find in his arms.

Only, she was scared of what she'd find on the other side. The part that came after they got through this battle with Tate Greer and Wes Matthews and the whole RevitaYou mess. When life went back to normal and he went back to being Lieutenant Tripp McKellar and she went back to being CSI expert Sadie Colton.

When they had to see each other at work and handle cases together and find a way to live a normal life again.

The danger that was so awful right now had also created a fake intimacy. One that hadn't had a place in the real world before and likely wouldn't again.

Because how did you make a go of a relationship that started in the midst of a crisis? Sure, her siblings might be walking proof that you could come out the other side happily in love, but she just didn't see that for herself. She'd known Tripp a long time and it hadn't happened for them. She'd be a fool to think that would change after the danger died down.

"I do still have dinner downstairs. I can heat up a burger for you. Throw some frozen french fries in the oven."

"You don't need to go to any trouble."

"It's no trouble. Besides, I have a few things I want to show you. I've been digging through files all day, and I want to get your opinion on a few theories I've put together."

She sensed it was a bit of an excuse to get her out of the room, but Sadie didn't care. A burger and fries and Tripp sounded like a nice way to finish out her evening.

She was strong enough to handle it. More, she could remember that the situation was temporary and enjoy it anyway.

As she got off the bed to follow Tripp downstairs, Sadie decided she would do just that.

TATE STOOD IN the shadow of Tripp's house, the cold air that swirled around him sharpening his senses. The scent of gasoline rose from the container by his feet. The night was cold, bitterly so, and the snow that had been predicted on the day before hadn't disappointed.

He'd likely do better to wait but he was running out of time. He needed to do this *now*.

It was time to end this.

Everything he had built, worked for, planned for; all of it had vanished in a matter of days. And the bitch sitting inside was at the root of it all.

It was shocking on some level. He'd run his business for a long time. He recruited carefully and he knew how to get around the cops and the Feds in equal measure.

And in a matter of weeks it had unraveled so badly, he'd be lucky to get out of Grand Rapids with nothing more than the money he'd stowed down in the Caymans.

Damn Matthews.

Tate huffed out a harsh breath, the air in front of him steaming with it. The bastard had been so slick and sure of himself. So convinced they'd make a good long go of this RevitaYou crap. And the results had been impressive. Hell, he'd looked at the users himself. Some of them actually *looked* ten years younger. The transformation had happened quickly and before they were even done with the first bottle, people were lining up for more.

As that line grew, Wes Matthews had spun quite a tale of profit beyond anyone's wildest imaginings.

Tate had spent most of his life convinced the straight and narrow path wasn't for him, but even he had thought about going legit on the product. It was too good and too effective not to think about actually putting it out to market and running a business to widely distribute it. The money would print itself.

Until it started killing people.

Because, as it turned out, you can't turn back time, no matter how hard you try to engineer it.

Now Matthews was gone, Gunther Johnson and Landon Street were in jail, and his traitorous little ex-fiancée was spilling her guts to the cops. And while the Caymans were looking better and better, he wasn't going anywhere until he dealt with all those damned loose ends.

Tate patted the box of matches safely tucked away in his pocket before he bent to pick up the gasoline can.

It was time to start recouping his investment.

TRIPP KNEW SOMETHING had changed, even if he couldn't fully put his finger on what it was. The tension that had hovered between him and Sadie this morning had vanished. Instead, what had replaced it was a spirit of collaboration from his partner, who seemed to have turned an emotional corner.

It was the only way he could characterize the "something" in his mind.

Even as he had to admit to himself that Sadie wasn't the only one who'd changed.

Her stormy exit from the kitchen that morning had left him with a lot to think about. More than a lot, if he were honest with himself.

And he didn't entirely care for some of his conclusions.

She'd said many things that made him think, but her parting shot had been the most effective.

In the end, you'll realize that they're just words. Safety. Security. Sanctuary. It's all an illusion anyway.

Was that the case?

He made his life under the working assumption that his job was to keep people safe. Yet her words had made him reconsider that and all he'd believed about himself.

If safety was an illusion, then maybe his job wasn't about keeping people safe at all. Maybe it was about holding back the dark so they remained just safe enough.

And so the dark remained just far enough away.

The exact opposite of Tate Greer, Capital X and the entire RevitaYou case that had consumed them all for the better part of six months. As the case had grown deeper, its secrets unfurling lead by lead, the dark had crept closer.

The capture of cop Joe McRath.

Followed by the uncovering of Capital X.

And then Sadie's kidnapping.

He'd believed he was doing his job, but was this all a lesson in dealing with the dark? In learning how to handle it when it inevitably came?

He'd been there before. Lila's death had decimated him, from the sheer violence of the act, the loss of their unborn child, and the unrelenting knowledge that it had happened because of him. A man he'd put in prison had gotten out and exacted the worst revenge anyone could imagine.

Tripp had borne its consequence every minute of every day since.

Yet even with that experience, he had never seen his role as defender and protector a useless act. He'd always believed in his ability to do his job and keep others safe.

And Sadie had upended that with a few well-placed jabs.

Only they hadn't been jabs. They'd been the serious assessment of a woman in the midst of a crisis. But they were also the words of someone who'd given her professional vow to serve and protect.

She wasn't a civilian, untrained in the world of criminal minds and the violent acts that stemmed from those places. She also wasn't ignorant of what went into his life day by day. The TV cop shows had it wrong. What looked like a life of swift action on a screen resembled that far less often in real life. Instead, he made his life on the tiresome reality of repeat offenders, avoidable crimes and endless reams of paperwork.

All while praying like crazy he'd avoid too many experiences like the rescue at the lake and the subsequent attack at the hospital.

The oven timer dinged and Sadie pulled out the cookie sheet of french fries. "These smell delicious." She smiled. "A most excellent idea for dinner."

"I have a few every now and again."

Sadie had already fixed her burger and, after scooping some fries into a bowl, met him at the kitchen table.

He was pleased to see her navigate her way around his home, comfortable even if she didn't fully realize it.

He snatched a fry, happy that she'd salted them perfectly.

"So what did you want to show me?" she asked.

"Don't you want to eat?"

"I can eat and listen at the same time." She dipped a fry in ketchup. "I want to hear your theories. See if they match any of my own."

"Okay." He pulled his empty plate from earlier closer and grabbed a further handful of fries for himself. "I feel like catching Matthews is the key to all this."

"Abigail's father is the linchpin."

"You think so, too?"

"I do." Sadie set down her burger and wiped her fingers on her napkin before continuing. "I talked to my sisters about it. Vikki in particular, who's the closest to Brody and knows how scared he is, is putting a lot of hope in the scheme Riley and Ashanti have cooked up."

"It's good. They know what's needed to both reel him in and do it in a way that makes sure Matthews can't get off on a technicality later."

"My brother does good work."

"He does."

Tripp considered the man he'd come to know since joining the GRPD. Riley Colton was rock-solid. He'd started Colton Investigations after Graham Colton's murder and, like many others in local law enforcement, Tripp had carried a bit of skepticism the job choice was fully altruistic. The trauma of one's parents' murders would leave anyone raw, wounded, and seeking a path for vengeance.

Only, Colton had done the opposite. He'd built a strong business, steeped in preparation, an ability to follow procedure, and exceedingly good instincts.

Tripp had seen it firsthand—and had been forced to eat a rather large serving of crow—on one of the first cases Riley had helped GRPD with, about four months after founding CI. They'd had a low-level drug trafficker who'd suddenly increased business a thousand-fold. The entire PD, out en masse, had been trying to figure out where the thug secured his access and his supply. It was Colton who'd traced the details back to a dealer in Chicago who'd set Grand Rapids in his sights as part of an expansion effort.

And it was Riley Colton who'd uncovered the information in a careful and methodical way. One that had allowed the GRPD and the Feds to put the trafficker and the dealer in Chicago in prison for life.

"Colton Investigations is a top-notch organization," Tripp added. "I've always thought so, but the respect he commands from the rest of the GRPD as well as the FBI is all further proof of that."

"As the oldest, Riley remembers more of my father's stories than the rest of us. He knew the cases that made our dad so mad. The ones where a criminal got off on a technicality or a lapse in procedure."

"That'll shape a person."

"It certainly did shape Riley."

Without knowing where the question came from, Tripp pressed her. "And what about you? What shaped you and made you want to join the GRPD?"

Sadie stared down at her plate, toying with a fry before looking back up at him. "My parents were still alive when I went into the academy. So I can't say it's their deaths that gave me any sort of calling to law enforcement."

"What did give the calling?"

"I'm not sure." Her gaze dropped back to the fry, which she swirled in ketchup. Although Tripp could only see a partial view of her face, he didn't miss the emotions that furrowed her brow. And when she finally looked back up, he sensed a change in her.

Just like earlier, he felt it once more. As if she'd come to some sort of decision and was ready to share it with him.

"That's not entirely true. I do know. I was a bit aimless after high school. I was a good student. One of the best, actually. But I was mousy and my head was always buried in a book. I was sort of your classic nerd."

"I'm struggling to believe that."

"Well, believe it. I had a glamourous twin and I was the proverbial ugly duckling."

Tripp couldn't see it, but he knew he had no place to argue with her. He also knew the ideas she carried contributed to who she was. How she saw herself. And while she might no longer look like that forlorn teenager, the experience was no less real to her.

While he simply waited for her to continue, those emotions continued to play over her face. For as open and caring as Sadie was, Tripp realized that he very rarely saw her emotions. She had a surprisingly strong poker face, easily conveying her concerns for others while keeping her own emotions firmly locked down.

"Anyway, I was a nerdy kid and I wasn't ready to

go to college. I wanted to, but something kept holding me back."

When she didn't elaborate, Tripp sensed it wasn't his place to ask. But he wanted to. And in the wanting, he realized just how badly he wanted to know *her*. All of her.

That was why, once again, he kept his thoughts to himself. He didn't share the intimate details of his life and he had no right to pry into hers.

But that didn't make the wanting less intense. Or make the interest fade away.

"Vikki was all excited about going into the Army and I wanted to share that excitement, only I didn't have it. I had the grades, but not the gumption."

"Gumption for what?"

"To leave Grand Rapids. To go out in the world. Even if it were just a few hours away at a state school. So I stayed. I took community college courses on subjects I really didn't care about and all the while wondered when I'd finally find something I did care about."

"What flipped the switch?"

"I started working out at the community college. I had a three-hour stretch between two of my classes. It didn't make sense to come home, and the classes weren't hard enough to bother with studying in the library. So I went to the gym. I started on the treadmill and worked my way up to weights. And the whole time, there was this woman there who was about my age. And she was always working really hard and seemed really focused. We struck up a conversation one day and she mentioned that she was applying to the academy."

"Who was it?"

"Rosie Archer. Now Rosie Santorini."

Tripp knew Rosie. She was one of his best detectives. She'd fast-tracked into her role as detective, a product of that hard work and determination Sadie mentioned. "That's an outstanding role model if I've ever seen one."

"She was. And she introduced me to a new career path. Every time I'd thought about college, it was through the lens of accounting or finance or something in the legal field. It never crossed my mind that I could make a go of things on the other side, focused on law enforcement."

"So you applied to the academy?"

"I did, but not at first. First, I was determined to get the education I needed. Now that I had a different purpose, I shifted into civics classes. If I was going to catch bad guys for a living, I wanted to make sure I understood the legal reasons why. And after I did that, I applied to the academy."

"Yet you ended up in CSI."

Sadie smiled at that, the first real smile he'd seen since they'd started their discussion. "Just one more tumbler in the lock."

"How so?"

"So I mentioned I was a reader..."

"Sure." He nodded, not sure where she was going but also recognizing what might appear aimless to others was all part of a definitive path for Sadie Colton.

"Once I realized that there was a way to use my love of mysteries and clues in my job. I was a goner."

"Nancy Drew's got nothing on you?"

"Something like that."

Sadie's smile fell, her expression changing so fast

that Tripp's pulse kicked up several notches. "What is it?"

"Do you smell it?"

She was already on her feet, moving toward the sliding glass doors that led to the back patio, when Tripp scented the mix of fire and gasoline. But it was the bright flicker through the window, visible over her shoulder, that had Tripp standing, as well.

"Tripp!" Sadie turned from the window. "The house is on fire!"

Chapter Twelve

Sadie struggled to get her bearings, the scents of gas and smoke so overwhelming she fought off a wave of dizziness. How had it happened so fast? One moment she and Tripp were talking and the next, they were simply overpowered. Tripp had already moved, his chair overturned where he'd pushed back from the kitchen table. After assessing the situation out the kitchen window, he'd gone to the front of the house to evaluate the damage.

All while she continued to stare out the window into the backyard.

There was something out there. Something more than fire. She knew it deep down in her bones.

Tate was out there.

"The fire's surrounding the house." Tripp raced back into the kitchen, the vivid flames outside the window tossing an odd glow over his features. "Sadie. Did you hear me?"

"Tate is outside."

"What?"

"Tate. He did that. That's why the fire is everywhere. Front and back in equal measure. He set it, Tripp."

She'd barely finished the words when Tripp's hand closed over hers, pulling her toward the front door. "We have to get out of here. Wrap up in a blanket and I'll carry our coats."

Sadie felt herself being led, the firm grip of his fingers like a vise over hers. He barreled through the living room toward the front foyer, pulling a blanket off the couch as they moved before stopping at the closet to drag out their jackets. With deft movements, he wrapped a thick scarf over his hand to open the front door.

Thoughts swimming, Sadie heard a voice almost outside of herself. "Tripp! No!"

With a force she had no idea she possessed, she clamped her free hand down over his wrist, dragging on their joined hands to keep him from opening the front door.

"Sadie! We have to get out of here."

"You can't go that way."

Smoke already filled the room and Tripp's gaze darted from her to the door and back again. "We have to get out."

"That's what Tate wants. There's no way he's letting us out of here. Either we burn inside or he'll smoke us out and take us down in plain sight. That's why the flames are all over. We can't go that way."

"Then we'll go out the back."

"How do we know his goons aren't with him?"

It was a factor they had to consider. Although the takedown at Sand Springs Lake had also secured several of Tate's goons, they had to assume he had more. And if he had more, they had to assume those men were also waiting outside the ring of fire consuming the house.

"The basement."

Tripp shook his head. "We don't have time."

With the smoke already impossibly thickening, they'd have to crawl into the center of the house to reach the basement door.

"It's our only way. You've got storm doors to get outside, right?"

It was a silly fact but one she'd thank herself for later if they got out of this alive. Sadie had always been intrigued by the idea of storm cellar doors that closed into the ground. The houses in this neighborhood were known for that feature.

"Yeah."

"We'll get outside that way. They won't expect us and you can get a better lay of the land."

"And if the fire's outside the perimeter of the cellar's storm doors?"

"We'll take our chances."

He looked about to argue but Sadie rolled right over any objection, screaming to be heard over the roar of the fire, "Get your weapon."

Tripp turned back to the closet and pulled out his service revolver before reaching deeper inside. He pulled out an extra gun and handed it over. "You still know how to use one of these?" he screamed.

She avoided the eye roll—well aware it would be barely visible through the smoke anyway—and took the gun. "I'm all set."

It was only then that the lights in the house flickered before going fully dark.

Tripp's hand on her wrist shifted, his fingers lacing with hers. "Get on the floor and stay close to me."

In the thick, dark smoke, they began to crawl for the interior of the house. It was the exact opposite choice of every instinct she possessed to get outside.

But, in her gut, Sadie knew it was their only shot at survival.

TRIPP MENTALLY COUNTED off the distance from the foyer to the basement door. It was off the hallway to a downstairs bedroom and, while it likely wasn't more than twenty feet, it felt like a mile. Smoke billowed so thick above them, he could only marvel at the fire's deadly speed.

But he took comfort from the steady presence of Sadie by his side where her arm brushed against his calf as they crawled toward their goal.

The noise and heat of the flames whirled around them, the blaze angry and shockingly loud. Along with the furious lap of the flames, the sounds of his house breaking and burning around him echoed in his ears like a raging nightmare. Still, he moved forward, determinedly onward toward the basement door and what he hoped was safety.

His shoulder hit the corner of the wall, but Tripp ignored the pain. That corner meant they'd turned the last few feet into the correct hallway. Reaching back, he felt for Sadie's shoulder so he could lean in as close as possible.

"We're at the door. I don't know how long the frame will hold, so you have to move across the basement as fast as you can." He shouted the words and still wasn't sure she'd heard them all through the rushing and whirling of flame. But he had to hope she understood. And what she'd missed, he'd manage himself, weaving a path through his basement.

With the scarf wrapped around his hand, he turned the knob. Darkness yawned beneath him but he had the sense of fresh, albeit musty, air. "Hold the handrail."

He felt Sadie brush past him in the dark before he reached out and closed the door behind them. The fire was gaining and it was only a matter of a few minutes before the house collapsed in on itself. Tripp was determined not to focus on that. The air was cleaner here and they'd make it.

They had to.

"I'm at the bottom." Sadie's voice floated over him, a disembodied sound that echoed off the thick concrete of the basement. Tripp took the last step, his feet touching the reassuring strength of the concrete. He grabbed her hand once more, his fingers tightening over hers just as a loud crash echoed above them.

The floorboards above their heads groaned with the weight and Tripp tightened his grip. "Let's go."

"Can we follow a wall?"

"We have to walk straight through the center. The stairs leading up and outside are directly opposite. It's the quickest way."

As if to punctuate his point, the floorboards groaned again, the wood above them coming to life with fire. It wasn't much—and the flames only added to the danger—but they also added the slightest bit of light.

"Come on!"

Tripp navigated them through the dark, desperately

trying to picture the items he had scattered around the basement. There was a weight bench, which he remembered only as his shin connected with a rack of hand weights. Ignoring the throbbing pain, he moved Sadie deftly around the object and toward the stairs.

That terrible groaning continued above them and as the fire spread, the flames added light to their way. Tripp could finally see the stairs in front of them, the concrete at their feet devoid of any further obstacles.

"There, Sadie!"

"I see it."

With the way visible, Tripp ran them toward the stairs, the heavy creaking finally growing too much. He heard the cracking house above him, shuddering as the structural damage finally caused the wood frame to give way.

Sadie screamed and he practically threw her into the stairwell as the burning house fell into the basement around them.

Smoke rushed into their alcove along with an intense heat Tripp had never felt before. It was like being inside an oven, and he knew they wouldn't be able to withstand it for much longer. Pushing past Sadie up the concrete steps, his hand hit the underside of the storm door and he felt around for the latch to unlock it.

"Tripp!" Sadie shouted from behind him as the flames leaped further into the stairwell, lapping at them with hungry hands.

Tripp dropped the coats he still carried onto the top stair. He fumbled with the metal lock that kept the storm doors barred from external intruders, working it with frantic fingers when the bolt didn't want to budge. The frigid temperatures outside had made it hard to move and the lock seemed impervious to the heat steadily climbing behind them.

"Tripp!"

As Sadie's panicked scream washed over him once more, Tripp felt the latch give way. On a thick, heavy squeak, the door lifted in his hands. The snow that had lay more than a foot deep on the ground added to the weight, but Tripp ignored it all as sweet, fresh air swept into the ever-widening opening.

"Here. Let me help." Sadie came up beside him, her arms stretching beside his to push the door up. "But we have to do it slowly. We don't know who's out there."

"Yeah, but we do know what's in here. And we have to take our chances."

Tripp used the opening to look out into his backyard. Although little had gone as he'd hoped, the one thing in their favor was that the fire was lapping against the frame of the house. The path out of the basement was free and clear of flames.

Bastard knew he couldn't keep that blaze going in the snow, Tripp thought grimly as his eyes tried to adjust to the dim light in the backyard. Sadie's warning still echoed through his mind, nearly as loud as the fire, that Tate and his goons would be standing guard wherever they chose to flee.

While that danger might be real, they had to get *out*. Much of the house had fallen inward, but a few walls were still standing. He and Sadie weren't safe where they were and, worse, they risked being locked in if one of those walls fell the wrong way.

"We have to move," Tripp whispered urgently.

"What if he's out there?"

"Then we take our chances. They're still better than where we are. Do you have the gun?"

"Yes."

"Here." Tripp fumbled for the coats on the step. "Put this on. I know it doesn't feel like it now, but the moment you get beyond the blaze, you're going to be freezing."

"From a frozen lake to a fiery inferno." Sadie's laughter came out slightly manic. "The man is a lunatic."

"Yeah, but we've got the element of surprise on our side. It's possible he's thought we didn't make it out since the moment the roof fell in."

It was a small hope, but Tripp decided he'd take it anyway. Even the smallest advantage of surprise was something and since his house was blazing like the fires of hell, there was no way his neighbors hadn't called it in already.

The danger might be real, but he'd bet his life Tate and his goons wouldn't stick around once the fire company arrived.

That meant he had only a few more precious minutes to take the bastard down. With a burst of strength against the heavy door, Tripp used the momentum of his body to walk up the last few concrete steps, pushing the door high and wide. He was going to take down Tate Greer.

Finally.

ONE MINUTE SHE was bracing herself against absurdly misplaced laughter and the next Tripp was on the move.

The basement door creaked and groaned on its metal hinges as Tripp lifted it wide and high before running up the last few steps and out into the yard. She called after him but it did nothing to slow him down.

Nor did he even acknowledge he'd heard her.

Instead he just kept moving, farther away from the house and into what could only be Tate's crosshairs.

"Damn fool man," she muttered before adding one of her favorite curses for good measure. And then she focused on her own situation, the increasing collapse of the house a steady reminder she needed to move, too.

Sadie checked the gun, the piece familiar to her, as it matched the one she'd carried as a rookie, and followed Tripp into the cold. The house kept making those horrible wrenching noises, its remnants' continuing fight to stay upright rapidly waning in the bitter night air.

Deep snow sucked at her feet, cold against the sneakers she'd had on all day. The temperature was a shock against the oven-like warmth she'd experienced in the basement, but she didn't have time to analyze the changes. All she could do was move.

The urge to get away from the house was strong, but her gaze swung like an arc over the property. Outside lights were on at the neighbors' on both sides but she saw no lights reflecting from windows or people coming out onto the street. She vaguely remembered a few comments Tripp mentioned about the people who lived on either side of him. An elderly couple, who were in Florida this time of year, flanked one side, and a young couple without children, who were rarely home in the evenings, the other.

That meant no one would be observing through windows, watching the flames engulf the house. Nor would they have any sense of intruders sneaking around the grounds.

While she wouldn't expect someone to risk themselves for her—and as a law enforcement professional she sorely wanted them to remain inside—an extra pair of eyes or a shout from a window that they'd called 911 would be more than welcome at this time. Since she'd get neither, she moved on, trying to get a sense of where Tripp had gone.

The footprints she'd seen in the snow faded at the edge of the house, the heat of the fire melting the ground cover. So instead, she moved back and away, sweeping in steady arcs just as she'd learned at the academy.

Tripp's backyard was long and deep, the snow-covered grass ending as it ran into a stretch of woods. As she stilled, considering those woods on her next sweep, she realized how easy it had been for Tate to hide there and lie in wait.

A shiver went through her that had nothing to do with the cold.

And everything to do with the knife she felt pressed against the thin and tender skin behind her ear.

TRIPP SAW IT all play out before him. He'd made a full perimeter around the house and it was only as he made the final turn into the backyard—giving the collapsing house a wide berth—that he saw his mistake.

The large, hulking form of Tate Greer had come up behind Sadie, one arm wrapping around her neck while the other held a wicked hunting knife up to the sensitive area just beneath her ear. The shout had al-

ready risen in his throat when Tripp pulled it back by
sheer force of will.

Greer had played them.

There was no one else waiting with him. He'd done
this all on his own. Tripp knew there were any number of clinical terms for it. Escalation. Psychopathy.
Violent tendencies. But to his mind, the situation was
far simpler.

Tate Greer was determined to finish what he'd
started.

The first whirl of fire engine sirens echoed in the
distance and Tripp knew there was no room to wait.

Greer was no doubt counting down, as well, and it
would be the closing bell to whatever horror the man
had in mind.

Sadie had stilled the moment the knife touched her
body and Tripp knew they were at a collective disadvantage. She couldn't see him and he had no way of knowing how her own rush of adrenaline was affecting her.

Could she react with the speed he needed?

Would she fall or fumble?

And could Tripp line up a shot in a way that had
Tate's reflexes moving the knife *away* from Sadie's
body instead of into it?

He considered himself a good marksman, but he was
no sniper. So aiming for Greer's head was out of the
question. The risk was too damn great.

And as the sound of sirens bore down, there was no
more time to think about it.

Resetting the safety and placing the gun in the back
waistband of his jeans, Tripp moved forward. The snow-
covered ground had a layer of ice and the only thing

keeping him from sounding an alert was the continued shriek and whine of fire behind him. That, coupled with the wail of sirens, did enough to hide the steady crunch of his boots on icy snow.

Despite the surrounding noise, Tate's voice rose over the din. "You were supposed to be so easy. You were my ticket into every damn database I needed. To the police. To Colton Investigations. I had it all planned and you ruined it."

"Go to hell."

Tripp smiled in spite of himself, Sadie's swift retort affirming that the empty laughter that had concerned him while they were still in the basement had given way to pragmatic disdain.

It was the first glimmer of hope they'd get out of this.

She just had to stay strong.

And he needed to make sure Greer had no idea he was closing in.

With careful steps to ensure the snow didn't make any additional noise, Tripp moved closer. An idea formed and he dug the gun from his waistband, turning the butt side out. As soon as he was in range, Tripp raised his left arm and slammed the butt of the weapon on Tate's head while using his dominant hand to hold his knife arm still.

"Sadie! Drop and move!"

Sadie did as she was told, falling to her knees in the snow.

The force of Tripp's revolver hit its mark, but only served to anger Greer further. The man whirled, using some fancy footwork of his own as he spun around to face Tripp, the knife blade glinting sharply in the light of the flames. Even with the solid blow to the head, the man never lost his balance. An excessively neat maneuver that left Greer on his feet and still in full, controlled possession of the knife.

Tripp had learned early on in his rookie year never to underestimate an opponent. Some of the smallest men he'd taken down had near superhuman strength and a larger criminal often lost ground to the inevitable inertia that kicked in once a body started moving in the wrong direction.

Tate Greer fit neither description. He was a big man, with the large proportions of a heavyweight fighter. And he had the quickness and speed of a lightweight.

A lethal combination.

Tripp reared back as Greer's knife arm shot out, slicing through the air nanoseconds before Tripp got out of the way. While the force of the movement would have put any normal person off balance, Greer retained his, bouncing on the balls of his feet. "She's not getting out of here alive, man. And neither are you."

He slammed forward again, an angry grizzly with sharp claws, his arm waving that blade through the crisp night air.

The very tip of the blade sliced through the thick sleeve of Tripp's coat. Fire shot up his arm at what would no doubt be a deep cut, but he ignored it, instead channeling the pain toward his foe.

Tate Greer was the enemy.

He and his thugs had terrorized the good people of Grand Rapids for years. Long before RevitaYou had even been a glimmer of an idea, Greer had been harming people by lending money illegally and then siccing his thugs on them.

And then he'd turned his sights on Sadie.

Using her. Manipulating her. And then kidnapping and trying to kill her.

Whatever vows Tripp had made to serve and protect seemed inadequate for the moment.

Greer was his prey.

And any and all pretense of capturing the man, through proper channels as a leader in the GRPD, had vanished. Tripp wanted vengeance and had no illusion it would be sanctioned by his employer.

Greer slashed out with the knife once more and Tripp leaped away from the blade before going on the offensive. He still had his gun and wanted to use it, but the brutal, near hand-to-hand-combat style of his opponent meant the weapon could either work for him or just as easily be turned against him.

As the wail of the sirens grew louder, Tripp knew he only had another minute at most. He feinted to the side before pivoting and bringing the butt of the gun down once more on Greer's body. He'd aimed for the head but the gun grazed just off of the guy's shoulder. Despite missing his target, the blow did finally dislodge Greer's footing. Only, instead of stumbling back from the force of Tripp's strike, the man windmilled his arms, the knife once more flashing in the light of the flames.

Greer used the change in momentum to his advantage, thrusting forward. His knife struck the heavy padding of Tripp's coat before plunging through the thick wool and into his waist. The jab was quick, the pain a piercing nuisance, before Greer pulled back, still trying to regain his balance in the still-fresh snow.

Tripp saw the knife rise, streaked with blood this time and ready to strike again, when blue and red lights flashed from the street, the sirens keening into the night.

Sadie shouted, racing closer to them, her gun extended and pointed directly at Greer. The man seemed to hover for an endless moment in indecision until she shot off a round, the bullet going just wide of him. It was enough to push Greer into motion. He turned tail and ran for the woods.

Orange flames still sparked into the sky behind them but Tripp ignored them and gave chase, Sadie's heavy footsteps audible behind him while the thick snow dragged on his feet. He saw Greer stumble with it, too, but the man had a large enough head start that Tripp wasn't able to reach him. Registering once more that he had a gun in his hand, he stopped and took aim.

Pain ran a searing path from his arm to his elbow where Greer's blade had sliced him, but Tripp held his position, lining up his shot. Without giving himself another moment to think—or to reconsider aiming at another's back—he fired off his shots.

Six in a row, all directed at the weaving figure heading for the woods.

On the fifth shot, he saw Greer jerk and stumble, but still, the man never lost his balance. Or his momentum. He just kept moving into the woods.

"Tripp!" Sadie moved up behind him, hanging on his arm and holding him still.

"I have to go after him." Tripp tried to run but she

seemed surprisingly strong, her hold able to root him to the spot.

"Tripp! You're hurt."

Her words registered dimly in his mind as he looked down to where she held tight to his forearm. He stared at her hand and the vise grip she had on his body, curious as to why her hand felt so heavy where it lay. And then his gaze drifted to the drops of red coloring the snow at his feet.

As the blood registered as his own, the adrenaline that had carried him through his backyard gave out. Along with the dizzying drop in blood pressure, a searing pain lit up his side. He saw the ground rise up, swift and immediate, before he felt Sadie's arms wrap tight around his chest, slowing his momentum.

And then the world went black.

Chapter Thirteen

Sadie glanced around the emergency waiting room, her siblings assembled in the various chairs nearest her. They were all there. Riley and Griffin held court at the doorway, refusing entry to anyone who didn't pass muster. Pippa and Kiely took point on conferring with the hospital staff and getting updates on Tripp's condition while also peppering the GRPD with questions every time an officer came in to pay respects.

Vikki sat by her side, her hands clutching Sadie's as she crooned over and over that they'd find Tate and put him away forever.

"That bastard is going to pay."

Vikki had said the same thing, in a variety of ways, with a variety of colorful descriptions, for the past hour. Sadie was grateful for the comfort but all she wanted was to see Tripp.

"Hey, Vik. Why don't you let me take over for a minute?"

Vikki stared up at Riley hovering in front of them. Sadie felt her twin's hesitation in the clutch of her hands before Vikki nodded. "I guess I could use some disgusting coffee out of a machine that's nearly as old as I am."

"That's my girl." Riley dug some change out of his pocket. "Would you mind getting me one, too?"

"Sure."

Sadie saw the subtle communication pass between Riley and Vikki. Under normal circumstances, she'd be annoyed they were communicating about her when she was right there. But, all things considered, she could hardly say she wouldn't be doing the same right now if the roles were reversed.

Riley took Vikki's seat, his arm going around Sadie's shoulders. She took the moment to snuggle into her brother, amazed to realize how good it felt to let down her guard.

To ease the burden that had hung over her for more than a month now.

She'd believed herself moving past the pain of Tate's betrayal, especially after the time she'd spent with her sisters, but now she had a new agony to deal with. One that went far deeper, even if she'd only spent a few days with Tripp.

What if he'd died?

Tate's stealth attack had caught them both off guard and they'd both inhaled a lot of ash and smoke. Now Tripp was dealing with a deep knife wound on top of it.

The fire had left her throat raw and scratchy but it had nothing on the tight ball of pain that lodged there as tears welled up at the thought of losing Tripp.

On her hard sob, Riley pulled her close. "Hey now."

"I can't—" She broke off, another sob shaking her body.

"Shhh." Riley let her cry it out, all the fear and tension, layered over the helpless uncertainty of whether or not Tripp would be okay.

"This is getting to be a habit with us," Riley said once her storm of tears had passed.

"A habit that's, once again, my fault."

"We're back to that?"

"Yes, we're back to that. Because the man I nearly married tried to kill me and the good lieutenant tonight. Because he damn near succeeded and even right now Tripp is in an OR and his house is in ashes."

"He's getting a blood transfusion, a serious shot of meds, and a round of stitches. No one's operating on him."

"It's all my fault."

"No, actually it's not."

Another set of tears welled, quieter and hotter than the first. While she wanted to regain some control, Sadie knew the key was letting it all out.

Something she hadn't done in the sheer rush of events. Instead, she'd watched as the paramedics transferred Tripp from the freezing cold ground onto a stretcher. She'd protested when they'd wanted to strap her onto one, too, but had finally relented when one of them forced oxygen on her. The pure air had felt too good in her battered lungs and suddenly she'd been too tired to argue.

Even if she hadn't been too tired to watch the still-leaping flames from the back window of the ambulance as they'd rushed her—for the second time in a week—to county hospital.

She'd been checked out and, despite being offered a chance to be monitored overnight, she'd refused. She had no interest in being hooked up to monitors and an IV, and confined to a bed again. Tate was still out there and he'd already proved a hospital entrance wasn't enough to deter him.

She'd be damned if she was going to put herself in danger again.

Because, once more, he'd escaped. Like a cat with nine lives. Every time they were close to taking him down, the man vanished. While Sadie understood she and Tripp had been at a disadvantage this evening with Tate's surprise attack, they'd still been serious opponents. Two trained cops, both armed.

Yet Tate had still escaped.

Riley spoke once more, his voice strong and firm and full of conviction. "It's not your fault, Sadie."

"I brought this. On all of us."

"Like Dad brought his and Mom's murders on himself? Like Abigail brought on her father's crimes when she came into Griffin's life? Or maybe it's like Flynn's being responsible for his half brother Landon's bad choices?"

Riley kept going before she could even get a word in. "The RevitaYou case has blown wide open and every one of us has been doing our level best to fight it with all we've got. Don't you dare go taking this on yourself."

"Real nice to use our parents on me."

Riley smiled down at her. "I'll use whatever it takes. You're not at fault here. None of us is. But we are all in control of what we do about it."

"When did you get so smart, big brother?"

"I've always been smart. It's just that no one wants to give me any credit for it. And that includes a very pregnant Charlize, who's been texting me nonstop for the past hour for updates."

She wrapped her arms around his waist, hugging him tight. "Consider it a public service."

"How's that?"

"As your siblings, we're honor-bound to make sure your head doesn't get too big."

The laughter started down low and deep and Sadie could feel her brother shaking against her. It was only as she pulled back and looked up at him that she saw the mischief filling his eyes. "Consider it a family condition."

"Oh, there's no doubt about that. Now go call Charlize," Sadie ordered.

A doctor came into the waiting room. "Is there a Sadie Colton here?"

She stood abruptly, smoothing her shirt against her hips. "That's me."

"Lieutenant McKellar has asked to see you. He's been quite insistent, as a matter of fact."

Riley, still holding her hand, gave it a tight squeeze before releasing it. "Go on. We'll all be right here."

"Thank you." Sadie bent to kiss Riley on the cheek. "For everything."

TRIPP REACHED FOR the small cup of water on the rolling table that fit across his hospital bed and winced at the sharp pain that radiated down his side. He knew he was more than lucky to be alive with nothing more than some stitches and enough antibiotics to fell an elephant, but the pain irritated him all the same.

Greer had vanished. And the shooting pain lancing

through Tripp's side seemed like one more mocking example of how he'd let the man get away.

Again.

He was well acquainted with slippery criminals. Hell, the majority of police work was hunting them down and doing your level best to catch them. But Greer's ongoing vanishing act had reduced Tripp to the level of a keystone cop. He'd had the man in his hands, for Pete's sake.

You also nearly took a stomach full of hunting knife, the more reasonable part of him chided through the self-recrimination. A fair argument that gave little comfort.

Or none at all.

"Tripp." Sadie appeared at the door, her voice gravelly and still layered with smoke when she spoke again. "You up for a bit of company?"

She'd changed clothes, the oversize sweatshirt rolled up several times at her wrists drowning her in the heavy material. The soot that had marred her skin—the last thing he remembered seeing before he'd passed out—had been washed off and, somewhere over the past few hours, she'd taken a shower. Her strawberry-blond hair shone under the recessed lighting of his room.

She was beautiful. And perfect. Something clenched hard and tight deep inside him at the realization that she was okay. And at the even bigger realization that she might have been killed tonight.

Sadie took a few steps into the room but remained near the door. "How are you feeling?"

"I'm fine."

A small frown marred her lips, matched by the slight

furrowing of the brow he'd come to adore. "I don't believe you."

"I am fine. But I can admit that I've also felt better."

"You were stabbed. And you inhaled so much smoke." She took a few steps closer. "When you fell down in the snow, I didn't know if you'd be okay. Or if—" She broke off, a hard sob escaping from her throat.

"Sadie, I'm fine." His heart broke as sobs racked her shoulders, dwarfed beneath the thick cotton of her sweatshirt. "Come here. Talk to me. I promise you, I'm okay."

She continued crying, the tears she seemed unable to control continuing to quake through her body. But she did move closer, coming to stand beside the bed. He ignored the pain that seared through his side as he sat up, readjusting so there was room beside him on the bed. He pulled her close, into the spot he'd made, before wrapping his arms around her. "Shh, now. It's fine."

She nestled into his arms, her body slowly calming. They both faced the doorway and he fitted his chin just over her head, holding her through the storm of tears. Even the pain in his side seemed to fade as he sank into the quiet with her, content to simply hold her.

To assure himself she was safe.

They'd made it through together. That was some sort of miracle, if he were honest with himself. Between the fire and the fight, the fact they were both here and relatively whole was…well, it really was a miracle.

That was a concept he hadn't thought about in a long time. Miracles. Wonder. Maybe even divine intervention. He'd stopped believing in all of it a long time ago, the reality of losing Lila and the baby too much to bear.

Or to continue to hope.

Yet, somehow, in the midst of all he'd experienced over the past few weeks, Sadie Colton had returned that to him. He did have hope that they'd get out of this. That Tate Greer and Wes Matthews would get their due. And that Capital X would, once and for all, be vanquished right along with the pure evil that was the RevitaYou supplement.

A fountain of youth that killed people. Vanity might be a sin, but Tripp was determined that no one else was going to die for it. And the people who had brought the drug to life would go down with the ship.

"Am I hurting you?" Sadie struggled to sit upright but he held on, holding her still.

"I'm fine."

"You just tightened up. I thought maybe you were in a lot of pain."

Tripp realized that he had tightened his hold as he'd thought about Capital X and RevitaYou, and relaxed a bit. "Sorry. Occupational hazard."

"Of what?"

He breathed in deep, the light, fresh scent of her adding to that unfurling hope in his heart. "Thinking about the day this whole RevitaYou thing is behind us all."

She laid a hand over his. "Do you think that will happen?"

"I do. We're close and getting closer every day. Make no mistake about it, today's incident was *because* of how close we are to arresting Matthews and Greer."

"Maybe."

Tripp heard the hesitation and let it go for a minute,

curious if she'd continue. When she didn't, he prodded her for more. "Maybe? That's all you've got?"

She shifted then, gently moving out of his arms. He wanted her to stay—nearly asked her to—but it was only because he realized that he wanted her in the same place forever that he held back.

Had he really gone *there*?

What right did he have to even think that way? Sadie had her entire future in front of her. She would heal from the pain Tate Greer had caused and she'd move on. She would and she deserved to.

And she deserved it with someone who wasn't damaged and broken. Like him.

He might have found a few vestiges of hope these past few days, but he knew who he was and he knew his lot in life. Marriage and a family weren't a part of that.

Sadie Colton was designed for marriage and a family. It was written in every pore. Seemed to halo her, shimmering as clear as if he could reach out and touch that future himself.

"I say maybe because Tate is still out there. So's Wes Matthews. My family hasn't found Brody yet, no matter how many text messages my sisters have sent him. I'd have added to their number if I hadn't just lost my second cell phone this week."

She sighed heavily, the hair framing her face blowing in the light gust. "All I'm saying is that while I hear you, I'm not sure we're going to get a neat bow wrapped around this one."

"Who said anything about bows?"

"You were getting dangerously close."

Tripp wasn't sure if he was offended or ready to

laugh. In light of all they'd been through, maybe that was a good thing. It meant that they could still *feel* something. Could still render emotion and find topics to argue about. To learn from one another and debate the facts.

For now, it would have to be enough.

His body might want more, but his mind knew better. He needed to stay strong and resist these inconvenient feelings for Sadie. Because no matter what she thought, he knew in his bones that this would end. Sooner rather than later, in fact.

Greer's days of running free were numbered.

And once that monster and his fellow villains were off the streets, life would go back to normal.

It would.

Because it had to.

SADIE FELT THE exhaustion down to her very marrow, yet sleep still eluded her as she struggled to get comfortable in the guest chair in his room. Tripp had finally dozed off about an hour before. She'd wanted to go say goodbye to her family, still hanging out in the waiting room, and send them home, and knew it would be an acceptable excuse to leave Tripp for a few minutes. As she'd hoped, by the time she'd returned to his room, his eyes were closed and he was snoring.

It was a sweet sound, which really meant she'd gone around the bend for this guy. She'd groused at her brothers for years for snoring like grizzlies, yet here was Tripp, likely just as loud, and she thought it was a symphony.

Because you've got it bad, Colton. B-A-D bad.

A fact she'd struggled with earlier when she'd left his arms. It had felt so good to lay there with him, practically intertwined on the small bed. She'd felt safe and secure, and in the cocoon of his arms she could let her fantasies go. There, with the masculine, woodsy scent of him surrounding her, she could pretend this wasn't temporary. More, she could believe that somehow they would find their way.

Together.

That was why she'd had to step away. Pull herself from that warm embrace and take the seat opposite his hospital bed. She'd stared at the beeping machines, the confirmation that his heart was still beating and blood still flowed in his veins. And she took heart that they'd survived yet again.

Because she'd rather be in a world with Tripp alive.

Beyond that truth, not much else mattered. Not her feelings for him or the increasingly urgent need she had to tell him—which was the path to disaster.

Yes, they'd grown close over the past week.

And yes, the feelings she'd always had for him had reawakened with the close proximity and intense experiences.

But it couldn't be anything else. And it was up to her to find acceptance in that.

"Sadie." Vikki whispered her name from the doorway and Sadie turned to find her twin standing there, her expression inscrutable. That was odd since she and Vikki always knew what the other was thinking.

Yet Vik's expression gave nothing away, even as Sadie sensed her sister had quite a lot to say.

She gave one last look at the monitor, then at Tripp,

before standing and following Vikki out into the hallway. "What is it, Vik? I thought you and Flynn were heading home with everyone else?"

"We were. But—" Vikki stilled, her green eyes clouding. Their eyes were the one match they shared as twins.

"What is it, Vikki?"

"We were already in the car and Flynn was almost out of the parking lot when I asked him to come back." Vikki's arms went wide before pulling Sadie close. "I almost lost you tonight and I just—" Vikki let out a long, hard sigh. "And I love you and I needed to see you again. Hold you again."

Sadie clung to her sister, the bond they'd shared their entire lives even stronger than the tight grip that held them in place now. It felt good to hold her sister. To feel the solid lines of her body and know that she was alive and well and whole.

"First the kidnapping from the safe house and now tonight." Vikki sighed again as a shudder seemed to echo through her body. "I can't lose you, Sadie. I just can't."

"You didn't, Vik. I'm okay. Really, I'm fine."

"I know." Vikki took a step back and shook her head. "I know. I'm looking at you and I know you're fine. And I keep telling myself that. And then I think about what might have happened and it washes through me once more."

Flynn let out a discreet cough before moving down the hallway. The GRPD had put two guards on the ward this time. They'd been apprised of who could come in and out, and allowed Flynn to pass. He moved up beside

Vikki and wrapped an arm around her. "We're both so glad you're all right, Sadie."

"I know."

Although she hadn't spent much time with Flynn since her sister had fallen in love with the Army MP while Sadie had been in the GRPD safe house, she knew he was a good man. He had the ringing endorsement of her family and she'd never seen Vikki so blissfully happy.

But seeing them now—their mutual support and affection for each other so obvious—made Sadie's heart happy. She *knew* the love Flynn felt for her sister—saw it in Vikki's love in return—and was beyond grateful.

It was proof that love could find its way in the darkest of times.

"You having a party out there?" Tripp's normally deep voice was still tinged with the husky aftereffects of smoke inhalation.

Sadie turned back toward his room. "Are you okay?"

He stared at her from the bed. "Sounded more interesting out there than in here."

Sadie walked into the room, gesturing Vikki and Flynn with her. "Do you need anything?"

"I'd like an opinion, actually."

"An opinion about what?" Sadie asked.

Vikki had already moved into motion, pouring Tripp a fresh glass of water from a pitcher on the counter. She brought it over, removing the older one that had likely grown warm.

"Thank you." Tripp used the controller on his bed to sit up and take the water from Vikki. After drinking deep, he eyed Flynn before setting the glass down. "I've got an idea."

"Something we can help you with?" Flynn asked.

"I think so. I need a few days to heal and Greer has already proved he can move around undetected. I'd feel a lot better if Sadie and I got out of town."

"I can't go anywhere—" Sadie started to protest.

But Vikki had already moved closer to Tripp. "You had me at 'out of town,' Lieutenant."

"I've got a private place. A small cabin. Hell—" Tripp laughed, the sound hoarse "—I usually have to use my GPS to find it. It'll be a great spot to lay low for a few days. Give us some time to analyze Greer's moves and what he might do next."

"I think it's a great idea. Inspired." Vikki was already turning to Sadie, her excitement crushing whatever it was Sadie wanted to say.

A few days out of touch from everyone…but *with* Tripp?

Sly fingers of need beckoned her forward, willing her to say yes to the idea, while the more pragmatic side of her was convinced she should say no.

A cabin so remote he needed GPS to find it?

"I can't just run away again. That's what I've been doing for more than a month now and it hasn't gotten me anywhere. I'm no safer now than I was before all this started." Sadie heard the arguments coming from her own lips and knew them for the lies they were.

Sure, on principle, she didn't want to turn tail and run from Tate Greer. But Tate had little to do with the silky voice that continued to keep her company in her head, suggesting that she'd actually like nothing more than *to* run away with Tripp for a few days.

Forever, really.

"It's a great idea, McKellar." Flynn nodded. "We can feed you any information you need out of Colton Investigations' HQ. And I'm sure Emmanuel can keep you apprised of whatever GRPD data you need."

"I've got full digital capabilities at my place," Tripp added, reinforcing that the transition would be both easy and seamless.

"But I—" Sadie stopped as Vikki appealed to her once more.

"Sadie, please. Go away for a little while. Help Tripp get better, and get off the grid for a few days. You've both been through so much. You need time away from this mess. From the fear and the sense that there's another shoe waiting to drop."

She knew she should argue. Or stall. Or demand a few days to think it over, but really, what was the point?

Tripp McKellar had just invited her to run away with him. He might not understand what that meant to her, but really, how often was a woman offered a chance to make her dreams come true?

Chapter Fourteen

Tripp watched Sadie putter around his cabin's kitchen from the comfort of his well-worn couch and wondered what he'd possibly been thinking inviting her up there. Sure, there'd been copious amounts of painkillers involved, but really, the drugs hadn't clouded his thoughts that much.

No, instead they'd blunted his ability to think three steps ahead of himself.

That was where he now found himself, healing with all the comfort of a riled grizzly while sporting a near constant erection.

It hadn't been this bad at his house. Maybe because she'd hid out much of the time in the guest room? Or maybe because her family had dropped in several times, effectively diminishing his more lustful thoughts about their baby sister?

Who knew?

All he did know was that after three days his side hurt like a beast, the stitches itchy as they healed, and Sadie Colton flitted around his cabin like his own personal angel of mercy.

She made his breakfast.

She refilled his coffee.

She plumped his pillows.

And all he wanted to do was wrap his arms around her, drag her down onto the old lumpy couch and make love to her until both of their eyes crossed. His desire was so great he'd even gotten over feeling embarrassed he had condoms in his gym bag. It was an oddly hopeful purchase he'd had no reason to make doing last month's shopping, yet had anyway.

Hopeful and now a taunting reminder from his worn-out GRPD duffel.

Tripp groaned at the injustice of it all.

"Tripp? Are you okay?" Sadie turned from where she stood at the kitchen counter, concern written across her face.

"I'm fine."

"You sounded like you were in pain."

"No." Unclenching his teeth, he tried to come up with something plausible. "I just moved the wrong way."

"Are your stitches okay?"

"I'm fine, Sadie."

The words came out sharper than he'd intended, but really, what was a man to do? Her light and sweetness and, hell, just *her*, was slowly driving him mad.

The computer Tripp had settled on the coffee table rang, an incoming video call lighting up the screen. He tapped the button to answer it. Literally saved by the bell. "McKellar here."

As the video came up, he saw several of his team members in one of the GRPD meeting rooms. Riley was also visible in the shot, along with Ashanti Silver.

"Looks like a full house," Tripp drawled.

"You better believe it, McKellar." His chief started right in. "We've got a lead on Matthews."

Sadie entered the living room, coming fully into view on screen. "Chief Fox. How are you?"

"Sadie. Good to see you."

"You, as well. Please tell us you're calling with some good news."

"You bet we are, little sister," Riley told her. "Matthews took the bait."

Although Tripp wouldn't go all the way to admitting to skepticism, he had definitely had his concerns that the honeypot plan to capture Wes Matthews wasn't going to pay dividends. Not because it was a bad idea, but because the notion that Matthews could still think about sex in the midst of his pyramid scheme going bad seemed like an impossible stretch.

Clearly, he'd underestimated the male libido.

Not that his was doing him any favors.

"Tell us what you've got."

Ashanti took over the video call, using the sharing feature to run through the most recent emails her "character" had shared with Matthews. A few of the images were quite graphic and Tripp couldn't help but side-eye Sadie.

To her credit, she was completely focused on the discussion. A true professional, all while that very libido Tripp was so busy condemning in Matthews was distracting him with Sadie.

"But the best was the conversation we had last night." The images on the screen fell off as the GRPD meeting room once again came into view. And then Ashanti played the recording of her call with Matthews.

Tripp listened as they talked of deals and investments and some money Ashanti's "character" wanted to invest. She purred a little, letting off the throttle when the discussion of investments shifted toward a face-to-face meeting.

"I don't believe he fell for this," Sadie said to Tripp, but added under her breath and low enough it didn't interrupt the replay, "But Abigail said it would work and she was right. She even suggested they pepper in big words and reference a few old movies that he loves. Listen to how smoothly Ashanti slid all of that in there. He's putty in her hands."

Matthews certainly was, Tripp thought to himself. He remained quiet, listening to the rest of the recording before interjecting. "Has he committed to a meeting yet?"

"Not yet," Ashanti said. "I think I'll get him on the next call, though."

"Do we still think he's in the Bahamas?" Tripp asked.

"That's still the latest intel from the Bureau," Chief Fox affirmed. "They've worked well with us on this and Agent Winston has played more than fair with me."

Tripp suspected that might have something to do with how well Kiely was working with her new fiancé, but who wanted to quibble? While he understood the situations that often dictated one side or the other to behave territorially, they were all after the same end goal. And Tripp had had little time or acceptance in his career for the politics that often existed between the Feds and the local government.

Part of why he'd always respected Cooper Winston was his willingness to do the same.

Taking down Capital X and Wes Matthews needed to be priority number one. It was good to know that everyone collectively felt that way.

As if reading his thoughts, Fox added, "Sadie, your sister Kiely has been a huge help on this, too."

"Thank you, sir. She wants to see this wrapped up, just like we all do."

"Without question." Fox changed gears, his next question deftly shining a spotlight directly on Tripp. "How are you feeling, McKellar? Healing up well?"

"Yes, sir. Feeling good as new."

"You keep telling yourself that," Chief Fox chuckled.

In minutes, the call had ended, Tripp's computer screen once again dark.

"That is encouraging news," Sadie said. "I really wasn't sure this was going to work. But it's so weird, it's just like Abigail said. Her father is highly susceptible to this approach." She shook her head before gesturing in the direction of the now dark computer screen. "I didn't want to believe it but it's hard to deny that sort of response."

"It's hardly a surprise."

Sadie stood and had only taken a few steps toward the kitchen when she stopped, cocking a hand on her hip. "What's not a surprise?"

"Men. Their egos. And body parts farther south. It's a cliché for a reason."

"Maybe," she said and shrugged. "I guess I wanted to give him a little more credit, though. I may hate his criminal line of work, but the guy did work hard to build up his pyramid scheme. Seems like an awful big waste to lose it all just because he couldn't keep it in his pants."

"That's still to be seen."

"I suppose."

Tripp continued, all that lingering frustration still roiling in his gut. "Besides, guys like him? Like Greer? They all think they're above getting caught."

"Are you okay? Your voice sounds strange."

Was he okay? Up until a few days ago, he would've said he was fine. More than fine. And then Sadie Colton had come into his life like a hurricane.

Yes, he had been attracted to her before. But it was hard to believe how quickly that slow burn had turned into an inferno.

"I'm fine."

"You keep saying that, and yet each time you do, I'm finding I believe you less and less."

"What do you want me to tell you?"

"The truth."

What *did* she want him to tell her? That he cared about her? That he suspected he felt more strongly toward her than he should or than he ever wanted to feel for another human being ever again?

Or maybe she wanted him to tell her how she decimated his willpower with the barest glance.

Perhaps what she *really* wanted to know was that she was in his blood and, no matter how much distance he put between them or how many times he told himself he couldn't touch her, they were racing toward some sort of inevitable cliff.

And it would take barely a glance to push him straight over the edge.

"At the risk of paraphrasing a movie line, I'm not sure you can handle this truth."

Whatever patience she was hanging on to vanished in an instant. "You have some nerve, treating me like my ideas have no place here, with this surly dismissal. This was your idea, may I remind you. *Your* idea to come sit here and hide out from Tate Greer."

"I know."

"So why are you acting like this? We just got some good news. Hell, great news." She heaved out a heavy breath. "And all you can do is sit there being an ass about it all."

"I'm not—" He got to his feet, the tug of pain in his side nothing compared to the desperate need that twisted and churned inside him. "You know what, I'm not doing this."

"Doing *what*, Tripp?"

He was nearly out of the room when her question stopped him. The confusion, yes, but something else.

The hurt.

And with that small note of hurt something inside him broke wide open. His resistance vanished and, with it, any and all ability to stay away from her.

He pivoted, marched straight back to her and pulled her into his arms. One minute they were on opposite sides and the next she was right in the moment with him, her mouth fused to his, kissing him back like her very life depended on it.

It was what he'd wanted. What he'd yearned for.

And as his hand slid down her back to settle on her hip, Tripp finally quit fighting it.

FINALLY.

That lone word rang over and over in her mind as Sadie held on to Tripp.

How long had she wanted this? Wanted *him*?

There had been times when it had felt like forever. She knew she'd been someone before the day, as a rookie, that she'd been introduced to Tripp. But so often she'd forgotten what life had been like before she'd met him. Before she'd lived with the reassuring knowledge that there was someone in the world as good and decent and honorable as Tripp McKellar.

And hot, her subconscious reminded her as Tripp deepened the kiss further. *Never forget wildly attractive and hot.* Because to her, Tripp was the perfect man.

"Sadie," he whispered against her lips.

She ignored it, especially since most of what had come out of that lush frame in the form of words over the past hour had only served to annoy her. She much preferred what they were doing now.

Maybe if they stayed like this, mouths fused, they could get past whatever irritation had somehow found its way beneath his skin.

"Sadie." He said her name more firmly before matching the words with a fixed hold on her shoulder, stilling her.

"What?"

"We shouldn't—"

She lifted a finger and pressed it against the lips that had so recently ravaged her own.

"If you say we shouldn't do this, I'm going to slug you. And I have two brothers, so don't think I don't know how to deliver a rock-solid punch. Both because they taught me how and because I've used it on each of them with considerable effectiveness."

"But we—"

She pressed harder. "No. I'm sick of excuses for why this is a bad idea."

He shifted one hand from her shoulder, capturing her finger in his. "Would you listen to me?"

"Why?"

"Because I'm trying to be responsible here. You're here in my home at my insistence. And I'm your boss. And less than five minutes ago we were on a work call with the chief of the Grand Rapids Police Department. *And* your brother," he added in what felt like a low-blow afterthought.

"I'm not sure what my brother or, come to think of it, the chief, has to do with us having sex."

"Who said we're having sex?"

"I did. And I want to. Unless you don't want to."

"Sadie—"

"Yes or no, Tripp. I'm not interested in any other answer you can possibly come up with. That goes for excuses, too. Or any other half-baked reason that comes out of those impressively creative lips of yours. It's a question with a binary answer."

"'Impressively creative'?" A lone eyebrow quirked over those endless pools of blue.

"Yes."

"We shouldn't do this. And those reasons you're brushing off so easily are actually real reasons."

The light of battle was no longer reflected in his eyes. Instead, all Sadie saw was a very real, impossible-to-ignore vulnerability. And she understood it, because in that blue gaze she saw herself.

"I want you, Tripp. Right here, right now. I don't care what comes after this time. Or what might happen once we're back in the office. We're two adults. And I've known you long enough to know that if we make love, you won't hold it against me at work."

"But I—" He stopped, his gaze never leaving hers. "Yes or no, right?"

"That's it, Tripp. Yes or no." She kept her hands on his shoulders, but otherwise remained still. And in the waiting, recognized he needed the same from her. "My answer is yes."

He looked down at her for one inscrutable minute and she waited, not even daring to breathe. He wanted her. She knew that. Recognized the same need she felt in herself for him.

But still, she waited.

Because whatever held him back went far deeper than worrying about work. Or a boss/employee relationship that barely held water as an argument since Tripp had minimal, if any, sway over the CSI team.

No. This was something more. Something that went far deeper than desire between a man and a woman. Something she'd sensed in him for so long. Something deeply felt that held him back.

"Yes."

That word was practically a growl, guttural with need, as he pulled her close. His mouth closed over hers and Sadie thrilled to the heat that rose once more between them. Pressing herself against him, delighting in the hard lines of his body and how they complemented the far softer lines of hers, she put everything she was into the kiss.

Into her *yes*.

The couch that had been his work space for the past few days suddenly seemed as good a choice as any, the two bedrooms they'd each been occupying down the hall much too far to walk.

She was done with waiting.

She wanted him here. Now. And there was no more time to lose.

The clothes they wore—his well-used gym gear sporting GRPD labels from a bag in his trunk and hers, more loaners from her sisters—vanished in moments, falling to the side of the couch with gentle thuds as one piece followed the next. With a soft sigh, she pressed her now naked chest to his, the heat of his skin warming her despite the cold that howled outside the door.

Her breasts ached for his touch, her nipples sensitive points where they rubbed against the coarse hair of his chest. Sadie ran her hands over it, that male covering tapering to a narrow line just below his stomach. She was careful to avoid the bandage that covered his healing stitches, instead following that line of hair where it trailed to something even more male, more impressive. And as her hand closed over the firm length of him, Tripp exhaled heavily against her lips.

"Sadie."

The heat of him branded her, hot and hard and pulsing with life in her palm. She moved then, tentative stroking motions from base to tip, growing bolder when his breath grew more ragged, his hold on her tighter.

Without breaking that steady pressure, Sadie continued the sweet battle between them. His hands roamed over her body, drawing sensations as his thumbs brushed her nipples before both hands fully cupped her breasts. She stilled briefly, her chest arching into his hands as her head fell back, his ministrations shooting molten need to her core. It was only as he grew bolder, the press of his own hands more urgent, that she resumed those steady strokes.

"Wait."

He nearly stumbled as he stepped away, cursing as he crossed the room. Although she immediately missed his touch, she could hardly argue with the sight of his taut butt and muscled back and thighs as he crossed the room to his gym bag. "What are you—" She stopped as she recognized the box he came up with after digging deeply in the bag, another round of curses bulleting from his lips.

A giggle started deep in her belly, rumbling to life as he stomped back to her. His face still bore the unmistakable signs of sexual tension, which only served to make her laugh harder.

"What's so funny?"

"You." His mouth dropped as he caught sight of her, but she rushed on. "The cursing and that petulant little frown is too cute for words."

"Cute wasn't quite the look I was going for."

She reached for the box, digging out a condom and tossing the container onto the coffee table as he continued to stare down at her. She tore the foil before looking up at him from beneath her lashes. "Ruggedly handsome work better?"

"Much."

"Then sit that ruggedly handsome yet still-healing body down on that couch and let me get to work."

The surly look vanished as he took a seat. "Yes, ma'am."

Sadie settled herself over his lap, straddling his thighs with her own. "Did you just 'ma'am' me?"

"I'm afraid I did." He rubbed his thumbs over her nipples once more as he nipped kisses along her jaw. "Ma'am."

"You're going to pay, McKellar." She unrolled the condom over him, with deliberate, agonizing slowness, amazed that sex could be as much about laughter and fun as it was about pleasure.

And as she centered herself over his sheathed body and began to move, Sadie realized something else.

Sex was also about joy. And fun. And, as her pleasure crested, unleashing wave after wave of sensation through her body, she knew it for love.

TRIPP HELD SADIE in his arms, his breathing still harsh and ragged against her neck. He'd buried his face there as he'd poured himself into her, holding her body tight against his.

They'd just had sex on his old, lumpy couch that had likely been constructed during the Kennedy administration and it was the best sex of his life.

No bed had ever been as comfortable and no woman had ever been as sweet. Or as utterly all-consuming as Sadie Colton.

She'd decimated him.

As he struggled to regain his breath, he was already thinking about when they could do it again. Because one taste of Sadie wasn't enough. A lifetime of Sadie wouldn't be enough.

And that was a sobering enough thought that he lifted his head from her neck and dropped it back against the couch.

He'd given in.

On some level, he supposed it was inevitable, but he'd believed himself strong enough to withstand her. Or, if not her, his maddening feelings for her, which he knew were misplaced. Because despite all evidence to the contrary, he and Sadie didn't have a future.

Even if he could see past the lessons he'd learned with Lila's death, he was still Sadie's boss. She might not directly report to him but he was still a superior in the department.

And besides, he wasn't past Lila.

He'd made a vow never to put another person's life at risk for his job. If Sadie was harmed because of him...

He'd never survive.

Sadie still straddled his lap but she shot him a warm, satisfied smile—clearly oblivious to his thoughts—as she slipped off to sit beside him. Reaching behind them, she dragged a blanket off the back of the couch and covered them both.

"How are your stitches?"

"Fine."

She gave him a dark side-eye as she settled the blanket into place. "Back to 'fine' again?"

Unwilling to pick a fight with the taste of her still on his tongue, he added, "Really, I'm good. The stitches are fine and I actually forgot they were there." Tripp patted the bandage, pleased to find the area tender but no worse for wear.

"Good."

He leaned over and pressed a kiss to her forehead, absurdly pleased when she snuggled into his side.

That, considering the direction of his thoughts, was the last thing he should be thinking. Yet there he went, lifting his arm to cradle her shoulders, snuggling her more tightly into the crook of his body. He felt himself fading lightly, the quiet rhythm of her breathing steadying his into the same cadence. His head nearly fell forward in sleep when she spoke once again.

"I'm glad we did that. And I'm counting the minutes until we can do it again."

Tripp's eyes popped open, his body immediately on full alert at the bold declaration. "You think we're going to do that again?"

"I sure as hell hope so, because one time is most certainly not enough."

He wanted to argue. Knew, really, that he *should* argue. But he felt too damn good to do anything but agree with her. "No, one time isn't nearly enough."

"Since I'm still smarting from the 'ma'am,' I'll do you one better and tell you I told you so."

Amused at the fact that sex had unleashed "chatty Sadie," he shifted so he could look down at her. "When did you tell me so?"

"How about every day since the day you rescued me? I can't believe you haven't seen the come-here-big-boy looks I've been throwing or felt the longing glances that bore into your back every time you turned around."

Come here, big boy? Maybe "chatty" wasn't quite the right term.

"For the record, I felt no longing glances and I'm not dignifying the 'big boy' comment with an answer."

"That doesn't make it any less true."

He supposed she was right, but he still wasn't going there. That made her abrupt leap off the couch, fully naked as the blanket fell away, enough to steal his breath away. But it was when she turned, giving him a full view of her gorgeous body, that he knew he was lost.

He'd made love to Sadie Colton. And it had been better and even more amazing than he'd imagined. And he'd imagined often and in great detail.

So yes, he couldn't wait to do it again.

Even if, somewhere in the recesses of his brain, he registered that she was talking to him.

"I'm glad we're on the same page. I'll make us a snack and then we can get to doing it again."

A snack?

The same page?

What page?

She continued, oblivious to his confusion at the rapid change in direction. "After all, once we get back to Grand Rapids, we have to give all this up. So I plan on getting my fill every possible moment until we do."

Chapter Fifteen

Tripp hefted the ax and slammed it against the block of wood, Sadie's words still rattling around in his mind like loose marbles.

After all, once we get back to Grand Rapids, we have to give all this up.

Give it up?

Hell, they'd barely started and she was already talking about giving it up? Not that it had stopped him from making love to her once again after their quick snack of peanut butter on crackers. Nor had it stopped him from taking full advantage of that lush body in the shower, either.

But now, out here in the freezing cold an hour later with a few split logs beside him, Tripp brought her words back in vivid detail.

I plan on getting my fill every possible moment until we do.

Get her fill? What was he, some stud pony here to do her bidding?

Even if you've been exactly that all afternoon, McKellar, an exceedingly *un*helpful voice volleyed right back in his mind, *you were the one who told her this couldn't be real. Why are you so upset she recognizes that?*

Because, damn it.

Because she matters.

"Damn it," he muttered, sick of the circular argument.

And even more sick of arguing with himself.

"Tripp McKellar!" Sadie shouted his name as she marched toward him. She'd dragged on a pair of large fishing waders he kept in the cabin's closet and the oversize boots had her high-stepping because they were made to fit him, not her. "What in the hell are you doing out here?"

"Isn't it obvious?" He hefted the ax once more, banging it down on a fresh, unsuspecting piece of wood.

"You've got stitches in your side, you jackass. You want to rip them all out?"

"I'm fine," he muttered, well aware his use of that phrase had reached monumentally ridiculous proportions. He reached for another small log but she had already moved up beside him and kicked it out of range.

"You really are a jackass. And that's plenty of wood. Especially since there's already more than enough in the metal stand beside the fireplace. Get inside."

"You've got no right to order me around."

"And you've got even less right to test my crappy nursing skills when those stitches come loose."

It was the hitch in her voice as she said that last part that stilled him.

He was being that exact jackass she accused him of being and there was no logic for it. But for some reason, three epic sessions of sex had left him emotionally raw instead of satiated and practically comatose.

That made even less sense than the anger that continued to roil and seethe at her dismissal of anything between them once they left the cabin.

Wasn't that what he'd wanted? No strings attached. Someone who recognized and understood he wasn't meant for a relationship.

Right?

Tripp tossed the ax back into the small shed alongside the house and followed Sadie back inside. His gaze alighted on the stack of wood beside the fireplace before quickly bumping away to stare at something else— anything else—that wouldn't make a liar out of him.

Only, his gaze caught on Sadie's lush body and the rounded curve of her ass and, once again, he was trapped.

Trapped with all these *thoughts* and *feelings* he had no business possessing. Worse, that he'd sworn would never be for him.

She whirled on him, unaware of his perusal. "Do you want to tell me why you were out there putting your health at risk?"

"My health is fine."

"You know, I saw a nearly full bottle of whiskey in the pantry. I think I'm going to start a drinking game. Every time Tripp McKellar says the word *fine*, I'm going to take a shot." She moved up right in his face, hers set in dark, dangerous lines. "I should be good and drunk by noon."

"I am fine. And you sure as hell weren't worrying about my stitches in the shower."

Those gorgeous green eyes went wide about a half second before flames shot through them, lighting her up like the winning screen on a video game. "Don't flatter yourself, baby cakes."

Tripp had no idea where it came from. He'd never been one to even mention sex to a woman before and here he was taunting Sadie with what had transpired between them. And then had to stand there while she shot it all straight back at him like a little firecracker, more than able to hold her own.

That flickering anger that had gnawed at him every time she'd mentioned Tate Greer over the past week flamed to life, white-hot and pure. It had broken his heart to see how Greer had left her feeling less than.

But looking at her now, Tripp saw a new truth. The woman standing before him was empowered. Bold. And he still wanted her more than he'd ever thought possible.

Without knowing who shifted first—and in the end, maybe it never mattered anyway—they moved into each other. The light of battle winked out, floating away like a wisp of smoke as they came together. Nothing in the world but the two of them.

She welcomed him with her mouth, opening beneath him as his tongue sought hers. As his hands molded her skin, a masterpiece coming to life beneath his fingers. As their breaths met and mingled, growing heavy with need.

"I want you," she whispered, half challenge, half plea, and he felt an answering response rise up deep from within. "Now."

"Yes." He reached for her, walking backward toward the bedroom as he held her against him. His hands were already at the hem of her sweatshirt, his fingers plying the warm skin at her waist. They'd barely reached the doorway when Sadie stumbled into him. His tight hold was the only reason they remained upright and he suddenly had an armful of woman as something cold and heavy brushed against his foot.

"Whoa." Tripp steadied her, his mind still hazy from her kisses. "Are you—"

He never got the question out as laughter shook her shoulders. Even as he tried to catch up, she nearly doubled over with it, one hand reaching out for balance on the bedroom door frame.

He had a momentary flash of good, old-fashioned, red-blooded male fear that she was laughing at him.

And then he saw it.

The huge fishing waders still clung to her feet, the thick soles planted against the floor, extending her feet to nearly double their size.

"Where did you even find those?"

His question only had her laughing harder. "Hall closet."

The catch-all box in the base of the closet drifted through his mind's eye. "It's a sexy look."

Tripp bent to remove them, his hands roaming over one firm thigh as he dislodged the boot. He did the same with her other leg, lingering longer than absolutely necessary, his pinky finger flicking against the sensitive skin at the very top of her thigh. He heard her quick rush of breath, the laughter fading away as if it had never been.

And once the boots had been removed, kicked and discarded into the hall, Tripp returned his hands to her waist, his mouth lingering over hers. "Now. Where were we, baby cakes?"

He felt her lips widen into a broad smile against his own as her arms wrapped around his neck. The storm of one battle ended just as a new, more delicious one took its place.

SADIE CONTEMPLATED THE cool air against her naked backside and realized that, for as generous a lover as Tripp McKellar was, the man was a serious blanket hog. Like a conquer-and-gather-up-all-the-covers sort of guy. But since the large body that shielded her front was practically a heater, she snuggled in closer and decided in the moment that it didn't matter.

Her thoughts were as lazy as the first rays of dawn filtering through the window, flitting from subject to subject with little effort. It wasn't a time of day she usually saw and it was a novel idea to simply lie there for a bit, enjoying the moment. And being wrapped up in Tripp.

How had this happened?

Well, she knew *how* it had happened. But the bigger question was why? And an even bigger one than that—why now?

They'd gone from colleagues to friends to lovers in the span of a week. And while she was wildly happy with the outcome, she knew it couldn't last.

Hadn't that been the real root of their fight?

The pitched battle they'd waged from the wood stump outside, through the living room and on into the bedroom, may have changed tone and tenor along with location, but she was smart enough to know its cause.

This couldn't last.

Hadn't she tried to acknowledge that? To be mature and open and honest, proving to Tripp she didn't have expectations about what was happening between them beyond these few days locked away from the world?

It had been rather broad-minded of me, really, she thought with no small measure of disgust. Until he'd picked a fight with her. And that only added to her confusion because wasn't that what he'd wanted?

So how had saying it somehow pissed him off?

Much as she wanted to lean back on her inexperience and blame it for their argument, she knew his reaction had had nothing to do with how many men she'd slept with. Instead, it'd had everything to do with putting a timeline on how long she'd sleep with *him*.

He'd even used that stupid excuse about being her boss.

Suddenly restless, Sadie slipped out of bed. Tripp never moved, the thick covers still clenched in his arms as he slept. She found her clothes in a pile near the door and silently pulled them on before closing the bedroom door behind her and heading out to the living room.

The cabin wasn't large but it had a spacious feel, with high beamed ceilings that gave a sense of openness in the main gathering area. She curled up on the couch, still restless with her thoughts as her gaze darted around the room. She could watch TV but she wasn't in the mood for news or any of the old reruns to be found this early in the morning. It was only when her gaze alighted on the various computers Tripp had set up that she decided to email Kiely.

Her older sister was a badass private investigator, full

of what her twin, Pippa, had always classified as vim, vigor and a solid dash of vixen. Kiely had never been a shy, retiring sort of woman and she'd be the perfect person to talk to about Tripp's out-of-line response to Sadie's magnanimous declaration of sexual freedom without strings.

Sadie loaded up her email, doing a quick scan of what had come in overnight. Pippa had sent the sisters a silly meme about Michigan winters and Sadie replied with a smile and a snowman emoji before opening a new window to type her note to Kiely. That made it all the more surprising when her video chat kicked in two minutes later, Kiely on the other side.

Her sister's face came to light on the screen, a small boy wrapped in her arms. Similar to the big man Sadie had left sleeping in the bedroom, the little guy had his arms wrapped around a blanket, only his eyes were wide-open and blinking in that sweet, chubby little face.

Alfie.

"Hey there." Sadie gave the camera a little wave. "Hi, Alfie." She didn't quite get a smile but she saw interest light in that little face.

"I saw you were online," Kiely said. "And since we were up, I thought we'd give our aunt Sadie a call."

Something clenched in her heart at the use of the word *aunt*. It was still so new, her sister's romance with Cooper bringing Alfie into their lives. She felt the same about Abigail and Griffin's baby, Maya. In a matter of months, Sadie had gone from not even being an aunt to having two little ones in her life with Riley and Charlize's baby on the way in the new year.

"I'm glad you did."

They talked for a few minutes, Alfie growing more animated and involved in the conversation. He was already talking and, while she missed a few things, Sadie managed to get most of what he was saying. And what she'd missed, Kiely easily filled in.

"You're getting good at this," Sadie said, her heart full.

"Good at what?"

"Toddler speak. You understand everything he says."

Kiely looked down at the baby as Alfie looked up and in that quiet glance, Sadie saw the truth. Her sister had, in a matter of a few short months, become a mother. She was changed—transformed, really—and it was beautiful to see.

Kiely beamed back, kissing the baby on the crown of his head. "That's because Alfie's so smart."

The small boy settled in Kiely's arms, his eyes blinking with tiredness.

"I can let you go."

Kiely shook her head. "He's a good sleeper and once he's out, noise doesn't bother him. Talk to me. I know something's going on, especially since you're never up at this hour unless you haven't gone to bed."

"That's not true."

"It's completely true and you know it. Spill."

Sadie let out a small sniff at being nailed so easily, but it was for show only. She desperately needed to talk and was beyond grateful Kiely was there to listen. And, just as her sister had promised, Alfie's eyes had already closed, his little head nestled against her sister.

"I slept with Tripp."

Kiely's answering grin was immediate and tinged

with those solid hints of the vixen Pippa had always accused her of being. "I knew it wouldn't take long."

"Kiely!"

Part of her wanted to be shocked but really, how could she be when her sister was right.

So very right.

She and Tripp hadn't lasted that many days in confinement before giving in to the attraction between them. The three days had felt like an eternity but really wasn't.

"He's an attractive man and you're a beautiful woman. And the air practically combusts around you. How could I have been wrong?"

"The air combusts?"

"Yeah, it does. Which is yet another reason Tate Greer was never right for you."

"I thought it was because he was a killer and a criminal."

Kiely waved a hand. "That, too, of course. But if I suspend all that for the briefest moment—"

Sadie tried to stop her—how did you just *suspend* criminal activity?—but Kiely steamrolled over it. "Seriously. If you hold that part of it for just a minute, you'll understand what I'm saying. None of us knew who or what he was and, really, how could we? But we all knew there wasn't a spark between you. That was what we all kept pushing up against when we tried to talk to you about him. We wanted to know if you were happy."

"I still say him being a criminal makes sparks a moot point."

Kiely eyed her through the video chat camera before cutting to the chase once more. "If you're having what

I presume is amazing sex with Lieutenant Hottie, what are you doing emailing me so early in the morning?"

"We had a fight last night."

"Did you get makeup sex?" When Sadie said nothing, Kiely only smiled again. "I'll take that as a yes."

"I'm still mad at him."

"Why?"

"Because I gave him a no-strings out to this whole thing. The world is upside down and this place is like a cocoon. But the real world is still outside. Tate's still not caught and neither is Wes Matthews. I'm a big girl and I know the score."

"And you told him all that?"

"I was much more eloquent."

"No wonder you pissed him off."

The solidarity and support she was so convinced she'd find from her sister was nowhere in evidence. Instead, Sadie's mouth dropped and she nearly shouted into the screen before she remembered the sleeping baby as well as the sleeping man in the next room.

"What is that supposed to mean?" she hissed instead.

"It means he wants to think he has no strings. But he sure as hell doesn't want you to actually tell him that."

"Why not?"

"Because it's not what he really wants."

Sadie flopped back on the couch, utterly confused and rapidly losing the thread of the conversation. "This is stupid. And not the regular sort of stupid but the multiple-O *stoooopid*." She elongated the middle of the word, pleased when her sister finally seemed to agree.

"Totally. But that's men for you." Kiely kissed the top of Alfie's head again before looking down at him.

"I have no idea how they start out this way but end up that way. But somehow they do."

"Tripp is a grown man. He knows what he wants and I'm trying to respect that. He had that awful thing that happened to him with his fiancée dying…" Sadie searched her sister's face. "I have to be okay with it if he doesn't want a relationship."

"For him?"

Sadie shook her head, the truth crystal clear. "For me. Or it'll decimate me."

Kiely's gaze softened, her tone quiet. "Only you can decide that. But I will tell you one thing. Don't let him off the hook too easily."

Sadie heard the stirring from the other room and stared at the closed door before turning her eyes back to her sister. "What's that supposed to mean?"

"It means your feelings matter, too. What you want matters, too. You need to believe that, Sadie."

The clear sound of another human moving around came from the bedroom. "I've got to go."

"Think about what I said?" Kiely added.

"I will."

Then the screen went dark and Sadie shut down her email just as Tripp came into the living room.

"Morning."

"Good morning."

"Everything okay?" His eyes were alert, even through the lingering vestiges of sleep.

"Yeah. Fine. My sister Kiely called me. The baby was up, so it gave them something to do."

Tripp nodded. "I thought I heard voices."

Before she could respond with some sort of excuse,

he headed for the kitchen, seemingly unconcerned she was already up or that she'd talked to her sister. She heard him open the fridge and the light scrape of a tin can against the countertop when he set it down to prep the coffee maker. Then she caught the sounds of water being added and coffee grounds hitting the filter.

How was it all so normal?

She got off the couch, not sure what she wanted to say yet deeply aware of the need to say it. And as she came upon him in the kitchen—his shoulders broad beneath a navy GRPD T-shirt, gray sweatpants riding low on his hips and his hair mussed from sleep—her sister's parting words rang loud and clear.

Your feelings matter, too. What you want matters, too.

"I'd like to know about before."

Tripp's gaze lifted off the coffee maker, the sleep fading a bit more. "Before what?"

"I'd like to know about your fiancée."

TRIPP WANTED TO be angry. Somewhere down low and deep, he wanted to find some ire to blunt the pain and surprise of Sadie's words.

Only nothing came.

Not fury or frustration, or even the smallest rub of irritation.

Funny, how he'd felt all of those emotions yesterday during their argument and now he couldn't find a bit of them. Couldn't conjure them up, no matter how hard he tried.

"You know about Lila?"

"Yes, Tripp. I'm sorry, but I've lived in Grand Rapids my whole life. Even if I hadn't joined the force, I'd have heard the story."

"But you did join the force."

"Everyone there knows what happened to you. To her." Sadie's voice was gentle, but there was something insistent there, too.

Or maybe it was something insistent inside him.

A driving need to get it all out. Maybe, by finally speaking the words, he'd remove the ashy taste from his tongue and the bitter remorse that always steamrolled him when he thought about Lila and the baby.

Maybe.

"I had a girlfriend named Lila. We'd been dating about six months when we found out she was pregnant."

Sadie's eyes went wide at the news of the baby but she remained silent. It was the proof he needed, though, that he had managed to keep that part of the story as his own. The entire GRPD might have known what happened to him but no one had known about the baby.

That seemed monumental, somehow. Like there actually was still *something* completely private about his grief.

"I'd already made detective a few years by then and had several cases under my belt. I made enemies. And one decided to enact his vengeance when he got out of jail on a technicality."

"Tripp." She laid a hand on his arm but he slipped away, moving to the cabinet to pull down a few mugs. Her touch felt good—too good—and there was no way he'd get through this if he let her touch him. So he made himself busy with the mugs and taking spoons from a drawer and even moving to the fridge to get milk.

All while telling her about the day that changed his life.

"We got engaged after we found out about the baby. Lila had a checkup that day and I was going straight to the doctor to meet her."

He paused, images of the day still so fresh in his mind. The hints of spring in the breeze. The sun that beat down, warming the still cool air. And the dark, nondescript car that rattled without its muffler, moving through the medical center's parking lot like a shark preying the waves.

He'd seen it, of course. Heard it first, really. But he'd had no idea what evil lay inside. Or the desperate heart that beat for revenge.

Tripp told Sadie those things as he leaned back against the counter sipping his coffee.

"We were at a medical center and I kept hoping that would be enough to save her. I rationalized it to myself. That by having doctors close by, she'd have to be okay." He stopped then, the images that were never too far away seeming to fill all the open kitchen space, pushing out the air so that his breath came hard and fast. "But I was wrong."

"I'm sorry."

"Of course you are. Everyone's sorry." Tripp finally glanced up, surfacing from the depths of his memories. "Everyone always is. But no one is sorrier than me."

With that, he set down his mug and walked out of the kitchen. He didn't really care if she had any questions or if there were any other details she needed to know. None of it really mattered anyway.

TATE EXTENDED A HAND, issuing a series of commands to Snake as he took a deep breath of the bracing cold air. They hadn't had any more snow, but it had remained frigid. The freezing temperatures seemed to hone the dog's reactions, his movements swift and immediate.

Which was exactly the response Tate needed right now.

Sadie and her police officer had vanished again. He'd called in every favor he'd had and no one had seen them or known where they'd gone. The two of them had basically disappeared four days ago and Tate had no idea where.

After three fruitless days spent trying to hunt them down, he'd had a vision overnight. An inspiration, really.

Snake returned when called, his back ramrod straight as he stared up at his master.

Tate flicked his gaze down to the dog, curious how a creature not nearly as smart as a human could be both tool and companion. He'd thought it before, until he'd had an epiphany while training Snake so many years before.

Discipline was nothing more than training with purpose.

All he needed to do was to use what the dog wanted as the reward to keep him in line. Praise. Food. Shelter. Pack. Whatever it was, identify that carrot and then dangle it at the end of a very long stick.

Each and every time, the dog responded in kind. It was time to do the same with Sadie.

She could hide, but all he really needed was the

proper point of leverage. A lone carrot to immediately pull her out of hiding.

He issued another command to Snake. And as he watched the dog bound over the cold ground as instructed, Tate considered the perfect place to snatch Sergeant Victoria Colton.

Chapter Sixteen

Tripp avoided the wood-chopping routine again, even as he knew there was nowhere inside the cabin that would put him far enough from Sadie.

But he tried.

After he left her unceremoniously in the kitchen, he'd walked off to the bedroom, taking a shower and adding plenty of time to shave, too. Even with meticulous swipes of his razor, he was still done too quickly, so he'd finally opted to sit quietly on the couch and focus on his computer.

Sadie had obviously sensed his reticence to talk further, keeping to herself and focusing on the other department laptop he had with him.

Somehow they made it through most of the morning before she finally spoke. "We should probably start thinking about how to get out of here."

Tripp glanced up from the report he was reading. "Greer's still out there."

"Yeah. And we're stuck in here. I read Riley's report this morning and Ashanti's getting closer on the work with Matthews."

"So we stay put until it's done. Until we know you're safe."

She ignored his point and kept on pressing hers. "I still keep going back to the bigger idea that the only way we end this is to pit Tate and Wes Matthews against each other."

"Tate's trying to kill you."

"So we make sure he doesn't succeed."

He'd spent enough time with Sadie now to know that she wasn't nearly as flippant as the comment suggested. But still, he couldn't understand how she could be so blasé. Tate Greer was a threat. Tripp had several GRPD team members hunting for the man even now, trying to find him in any possible location anyone had ever placed him. All to no avail.

He'd ghosted them once again.

And Tripp didn't want Sadie anywhere near him when the man decided to reappear.

"It's not like we set you up as bait in the hospital or at my house. You were hidden away and that didn't stop him."

"I need to go back to living my life. Between a month in the safe house and now another week of running, I need something different."

Or she needed away from him.

Underneath, Tripp wondered if that was the real truth here and it drew a harsh stab of pain low in his gut.

He'd believed himself unable—and, more to the point, unwilling—to care for anyone again. But somehow, some way, Sadie had gotten to him. Having sex with her had made it all more real, more tangible, somehow.

But it was being with her. Spending time with her

and seeing her at her most personal and intimate that had allowed him to really see her.

Yes, he'd been fascinated before. And he'd even been smitten. But now?

The word *love* played through his mind, consuming him with all the impact of an avalanche.

He couldn't be in love with Sadie. Not now, not ever.

"You can go back to living your life after Greer's caught."

"That's not your decision to make."

Although the declaration was pointed, there wasn't a trace of anger in her tone. Yet it was as effective as waving red before a bull. "Don't brush me off or dismiss me like I don't matter, Sadie. It's my job to keep you safe and I'm going to do it."

"It's my job to keep myself safe. I got myself into this and, while I appreciate all you've done, it's time to go home."

"And what if something happens to you?"

"Then I'll face the consequences." She set the computer down on the coffee table and turned to him, eyes pleading. "I've spent the past five weeks hiding from my life. I haven't worked. Haven't seen my family for much of that. I haven't even been inside my own home."

You were with me, that small, traitorous inner voice taunted, before going in for the kill. *Where you should be, always.*

Only, to hear her now, that time away hadn't been enough. What was between them wasn't enough to make her stay. That was rich, coming from a man who refused to admit he cared for her. Maybe even loved her.

But, like always, he fell back on what he knew. What

was tangible to him. "You said something to me the other day. About safety being an illusion. Do you believe that?"

"Yes."

"Then you make my life's work and the work of everyone else at the GRPD a lie."

"That's wildly unfair."

"Why? Isn't that what you're saying? If there's no such thing as safety and security, why does any of the work we do matter?"

Although she'd remained calm and measured up to now, Tripp saw her fight for composure. "My parents were murdered. Your fiancée and child were murdered. I almost married a man who wants to kill me. What safety is there in a world where any of those things can happen?"

Once again, a brick wall of disagreement seemed to have sprung up between them. "So you acknowledge it. Work with it. You don't go putting yourself in the crosshairs of a killer."

"No, Tripp. Instead, you deny any and all happiness in life. You deny yourself love and someone who cares for you because something may happen. You're accusing me of wanting to get back to my life but you refuse to live one."

Tripp's phone went off, the heavy ring interrupting the still rippling waves of her accusation. He saw Emmanuel's name on the caller ID screen at the same time a text came in from Cooper Winston.

"McKellar," he answered.

"Is Sadie with you?" Iglesias's question was out without preamble.

"Yeah. She has been for several days."

"Is Vikki with you?"

Ice pitted in the center of his stomach as Tripp shot a glance at Sadie. "No. Why?"

"She hasn't been seen since this morning."

Tripp glanced at the sun filtering through the window. "It's barely noon."

"Flynn is going out of his mind. They were supposed to meet for an early lunch and when she didn't show, he got worried. She hasn't been to work all morning."

"What's going on?" Sadie moved beside him, her gaze intent.

"Put me on speaker," Iglesias ordered.

Tripp did as asked, setting his phone on the table. He reached for Sadie's hand, not caring about the argument or their philosophical differences on life and love. She was going to need every bit of support he could give her.

"Tell her," Tripp ordered, willing everything he felt—and all he couldn't say—into their joined hands.

"Vikki's gone."

SADIE HEARD THE disembodied voice of her future brother-in-law float off the coffee table and tried to process what Emmanuel was saying.

Vikki was gone? She'd never made it to work or a lunch date with Flynn. Nor was she answering her phone.

She wanted to ask questions—knew she should be asking questions—yet nothing came to mind.

Her sister was gone.

They were twins, damn it! Shouldn't she have felt something? Shouldn't she have known?

But she'd been here, hidden away. It was just like she'd told Tripp, only now, somehow, it seemed worse. She hadn't just run from her life, she'd put her sister in the crosshairs of a killer.

Because while she had no questions, she had plenty of self-recrimination.

"It's Tate Greer."

"That's what we think," Emmanuel affirmed.

"I know it is. He couldn't find me, so he's gone after the one person he knew could draw me out."

While the same would be true of any of her siblings, Sadie had no doubt it was deliberate and purposeful to take her twin.

"Are there any leads on where she is? Any traffic or street cams?" Tripp took over the conversation.

"The team's been scouring anything they can find," Emmanuel said. "But nothing's hit yet."

"We'll be there in an hour," Sadie interjected into the conversation. When Tripp did nothing more than look at her and nod, she pressed on. "There are going to be a limited number of places Tate can take her. Have Gunther Johnson brought up to Interview."

They ended the call, even as the face of Tripp's phone continued to light up with messages. Cooper texted again, followed by her brother. She made a quick call to Riley, assuring him they were headed back to the city. When he'd tried to argue with her to stay put, she'd hung up on him.

And in under a half hour they'd packed up and were on their way to Grand Rapids.

The sun was bright in the sky as they drove toward the city. It was mid-December and it dawned on her as

Tripp turned onto the interstate that it was coming on Christmas and she hadn't even thought about it. She'd spent so long locked in the safe house, whisked away from her life and her family, that when it had become too overwhelming to think about the holidays—and missing everyone—she'd shut it all out.

Only now, it all came flooding back.

"You've been quiet. How are you doing?" Tripp asked.

"Thinking about Christmas."

"It's so soon. Hard to believe it's here again."

"I made a deliberate effort to put it out of my mind in the safe house. And with all that's been going on, I continued to forget. But that doesn't mean it's not almost here." On a hard sigh, she remembered something else. "Oh, Tripp. Your poor house. What are you going to do?"

"Get a new one. It wasn't like I spent that much time in the old one."

She heard the flat assessment and recognized that he wasn't making up the casual response. Losing his house—his home—didn't seem to have that big an effect on him. "You don't sound that upset."

"It's a house."

She had no idea why she kept pressing the subject, but suddenly it seemed important. Huge, actually. "But you won't be in it for the holidays."

"I usually work through the holidays, so I don't bother with a tree or decorations."

Sadie thought about the small tree she put up each year in her apartment. She'd dubbed him Herman because he had a square, boxy shape that reminded her of

Herman Munster. It was silly and stupid, but she smiled each year when she pulled Herman out of the storage closet and set him up in her front window. And each January, when she carefully nestled him back in his box, she knew that she'd see him again.

Tripp had none of that. Whether by choice or now by habit, it didn't make things any less bleak. Or true.

But as she stared down the possibility that her sister would be hurt, or worse, Sadie understood it. She'd been so angry at Tripp's refusal to see all that could be, between them and, more broadly, in life. And then she'd been sad when he'd simply walked out of the kitchen this morning after sharing the details of Lila's death.

But now? Now she understood.

If something happened to her twin, Sadie had no idea what she'd do. It had been hard enough to lose her parents, but she and her siblings had found a way forward.

Yet Vikki's life being in danger was entirely different somehow.

The inability to believe in a world that contained light and love, and only risk if you tried for those things, suddenly made sense.

And with it, Tripp's determination to avoid it all.

TRIPP STOOD OUTSIDE the interview room, Sadie at his side. She'd been quiet since their odd diversion of a conversation in the car about the holidays and he wasn't sure what to make of it.

Sadie was strong enough for this, of that he had no doubt. Steely determination poured from her and he had no qualms about putting her in front of Johnson again.

It was the fact that she had to that still chewed him up.

How had it come to this?

And how had they never even considered the possibility that by leaving town, Tate would turn his sights on a new target.

The ever-petulant Gunther Johnson was brought into Interview and Tripp and Sadie entered shortly after him. One of the guards who'd escorted Johnson to the room fitted the handcuffs to the table locks and, in moments, the young man was seated, his careless sneer firmly in place.

"Look who's back."

Since Gunther had showed little but sullen attitude for the past few months, it was something of a surprise to see him initiate the conversation.

"We've got more questions for you."

"Why else would I be here?" Gunther said before turning his attention to Sadie. "That bruise has nearly faded away."

She touched her jaw. "How sweet of you to show you care."

Something dark and unexpected flashed across his face. "I don't go around beating women."

"Never said you did. But your boss certainly has no problem with it. Which is why we're here."

Although Tripp and Sadie hadn't overly prepped for the meeting, they had talked broad strategy. The idea was to put Johnson on the defensive and then pepper in how Greer and Matthews were going to take the score and run for the hills.

All part of Sadie's continued push to pit one of them

against the other. So it was strange to see her employ such a risky tactic as empathy.

"You still haven't caught him yet?"

"You know we haven't, Gunther." Sadie leaned in. "Because if we had, your life in here would've gotten a lot harder. Isn't that right?"

"Tate and I are square."

"Until he pegs you for the one who gave him up to the GRPD." She traced a small pattern on the table. "I can see to it that he finds out that little detail."

"You don't know jack, lady."

"I know plenty. And since I'm about to become the bait to get my sister back from the bastard, I'd say I know a hell of a lot more than you."

"What about your sister?"

"When he couldn't get to me, he took my twin sister. For revenge. To draw me out. His set of twisted reasoning really doesn't matter, does it? Because I'm here. And I need your help."

"Why should I help you?"

"Because I'm asking. Because an innocent woman's life is at stake. But if those aren't reason enough, I'll give you one more."

Gunther didn't respond though his interest was unmistakable.

"Wes and Tate don't deserve to get off scot-free in this whole thing, while you're stuck in here. I'm just a worker bee in CSI, but I've been around this place for a long time and I know how it works. The lawyers are going to go to town on what you know, who you know, and what you were part of. Especially if Tate and Wes get away and they don't have them to play with."

"That's B.S."

"No, it's not. It's truth. My father was a lawyer and my older sister followed in his footsteps. I know how hard she works to make sure guilty people pay." Sadie eyed him, never breaking her intensity. "And no one's going to cut you a break if they know you had an opportunity to help and didn't take it."

Just as in her first meeting with Gunther, Tripp was impressed with how smoothly Sadie handled the interview. And in her approach, he saw something else. For all her efforts to get answers and get through to Gunther, she never dismissed him. He'd observed a lot of interviewers through the years and knew it was unfortunately all too easy to forget the person sitting opposite you actually *was* a person. Instead, it was easier to create distance with labels like "perp" and "criminal" as a way to deal with sad wastes of life.

Only, Sadie didn't do that.

And it was fascinating to see how Gunther responded to her willingness to see his humanity.

"You're not playing me?"

"No, I'm not. I want my sister back and I need your help."

Tripp chose that moment to step in. He'd observed the young man for nearly three months now, unable to understand how Gunther would trade his life for such a dead-end choice as working for Capital X. What he hadn't done in all that time was see Gunther as anything other than a criminal.

It was time to change his approach.

"Gunther, this is your chance to step up."

"What's in it for me?" Gunther's ice-blue eyes assessed him, but for the first time they appeared to actually be considering the conversation instead of actively projecting contempt.

Tripp refused to drop into his historic default and assume the guy would make a poor choice. "You've got a chance to do the right thing."

Gunther stared down at the table and gave no indication one way or the other. Tripp shot a side-glance to Sadie and felt his heart stick in his throat at the desperate hope that lined her face.

She was depending on whatever possible shred of decency might still be in Gunther Johnson's heart. When they'd walked into the room, Tripp would have said that was impossible.

Now, after the guy had been exposed to a few rounds with Sadie Colton... Tripp wasn't so sure.

He reached out under the table, extending his fingers so they just brushed against hers. It was silent support, but as he touched her skin, Tripp recognized the comfort he was taking in return.

"Guy has a few old warehouses just outside of town."

"Where?" Tripp prompted before tossing out a few main thoroughfares that ran out of town toward the suburbs.

Gunther nodded on the last one. "You know it then. He's had 'em for years. Bought them on the cheap when they got all sad and abandoned. He..." Gunther hesitated before huffing out a low sigh. "He uses them when he needs to rough people up."

Tripp considered Gunther's description and the truth beneath it all. Greer, and by extension, Capital X, had been close all along.

Tripp glanced at Sadie but she was already rising, gratitude rolling off her in waves. "Thank you, Gunther. I won't forget this, and I will make sure my family doesn't forget it, too."

Tripp stood as the kid nodded, his eyes still that cool, calculating blue. Tripp didn't miss the way they followed Sadie as she rushed from the interview room. "I know I'm no prize, but women don't deserve that crap."

"What you did today, Gunther? It matters."

Although Tripp knew the young man's deeds wouldn't be erased by one act of decency, he also had hope that this could be the beginning of something new. Assuming the kid had played straight with them, Tripp would do what he could to ensure Gunther was treated fairly.

But for now he had to follow Sadie.

And this ridiculous idea she had to set herself up as bait.

"I'M NOT ARGUING with you." Sadie stared Tripp down before turning to her brother. The high, wide windows of the refurbished warehouse about a mile from Tate's hideout eclipsed Riley, the purple light of a winter afternoon filling the space behind him. "Either of you."

"You can't trade yourself for Vikki." Tripp had tried the argument several times and now Riley had started in. Despite his concern, Sadie steamrolled the argument.

"I'm the only one who can. Tate wants me. And he's using Vikki to get to me. His behavior keeps escalating and we know he's desperate. This will end it."

"What if we can't get to you?" Tripp asked.

It broke her heart a little to hear the hitch in his voice. But still, she remained strong.

"What do you think all these people are going to do?" Sadie pointed to the assembled police teams prepping and planning around them. The GRPD had commandeered the refurbished warehouse space, the home of a design firm that would be out all afternoon for its annual holiday party.

It had been sheer, blind luck that one of Tripp's detectives had known the owner of the warehouse and had asked to use the space, only to find out during the call the extra stroke of good luck that the place would be empty.

Sadie kept telling herself that stroke of good fortune was the proof that it would all work out.

That Vikki was okay.

And that she'd be okay, too.

"You don't have to do this, squirt." Riley pulled her close, wrapping her tightly in his arms. "You really don't."

"Yeah, I do."

Riley only hugged her harder before moving off to ask more questions of the two SWAT leads managing the op.

Once he was gone, Sadie was left alone with Tripp. Or mostly alone, if she ignored the fifty or so people milling around them, all preparing for the meet with Tate.

"Your brother's right." Tripp stepped closer but didn't touch her. "SWAT's here. We can get eyes in there and get Vikki out."

"This is quicker. And it's the easiest way to get what we want."

"And if Greer suspects you've got backup?"

"Tate's known for a while I've got backup. Part of me thinks that's what all this is about. He knows as well as I do that this needs to end, and he wants to show off how strong he is."

"That is why the professionals need to handle it."

"The professionals *are* handling it." Sadie strode closer and ran the tips of her fingers over his knuckles. The touch was light—as light as his had been in the interview room when they'd spoken with Gunther—and that made it all the more powerful.

"I can do this. And more to the point, I need to do this. I'm a trained cop and I know how to handle myself on an op. And my sister is inside that warehouse."

Sadie took some comfort from the fact that surveillance had confirmed Vikki was in the building and alive. But Sadie had grown impatient with waiting, ready to move in and get this done.

She'd let Tate into her life. And while she was coming to accept that she didn't need to emotionally flog herself over that fact for the rest of her life, she did need to act.

To save Vikki.

And, maybe, to save herself.

Chapter Seventeen

Tripp ignored the unrelenting fear that gnawed at him with the sharpest of teeth and focused on the team. Everyone had fanned out into their prearranged spots, with SWAT taking point on another warehouse rooftop a building's width away. A sniper, two GRPD detectives and a K-9 trainer capable of handling Greer's dog were also positioned behind the warehouse, determined to catch Tate or his henchman should one of them run out the back.

The intel on the building was solid. Heat sensors had mapped out three people inside as well as the dog. What was presumably Tate and Vikki, based on how one body never moved while the other wove in and around it, were in the center of the building, the dog pacing in time. A third heat signature was positioned near the back entrance.

SWAT had tried to get eyes on that last individual to assess what they'd be up against, but the figure remained stubbornly in place, not moving or making rounds.

It was that third figure that scared Tripp. They were

ready for Tate and had a properly trained handler focused on the dog. But the third person was a wild card.

"She's moving in." The comm device in his ear signaled that Sadie was on the move.

Tripp watched from his position, hidden at the edge of the same building SWAT had commandeered.

And prayed this wasn't the last time he'd see her alive.

SADIE HAD CONSIDERED how she was going to play this meeting with Tate ever since she'd discovered Vikki had been taken. She'd downplayed the risk to Tripp and her brother and the rest of her family, but never once had she downplayed it to herself.

Tate Greer was dangerous. And there was no way he was going down without a fight.

He'd lost all he could lose and that made him even more deadly than he'd been before. As the head of Capital X, the risk in his life was matched only by all the pieces he controlled. His staff. The people he roughed up when they didn't pay. And all those under the thumb of his criminal enterprise.

But the RevitaYou scam had seen it all vanish, cracking his organization wide-open.

Now he had nothing left to protect. Except his pride.

It was for that reason Sadie had finally settled on her approach. Since she'd spent the past six weeks with her own pride in shambles, it turned out that *that* was the hill she was willing to die on.

The warehouse had a large, covered entrance and she stood there, laying hard on the doorbell that buzzed for after-hours visitors. The GRPD and the Feds had not been able to contact Tate, every call in to him going to voice mail. But he had allowed Vikki a tearful call out to Flynn. Sadie's future brother-in-law had nearly chewed through the phone. It was only through sheer dint of will and his extensive military training that he'd finally been talked into waiting in the SWAT van. If given the chance, he'd have fought Sadie to meet Tate himself, but it was SWAT who'd finally helped her win the argument.

The team leader's report on the interior layout, perimeter access and available sight lines, not to mention the minimal but still existent traffic in the warehouse district, meant they wanted as few extraneous people involved as possible. Anyone other than Sadie risked riling Tate up instead of getting Vikki out.

Sadie lifted her finger then laid it on the buzzer again. The distant sound of a dog barking registered and she nearly stopped the buzzing, having no interest in meeting Snake face-to-face again.

But then she thought better of it.

This was as much a mental game as a physical battle and she needed all the advantage she could get.

The door cracked open, a large gun pointing directly at her face spearing through it. The sound of the dog's whining filled the air, but at least the barking had stopped.

"About damn time you got here." Tate's hand snaked out and covered her wrist, dragging her inside. She'd barely cleared the door when he re-aimed the gun at her. "Take the coat off. Empty your pockets and purse."

"I don't have a gun." She kept her tone flat and even, unwilling to rise to his bait no matter the subject.

"Yeah, right."

She held up her hands before moving them slowly to her coat to strip it off, letting it drop to the floor. She did the same with her bag, dumping it over first so the contents fell out—her wallet, a brush and a pack of gum.

The items had been deliberate choices, all designed to keep Tate thinking she'd subserviently come to save her sister. What he had no way of knowing was that the gum was a sweet little listening device Ashanti had cooked up about a year ago, or that a Taser had been neatly embedded in the material of the purse. A small switch in the handle would turn the purse into a lethal game changer the moment Sadie confirmed Vikki was okay and was within proper range of Tate.

She considered how easy it had been to enter as she bent to stuff the items back into the purse. It felt like the tide turning in their favor, but was it too easy?

The last briefing from SWAT ran through her mind. The only real identified unknown was the third person in the warehouse. No one had put eyes on the guy and a quick run of Tate's known associates hadn't turned up anyone not already captured. That didn't necessarily mean anything. Tate had eluded arrest for so long, there was no telling how many tentacles he had stuck in any number of places around Grand Rapids.

So she'd keep watch and stay aware. *He* didn't know she knew there was another goon in the place and she needed to keep it that way.

She stood and Tate moved behind her, pushing her forward with the tip of the gun against her back. She stepped forward quickly, arching away from the gun as her gaze discreetly roamed the warehouse.

Where was Tate's henchman?

And then she saw Vikki and all thoughts of anyone else vanished. Her psycho ex, the gun and the dog were all forgotten as Sadie raced to where Vikki sat, strapped to a wooden chair, her green eyes wide pools of fear in her face.

"Vikki!" Sadie wrapped her arms around her twin, pulling her close and whispering as fast as she could, "It's going to be okay."

Vikki's hands and feet were bound but Tate hadn't gagged her and Sadie felt the press of lips against her cheek and a hard shudder when Vikki exhaled. "You're okay."

"You are, too." Sadie stepped back, concerned by her sister's pale face and fear-filled eyes. Vikki was terrified, which only served to give Sadie's anger a laser-sharp focus.

"He wouldn't tell me anything and I thought he had you."

"Shh, now." Sadie tried to pull Vikki close but Tate had already come between them, pushing Sadie out of the way.

"Aww, isn't this sweet?"

"I'm here now, so you can let her go." Sadie clutched the strap of her electrified bag and refused to cower. She wanted Vikki out of there and then she could distract Tate or subdue him until SWAT found an opening.

Tate pointed the gun at Sadie again, waving it in her face before using it as a pointer against her chest. "You aren't the one giving orders."

"I'm the one you wanted here. Let Vikki go."

Tate's lips curled, an evil mockery of a smile.

God, how had she ever thought herself in love with this man? The very idea of touching him made her skin crawl.

For the past six weeks, thoughts like that had dragged her down, making her feel less than. But in that moment, staring Tate down, Sadie felt the sands shift.

She knew what love was. Real, true love. For Tripp.

Funny how simple it all was now that she had the single-minded clarity to see it.

Tate had betrayed her. If it were simply a case of a romance gone bad, she'd have had to live with that. But it wasn't. He'd proved beyond any doubt that there was nothing good inside him. She could continue to wallow in that, or she could revel in the fact that she'd found this man's antithesis.

Thanks to Tripp McKellar, her faith in other people had been restored. He was good and decent and honest. And while she might think his theories on not forming attachments were stupid, in the end, it didn't matter.

Because she loved him.

And in the loving, she'd found herself again.

TRIPP SWORE AS he stared at the front of the warehouse, the quiet drone of comms humming in his ear. They'd cleared all unnecessary chatter off the line, leaving it mainly to SWAT and the department's hostage negotiator. And despite the fact Sadie had been in there for over ten minutes, no one could see her or even think about getting a shot off.

But they could hear her.

The GRPD's tech wizard had connected the interior comm units to the small listening device Ashanti had created and planted in Sadie's bag, all while keeping the department's comms open and working so everyone had the same intel.

Right now, it was all they had.

Tate hadn't given them anything to work with when he'd opened the warehouse door. He'd handled it by the book, minimizing any exposure to himself as he kept Sadie firmly in front of him, effectively blocking himself.

No matter how well trained the sniper, some shots were still impossible.

The deep-seated desire to run in there was maddening and Tripp wondered how he'd let her do this. As lieutenant, he had a fair amount of say in the ops the GRPD ran and how they were executed. Yet he'd let her go barreling into this situation like John Wayne at her own personal *High Noon*.

Only…

Only it wasn't about *letting* her do anything. She was a grown woman with a strong mind and a high degree of capability. They hadn't sent a civilian in to manage this.

They'd sent a cop.

He'd do well to remember that.

And he'd damn near convinced himself she'd be okay when the voice of one of the SWAT leads came through his earpiece. "Third heat signature is moving. Out of the back of the warehouse and into the main. Moving slow but heading toward the cluster of people in the middle."

The wild card they didn't know what to do with.

Tripp's hands curled into fists and he stared at the warehouse door, willing the events inside to go Sadie's way.

He knew he should wait.

Knew that Sadie and Vikki's lives depended on it.

But he was a cop, too. They might have sent a cop, but there was no way he could let her do this alone.

Before anyone could stop him, Tripp raced toward the warehouse.

SADIE KNEW SHE couldn't use the Taser bag too quickly, but everything inside her screamed to get it done. *Get Tate and the dog. Deal with the third man. Get Vikki out.* Backup was so close, the moment she gave the shout, her little pack of gum would alert SWAT to move in.

But Tate's gaze was unrelenting, the gun never moving from where it targeted her chest.

For a split second, all the hope she'd carried inside and on into saving Vikki died. What was she doing there? She had no gun. No body armor. And she was staring down a madman.

Had she really thought she could do this?

Tate had outsmarted her at every step. From their first date on through to the house fire the other day. Did she honestly think she could win now?

"Why'd you do it?" She had no idea where the question came from, but once it was out, there was no holding it back. "Why me?"

That dark grin never faded, but Tate did cock his head, assessing her. "I thought you'd be an easy mark."

Thought?

"You thought wrong."

"Yeah, I did. You never gave me the intel I needed. You protected your family and the damn police department like their secrets were gold. And—" that grin grew darker even as the gun seemed to grow steadier "—I never wanted to be married anyway. I guess I'm really a lifetime bachelor, after all."

"Let my sister go. This is about you and me."

"I don't think I will."

"Then prepare for the full force of the US military to hunt your ass when you take one of their own. And you can put her sergeant fiancé at the front of that line."

Despite the truth of Sadie's words, Tate only laughed. "Keep dreaming, sweetheart."

"So this is the end?" Sadie's hand clenched tighter on her purse and she calculated how she could rush Tate with it and still prevent him from taking a shot.

And realized she couldn't.

Because she hadn't fully calculated the risk to Vikki. And, for all her planning, a man with a gun still trumped a woman with a Taser.

"It sure is, sweetheart. Good thing I still have the credit from our canceled honeymoon in Aruba. I think I may take that trip once this is all over."

Tate's hand never wavered and Sadie eyed her sister, desperate to communicate all her love. She wasn't going down without a fight, and there was no way she was leaving Vikki to Tate's sick and twisted goals. Because once she was gone, she had no doubt he'd turn the gun on Vikki before SWAT could get inside.

"You'll take that honeymoon over my dead body."

Tate nodded. "That's the whole idea."

Sadie moved then, flipping the small switch on the purse just as Ashanti had taught her. The bag hummed in her palm and she swung wide as she moved, determined to hit Tate with the broadside of the fabric.

As she moved, a gunshot rang out and, despite the near deafening sound, her forward momentum never slowed with the bullet's impact. Instead, she connected with the large figure that raced toward them, even as her body continued onward. Tate seemed to disintegrate in front of her, his large frame crumpling to the floor as her own body tangled with Tripp.

Tripp who took the brunt of Tate's bullet, his heavy body slamming against hers from the force.

The dog moved, too, but Ashanti's invention was Sadie's saving grace. She swung the bag wide, hitting the full left side of the animal. An immediate whine went up as Snake stiffened before falling to the ground in convulsions.

Sadie dropped the bag, twisting to hold on to Tripp's shoulders, all while trying to assess where the shot that hit Tripp had come from.

And saw Brody twenty feet away, a gun in his outstretched hands.

"Brody!" She shouted to him as the SWAT team rushed the warehouse.

But it was Vikki's warning that filled the room, intent on stemming the tide of firepower moving in.

"Don't shoot! That's our brother!"

Tripp registered the shouts of the sisters and put every bit of force and command he could into his voice from his position on the floor. His chest streamed with fire from where Greer's bullet had hit his vest, but he struggled to his feet. "Stand down! Do not shoot!"

He kept repeating himself, his voice echoing through the warehouse and on back into his ear via their comms.

As the adrenaline-fueled shouts of SWAT calmed, Tripp's gaze swung frantically. And found Sadie huddled over her sister as one of the snipers worked on removing the ties holding Vikki in place.

Brody Higgins stood beside them both, his hands in the air and his eyes wide in his face as they kept shifting to Tate Greer's lifeless form on the floor.

Flynn flew past Tripp into the warehouse, going straight to Vikki. The hostage negotiator working with SWAT was on his heels, moving to Brody. Tripp could do nothing but stand there, taking it all in even as the edges blurred so there was nothing to see but Sadie.

She'd done it.

She'd brought down Tate Greer and whatever was left of Capital X, and saved her sister. She'd known it was the right move and he'd doubted her.

Just like he'd doubted all along. Himself. His feelings. And all that was between them.

Sadie walked to him, moving in close but not touching. "It's finally over."

"All thanks to you."

"And to you." She tapped the vest. "I know a bullet to the vest isn't lethal, but it hurts like hell."

He laid a hand over hers. "I'm good."

"Tripp. It's over." She dropped her hand and turned to survey the room that, in a matter of minutes, had transformed with several teams from the GRPD as well as the FBI. And, mixed in with them all, was a bunch of Coltons. "Brody killed Tate."

"He did. And you were amazing." Tripp could only

stare at her, all the things he wanted to say stuck somewhere in the middle of his chest. He loved her.

And he wanted to be with her.

But hadn't this showdown proved him right?

The world was dark and dangerous, and if he'd lost her, he would have been lost himself.

"I want to thank you, Tripp. For everything. You're the reason I got out of Tate's clutches at the lake. And you made sure I was safe after the hospital and the fire. Thank you." She moved in closer, rising on tiptoes to press a kiss to his lips.

It was more chaste than any they'd shared so far, but it packed a far greater punch.

Because in this kiss, he'd felt her goodbye.

SADIE WAS BREAKING apart inside as she stepped back, but she refused to give in. Refused to take it easy on Tripp and accept a relationship that was half measure. She loved him and she wanted a life with him. A whole life, not one loaded with strings or laden with fear.

They were strong and they were capable. And they channeled those qualities into doing a job that mattered. If there was danger tied to it, they'd both long accepted the personal risk. Each was entitled to *be* a person. To having a personal life.

And to finding and keeping love.

But she couldn't tell him that. He had to find it all on his own. Had to understand it in his bones.

Riley rushed up to them. Oblivious to the quiet moment, he pulled her into a bone-crushing hug before stepping back and turning to Tripp. "McKellar. Wes Matthews bit."

"Ashanti said she was close," Sadie interjected.

"Closer than we realized. Matthews is smitten and decided to surprise her. He's on a private plane landing in an hour in Florida. Ashanti's already on a plane with the FBI. Chief Fox has a team already coming together to watch the takedown. He wants you there if you're up for it."

Tripp nodded at her brother before turning to Sadie. "I'm sorry."

"Go. We're done here."

His gaze narrowed and she knew he'd heard exactly what she'd meant.

They were done.

Because she wasn't living half a life any longer. She deserved better.

And so did he.

TRIPP STARED AT the large screen in the GRPD's biggest conference room, communications flowing fast and furious from the speakerphone in the center of the oversize table. Matthews's plane would arrive in Florida in ten minutes. Air traffic control had already granted permission to land and the small aircraft was in final descent now.

He should feel triumphant. Satisfied. The RevitaYou case was nearly closed.

We're done here.

Who knew Sadie's comment would be so prophetic? Or as much about them as the case?

"Ashanti's in position." The announcement flowed through his comm unit, Cooper's voice calm as he relayed directives from inside the private terminal.

The takedown was all mapped out. Matthews was on US soil but he had to willingly go with Ashanti. Any appearance of coercion wouldn't look good when this case finally went to trial.

Tripp had every confidence Ashanti could pull it off. She looked the part of a wealthy investor, her pretty skin set off to perfection against a winter-white suit.

"Plane's on the ground." Cooper affirmed through the comms.

And then they let it all roll.

Tripp listened to Ashanti's smooth purr as she met Matthews for the first time. The lighthearted lines she drawled so effortlessly played to his ego and his intense love of old movies. She had a ready reference from *Casablanca* as they strolled from the terminal toward the waiting limousine outside.

And she was more than happy to channel *Citizen Kane* once she got him to the car.

But it was her last and final reference—to *The Wizard of Oz*—that put the Feds in motion. Just like they'd planned, the moment Ashanti confirmed they weren't in Kansas anymore, Cooper and his team moved in.

Tripp wanted to enjoy it. Wanted to revel in the reality that this was all finally behind them.

Come Monday, he'd go back to his old life.

One that didn't include spending his days with Sadie.

He heard the words flow through the speakerphone. Saw the video feed that matched up on the west wall. And cheered with the rest of the team when Cooper's boss held his badge at eye level in Matthews's face.

"Wes Matthews, you're under arrest."

"Wh-what?" the man sputtered, his eyes shooting to

Ashanti before swinging back to the large man standing much too close for comfort. "This is ridiculous. I'm here on a personal matter."

Ashanti smiled then stepped back a few feet. "Actually, you're here at the government's request. I'm just doing my patriotic duty."

Before Matthews could sputter out another word, Ashanti turned on one very fine heel and walked away.

Tripp knew her husband waited in another SUV a few feet beyond. A beloved Grand Rapids teacher, he was equally loved by his wife. And despite the thousand plus miles of distance, Tripp also knew what awaited Ashanti when she reached him.

Support.

Mutual respect.

The absolute certainty another had your back.

And, damn it, he'd had that. With Sadie. He'd had all of it and he'd thrown it away because…

Because of Lila?

The FBI read Matthews his rights and informed him of the charges.

Because of the baby?

The man spluttered and cursed the whole time as several FBI team members moved in and secured him in cuffs.

Because he was stupid.

It was the only answer left. Because he'd finally found forever and he would be the world's biggest fool to let it go.

SADIE LOOKED AROUND the small library of the home she'd grown up in and wondered how she'd ended up back here. Not the literal here, since she regularly visited her brother or came over on CI business.

But since she'd already been given one of the guest bedrooms for the night and even had a toothbrush set out on the sink, the proverbial "here" seemed pervasive.

The house doubled as CI headquarters and Riley had already pulled her aside to discuss how he wanted to further expand the business. Ashanti's successful work on the Wes Matthews situation had further confirmed Riley's instincts.

Colton Investigations frequently worked with law enforcement, and the more skilled individuals he carried on his payroll, the more cases the firm could work.

That was why he wanted Sadie to come work for him. As CI's first crime scene investigator.

Sadie rolled the idea around, more and more convinced it was the right choice. As an ex-FBI agent himself, her brother had vast resources, and she'd already told him that he'd need to invest in state-of-the-art equipment if she was going to even consider it. Riley had not only said yes, he'd given her a budget she could work with, and she was already dreaming of the great new tools she could buy.

But it also meant coming home.

She'd keep her apartment and continue living on her own, but making this choice meant she would be tying her life even more tightly to her siblings. And while part of her questioned if she lacked independence, a bigger part of her thought it sounded nice.

Better than nice, actually, especially with Vikki joining CI full time, too. To be part of the family business and use her knowledge doing a job she loved.

She and Vikki had spent about an hour together earlier, talking through what had happened and how happy they were to be back together. By the end, Sadie had known how badly Vik wanted to get to Flynn and she'd sent her off then wended her way through the house to a quiet room not full to bursting with Coltons.

She loved her family, but a bit of quiet was welcome.

"Sadie."

Vikki was back and stood at the door. "Someone's here to see you."

Her twin slowly backed out of the entryway as Tripp filled it. And in that moment Sadie finally understood what she'd been feeling.

Like Vikki had wanted the comfort of being with Flynn, all Sadie wanted was Tripp. And she'd accepted that what she'd wanted wasn't possible.

Only, he was here. Now.

And that feeling of safety only intensified, wrapping her in its tight, warm arms. "Hi."

"Hey."

"I heard the FBI took down Matthews."

"It was textbook, thanks to Ashanti. And that is good, since we're going to need every advantage when this goes to trial. And Brody is home and safe."

Sadie nodded, well aware of the risks if things hadn't been handled to the letter. Namely, that Wes would get off and find some way to replicate the project elsewhere.

Tripp continued to stand there, discomfort riding his shoulders like a cloak. "So, um, look... You said something to me. After we talked last. About it all being over."

Hope fluttered once more in her chest but Sadie

pushed it down. She couldn't go there. Couldn't let herself believe things might be different for them. "Because it is."

Tripp stepped into the room, carefully closing the French doors before turning back to face her. "Did you mean Greer and Matthews and RevitaYou? Or did you mean you and me?"

"Does it matter?"

"It does." He moved closer. "To me."

"Why?"

"Because I'm done hiding, Sadie. I'm done living half a life. And I'm done believing that having no one in my life is better than risking loving someone."

"I'm glad to hear it."

He stared at her, those steady blue eyes never leaving hers. "Does that mean you'll give me another chance?"

"At what, exactly?"

"At us. At being a couple. At making a life together."

She wanted nothing more, but she couldn't quite let him off that easily. "You're not still upset that it might be awkward at work?"

"No."

"And you need a place to live. You thinking of freeloading off of me for a while?"

A small smile twitched the corners of his lips. "If you'll have me."

"And what about a Christmas tree?"

"What about one?"

"I'm putting up Herman once I get home. I'm not living without a Christmas tree."

"Herman?" His eyebrows narrowed in confusion.

"The tree."

"Oh. Then I won't, either."

She opened her arms. "Come here, Tripp. Please."

It was only once he pulled her close that she let him off the hook. "Even if you feel weird at work or leave your clothes laying around my apartment or hate the Christmas tree, I'm going to love you anyway. I hope you know that."

"Good. Because I'm going to love you, too. Because I do love you. I love you more than I ever thought possible."

"I love you, too." She pulled him in for a kiss, reveling in the fact that he was there and they were together.

It was only long moments later, when the kiss had faded and they had their heads pressed together, that she remembered her news.

"I do have one more thing to tell you."

"Oh?" Interest sparked in those blue depths. "What is it?"

"I quit. Consider this my two weeks' notice."

Epilogue

Christmas Eve

Alfie raced through Riley's living room as fast as his toddler's gait would carry him. He had speed but was still a bit wobbly on his feet. Sadie let out a quick sigh of relief as she saw Tripp put a steadying hand on an antique manger set that had been her grandmother's.

Now that there were small children in the house, it looked like they'd need to reconsider the placement of some of the holiday decorations. An idea that only made the smile she couldn't seem to stop grow wider.

Then she smiled even more broadly when Tripp reached down and plucked Alfie up, holding him high above his head. The little boy giggled. "Uncle Tip! Airplane, Uncle Tip!"

"Uncle Tip" obliged, moving the boy around in the air before walking him to the tree so he could touch one of the more precious ornaments on a high branch.

"Watch out, Tripp," Kiely admonished as she walked into the living room with a large tray of desserts. "Those little fists are quick."

"Good thing I'm quicker," Tripp said, closing a

hand over Alfie's just before his fingers made contact with crystal.

Tripp then leaned in and made raspberries against the boy's belly, sending Alfie into gales of laughter and effectively distracting him from the tree.

Cooper, following behind Kiely, extended his hands for his son. "Is this one making trouble?"

Tripp gave the boy a quick kiss on the head before he passed him over. "Only the best kind."

"There's a best kind?" Kiely asked.

"When you're two, it's all the best kind."

With his precious charge deposited in his father's arms, Tripp came and took the seat beside Sadie. Just like they always did now, his hand covered hers, their fingers linking. It felt so right—and so natural—Sadie couldn't believe how quickly that simple touch had become a necessity.

Just like Tripp.

The time had seemed to pass in a blur, the RevitaYou case wrapping up with record speed. With Tate Greer dead and Wes Matthews in federal custody, the work had shifted to the federal prosecutors who'd taken over.

It had also left the two of them some quiet time together to settle into their relationship. As part of that, they'd also spent time with her family. Tripp had settled in well to the "Colton Chaos" as she liked to think of it, taking all of them in stride. It helped that he knew so many of them through work, but Tripp had seamlessly moved into a more personal relationship with each of them. Riley, in particular, had warmed to Tripp, their already strong work friendship morphing into a more brotherly relationship.

As if she'd conjured him, Riley entered the room, his hand on Charlize's extended belly before he gently situated her in a chair by the fire. Once he was satisfied she was comfortable, he turned to face them all.

"I think he's going to make a speech," Sadie leaned over and said to Tripp. "Settle in."

Tripp pressed a quick kiss to her cheek. "I'm ready to be inspired."

Sadie couldn't resist sticking her tongue out at her brother before whispering back to Tripp, "You're a traitor to the cause."

Riley waited as everyone quieted, his gaze slowly moving around the living room. Sadie's eyes followed and, despite her teasing over Riley's assumption of de facto elder statesman, she understood his pride. It was an awesome sight to see them all there.

Griffin and Abigail sat on the floor, Maya nestled in Abigail's lap, a stuffed reindeer in her small hand. Vikki and Flynn sat beside Pippa and Emmanuel on one of the large couches that bookended the room, while Kiely and Cooper kept Alfie occupied between them on a matched love seat. And Brody had taken a seat on the end of the couch where Sadie and Tripp sat, opposite to Riley.

Sadie gave Tripp one last kiss before scooting over to sit beside her brother in spirit. Brody had saved her and Vikki. He'd finally decided to take things into his own hands, ending the threat Tate had posed, determined to keep them all safe.

"If I haven't said it lately, thank you." Sadie tucked her hand in the crook of his elbow. "For everything."

Brody blushed but nodded. "I did what I had to do for my family."

"You did."

Riley raised his glass. "As we approach the holiday, we're all here and all together. Our family has faced innumerable challenges this year, but as we come to the close of it, we're stronger than ever. All while growing quite a bit."

"Colton world domination!" Kiely shouted at her brother, eliciting a laugh all the way around. But she was the first to lift her glass in return, everyone else following suit.

"To family!" Riley said, his glass high.

"To family," they all responded in kind.

Sadie gave Brody a large hug before shifting back to extend her hand to Tripp. As his fingers closed over hers, she knew she'd found her place. She'd always had one as a Colton, but now she had another one.

With Tripp.

The man she loved.

As the lights of the tree shone down on all of them, Sadie settled into the joy and beauty of her present.

And knew the future had never been brighter.

* * * * *

COMING SOON!

We really hope you enjoyed reading this book.
If you're looking for more romance, be sure to
head to the shops when new books are
available on

Thursday 10th December

LET'S TALK
Romance

For exclusive extracts, competitions
and special offers, find us online:

f facebook.com/millsandboon

y @MillsandBoon

⊙ @MillsandBoonUK

Get in touch on 01413 063232

JOIN US ON SOCIAL MEDIA!

Stay up to date with our latest releases, author
news and gossip, special offers and discounts, and
all the behind-the-scenes action
from Mills & Boon...

 millsandboon

 millsandboonuk

 millsandboon

It might just be true love...

MILLS & BOON

HISTORICAL

Awaken the romance of the past

Escape with historical heroes from time gone by. Whether your passion is for wicked Regency Rakes, muscled Viking warriors or rugged Highlanders, indulge your fantasies and awaken the romance of the past.

MILLS & BOON

MODERN

Power and Passion

Prepare to be swept off your feet by sophisticated, sexy and seductive heroes, in some of the world's most glamourous and romantic locations, where power and passion collide.

MILLS & BOON
True Love
Romance from the Heart

Celebrate true love with tender stories of
heartfelt romance, from the rush of falling
in love to the joy a new baby can bring,
and a focus on the emotional
heart of a relationship.